Lake
Turkana

KENYA

Lake Victoria

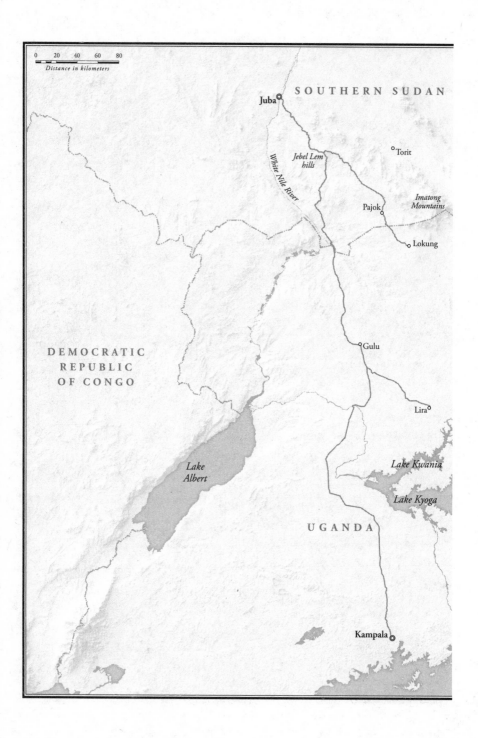

0   20   40   60   80
Distance in kilometers

SOUTHERN SUDAN

Juba

Torit

Jebel Lem
hills

White Nile River

Imatong
Mountains

Pajok

Lokung

DEMOCRATIC
REPUBLIC
OF CONGO

Gulu

Lira

Lake Kwania

Lake
Albert

Lake Kyoga

UGANDA

Kampala

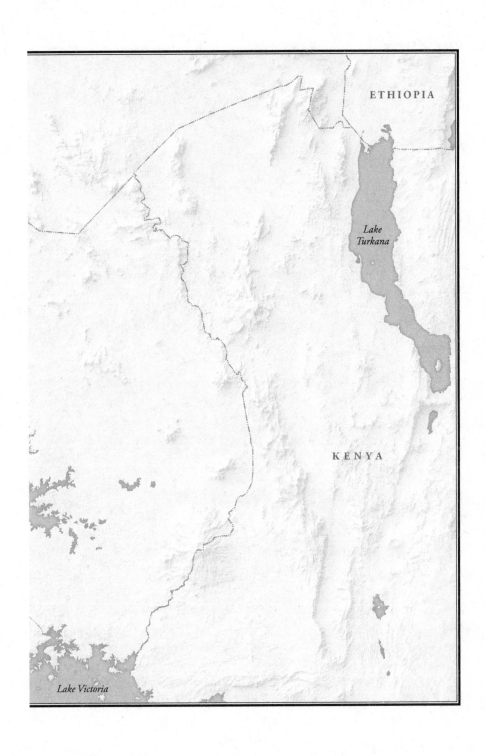

PRAISE FOR MARK SULLIVAN

"Mark Sullivan's *All the Glimmering Stars* is the pinnacle of an already distinguished career. A searing piece of historical fiction steeped in a years-long deep dive into the horrors of child soldiering, it is at its core something tender and rare: a love story between two profoundly good people striving for light in unimaginable darkness. It is a joy and an inspiration."

—Gregg Hurwitz, *New York Times* bestselling author of the Orphan X series

"Set amid the harrowing chaos of Joseph Kony's cultlike regime and his abducted children turned soldiers, an extraordinary narrative of love and unwavering resilience emerges. The intertwined journey of Anthony Opoka and Florence Okori stands as a luminous symbol of hope. Their love becomes a refuge, a testament to the human spirit's endurance."

—Jamie Ford, *New York Times* bestselling author of
The Many Daughters of Afong Moy

"An incredible story, beautifully written, and a fine and noble book."

—James Patterson, *New York Times* bestselling author

"Exciting . . . taut thriller . . . *Beneath a Scarlet Sky* tells the true story of one young Italian's efforts to thwart the Nazis."

—Shelf Awareness

"Meticulous research highlights this World War II novel of a youth growing into manhood . . . a captivating read . . ."

—RT Book Reviews

"Sprawling, stirring, like the richest of stories, and played out on a canvas of heroism and tragedy, *Beneath a Scarlet Sky* is like one of those iconic World War II black and white photos: a face of hope and tears, the story of a small life that ended up mattering in a big way."

—Andrew Gross, *New York Times* bestselling author of *The One Man*

"Action, adventure, love, war, and an epic hero—all set against the backdrop of one of history's darkest moments—Mark Sullivan's *Beneath a Scarlet Sky* has everything one can ask for in an exceptional World War II novel."

—Tess Gerritsen, *New York Times* bestselling author of *Playing with Fire*

"This is full-force Mark Sullivan—muscular, soulful prose evincing an artist's touch and a journalist's eye. *Beneath a Scarlet Sky* conjures an era with a magician's ease, weaving the rich tapestry of a wartime epic. World War II Italy has never been more alive to me."

—Gregg Hurwitz, *New York Times* bestselling author of *The Nowhere Man*

"*Beneath a Scarlet Sky* has everything—heroism, courage, terror, true love, revenge, compassion in the face of the worst human evils. Sullivan shows us war as it really is, with all its complexities, conflicting loyalties, and unresolved questions, but most of all, he brings us the extraordinary figure of Pino Lella, whose determination to live *con smania*—with passion—saved him."

—Joseph Finder, *New York Times* bestselling author of *Suspicion* and *The Switch*

"After his triumphant novel *Beneath a Scarlet Sky*, Mark Sullivan delivers another stunning tour de force . . . An inspirational true story featuring human strength, faith, and endurance against all odds."

—Authorlink

"[Sullivan's] got an extraordinary imagination, paired with a real talent for creating realistic scenes, both hair-raising times of danger—like being strafed— and intimate moments of pain."

—Historical Novel Society

"Mark Sullivan has done a fantastic job reliving this harrowing story . . . If you're a fan of historical novels this is one of the best that will come out this year or any year."

—Red Carpet Crash

"Sullivan brings to life another little-known tale of perseverance and bravery in the face of incredible hardship."

—She Reads

"A simply riveting read from cover to cover, *The Last Green Valley* is a deftly crafted novel that showcases experienced author Mark Sullivan's exceptional narrative storytelling skills combined with exceptional originality."

—Midwest Book Review

"I hail Mark Sullivan for doing it again—taking very real, very human stories set during the most intense period in recent world history and providing us with a work of historical fiction that we will not forget anytime soon."

—Bookreporter

"Mark Sullivan has done it again! *The Last Green Valley* is a compelling and inspiring story of heroism and courage."

—Kristin Hannah, #1 *New York Times* bestselling author of *The Nightingale* and *The Great Alone*

"Mark Sullivan weaves together history and memory in an epic journey of love and resilience. One of the most riveting, page-turning books I've read in a long time."

—Heather Morris, #1 international and *New York Times* bestselling author of *The Tattooist of Auschwitz*

"Sullivan again demonstrates his gift for finding little-known embers of history and breathing life into them until they glow and shine in ways that are both moving and memorable."

—Pam Jenoff, *New York Times* bestselling author of *The Lost Girls of Paris*

"Mark is one of the most gifted and successful novelists of our generation. His ability to weave drama, morality, and emotion through wonderfully captivating stories of the human spirit puts him among the greats."

—Tony Robbins, #1 *New York Times* bestselling author and the nation's #1 life and business strategist

ALL THE
GLIMMERING
STARS

Published by Lake Union Publishing, Seattle

www.apub.com

Amazon, the Amazon logo, and Lake Union Publishing are trademarks of Amazon.com, Inc., or its affiliates.

ISBN-13: 9781542038126 (hardcover)
ISBN-13: 9781542038119 (paperback)
ISBN-13: 9781542038102 (digital)

Cover design by David Drummond
Cover illustration by David Cooper

Printed in the United States of America

First edition

ALL THE GLIMMERING STARS

A NOVEL

MARK
SULLIVAN

LAKE UNION
PUBLISHING

*In memory of Mark Rausenberger and all the children who
never escaped the Great Teacher.*

"I did not look at my life and our story as something with value that others would want to know. But helping with this book gave what Anthony and I went through so much more meaning, and I began to see that people would want to know what happened to us and how we survived. Today, I hope our story can spread the power of love, heal people, and help keep children out of wars forever."

—*Florence Okori Opoka*

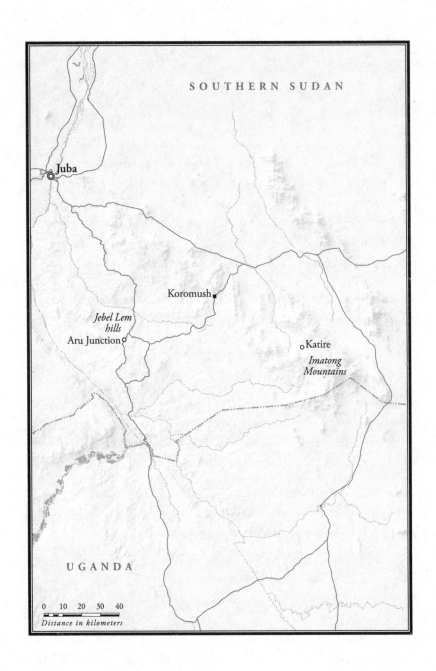

SOUTHERN SUDAN

Juba

Koromush

Jebel Lem hills
Aru Junction

Katire

Imatong Mountains

UGANDA

0   10   20   30   40

Distance in kilometers

Chapter One

December 28, 1994
Koromush Barracks, Southern Sudan

It was early yet.

Darkness lay upon the sultry land, savanna country that rose toward steep, cloud-wreathed mountains to the east. Among the many scattered acacia and thorn trees, elephant grass grew as tall as a man and wavered in the humid breeze and the dim, pale light of a crescent moon.

They'll come in the high grass where we can't see them, thought Phillip Bol, a sergeant in the Sudanese People's Liberation Army. *They always do.*

Sergeant Bol was born a member of the Dinka tribe, and like many of his people, he was very tall, gaunt, and wide-shouldered. A decent and well-natured man out of combat, Bol was also a battle-hardened soldier fighting in a three-way war for control of his homeland.

But that morning, the sergeant's stomach roiled, and saliva soured at the back of his throat as he stood in a trench at the top of a hill, staring through binoculars at a sea of grass stretching out beyond a sixty-meter strip they'd burned around the base of the steep rise earlier in the day.

We may not see them until they hit the burn, but we'll hear them, by God. We'll hear them from a long way.

Bol glanced to his left and right, seeing the dim silhouettes of his men set at ten-meter intervals across the hillside, also staring out at the sea of grass, some veterans locked in memory and some new to service, no doubt contemplating the rumors they'd heard about the savanna and the invisible choir that would soon be upon them. Scouts had located units of the Lord's Resistance Army less than five kilometers away. The fight would not be long in coming now.

The sergeant drank from his canteen and ate a dried date to calm his gut. He wondered how many of his men would tremble at the singing. Then he wondered how many might run in sheer terror at the choir, for the soldiers of the Lord's Resistance Army were pound for pound the most formidable on earth, many of them veterans of years of near-constant training and combat.

Led by a fanatical, false messiah, LRA forces were either fearless or dead, a fact that made even a man like Sergeant Bol dread the night and the hymns that would soon lilt and threaten over the grasslands, as if given voice by sirens and false angels.

The sergeant glanced at his watch, seeing dawn was not far off. He called softly to the men closest to him, "Pass it along. No noise now. No talking. No movement. We want to hear them first. And no one runs in my unit. No one!"

Bol listened to his orders repeated along the line and in and out of the trenches before all fell silent save the buzz of insects, the cluck and fluttering of birds on their roost, and the gentle washing of the high grass. An elephant trumpeted the coming day back to the south, back beyond the barracks and armory the sergeant's commander believed the LRA was planning to attack. The first smudge of light began to show to the east.

The sergeant was aware of the hollow sound of his breath and, far to the west, the wah-wah, cough-like call of a leopard declaring his dominance before a strange quiet enveloped the land. The breeze stopped blowing. The grass stilled. There was only the whine of bugs for twenty minutes, long enough for the eastern horizon to glow before the rising sun and for Sergeant Bol to wonder whether the scouts were wrong.

The singing began at six, and at a fair distance out in front of Bol's position, indistinct at first, soft, almost sweet. It built force not with deep-toned basses and tenors, raucous warriors itching for a fight. Instead, he heard many sopranos and altos gathering as both a choir and an army, which began to advance through the high grass toward the ridge where the sergeant and his men waited.

"*Polo, polo, yesu Lara,*" they sang in the Acholi language of northern Uganda. "Heaven, heaven, Jesus save me."

The sergeant had heard the deadly chorus before, of course, but there was something about the wavering, high tone of the singing, almost ethereal in its innocence and menace, that made his skin crawl. He swallowed hard and heard some of his men shifting uncomfortably behind their rifles.

Sergeant Bol told himself to settle down and peered through his binoculars, seeing in the building golden light that the grass was moving some three hundred meters out and a good hundred meters side to side, as if this battle group of the Lord's Resistance Army were a long, horizontal wave swelling his way in a full-frontal assault.

"Here they come," he muttered.

"I don't see their heads above the grass," said a soldier to the sergeant's right.

"Because they're short," Bol grunted back, binoculars still pressed to his eyes. "And Kony will have them smeared with shea butter, all but invisible in that grass until they hit the burn and they're right on top of us."

As the wave came closer and closer, the sergeant could hear the elephant grass rustling over the choir, who were clapping in unison now and still singing their hymn of beseeching and faith.

> *Polo, polo, yesu Lara.*
> Heaven, heaven, Jesus save me.
> Heaven should come to rescue us in our lives,
> And we shall never leave the way to heaven.
> *Polo, polo, yesu Lara.*
> Heaven, heaven, Jesus save me.

"Light them up," Sergeant Bol said into his radio.

To his left, he saw a soldier get to his feet and say, "I can't do it."

"Get down, Private," the sergeant said.

"I didn't sign up for this, Sergeant. I won't do this."

"Private!"

"I can't," the soldier choked. "Even if they're armed to the teeth, I can't kill them, and I won't be killed by them."

He climbed out of the trench, took off running down the back of the hill toward the barracks a moment before a flare rocketed from the far end of the trench, arced, and exploded high over the savanna, fully revealing the choir in the golden grass: dozens of children and teenagers, all smeared with shea butter that made their skin look chalked, and all singing the same hymn.

3

Mark Sullivan

"*Polo, polo, yesu Lara.* Heaven, heaven, Jesus save me."

Bol saw that the boys at the very front of the attack were all bare-chested. They were unarmed as well, terrified, and clapping as they marched into the burnt field, eyes toward heaven and elbows entwined. The rest of the child soldiers of the Lord's Resistance Army carried AK-47s and shoulder-fired rocket launchers that they swung toward the sergeant and his men before they left the grass and opened fire.

SEVEN YEARS EARLIER

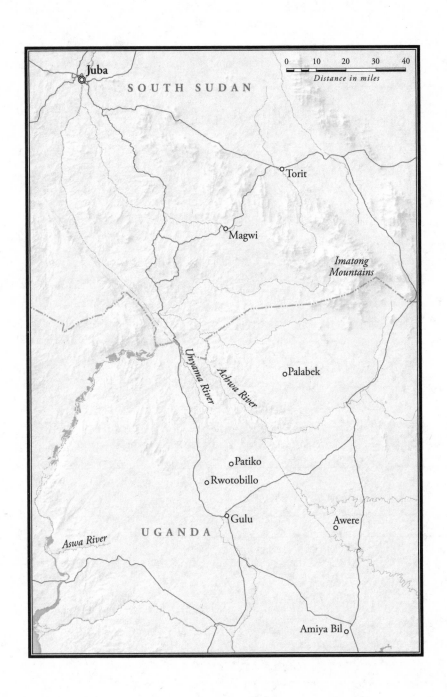

Chapter Two

June 1987
Rwotobilo, Uganda

Anthony Opoka was seven when his father began teaching him the intricacies of the African night sky.

The lessons started late one hot afternoon, with tall, lean George Opoka hurrying from his crop field through the bush toward a tiny village some 150 kilometers north of Kampala and less than 10 kilometers north of the smaller city of Gulu. George, on edge, craned his head every which way, looking for danger.

Random threat was a constant in the bush of the central highlands. Leopards, lions, hyenas, cape buffalo, and elephants roamed in the thick cover. So did poisonous snakes and, worst of all, disaffected soldiers from the five-year Ugandan Civil War, which had ended the year before with the victory of the army of Yoweri Museveni, now president of the country.

Exiting the thick cover, George slowed as he approached an oval-shaped hut made of mud and cow dung sunbaked as hard as cement. The hut had a new thatch roof shaped like an upside-down bowl that would shed water when the rainy season came.

A pretty woman in her twenties wearing a fitted bodice and wraparound skirt in bright greens and black sat outside the hut, tending a cook fire. Beyond her, youngsters were playing.

"Acoko Florence," George said, putting his hand on his chest, "how is it that you are more beautiful than ever?"

His third wife rolled her eyes and said, "You say that every day."

"And it is true every day! It is also true that Anthony will come with me tonight."

"Isn't he young yet, *Omera*?"

Omera meant brother in their Acholi language and was a term of both affection and respect that almost everyone used with George, who was known far and wide as a truly good man.

"I was taught at six, and he will be eight in October," George said. "It's time for Anthony to leave his mother's house from time to time and learn to become a man."

"A boy of seven cannot become a man," his wife said, sounding upset.

"He can be taught to become a human, then," George said, smiling.

Acoko would not look at George.

"What's the matter?"

She shook her head. "I know Anthony is not your firstborn, but he is mine, and my joy."

"Which makes what I have to teach him even more important."

His wife looked like she wanted to argue, but then sighed. "He is your son, and you are his father. I guess you know best about these kinds of things."

George studied his wife, who was normally full of good cheer and witty banter. Acoko had seemed smaller to him lately, less full of life, but before he could comment on that, she had gone inside the hut. She soon emerged with Anthony, who was waking up from a nap, grumpy and rubbing his eyes.

Anthony was all legs and arms, with a strong torso and a face that brightened when he saw his father. He ran to George and hugged him. George hugged him back, for he loved all his wives and all his children and believed in showering them with affection.

"Are you ready to go to human school?" George asked, winking at Acoko.

Anthony pulled back from his father, puzzled. "School is closed for break."

"This will be a different kind of school, one that could save your life someday."

The boy's brow knitted. He peered over at his mother, who was worrying her hands. Anthony adored his mother and walked over to her. "Can I, Mom?"

Acoko's smile was bittersweet as she put her hand under her son's chin and looked into his eyes. "You can and you must. Your father says he has much to teach you about being a human tonight."

Anthony grabbed his mother around the waist and squeezed tight. She raised her head to gaze at her husband as if to say, *Keep the good and gentle soul I have raised safe. And bring him home to me.*

George understood, smiled, and nodded to her.

"Go on," Acoko said, and gave Anthony a tickle in the ribs. "Time for human school."

Anthony peered up at her, grinning. "I'll be back before long, Mom."

"And I'll wait right here for you," she said.

———

As Anthony walked barefoot through the village with his father, his chest swelled with pride. Almost everyone loved Omera George, and here Anthony was being singled out for his special attention. Two of his father's other wives and several of Anthony's half brothers and sisters noticed. They broke away from what they were doing to call to Anthony and his father in greeting and in curiosity.

"Where are you going?" asked Charles, one of Anthony's younger half brothers and closest friends.

"To become a human," Anthony said.

"What?" his uncle Paul said.

"It's a secret, Brother," George announced, which only made Charles, Uncle Paul, and George's other children and wives even more curious.

"Can I come, too?" asked Albert, another younger half brother, only five.

"Not tonight, Albert," his father said gently. "Tonight belongs to Anthony."

Anthony rolled back his shoulders and made a face at his disappointed little brothers as he and his father walked off into the bush.

It's my night with my father, the boy thought happily. *Mine and mine alone.*

When they were out of sight and hearing of the others, George slowed and looked down at his son.

"Anthony, I wanted you to know that you are a special, special boy."

"I am?"

"You are. The way you love to run. The way you're quick to help your mother and work at school. The way you play with your brothers. Not many boys are like you. I wanted you to know that I see it. So does your mother. You are special."

Anthony felt warm inside, seen, understood, and filled up in a rare way. He beamed back at his father, thinking, *I am special.* George patted him on the shoulder, started walking again, and he followed, still basking in the praise and the rare warmth around his heart.

"Up until now, Anthony, we have kept you close to home," George said. "Your life has been between here and the school."

"And the market," Anthony said, and it was true when he thought about it: his life up to that point had unfolded in a very, very small area. He had not even been to Gulu, which he imagined as an exotic place bustling with people and strange new sights.

George said, "You need to start looking around yourself. Try to see things that will help tell you where you are and where you are going."

Anthony looked at all the brush and the trees around them, not quite grasping what his father was trying to tell him.

"Follow me," George said. "It will be easier to understand if I show you."

They took foot and game paths through lush thickets that smelled of blooming flowers to the edge of a ridge that overlooked a low green valley, where women pounded millet and men hoed gardens and smoke curled over fires lit for cooking.

George gestured behind them at three huge trees growing in a loose, crisscrossing cluster. "Those are the tallest trees for the longest way, can you see that?"

Anthony could see that but wondered if he'd be able to spot them from far away. His father gestured to the geographic features in the distance. To the northwest, the Kilak hills rose. To the northeast, he showed him a far-off round top near the town of Patiko.

"Those are landmarks. They don't move. If you can see both those high points, face your right shoulder to the hills and the left toward the round top. You will be looking south toward these three trees, and home. Do you see?"

Anthony nodded uncertainly.

Then, to the south, southeast, his father pointed out two hills well across the valley floor, set at right angles to each other and a good ten kilometers apart. George made his son notice how one had spires of rock jutting up out of the brush near the top, and how the closest hill had bare rock on top, no brush. That bald hill was higher than anything around.

"That's Awere Hill, where the crazy man preaches these days," George said. "So, you keep Awere Hill on your left and our three trees behind you, and you will go straight south to Gulu. Coming back, you keep Awere Hill on your right and the hills at Kilak and Patiko in front of you, and you'll come straight north until you see the three big trees and home. Understand?"

Anthony saw it now and nodded.

"Good. Smart boy."

At the praise, Anthony felt that rare inner warmth again. "Who's the crazy man, Dad?"

His father hesitated before replying, "His name is Joseph Kony. He lives near the hills and is the cousin of a crazy woman named Alice Auma, who called herself Lakwena, 'the Messenger.'"

"Messenger of what?"

"Who knows?" George said. "Alice claimed she could see the future, and convinced her followers, including Kony, that she could turn rocks into bombs. After Museveni won, she declared war on the new government. Kony refused to join his cousin and started wearing white robes and preaching on Awere Hill soon afterward. They say he can call thunderstorms and has powers far greater than Lakwena. More people go there every night to hear him preach and see him call storms."

Anthony stared far across the valley at the rock dome of Awere Hill, trying to imagine a man who could call thunder and lightning and rain.

His father, acting like he wished he had not mentioned Kony at all, said, "You're not going anywhere near Awere Hill. No one in their right mind goes there anymore."

"But I can use it as a landmark?"

George's shoulders dropped in relief. "Yes. That's right."

"What about in the dark? What if I can't see any of these hills?"

His father smiled. "Very good point."

———

George led him to a rocky outcropping free of trees and brush as a moonless twilight settled over the land.

"Why are we here, Dad?" Anthony asked, looking out over the now-indistinct canopy of the bush. "What's down there for me to see?"

He could sense his father smiling when he put his great hand on his shoulder. "You're not here to look down, Anthony. You are here to look up."

The boy lifted his eyes and saw the silhouette of George pointing at the great dome of the night sky and the stars appearing in every direction and more by the second, clustered and alone.

Anthony said, "I like looking at stars. They're beautiful."

"I do, too, but stars are much more," George said. "They can be your guide, your compass, and your map. When I was about your age, an old Acholi medicine man taught me that if you can learn the stars by their positions in the sky, you can find your way home or anywhere you want to go, even on a night as dark as this one."

Anthony listened as his father pointed out clusters of stars that almost never moved, and others that came and went at dawn and dusk and with the turning of the seasons. Once you had them memorized, he said, you could use them to figure out your location and direction.

"The medicine man also told me that our spirits come from stars and return to stars when we die. So, when you look up at the stars, Anthony, you may also be seeing the spirits of your ancestors and the souls of your children shining back at you."

The boy peered up at all the glimmering stars in the vast blackness of the night sky. "Is that true, Dad?"

George put his arms around Anthony's shoulders. "I don't know. But I like to think so."

Anthony hugged his father back. "Then I do, too."

On their way home, George said that in addition to learning about stars, he had to start thinking and acting more like a man now, not a little boy.

"But I'm only seven, Dad."

His father laughed. "Yes, your mother says the same thing. A human, then. But this is when it starts, Anthony. You are a boy now, but in the future, I want to be able to look at you and know what a good human you have become, someone who does the right thing, stands up for himself, who knows right from wrong; a human who treats people fairly and expects to be treated fairly, who knows his business and his work, and feels responsible for feeding and sheltering his family; a human who knows how to love and to learn from his wife, and how to teach his children well so they can teach their children well so that the story and skills of a good and decent life go on."

"How do I remember all that?"

"You don't have to. Not right now. But it all comes down to this, Anthony. Try to be a better human in some way every day. And whenever you are confused about anything in life, not sure what to do, ask yourself this question: What would a good human do?"

Anthony felt his father's passion even in the darkness. It made his skin tingle and fired the warmth in his chest again.

"What would a good human do?" Anthony said. "I will remember that."

"Good. And just one more question to remember: How can I be happy today?"

"I already am happy," Anthony said, trying to keep up, and amazed at his father's animal eyes at night.

George chuckled in front of him. "You are. For the most part. But do you know how to be happy when you are sad or afraid?"

"Go play with my friends?"

"Good. And here's another one: look for the good things in your life and be thankful. You will always feel happier if you do and less afraid if you do. I don't know why. But it's true."

They soon reentered the village and moved toward the fires, which were burning low and in embers. Anthony smiled when he saw his mother getting up from the reed mat that she'd been sitting on by the fire.

"You've been gone a long time," Acoko said. "I was becoming worried."

"He's safe and has no broken bones," George said. "But I think he's tired."

"And hungry? I saved some of the millet, plantain, and spicy okra sauce you like."

"Yes, please," Anthony said, suddenly sleepy and very hungry.

George hugged him. "A good first night, I think. You pick up things fast."

Anthony hugged him back. "I like learning new things."

"Then you have half the battle won."

His father went off to check the rest of his family and the family of his brother, Paul. Anthony's uncle lived very close by, almost beneath the three towering trees.

13

His mother put a spoon and a metal plate of piping-hot food in front of Anthony. "Eat or you'll never grow up to be the big, strong man you need to be."

"I already am stronger than the other boys because I like to run. Dad says it makes me special." He felt it again, that rare warmth filling him, and beamed at her.

"Then eat, special boy," she insisted. "Eat so you can run far and fast."

Anthony spooned the dish into his mouth, savoring all the tastes, and finding himself thankful for it in a way he never had before.

"It's so good," he said. "Thank you, Mom."

That pleased her. "I am glad you like it. What did your father teach you?"

"About stars. And how to be a good human. And about landmarks like Awere Hill and the three trees near Uncle Paul's."

"What about stars?"

"A lot of stuff. With stars, you can find your way in the dark and not be afraid."

Acoko's face clouded. "You may learn to know your way in the dark, but you should always be afraid of what lives and roams around at night. Always."

"Dad said I need to learn to be happy instead of being afraid."

His mother snorted. "George is a good man, but a fool now and then. Life isn't all about happiness, Anthony. It's about survival. Sometimes life is so hard you just have to survive it."

Anthony did not know why Acoko called his dad a fool, and it made him a little angry when he wanted to again have that rare, warm feeling of being filled up again, basking in George's praise.

"Well," he said. "Dad says I'm special because I work hard at school and help you and I'm a good friend."

His mother hesitated, then softened, rubbed his head and hugged him. "You are all that, little one. You are all that."

Chapter Three

September 1988
Amia'bil, Uganda

Some sixty kilometers southeast of Anthony's village and just outside of the city of Lira, Florence Okori was not feeling well and did not want to get out of bed.

Ordinarily, four-year-old Florence was among the first to arise in her extended family. The young girl loved being up early, hearing cocks crow before dawn, the cattle lowing and shaking their bells, the goats blatting and protesting to each other. The slap of her mother's sandals.

Florence's mother, Josca, was always up early by necessity. Flo usually got up voluntarily to follow her mom down the path from the family's compound of huts to the active stream where they fetched water in buckets and blue jerry cans and sang gospel hymns in the low light as they struggled back up the hill under the weight of their burdens.

Thanks to water hauling and near-constant movement from dawn to dusk, Florence was as fit and as strong as she could be. Moreover, the routine and rhythm of her daily and seasonal life—planting and tending and harvesting—all pleased her at a deep level. There was firewood to gather, yams and cotton to hoe, and mangoes to be picked today. And maybe a trip into the bush with her father to gather medicinal plants. And school was starting next week!

Get up, Flo, she thought drowsily. *Everything is about to get very exciting for you!*

Just the day before, her mother had said those words after Florence's father, Constantine, signed the papers and paid the tuition for her to start school.

All things considered, Flo should have been wide awake and alert by now, up, and pestering Josca with questions about what she would need for school and what it would be like and who her teacher might be. But she wasn't wide awake or alert. Not in the least.

Hearing the blanket across the door of her mother's hut flap open followed by the gentle slapping of Josca's sandals, Florence tried to force herself awake. She couldn't just leave her mother to fetch water alone.

Her eyes fluttered open. Her head ached. She'd slept outside, as she often did, and could now see her mother moving about in the dimness.

Florence willed herself to throw back the sheet she slept under and got over onto her knees and hands, where she felt dizzy for a moment. Her muscles ached as she struggled to her feet and then coughed and shivered in the warm, humid air.

"Good morning, Florence," Josca said. "Thank you for starting another day with me." Her mother hugged her and then said, "You are hot and yet you shiver, child."

"I'm all right," Florence said, feeling a burning sensation behind her ears and across the top of her brow. She thought that if she did not start to the stream now, she might not make it. "I'll take the buckets."

Her mother gave them to her and carried two blue jerry cans as she led the way in the gathering light past the family garden and bamboo plot to a narrow path that led downhill seventy-five meters to a dam built with a notch in it to allow the water to flow briskly. Josca filled the buckets first.

"You can start back while I fill the cans," her mother said.

"Okay, Mama," Florence said, fighting off another swirl of dizziness as she squatted to pick up the full buckets, one in each hand.

Florence turned and started up the short, steep bank, still clad in deep shadows. She smelled fire smoke and then something sharper, like the dried cinnamon her father liked to snap into his tea. Suddenly, her throat felt swollen and sore, and she had to cough.

Then it felt like bumps were swelling across her forehead and in her mouth! Her focus left the path she was climbing for the soreness in her throat, the need to cough, the bumps, and that odd scent of cinnamon in the air.

She stumbled and almost fell and spilled the buckets. Somehow, the four-year-old kept her feet and most of the water inside. Florence was surprised to have tripped; she thought she knew the path so well she could have walked it in the pitch dark, telling you where every root and loose rock lay. But now her head pounded. Her breathing became labored. She heard the thrum of blood in her temples, felt the skin on her arms prickle so hot she wanted to set the buckets down to scratch.

Florence told herself to get to the top of the steep incline before putting the buckets down. Taking one cautious step and then another, she felt as if she would make it, but then that rush of blood at her temples became a waterfall, making her swoon. She heard the buckets hit the ground and felt her ankles sloshed with water before she realized she had dropped them and was falling backward.

She hit with a thud and slid, starting to cry, aware of her mother yelling, "Florence!"

Josca was to her in seconds, cradling Florence as she moaned, "Something's wrong, Mama. There are bumps in my mouth and everything hurts. I'm so hot I can't stand up."

"Help!" her mother yelled up the hill. "Constantine! Help!"

Sunrise was still fifteen minutes off. Josca got Florence to a level place and was putting a damp rag on her forehead when her father came running down the slope with a flashlight.

"She's burning up," her mother said. "She's got a rash on her forehead and bumps in her mouth."

Florence was hazily aware of her father telling her to open her mouth and shut her eyes so he could shine the light. When she did, it was as if she were falling again, getting farther and farther from the beam of light playing in her face.

"There are spots on the bumps," Constantine said. "I think it's measles."

"Measles!" Florence was fading in and out of consciousness, but she heard the fear and defeat in her mother's voice. "What do we do?"

"We need to get her away from the other children. We take her to the hospital in Lira. They'll know how to treat her."

"Is she going to . . . ?"

"Her best chance is the hospital, Josca. I'll take her."

"I'm going with you."

The equatorial heat rose with the sun as Constantine lifted his sweat-drenched little girl into the small cart he'd hitched to their donkey. Lying on her back, groaning at the pain in her muscles and bones, Florence would barely remember her mother's terrified face floating over her before the fever spiked again and higher and the brilliant glare of the early-morning sun and the deep-blue sky framed by wavering banana leaves turned to red dots and then black dots that ate everything whole.

———

Josca saw her daughter's head loll and then arch back in some kind of convulsion. Florence's tongue sought the air and danced while her mother screamed to her husband. Almost as soon as it began, the little girl collapsed and lay still but for twitching. Flecks of white foam gathered in the corners of her lips.

"Oh sweet Jesus, no," Josca moaned.

"She's still breathing," Constantine said. "She's not done fighting yet."

He beat at the donkey's ass with a stick, and they broke into a trot. Josca ran beside the cart, looking for signs her daughter was coming around. Aside from the twitching and the occasional grimace, the four-year-old did not move, floating between life and eternity.

Please, God, not this one, Josca prayed as she ran. *Do not take this one from me. Florence is special. I can feel it in my love for her. She was made for greater things, Lord. Please. Let my baby girl live, and I will let love do the rest. I promise you that.*

It took them an hour to reach the hospital in Lira. To Josca's dismay, there were a dozen other mothers and fathers already lined up with coughing, feverish young children.

A male nurse wearing a mask was doing triage on the hospital's veranda. Josca ran to the front of the line and told the nurse that Florence had just suffered some kind of fit. It wasn't until she described the white foam at the corners of her lips and Constantine yelled that she was having another seizure that the nurse told her to bring the girl forward and fast.

Florence's second seizure stopped, but the twitches and tics that followed were bigger than after the first. Nurses rushed out with a gurney. They put Florence on it and sped her inside.

When Josca and Constantine tried to follow, another nurse stopped them.

"This hospital is in full quarantine. You've done what you can. Leave your names and where you live. When we know more, we'll send someone to find you."

"How long does it last?"

"Most people have nine to fourteen days of it. But for some kids, the fevers hit a lot harder and longer."

"Isn't there anything we can do?" Constantine asked.

"You can pray." The nurse turned away.

Josca felt helpless and fell against her husband.

"I'm praying that the disease is short, and she lives," Constantine said, hugging her.

"I am, too," his wife said. "But we've already lost four babies. What if we lose our Flo?"

Her husband looked off and could not answer.

———

For nearly two weeks, Florence fought the measles virus, which had ripped through unvaccinated parts of Uganda and overwhelmed hospitals and medical clinics. Her fevers spiked several times a day. She had to be fed fluids intravenously. The seizures, however, did not return.

She had no idea where she was when she finally roused in the evening after thirteen days unconscious. Her eyes lazily opened, seeing a woman in a sharp-white outfit coming toward her.

"Florence awakes," the woman said. "I am Miss Catherine, your nurse. Are you thirsty?"

Florence nodded in a daze. The nurse got her a cup of water.

"Can you sit up?"

The girl tried, but her body felt wooden, almost paralyzed.

"No."

Miss Catherine sat her up and poured water into her mouth. Flo drank it greedily, only to choke and sputter when some went down the wrong way. The nurse clapped her back, and she went off into an extended coughing jag.

"Your fever's down considerably, and the Koplik's spots in your mouth are almost gone," Miss Catherine said. "But that cough is going to stick around awhile, and you're going to be weak for a long time."

"I can't move my arms and legs," Florence said, afraid.

The nurse reached down and pinched her forearm.

"Ouch!"

"Aha," Miss Catherine said, and reached for her leg. "How about here?"

"That hurt, too!"

"That's a good thing. And now I have to take care of others."

For the first time, Florence looked around the room and realized it was wall to wall with beds filled with children, most of them sleeping.

"How many are here?"

"Thirty," she said. "And I'm responsible for all of you."

"How long do I have to be here?" she asked as the nurse got ready to leave her side.

"Until the fevers are gone and the doctor says you can leave."

———

Flo's fevers were not gone. Indeed, the following day, they returned with a vengeance, spiking above thirty-nine Celsius, which miraculously did not result in a fit but in nightmares and bizarre hallucinations where she believed she was no longer in the hospital but home with Josca and Constantine and all her brothers and sisters.

In one, she was walking to the store with her oldest brother, Owen, who was her favorite. Florence kept coughing and saying she did not know if she could make it. Owen kept telling her that everything was going to be okay, that she would get there. She took heart from her brother's soothing words only to notice that he was having trouble keeping up with her.

In reality, Owen was in his late teens, strong, and he worked hard all day. But in her nightmares, he kept trying to catch his breath and fell farther and farther behind until she could barely see him back there in the twilight. And then her big brother was gone.

Caught in the grip of the hallucination, Florence felt gut-punched by a loneliness she'd never known before, cast adrift in the night, trying desperately to find Owen and her way home to her mom and dad but not succeeding. She became hysterical and cried for what seemed like days.

"Shhhh now, Florence," Miss Catherine said when the girl woke up blubbering from yet another fever during her second month in the measles ward. "It was just a dream and I'm here."

"But I want to go home," she said weakly.

Behind the nurse, something squeaked. Miss Catherine looked over her shoulder, seeing what Florence was also seeing: two of the orderlies settling a sheet over a little boy's gaunt body on a gurney.

Florence did not have the strength to be frightened. "What will they do with him?"

"He'll be buried," the nurse said.

"Did he die from measles?"

"From complications from the measles, yes."

"I don't want to die, Miss Catherine."

The nurse looked stricken. "Oh, I know, honey. I don't want you to die, or anyone else in this wretched place."

"Will it help if I pray?" Florence asked.

"Of course. But if you wish your prayers to be heard, you must bow your head with a heart that is already at peace and glowing with gratitude."

"What is gratitude?"

"It's when you're thankful for something in your life. You're thankful to be alive. Or for the food you eat. Or this bed you sleep on. When you are thankful, your heart will not ache, and you will be heard."

The nurse kissed her on the forehead and walked away.

Florence closed her eyes, clasped her hands the way her mother did in church, and silently gave thanks for not dying, for the hospital, and for Miss Catherine. She did feel better—a little, anyway—and then prayed that no more children would die and that she would go home.

———

Weakened by the disease, however, more and more children in the packed measles ward began to die, as many as five a week. Florence saw them put under sheets and rolled out in the middle of the day and the middle of the night. Death, it seemed to her, had no clock. And the kids she did see leaving the hospital alive were all on crutches or in wheelchairs, unable to support themselves on their disease-withered limbs.

Florence turned five alone on December 1. The fevers finally stopped spiking two weeks later. But Miss Catherine told her she was still too weak to try to go home.

She felt no better or stronger in the days that followed. Then, one afternoon, when she thought she might never leave the measles ward, she woke up from a nap to find Josca and the nurse by her bed.

"Mama?" she said, starting to cry.

Her mother cried, too, and hugged her. "I've come to take you home, baby."

Miss Catherine said, "You're taking her against doctor's orders."

"Too many children are dying in here, and you said her fevers are gone," Josca said. "I'll care for Florence at home. Besides, it's Christmas tomorrow. I won't have her in here on the Lord's birthday."

The nurse did not look happy but helped Florence into her clothes and brought her a wheelchair. She'd lost so much weight, Josca said she looked like a little bird as they wheeled her out of the hospital three months after she'd entered.

"Goodbye, Florence," Miss Catherine said.

"I want to be a nurse like you someday," Florence said. "You get to wear a nice uniform and you help people."

"I guess I do," the nurse said, smiling, before looking at Josca. "The wheelchair stays, unfortunately."

"Oh," Florence's mother said. "My husband is using the cart to sell the cotton. But it doesn't matter."

With that, and in one motion, Josca picked up Florence and walked away with her. Flo could not remember the last time her mother had held her or carried her like this, and she melted into her mother's neck, her familiar smell, the fact that it was Christmas Eve and she was going home.

Josca managed to carry Florence in a cradle hold for more than a kilometer before shifting her grip and continuing on. By the end of the second kilometer and when they were no more than another kilometer from their little village, Florence felt her mother's strength flag.

"You can put me down, Mama," she said. "You don't have to carry me all the way without resting."

To her surprise, Josca shifted her grip again and set off even faster toward home, whispering fiercely in her ear, "You are my daughter, Florence. I love you with all my heart and soul. And love is the strongest force there is. If I had to, I would carry you forever."

———

Florence's skin prickled enjoyably, and her brain and heart and, quickly, her entire body flooded with the most beautiful emotions. She could feel the rush of love coming from her mother, started to cry with joy, and knew she would never forget the moment or how good and safe and protected she felt going home.

When Josca carried Florence back into the compound she'd left feverish and hallucinating three months before, her sisters and brothers were already starting to prepare for the Christmas feast, cutting yams into cubes, slicing onions, and tending to the pot simmering over the smoldering cook fire. They saw Florence and cheered and crowded around her after her mother laid her on a mat in the shade, welcoming her home.

"I knew you were going to make it, Shorty," said Owen. "Otherwise, I wouldn't have anyone to joke with."

"I missed you, Flo," said Margaret, who was three.

Florence smiled weakly. "I missed you, too. All of you. I dreamed of all of you."

"Florence grew, I think," said her older sister Rosa, who was fifteen. "Longer legs."

Frowning, Florence looked down at her legs, seeing them spindlier than she remembered.

"They are long, like spider legs," said a younger boy with a freshly shaved head and a missing upper front tooth. "Florence the spider!"

"Knock it off, Jasper," Owen said, gently swatting Florence's favorite cousin, who was a few months older than she was, smart, and always getting into one sort of mischief or another.

"Don't worry," Florence said. "I'll spin a web and catch Jasper in it."

"What am I?" Jasper said. "A bug?"

Her siblings all laughed; then a man's voice said, "What's going on?"

They parted to reveal their father, an intense, wiry little man who seemed in perpetual motion. Rare was the time when Constantine Okori smiled or slowed, much less stopped, from dawn to dusk. Unless it was a big holiday like this one. He carried two burlap bags that he set down on the ground. A chicken squawked and sputtered in one of them.

"Look who is home," Josca told him, stepping aside.

Constantine's eyes went wide. "Flo!" he cried, and rushed over to kneel beside her and put his hand gently on her forehead. "They wouldn't let us in to see you. But your mother and I prayed for you every day."

"I know," Florence said, grinning at him.

Constantine smiled, then looked at his wife. "Our prodigal daughter has come home."

Josca's brows knitted. "There is nothing prodigal or wasteful about Florence."

"Oh, you know what I mean," he said, the smile building. "She's home, and that is the best Christmas present and a cause for a great celebration. Certainly, for more beer than I bought."

His wife's frown deepened. She was evangelical and did not drink. Florence's father was Catholic and liked to drink beer very much on holidays.

"Start with the beer you have, will you?" Josca said.

Constantine looked ready to argue, but then shrugged and said, "I'm having one right now. To welcome our little girl home."

"Did you get the chickens?" she called after him as he went back to the bags.

"Two of them. Big capons. And everything else you asked for."

He reached into one of the bags and drew out a tall bottle of Nile beer. He used a pocketknife to flip the top and took a swig.

"Nice," he said, smacking his lips. "Still cold."

"Don't you have anything for Florence in your bag?" Josca asked. "Something to welcome her home?"

"I'm okay, Mama," Florence said. "I'm just so happy to be here."

But something seemed to dawn on Constantine, because he smiled and went back into his bag. "Even though I didn't know our dear Florence was coming home for Christmas Eve, something made me buy this after I got a good price for the cotton."

He pulled out a small chocolate bar and walked with it and his beer back to kneel by Florence once more. "Enjoy it, sweet one."

She didn't have it in her to tell him she was feeling a little sick to her stomach, so she said, "Can we save it for tomorrow, Papa? For Christmas?"

"We can," he said. "But why not try just a little?"

"Okay," she said, and got up on one elbow while her father broke off a corner. She put it in her mouth, and a wave of delight pulsed through her. "That's so good."

"Can I have a piece, Uncle Constantine?" Jasper asked.

Florence's father had a soft spot for his nephew, whose parents had died in a bus accident the year before. But he said, "Not now, Jasper. Not until tomorrow."

"Oh," the boy said, more than a little disappointed. "But there will be some tomorrow?"

"That's the plan."

"Oh," he said, smiling now. "That's good!"

"In the meantime, help your cousins and auntie with the firewood."

"Already done!" Jasper said. "Enough for tomorrow, too. And I swept the entire compound for Auntie."

Josca nodded. "He did. I didn't even have to tell him."

Jasper beamed and threw his shoulders back.

Constantine said, "Then sit and visit with Flo for now. Everyone else, back to your chores. It'll be dark before you know it."

———

While her other brothers and sisters went back to what they'd been doing, Jasper came a few meters closer to Florence before stopping, worry on his face.

"I can't get it from you, can I?"

"No," Josca said, patting Florence on the shoulder before getting to her feet and moving toward the fire. "The nurses said that's over early."

Jasper hesitated before coming to sit on the mat beside her. "What's the hospital like?"

Florence felt tired, but said, "Lots of kids and no play. I hated it. Except for Miss Catherine. My nurse."

Jasper thought about that. "Is it true you got spots everywhere? Like a leopard?"

"She had a rash, Jasper," Josca called over.

"But spots in her mouth like a leopard?"

Florence laughed and then coughed. "Leopards don't have spots in their mouths."

"How do you know?" Jasper said. "You ever looked in a leopard's mouth?"

"Hope I never have to. But I'm pretty sure they don't have spots in them."

"But you did."

"Measles does that. But they're gone now."

"Let me see."

Florence opened her mouth wide.

"Wow, Flo," Jasper said. "You've got a really, really big mouth."

Florence snorted. Her cousin was always saying things like that.

"Go away, Jasper," she said, yawning. "I'm going to sleep."

"Aren't you happy to be home?"

She looked all around the compound, remembered the total love she felt being in her mother's arms on the way home, and smiled as her eyes fluttered shut.

"More than happy, Jasper. This is the best Christmas present ever."

Chapter Four

May 1992
Rwotobilo, Uganda

Twelve-year-old Anthony Opoka tried to run everywhere he went, all day long. From his sleeping hut to the borehole well, from the well to the garden he tended, and then the entire way to school, nearly two kilometers, and back again in the late afternoon.

Anthony had been running like this almost every day since the May before, training himself to be fast over distance for the district footrace qualifiers and the district race itself. He had recently won his qualifier, as he had a year ago when he came in second at the district event. He had vowed that would not happen twice.

I'm going to win, he'd told his father and mother and brothers and sisters repeatedly. *I am going to beat that kid Patrick. You watch me. I will be district champion.*

Every time Anthony said it, he felt some of that rare warmth in his chest. If he closed his eyes, he could see everyone cheering for him as he crossed the finish line. *District champ!*

George had encouraged this way of thinking, as he always did when they went off together and talked about becoming a human instead of a boy. But his mother kept reminding him that anything could happen, that he could fail in a dozen ways he could never expect. She'd done it just the night before, knowing that today was the day. Today was the district race.

I won't fail, he'd told her, frowning. *Everyone will know who I am.*

Acoko shook her head. *Sometimes I think you need people telling you how good you are, how special you are, all the time, Anthony.*

What's wrong with that?

You should know you're good without having to be told. It should come from inside you.

Anthony had felt a little deflated because he'd realized that his mother rarely praised him and instead pointed out his shortcomings and invented ways his hopes could be dashed.

"I'm going, Mama," he called to her as she cleaned pots that morning.

"I see," she said, not looking up. "Good luck."

"I will be district champion!"

"I heard you. Run hard."

There was little enthusiasm in her voice, and he set off for school, wishing his father were not in Gulu and wondering again why Acoko had become so gloomy in the past year. She slept a lot. And Anthony had discovered her alone and crying more than once in recent months.

He tried not to think about his mother as he walked. But he loved Acoko and knew that she loved him, and he simply could not understand what made her increasingly sad. He'd even asked his father about it the other day, and for once, George had few answers.

Some people just become that way, he said. *Life disappoints them over and over again, so they come to expect it in a way.*

Anthony was rarely disappointed by life. He loved to laugh, was constantly amazed by new things, and adored school, especially math and languages. His teachers said that before long, he would be elected head boy, so he had embraced that goal in the same way he'd embraced trying to be better than the day before, being a good human, and training for the yearly races by running everywhere and by seeing himself cross the finish line ahead of Patrick Lumumba over and over again.

Storm clouds were forming in the west. The wind picked up as he broke into a jog and passed the abandoned home of his late uncle John and felt slightly sick to his stomach. His uncle had been killed by soldiers with the Lord's Resistance Army, fanatics loyal to that crazy preacher from Awere Hill. They had attacked his uncle and other patrons of a hotel in Gulu. Every time Anthony ran past his dead uncle's abandoned home, he heard his father telling him to watch out for LRA soldiers because they were kidnapping boys, and to stay away from all soldiers and military if he could manage it.

The worst thing you can do in life is to become a soldier, George often told him. *Being a soldier is all about the power of one man over another. Before you were born, Idi Amin's men beat me because they had the power to do it. When Museveni won the war, his men beat me because they had the power to do it. And Joseph Kony's men killed my brother for the same reason. Please, Anthony, whatever you do in life, do not become a soldier. Do not hold power over others.*

———

By the time he reached the school, his younger half brothers, Albert and Charles, were already there and playing tag with friends near a line of jitneys and buses. When they saw Anthony, they crowded around him.

"My brother will win," Charles announced. "He will be district champion."

"You don't know that," another kid said.

Albert got defensive. "We do know, and you know why? Because Anthony has trained hard, and he has already seen himself winning hundreds of times when he closes his eyes."

"Thousands," Anthony said.

"What if Patrick Lumumba has seen it that many times, too?"

Before he could reply, the teachers came out of the school and told everyone to get in one of the vehicles. Anthony, as school champ, rode with the teachers and headmaster, who asked him if he was nervous to be running in the open division, against kids as old as fourteen.

"I'll be nervous afterward," he said.

But when they pulled up to the secondary-school grounds, where the races were to be held, he saw hundreds of excited students streaming out of other jitneys and buses; and right in the middle of the crowd, standing taller than almost everyone around him, was Patrick.

He looks like a man! Anthony thought, his heart racing. *How is it possible for someone to grow that much in one year?*

Doubt began to seep into his thoughts. *I can't outrun a man. I'll have to take two strides for his one. I have no chance. No one in the race has a chance.*

Getting out of the bus, he felt defeated until Charles and Albert came beside him.

"You ready?" Albert asked.

"Did you see Patrick?" Anthony said, gesturing over at the boy who'd bested him the year before.

"Oooh, he's huge!" Charles said.

"I know. It's over."

"Over?" Albert said. "It's not over. Who cares if he grew a bunch? Maybe he can't run as fast because he grew a bunch."

"I don't know."

Charles said, "You can't race thinking, 'I don't know.'"

Albert nodded, said, "What would Dad tell you?"

Anthony thought about that, hearing his father tell him not to defeat himself before he tried something new. *You must believe you will do it before you can do it.*

He repeated that to himself several times and closed his eyes, trying to see himself ahead of Patrick, crossing the finish line with him far behind. But Anthony kept seeing his nemesis running slightly ahead of him.

Well, he thought, *maybe I can catch up and tie him.*

He'd no sooner had that idea than a plan formed in his mind, and he saw it clearly. When he opened his eyes, he smiled at his younger brothers and said, "Now, I believe."

"That's right, you do!" Charles said.

"You do, you do!" Albert said.

Whistles began blowing. Someone from the district had a bullhorn and used it to call the footrace champions from fifteen different schools, boys and girls.

The girls went first, taking off in a long line, all of them sprinting toward a flag on a pole some five hundred meters away. Within the first two hundred meters, gaps began to open in the field as several girls became winded by the pace.

Feeling sure he was right now, Anthony cheered for the girl who'd been well back in the pack at the start and passed four girls coming around the flagpole. She caught another girl with two hundred meters to go, and her schoolmates went wild as she closed on the leader.

But before she could fully catch up, the first girl crossed the line, gasping and gripping her side as she fell to the ground. The disappointment on the face of the runner-up hit Anthony deep inside his chest. Then the whistles and bullhorn returned, calling the boys to the starting line. Anthony saw the girl who'd come in second wiping at her eyes.

Not today, he thought, hearing the first rumble of thunder in the distance.

He looked at the dark clouds, but figured they were at least a half hour away.

They called the boys to the starting line. Anthony went to the middle. Patrick Lumumba came up last and pushed his way in to Anthony's immediate right, looking like he'd gained eight kilos in addition to the height.

"I'm always a little late," Patrick said to Anthony. "And I am going to bury you, Opoka."

"Of course you are," Anthony said. "Anyone can see that. I'm running for second place."

The bigger boy looked down at him. "Good. You do that."

At the crack of the pistol, half the boys in the field of fifteen took off as many of the girls had, in a full sprint. Patrick loped along behind them, his long legs chewing up just enough ground to stay in range. Anthony purposefully fell one boy behind Patrick halfway to the flag and the five-hundred-meter mark.

By the time they were fifty meters from the flag and the turn toward home, the boys who'd fancied themselves cheetahs were cramping and slowing. Patrick picked off three before the pole. Anthony passed the boy in front of him and shifted slightly left to stay directly behind last year's winner rounding the flag.

Patrick picked up the pace. Anthony stayed with him as they closed in and passed the boy in fifth and then the one in fourth. He could see the three leaders with their heads thrown back and their shoulders stiffening at the 750-meter mark. Patrick passed the boy in third with two hundred meters to go.

But as he did, Anthony noticed Patrick's head beginning to tilt back, searching for more air. The second he saw that, he realized how good he felt and did not hesitate with one hundred meters left. Anthony swung slightly right of the boy in second and broke into a full sprint.

He went past the boy, who grunted in surprise. Anthony focused ahead of Patrick and told himself to drive his arms and legs all the way through the finish.

Anthony came even with Patrick with twenty-five meters to go and moved ahead at twenty meters, hearing him gasp behind him, and then the pounding of his feet trying to catch him. He felt the bigger boy closing the distance, but when he crossed the finish line, the kid who'd bested him the year before was still a half stride off the pace.

Throwing his arms overhead and filled with joy, Anthony slowed, gasping for air and turning to see Patrick limp, moan, and grab at the back of his leg.

"Tore it," he snarled. "Tore it or I would have had you, Opoka."

"But you didn't," Anthony said, breaking into a grin when Charles and the rest of his school came to him, cheering. They hoisted him up on their shoulders and paraded him around the secondary-school grounds.

He felt filled up again with that rare warmth, basking in the glory and the praise. He'd earned it. Everyone said so.

Lightning flashed several kilometers to the north followed by crashes of thunder as the dark clouds began to release curtains of rain. But where the race was being held, the sun still shone strong and hot. As far as he could tell, the storm was going to miss them completely. The teachers and headmasters must have thought so as well because they did not protest when the man with the bullhorn called the students to get in line for lunch.

Anthony kept drinking water and walked around continuing to accept the congratulations of kids and teachers from his and other schools. He spotted Patrick and several of the other boys from the race sitting in the river that ran through the area. Patrick saw him looking his way, scowled, and pivoted his head to say something to Joshua, the boy who'd come in third.

Anthony didn't care. He'd won the race fair and square even if Patrick had torn his hamstring in the final meters. If he was going to be a spoilsport, there was little Anthony could do about it, and besides, he was starting to feel hungry.

Charles and Albert waved him over and let him cut in front of them in line. They'd gotten plates of food and were sitting in the shade eating when dark clouds took the sun. Anthony saw birds flush from a tributary of the Aswa River beyond the flagpole. He wouldn't have taken much notice if not for more birds whirling out of the tangle along the river, closer this time, and then again over the course of perhaps thirty seconds. He'd heard his father talk about leopards using the waterways to prowl and hunt. But that was usually at night and not in this kind of heat.

Right?

Two hundred meters away, more birds flushed out of the river bottom. Anthony set down his plate and got to his feet, hearing a low, persistent roar coming closer. He took five steps toward the river, seeing Patrick, Joshua, and two other boys standing up in the knee-deep water and turning to look behind them.

One boy managed to scream before a reddish-brown wall of rainwater the thunderstorm had dumped upstream slammed into them and swept them all away. For a split second, Anthony stood there, astonished, before instinct took over and he began to sprint downstream.

———

As fast as he was, Anthony was not fast enough to get ahead of the wave. The closest he got was forty meters, and there the water was frothy and ripping. He caught a glimpse of Joshua before the river took a hard turn left. The kid's head was above water and facing back at Anthony when he vanished against the near bank.

Rounding that turn, he saw two of the boys crawling out and collapsing in the grass, and then, farther downriver, he spotted Patrick, almost to the opposite bank and holding on to saplings that were bent like upside-down fishhooks. The stormwater raged and roiled around the bigger boy, who was screaming for help.

A close thunderclap behind Anthony threw him into another gear. He raced past the two other boys, who still lay there coughing up water. When he reached the bank opposite Patrick, it began to pour. Water kept crashing into the chest and over the head of his rival, and the river continued to rise, almost over its banks now.

Anthony kind of knew how to swim. George's brother, his uncle Paul, had taught him. But the only times he'd swum were when the water was almost still and nowhere near as deep. He looked behind him to see a mob of other boys and teachers running to the boys on the bank.

"Here!" Anthony screamed. "Patrick's here!"

Charles, Albert, and the headmaster from their school reached him first, followed by seven of the teachers.

"We have no rope," Anthony said. "We'll have to make a chain to get to him."

When the teachers looked at the water with horror in their eyes, he said, "I'll go first. Take your belts off and loop them together. Fast!"

In less than thirty seconds, they'd fashioned a length of interconnected loops, and more teachers were arriving and putting their belts on the back end of the chain when Anthony looked over to see Patrick almost submerged. He put his head and arms through the front belt, so that it rode beneath his armpits, and moved upstream fifteen meters.

"Drag me out if I go under!" Anthony said, as some of the teachers and older boys began putting the belts up under their armpits as he had. "The more weight behind me the better!"

Then, before he could talk himself out of it, Anthony jumped off the bank, went under, but almost immediately popped back up and stalled there, water pouring over the back of his head and making it almost impossible to see. The teacher behind him got into the water, and the one after that.

Anthony could almost stand upright as more of the people belted together entered the raging river and anchored him. He began to shuffle and wade sideways, but when he did, he hit a deep hole and went under again. This time he surfaced sideways to the man behind him, and yelled, "It's deep here!"

More students and teachers on the belt line climbed down into the river. Anthony stopped trying to find footing and did everything he could not to be swept back to the near bank. Another minute and more links in the human chain and he was almost to Patrick, who kept twisting his head away from Anthony to get his face out of the water long enough to breathe.

"Patrick!" he yelled. "Turn to me!"

Anthony stretched out his hand toward the boy, who still had a death grip on the saplings. Patrick turned his head, tried to see Anthony, but his face was awash. Sputtering, choking, he looked away.

"You have to turn and reach out to me!" Anthony yelled.

"I can't let go! I'll be taken!"

Anthony screamed to the people behind him that they needed one more person in the river and for everyone anchoring the chain to take two steps forward. A moment later, he felt the slack and took two hard pulls and kicks and went underwater. He slammed into Patrick.

Grabbing the bigger boy tight around the waist, Anthony tried to get his head up out of the raging river. But Patrick began to fight him. Anthony let go one hand, grabbed his rival by the neck, and used the leverage to surface.

"Let go!" Patrick yelled.

"No! Let your left hand go and grab the belt around my chest."

"I can't! I—"

"Trust me, Patrick! I've got you! You're not dying! Not today!"

Finally, the bigger boy's hand came off the saplings and stabbed out at Anthony as he fought to hold Patrick in place. He felt fingers grab the belt.

"Let go! I've got you!"

Both their heads were up out of the river water now and only centimeters apart in the pouring rain. He and Patrick stared into each other's eyes as the bigger boy let go of the saplings and swung with the current as he grabbed hold of the belt around Anthony, his full weight now dangling downstream in the rushing current.

"Pull us in!" Anthony yelled. "Everyone, go to the bank! Pull to the bank!"

Both of them went under at the first pull and the second. But neither of them relaxed their grips, and they surfaced both times, grinning madly at each other.

"I'm not dying," Patrick said.

"Not today," Anthony said.

Six pulls later, Patrick said, "I can feel the bottom!"

"I can't!" Anthony said.

"Don't worry," Patrick said. "I've got *you* now."

A minute later, they were being dragged up onto the bank, where they unbuckled the belts and everyone on the chain fell over on their backs in the pouring tropical rain. Anthony felt more exhausted and more alive than he ever had. People began to cheer and clap. He looked up and saw everyone from the race—athletes, coaches, teachers, and students alike—all there, all elated to see four of the boys survive the flash flood.

But then he felt sick to his stomach. "I saw him," he said to Patrick. "Joshua, the kid in third, before he went under. I don't think he made it."

Patrick's face fell. "I liked him. He was happy to be third."

Anthony said nothing, bewildered at the crosscurrent of emotions rolling through him, happy to have won, happy to be alive, happy Patrick was alive, and thoroughly shocked at Joshua's drowning. He wondered how he could feel all these things at once.

"We made it," Patrick said as the downpour began to lighten. "Because of you, Opoka."

"Because of everyone who went into the river after you, Patrick. I just went first."

"I'm serious," the bigger boy said, struggling to his feet.

When Anthony got up beside him, Patrick said, "You saved my life. I won't forget. Ever." He stuck out his paw of a hand, and Anthony shook it. "Oh, and I'm going to beat you next year. There's no way I'm losing two in a row."

Anthony laughed. "The only way you win is if I retire from competition."

Patrick laughed. "You caught me in my growth-spurt year. You watch, when you grow, you'll lose some of your speed."

"Tell it to your hamstring," Anthony said. "I'm not slowing down. Ever."

By the time they returned to the schoolyard, the storm had passed, though the river was still running hard. When he and Patrick said goodbye and got back in their respective jitneys for the rides back to their schools, Anthony remained at odds with all the emotions swirling in him except one—the dead-certain feeling that swelled in his chest when he realized he'd just made a close friend.

Chapter Five

April 1993
Amia'bil, Uganda

Nine-year-old Florence Okori was as happy as she'd ever been as she walked to school with her friends that cloudy morning early in the rainy season, feeling like anything was possible, even going out to see the bigger world.

"Someday I will go to America," she announced, which provoked laughter from her cousin Jasper.

"And how will you pay for that?" Jasper asked.

"From the money I will get by becoming a nurse," she said confidently.

"Do you know how hard that is? Becoming a nurse?"

"No harder than surviving measles," she said, and lifted her chin.

It had taken two full years for Florence to recover after Josca brought her home from hospital. Her mother had passed on many of her chores to her husband and older daughters to focus wholly on Florence in the first few months of recuperation.

Florence had lost almost half her weight in the measles ward, and she'd been so weak she could barely sit by herself. Some days she never woke up. Josca made her soups with bone broths and added meat whenever Constantine could afford it.

Her mother carried Florence everywhere. If she was fetching water, she sat Florence at the top of the grade, where she could watch. If she was hoeing in the gardens, Josca brought her along, setting her on a mat in the shade while she toiled. And when she went to church, Florence was cradled in Josca's arms.

Day after day, she basked in her mother's pure love. Despite the good food and the constant attention from Josca, the recovery was excruciatingly slow. Florence kept having minor relapses of fever. She overheard several women in the village tell her mother that she should not focus so much on Florence, that the likelihood was she would dwindle and die as so many others had.

But every time her mother heard any comment like that, she laughed and told them that Florence was going to live and grow up to be a nurse and show them all what a Ugandan girl could do when she put her mind to it. And every time she heard her mother defend her and speak so glowingly of her future, Flo loved Josca all the more.

Her siblings also went out of their way to help her and make her understand how incredible it was that she had survived. This was especially true of her oldest brother, Owen, who loved to tease and make her laugh.

The illness was gone for good by the following Christmas, and Florence had begun to use her arms tentatively. Her mother still carried her everywhere, even when she began to get her leg strength back.

You don't need to carry me anymore, she told Josca one day. *It makes you too tired.*

Florence, you are my daughter, her mother said. *I would carry you forever if I had to.*

Once again, Josca's devotion deeply touched Florence, made her feel whole, but she said, *I love you, too, Mama, but I need to try on my own now.*

———

Within weeks, she'd been able to stand and walk hesitantly with Josca's help into church past the women who'd told her mother to just let her die. With every day that followed, she got slightly stronger. By the end of August, some twenty months after coming home, she was once again rising with her mother, fetching water, and helping in the gardens.

Florence was almost seven when she finally started school. She felt lost the first month. But she worked hard and asked lots of questions when she didn't understand something. Once she did understand, she never forgot and quickly caught up to students her own age.

The teachers noticed. One in particular, Mr. Alonsius, was so good at explaining things that she wanted to work harder. Two of Florence's older sisters were in secondary school and wanted to be teachers like Mr. Alonsius. She would hear her mother tell them that to teach well, you had to learn well, and to study diligently in school.

One by one, however, her older sisters had gotten married and carried on the way their families had for generations—farming, bartering, most times living a hand-to-mouth existence.

When Josca saw Florence begin to achieve high marks, however, she became adamant that this daughter would not have the same kind of life. Florence would be different. She would go to school, learn, and eventually become a nurse to help people all over Uganda.

The other girls can marry, but not you, not at first, Josca always said. *You'll go to school, get a job as a nurse, and make money for yourself.*

And for you, Mama, said Florence, who by that time considered Josca her best friend.

Her mother taught her to put her mind not only to her studies but to business as well.

If you know how to make something for one price and sell it for more, you will never go hungry, Josca said after showing her how to make soap and to take it to the market to sell.

Florence had followed her mother's teaching about business and was soon making soap by herself and growing cash crops like cotton and melons that she could sell to have money of her own. She had also taken to following Constantine into the bush to gather medicinal plants. She adored these trips. Searching for medicinal plants, her father came alive, excited, and so eager to tell her what they were and how to use them to help others. Goosefoot leaves to reduce swelling. Bitter leaf for diabetes and joint pain. Beetroot to fight cancer.

Most people just walk by, only interested if it's corn or tomatoes in their gardens, he'd said more than once. *But the bush holds secrets. You just have to learn to see them.*

By the time she finished her second year of schooling, Florence had become one of the top students in her class. Mr. Alonsius had been so pleased with her performance, he'd given her two notebooks and two pens on the first day of school the prior September.

One notebook is for your studies, he said. *The other is for your thoughts and dreams.*

Florence was stunned. The notebooks and pens were literally the first new things she had ever owned herself, and she instantly became proud and protective of them. Every night, as Mr. Alonsius taught her, she wrote something down about her day and then about her dreams of the future, of becoming a nurse, seeing America, and so much more.

———

Those precious notebooks were in the little book bag Josca had sewn for Florence when she, her cousin Jasper, and their friends finally reached the schoolyard to find kids already playing football with a taped-up ball. The one-level elementary school comprised a long main concrete building and two shorter wings. Florence ran to the right-hand wing and entered the second classroom. She put her book bag at her desk and went out to join the game.

Before she could get there, Mr. Alonsius, who was always smiling and always crisply dressed, called to her, "Florence Okori! Did you write down your dreams last night?"

She nodded, grinned. "I will go to the nursing school in Kampala, Teacher! The best one!"

Her favorite teacher tapped a finger at his temple. "Good girl. That is the way to think your way ahead in this life!"

It was true. Ever since Florence had begun writing down her dreams, her imaginings of her future life, many of them had come to pass. When she had wanted a nice dress for her First Communion, her father had surprised her with the materials that her mother fashioned into a nicer garment than she'd ever imagined. And when she'd written about herself getting high grades on big tests in math, they had happened as well.

Just the night before, she had written down how she would ace her final exams in the coming weeks, and how, as she had told her teacher, in the coming years, she would attend the nursing school at the university in Kampala. As she ran off to kick the ball around with her classmates, in her mind she saw herself walking out the door of that school dressed in a sharp-white uniform.

Miss Florence, the nurse!

She'd no sooner had that thought than Jasper and her friends stopped playing and gaped at something behind her. Some of the girls started laughing. But
Jasper and the other boys grew tense and afraid.

Florence spun around and saw nine naked men wearing only colorful hats
as they entered the schoolyard. Four of them carried spears. Two held primitive
bows and arrows. The other three held AK-47s.

Mr. Alonsius started toward them. A gunman wearing a red hat lifted his
weapon and fired a burst into the air, freezing Flo's teacher and causing many
children to shriek and run.

Florence had never met men from this tribe before, but she knew who they
were the second she saw them. They were Karimojong, nomadic warriors, who
did not believe in wearing much more than a bolt of cloth over their shoulders,
and then only in the cold seasons. They were from far northeastern Uganda, hard
by the border with Kenya, and thought all livestock was theirs to steal, and all
villages theirs to raid and loot.

"Please," Mr. Alonsius said, his hands raised. "This is a school. There are no
cattle here."

Red Hat, as Florence would later call him, spit at her teacher's feet. "Why
do you rot their brains, Teacher? Why do you teach them to wear clothes and
follow dictators?"

"They are children."

"I am not talking about them," Red Hat sneered. "I am talking about you."

Mr. Alonsius swallowed hard. "What do you want?"

"Your clothes, to start. All of them. And the clothes of all the male teachers."

"Or what? You will shoot me?"

"I would not waste the bullet," Red Hat said, and gestured to one of the
men with a bow and arrows. "But my brother, he will shoot you in a way that
gives you so much pain you will hurry to take off your clothes before another
arrow sticks in your ass."

The naked man with the bow drew an arrow from his quiver, nocked it, and
grinned. "Turn around," he said. "Give me a target, Teacher Man."

"Or take off your clothes," Red Hat said, "and put them here in front of me."

After a long moment, Mr. Alonsius began to unbutton his white tunic.
Florence felt so angry she had to fight not to shout at the men. When her teacher

unbuckled his belt and pants and dropped them, she saw the humiliation on his face and wanted to cry.

Red Hat gestured at Mr. Alonsius's white briefs. "Especially those."

Florence would not watch. She stared at the ground, hearing Red Hat order the other male teachers to strip and put their clothes in a pile, before telling one of his men to get gasoline from Mr. Alonsius's motorcycle, parked in the shade of a tree where so many of Florence's classes had been held over the years.

"This is wrong," she heard Jasper whisper behind her.

"Don't say anything," she hissed back. "Or you'll be naked, too!"

A whoosh noise caused Florence to raise her head. Mr. Alonsius and the other three male teachers stood there, covering their genitals with their hands while watching most of their clothes go up in flames. The rest of their clothes had been wrapped around branch limbs and set afire.

Red Hat's men held the burning branches like torches, which they carried to the thatch-roofed classrooms and lit them one by one, starting with the left wing of the school.

"This will stop your brains from rotting," Red Hat said, more to the children than the teachers. "You will remember this day."

Florence watched in horror as the main building burned and the Karimojong men walked to the right-hand wing, the wing that held her classroom. One of them hurled a torch onto the roof, and it quickly caught and raged. At first, she was so shocked she could not move, could not feel anything but fear about what might happen next.

But as she watched the fire take the roof of her classroom, she understood what was still there and felt gutted. Florence fell to her knees when the roof collapsed and flames came out the door, and she wept in despair, watching her beloved book of dreams go up in smoke and ash.

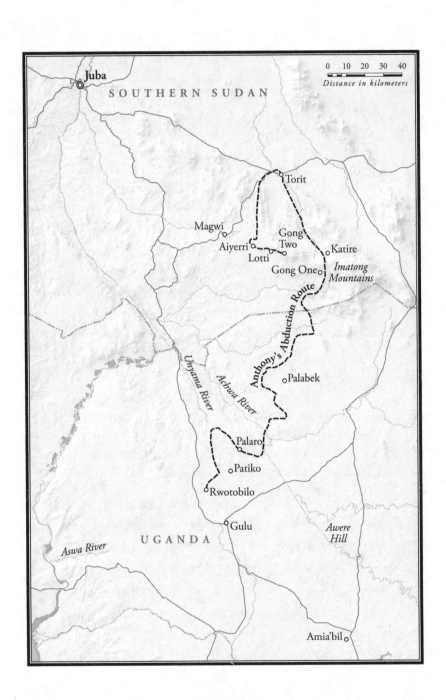

Chapter Six

September 14, 1994
Rwotobilo, Uganda

Anthony Opoka left day two of school that year sporting the biggest grin of his life.

"I knew you'd win, Anthony," said ten-year-old Charles, who ran up behind him.

"So did I," said twelve-year-old Albert, who was still limping from a fall he'd taken back in May. "Who else would be a better head boy? Our big brother is the smartest in his class."

"I don't know about that," said Anthony, who was fourteen, with a birthday coming the following month. "But I do like math and languages."

"You also get along with everyone," Charles said. "Even the teachers."

Anthony shrugged. "Why not get along with everyone? Who needs enemies?"

"And you are still the fastest boy for your age in the entire district," Albert said. "That counted. I am sure of it."

Ordinarily, that kind of praise would have filled him with that rare warmth. But for the first time since the faculty vote was taken earlier that afternoon, the grin faded from his face. Albert was correct. He was the reigning district champion in the one-kilometer race and had been for the past three years. But that distinction did not please him the way it once had.

The day he'd beaten Patrick Lumumba as a twelve-year-old had been one of the highlights of his life. Not only had he won the race, but he'd helped save a life and made a great friend. Anthony had felt strongly in his heart the last time he saw Patrick that, somehow, they were destined to be big parts of each other's lives.

But then, late in November of 1992, the headmaster had pulled Anthony aside to give him dreadful news. As had been happening more and more often in those days, a band of Lord's Resistance Army soldiers had come hunting for recruits to join Joseph Kony's war. The LRA attacked Patrick's village in the middle of the night. Patrick was abducted and dragged off, his wrists tied behind his back.

When Anthony had run in the district race the next May, he'd had no competition to speak of and felt sad that Patrick had not been there to push him. He'd felt the same way running in the district race this year; without Patrick racing him, the victory had felt hollow.

Moreover, his friend's abduction and a series of others in the past eighteen months had changed other aspects of his life. Made it smaller, certainly. No longer were they free to roam alone out of their family's compounds or off the route to and from school. Under George's orders, the boys moved together, or they did not move at all.

The past rainy season, the LRA raids had become more frequent and more brutal. The threat hung everywhere in the air.

The vague discomfort Anthony had felt learning about Joseph Kony as a seven-year-old had turned into anger at the kidnapping of Patrick Lumumba, and then to an almost constant fear that he and his brothers might eventually be taken. Many parents, including the Opokas, had started sending their kids into Gulu after sunset, long lines of children streaming into the city at dusk, sleeping on mats and blankets under sodium lights near the police and army barracks.

At first, Anthony had led his brothers and sisters on these long walks, navigating by the stars and the various landmarks. But within two weeks, Charles and Albert could have led the way. And now, after almost four months of walking in the dark, any of his brothers or sisters could have done the route alone.

———

As the Opoka boys made their way home from school that afternoon, a Ugandan army helicopter chugged north from Gulu and flew in arcs over the bush and villages, including Rwotobilo. Despite his father's general distaste for soldiers of any uniform, Anthony felt comforted by the gunship passing overhead as they approached their village. In response to the kidnappings by the LRA, President Museveni had sent more men and helicopters to try to stop them. Anthony hoped they succeeded and put an end to Kony and his followers.

When they reached home, Charles and Albert ran off to tell their mothers about Anthony's election. Anthony retrieved his hoe and was about to pick up where he'd left off weeding tomatoes the afternoon before, but then stopped in front of his own mother's hut, empty, abandoned. He felt even sadder than when he had been thinking about Patrick.

"Where is that head boy?" his father called out, laughing and clapping his hands as he came into the clearing. "I am so proud!"

George walked over and threw his arms around his son. "A leader. This is what you are, Anthony. And everyone sees it."

Anthony felt that warm feeling inside and tried to bask in his father's attention and praise. But his eyes misted over when he said, "Everyone except Mom."

George's face fell a little. "Your mother will know soon enough."

Acoko had left earlier in the year, gone home to live with her family. She said she had to help take care of her mother, who was ill, but she'd also told George that she did not know if she wanted to be married to him anymore. And she'd told Anthony that while she still loved him with all her heart, he was better off with his father for the time being.

She should have been here, he thought a little bitterly. *She should have been here to learn that I was elected head boy instead of abandoning us like that.*

Instead, he said, "How will she know?"

"Because you will tell her," George said. "She sent me a letter a few days ago. She said she is feeling better and wants to see you. I will give you the jitney fare this weekend."

"But you should come, too."

His father smiled sadly. "She did not ask to see me, Anthony. When she does, I will."

Anthony felt bad about his parents' fractured relationship but nodded. "I'll go see her."

"Good," George said. "Homework?"

"None yet. I'm going to finish weeding the tomatoes before we walk to Gulu."

"Not tonight. I need you all here first thing to harvest the corn and the eggplant. You, Albert, and Charles will sleep here. I have to go to my friend's store and sleep there to protect it, but I will be back right after dawn."

"Will you bring the baskets?"

"And the burlap tarps," George said before breaking into a grin again. "Head boy! It is a great honor, and it means I am almost done with my job, and we can be friends."

Anthony looked at his father, puzzled. "Almost done with your job?"

"Teaching you to be a good human."

"And because of that we can be friends now?"

"I hope so," he said, smiling. "Look. When I was about to become a father for the first time, I asked my mother what my job was as a parent. She said it was simple: From birth to age five, love them no matter what. From five to age fifteen, teach them as best you can. From fifteen on, be their friend because they will need that more than your unasked-for advice or guidance."

It kind of made sense to Anthony. "But I still have one more month to learn, right?"

George laughed. "Of course. And I'll see you first thing in the morning."

He turned and began to walk away.

"Dad?" Anthony called.

His father looked over his shoulder, his eyebrows up.

"I love you," Anthony said, feeling a ball of emotion in his throat.

"I love you, too, Anthony," George said. "You are a very special . . . young man."

Those words echoed in Anthony's ears along with the congratulations he'd heard earlier from teachers and fellow students as he weeded in the fading light, wondering if his mother would be happy at his becoming head boy, whether she would fill him with rare warmth. He smelled something savory cooking on the fire by Charles's mother's place and, when the wind shifted, the odors of an equally mouthwatering meal from Albert's mother's cook pot a hundred meters away, close to Uncle Paul's compound beneath the three tall trees.

Anthony looked out at the rose-colored sky in the west and whispered, "Thank you for today. And bless my mother and make her happy when she sees me."

He laid down the hoe at last light and headed toward Charles's mother's hut, where he ate a little, and then went to Albert's mother's hut and ate a little more. Afterward, as he lay down on his mat in his little hut and pulled the sheet up over his shoulders, he decided that, all in all, this had been one of the best days of his life.

Maybe even the best.

———

Hours later, Anthony awoke in the dark, excited for what lay ahead. They would finally harvest the corn and eggplant, and George would haul them to his friend's store for sale while he, Charles, and Albert went off to school, and his first real day as head boy.

He dressed and went to the corn patch when he could barely see. He started tearing ears off the stalks and piling them in small pyramids. By the time he'd finished a row, the first rays of sun had broken the horizon. Cows lowed in the distance. Goats blatted and the bells around their necks tinkled. There was the faintest smell of woodsmoke and spice on the wind.

Then he thought he heard a woman yelling to the west and across the road, probably the neighbors who were jealous of all of George's small businesses and successes. The woman stopped crying out almost immediately, and Anthony didn't think much of it as he continued to harvest the corn. Charles stumbled up, yawning and rubbing his eyes.

"You're almost done," Charles said.

"Because I got up on time," Anthony said. "Where's Albert?"

"Sleeping?"

Beyond the field and across the road, a guinea fowl flushed from the tall, dew-soaked grass. The bird flew low and arced away, cackling. And then another flushed, almost immediately landing in the road and running off, chirping in alarm. Anthony watched the grass.

"I'll go get him," Charles said.

His younger brother was turning to go when Anthony saw something that took his breath away as cleanly as a punch to the solar plexus. In the first strong sun rays hitting the wet high grass, he saw the glint of something metal. Then he saw the grass move, and it became the barrel and bayonet of an automatic war rifle held high by a filthy, bare-chested creature, his long hair in dreadlocks. He was no more than eighty meters off when he stepped out on the road.

"Charles!" Anthony hissed. "LRA! Run! Hide!"

His younger brother needed no more motivation than that. Charles bolted into the brush between the crop field and Albert's hut. Anthony got low and ran back up the picked corn rows before entering the thicker vegetation that separated the field from Acoko's abandoned hut and Charles's mother's place. He wanted to take off in an all-out sprint, heading toward that high point his father took him to when they looked at the stars. It was rocky there. He could get hidden among the boulders while still being able to watch the country all around.

But if Anthony ran, he knew he'd break branches. He might flush birds. LRA soldiers lived full time in the bush. They'd see the signs and come after him, find his tracks.

Heart racing and breathing hard now, he forced himself to slow down, to push branches aside rather than break them, and to look ahead, seeing the outline of Charles's mother's hut. As he veered around it, still back in the brush a good forty meters, he heard shouting, this time from Albert's mother.

"No!" she said. "Don't you dare take him!"

Charles broke from the brush on the other side of his mother's place. He was running for his life, with the bare-chested guy hot on his tail. The LRA soldier grabbed Anthony's youngest brother by the hair and yanked him full off his feet before slamming him down hard.

"What are you doing to him?" Charles's mother screamed.

The ten-year-old was rolling around on the ground, holding on to his head, and moaning.

"He is coming with us," the gunman said, aiming an AK-47 at her and kicking Charles in the ribs. "Get up, you."

Anthony couldn't just stand there anymore. He did the only thing he could think of and walked forward, purposefully breaking branches until the LRA soldier heard him and aimed the rifle Anthony's way. Arms up, he stepped out.

"Don't take him. He's only ten. And you've hurt his head. He's no good to you, man."

The gunman looked at Charles moaning on the ground, and then back again at Anthony.

"Turn around, Recruit," he said, gesturing with the muzzle of his gun. "Start walking."

———

When they reached the road to the school, the LRA soldier tied Anthony's wrists in front of him with twine. Beneath the filth, the soldier looked to be in his late teens. They marched to a crossroads west of Rwotobilo, where three other gunmen brought out six boys, all bound, all petrified.

From that point forward, they rarely used roads except to cross them. When they did, one of the LRA gunmen would sweep their tracks out of the reddish dirt. They walked single file, a formation they called "the rail," sticking to game trails, skirting the paths between settlements and fields. For the first hour, Anthony walked in a daze of fear; he'd heard horrible stories about the LRA and how they treated their "recruits."

The heat built. Behind them in the distance, Anthony heard the chugging of a helicopter. The LRA soldiers heard the gunship as well and picked up the pace into a fast march. Anthony realized he was already so far from home he did not know where he was. Every time they came to a clearing, he'd crane his head around, looking for landmarks and finding none; the vine-choked trees and canopy were just too dense to see through.

Finally, in the fifth opening, he spotted the Kilak hills to the northwest and then the ones near Lamwo, probably thirty kilometers away, but roughly in their line of travel.

Northeast, Anthony thought. *We're going northeast, which means home is southwest, almost directly behind me.*

He looked back when he got the chance, trying to spot the three big trees near Rwotobilo, but could not.

The sun swiftly became the enemy. As they moved through the thick cover, the heat was oppressive and saturated with humidity. One boy, the smallest of them all, asked for water and was denied.

"No water for recruits until sundown," said the bare-chested gunman who'd taken Anthony and was called Henry. "Show us how strong you are. Keep up. Or die."

Anthony fought off the urge to panic at that thought. In his mind, he changed, became not the valued son, not the head boy, but the runner. He thought about all the training he'd done over the past three years, the long distances he'd covered, and entered that place of grit where he was willing to accept the hardship as necessary, not for competition now, but for survival. To conserve energy, he started by forcing himself to relax, to move more fluidly and from his hips, with as little tension in his shoulders and core as possible. He could no longer hear the helicopter, but they continued to march for hours at that hard pace, pausing only to wait for a road to clear, or to be joined by more LRA soldiers and more abductees.

There were eighteen kidnapped boys and nine rebel gunmen by the time the sun reigned high overhead, beating down on them, merciless. Some of the boys began to stagger. No matter how hard he tried not to think about it, Anthony's mouth grew more and more parched. *How long can we keep going like this without water? How long can I?*

As they worked through the densest vegetation and crossed small streams, Anthony took to dragging his hands against the wetter leaves and rocks and then licking his fingers, using the moisture to cut his thirst. Then, miraculously, around midafternoon, a thunderstorm came and soaked them all.

"You're lucky," Henry announced. "A third of the recruits usually die from thirst the first day. I know I almost did."

Two more abducted boys and another soldier met them on the banks of the west fork of the Unyama River later in the day. The waterway was perhaps thirty meters across there, but deep, and with the storm runoff, the current was fast enough to remind Anthony of the time he and the teachers had saved Patrick Lumumba's life during the flash flood.

Someone had tied a rope to trees on both riverbanks. The LRA soldiers began shouting at the abductees, telling them to grab the rope and pull themselves across. Several boys looked like they'd rather walk off a cliff.

"I can't swim," said the smallest boy, the one who'd asked for water.

"Then hold on tight," Henry said. "Or drown."

Anthony said, "Hold left hand facing forward, right hand facing back. Better grip."

Henry hit him in the stomach with the butt of his rifle. "Shut up."

The blow knocked the wind from Anthony, but he saw the small boy do as he'd instructed and drag himself across the rope. More of the abducted boys went into the water and crossed. By the time it was Anthony's turn, he'd gotten back his wind. In the water, he purposefully ducked his head and drank before climbing to the other side.

All twenty recruits made the crossing alive, and soon they were headed through waist-deep grass toward a hill in the distance. They climbed to the top of that hill as the sun was starting to set and were told to stop and sit. They would eat and then push on through the night. Despite the heat pulsing from the rocks all around and beneath them, several of the boys were shivering and staring at the ground, lost in their fears. The smallest boy sat beside Anthony.

"Thank you," he said. "For telling me how to hold the rope."

Anthony nodded.

"I'm James," the boy said.

"Anthony."

"Shut up, you two," Henry said. "No talking."

Anthony said he had to pee, then got up, walked to the edge of the hill, squinting toward the low-angle sun. As he urinated, he peered back across the valley floor, searching for the three tall, crisscrossing trees at Rwotobilo. And in the final rays of the setting sun, he found them, saw them silhouetted against the horizon like a distant beacon calling him home.

"You, sit down, you're not going anywhere," said Henry, who'd walked up behind him.

Anthony followed the order, but not before burning the image in his memory. After they had fed him a porridge of greens, cassava, and beans, he studied the stellar night sky, fixing on a cluster of three stars low on the western horizon and a single bright one to the east.

He memorized their position in the sky in relationship to the direction they had traveled during the day and told himself he could find this place again.

I will, Anthony promised himself. *I will find this hill again.*

Chapter Seven

September 16, 1994
Southwest of Patiko, Uganda

They walked at night and hid from gunships during the day. Henry and the other LRA soldiers kept rotating Anthony's and the boys' places on the rail, and they kept changing directions. It was confusing, which seemed to be the point.

They had taken off their wrist bonds to allow them to grab on to things in the dark. But any complaint or question would bring a kick or a strike. Any attempt to talk to another abductee would bring a kick or a strike. If one of the boys cried after being struck, he was hit again and told to stop or he would die.

With every step deeper into the wilds of northern Uganda, Anthony felt more alone. Moving through unfamiliar terrain in the elephant grass and thorn brush, he'd had trouble seeing his three stars in the west and the one bright one in the east and became increasingly disoriented and anxious.

What if I can't find my way home?

Shortly after sunrise on the third day of his captivity, with that question still haunting him, Anthony collapsed with the other boys near a stream and slept until someone handed him a bowl of that bean-and-green mush again. One of the LRA soldiers had killed a warthog, and they were now roasting it over an open fire.

He looked at the porridge, smelled the pork, listened to his stomach growl, and heard Acoko's voice in his head. *If you want to run far and fast, you have to eat, Anthony. Eat as much as you can.*

Anthony imagined the vile porridge as the most succulent pork chop he'd ever had and tore into the mush, eating every bit of it. Afterward, he drank from the stream, then lay down and was about to sleep when he noticed the smallest boy, James, opposite him, eyes already closed, curled up in a fetal position, sucking his thumb.

Back at home and in school, a boy that old sucking his thumb would have brought ribbing and maybe jeers. But to Anthony at that moment, it spoke of an earlier and simpler time of innocence and made him want to cry. He started to close his eyes against the tears when he heard the crackle of a radio.

"Seven Alpha, Seven Alpha," a man in a wavery voice called over the radio in Acholi. "Monkey, Lion, Kudu, come back."

Another voice answered, "Monkey back."

A third voice answered, "Kudu back."

A fourth voice, not on the radio, and very close to Anthony, said, "Lion back."

Anthony crawled toward "Lion" and soon saw an LRA soldier with his back to him, operating a shortwave radio and scribbling on a notepad when the original caller began reading out a list of letters and numerals that baffled Anthony.

When he was done, a new voice came on, also male. "This is Six Bravo. Repeat Six Bravo for Two Victor."

"Roger, Six Bravo," Lion said.

"Tell Two Victor to wait for the storm, when the birds are down, to move to RV. Over."

"Roger, over and out, Six Bravo."

At that, the operator got up, left the radio, and hurried off.

Not knowing what to make of it, Anthony crawled back opposite James and tried to sleep.

———

They stayed there, hidden, for four more days. It was late afternoon September 20, 1994, when Henry came through, kicking all the abducted boys awake again. They were given another bowl of the mush and told to drink from the stream.

The sky, which had been brilliant blue after sunrise, turned leaden and threatening with rain and a building wind as they set off on what Anthony assumed was a bearing roughly north- northwest. Even if they got out into more open areas, with a lighter tree canopy, he would not be able to see the stars, and it bothered him as the day dimmed toward twilight.

The first drops of rain touched his skin as the single-track path they followed through thick forest opened into more savanna-like country. Forty other abducted boys were sitting there on the edge of the forest, watched by fifteen LRA men with automatic weapons. Another thirty boys sat out farther in the grass under the watch of ten rebel soldiers.

One of the LRA men whistled loudly. The abducted boys in the grass were all prodded to their feet and moved forward of Anthony's group. Shrouds of rain began to billow and fall. The thirty boys who'd been sitting farthest from the forest went toward the very front of the rail, perhaps seventy meters through the downpour from Anthony, so he wasn't sure at first. But then he studied this one boy in that group, seeing him move with a slight but more-than-familiar limp.

"Albert!" he almost shouted before catching himself.

Worry exploded through Anthony as he lost sight of his younger brother and realized Albert had been living this same nightmare. How was he keeping up with his limp? It looked worse than before.

Then the LRA men brought ropes and tied them around their waists, one boy to the next, in three linked rails of thirty. Someone whistled again. They began to march, the warm rain pelting them from their left. Even after sundown and with so much rain falling, the vast pale grasslands made it easier to see than in the forest.

Anthony focused on putting one foot down after another on the trail, which became muddier and slipperier through the night, telling himself whenever he felt like he couldn't go on that if Albert could keep moving, he could. The rain slowed for a time. There was a break in the clouds that allowed moonlight to shine down so the savanna turned brighter still.

More whistles. They were urged to pick up the pace. The rails of thirty boys shuffled fast in the dim light, covering ground like centipedes. If someone tripped and fell against their rope, the entire group hung up or slammed into each other like dominoes, slowing progress. Then there was bellowing from the LRA soldiers, telling them to haul the fallen back to their feet, or face the machine guns. Pulled back and forth, Anthony struggled not to lose his balance before the rail started sputtering into a steady pace again.

It went on for hours like this without a break. Anthony started to feel chilled, and his thoughts became somewhat incoherent as the rain returned, even heavier than before. Dawn came, dim and gray and slanted. The LRA soldiers goaded the boys to move even faster toward a high, rocky hill near Patiko, Uganda, about thirty-five kilometers north of Rwotobilo.

Anthony had no idea how long they'd been running in short, choppy strides, careful not to kick the heel of the boy in front of him and break toes, when behind him someone fell yet again, near the base of a big, rocky hill that loomed just ahead of them. The rope pulled him backward and he almost fell. The rail halted.

"Get up!" Henry roared. "Get up and move!"

Anthony turned around and looked to his rear, seeing five or six boys struggling to their feet in the low light, covered in dirt, and looking battered and out of it.

"Get up!"

"I can't!" one boy cried.

The other recruits who'd just stood up were looking behind them and down where Anthony could not see.

"I can't," the boy sobbed. "I just can't."

Henry whistled. LRA soldiers converged on both sides of Anthony's group of thirty and began untying them all, front to back. Anthony was gingerly feeling where the rope had chafed his waist when the boys behind him moved aside to reveal the last boy in the rail, the smallest boy in the group, little James, sitting there in the rain and the mud, cross-legged and sniveling.

"Bring him up to the top!" Henry shouted.

Four of the LRA men grabbed James beneath the armpits and cut him free of the rope. They dragged him uphill past Anthony.

"What are they going to do?" Anthony asked the boy in front of him.

Anthony had no sooner said it than he felt himself grabbed hard by his right arm and jerked around to find a big, tall LRA gunman dragging him away from the rail, almost in the opposite direction of James. No one watched. Everyone was focused on the crying boy.

Anthony felt like he was about to die.

"You do not speak," the soldier growled quietly as he slowed. "You stay silent, Recruit."

He stopped and turned to face Anthony, a wild-looking guy with dreads and a scraggly beard and a body that looked sculpted.

The gunman's eyes danced over Anthony, as if examining a relic from a forgotten past, before he whispered hoarsely, "Do you understand, Opoka?"

Anthony gazed in shock, realizing first that behind the wild hair and beard and filth, the soldier was younger than he'd thought at first glance. Then he noticed the shape of the lips and the angle of the eyes.

"Patrick?" he whispered. "Is that you?"

———

Patrick grabbed Anthony by the collar and hoisted him up on his toes just as Henry and other LRA men began shouting a couple hundred meters away. "Shut up and listen," Patrick said. "Your life depends on it, Opoka. Do you understand?"

Anthony nodded.

"They may make you do a terrible thing now. If you refuse, they'll treat you like that kid. Except it will be worse for you."

"What—"

"Shut up and listen! You do not know me. You do not know Albert. You cannot tell anyone he is your brother or that I am your friend."

"Why?"

Patrick shook him. "I'm trying to rescue you, Opoka. Let go the saplings and trust me."

"Okay. Okay."

"Whatever you do, don't try to escape. They have expert trackers. They'll find you."

It was actually all Anthony had thought about at many points during the long night. Escape. Going home.

"Opoka."

"Okay. I heard you."

Patrick released him, punched his chest, knocked him down.

Anthony hit the ground hard. "What are you—?"

"Shut up, Recruit!" Patrick shouted, and grabbed him again by the collar of his shirt, lurched Anthony to his feet, and basically dragged him up the hill past LRA soldiers standing guard on the slope.

When Patrick and Anthony reached the top, a bonfire had been built and the other boys had been released from the ropes that held them to their rails and moved into a great circle around the fire. Beside the fire, James was pinned to the earth face down by stakes and ropes.

"No," he was whining. "Why are you doing this?"

"Because you could not keep up," Henry said. "We told you, you had to keep up. Or die. And now you are going to die."

"What?" James screamed, trying to twist his head around. "No, please, I'll keep up now."

"Too late," Henry said.

"I promise!"

An LRA officer Anthony had never seen before came over and stood in front of a group of boys from another rail. One of them was his brother Albert.

Ignoring James's pleas and cries, the officer said, "You are now going to prove yourself. You will prove yourself to us by each of you stomping on him, one by one."

Anthony thought he'd heard him wrong, but then the officer repeated it, and he felt as if he were going to be sick. He looked back at Patrick, who was standing about ten meters away, staring straight ahead.

"If you refuse, if you look away, you will join him," the officer warned them all. "If you cry after you stomp, you will join him. You will do this as if he is a worthless animal. Do you understand? Good, you, go."

He jabbed the muzzle of his rifle at an older boy, who began to breathe fast and hard.

"You want to join him?" the officer asked, nodding at James. Then he looked all around. "Does anyone want to join him?"

The older boy marched toward James, who began to whine and screech. Anthony heard the order to watch but could not. The sheer intensity of the situation flipped some kind of mental switch, a disconnection from reality that marred the sounds of the wind, the rain, and the fire crackling and blurred all movement.

Anthony tried to focus on the boys on the opposite side of the big ring, seeing their faces twitching, jaws grinding or slackening, the sweat pouring from their brows, their lips quivering and betraying their emotions when the thumb-sucker let out a sharp cry of pain at the first blow.

Feeling like he was lost in a nightmare, he thought he heard someone say, "Stop. We're taking a picture."

He swiveled his head, saw the older boy standing by the fire while an LRA soldier snapped his picture beside James, who was groaning and crying. One by one, the officer ordered twenty more boys from Albert's rail to come forward and stomp on the slow and innocent one. When it was finally Albert's turn, he had to walk right by Anthony. Their gazes locked in for a moment, and he swore all he could see was torment in his younger brother. Albert limped on as if approaching a cliff.

Anthony still could only watch the reactions of the boys opposite him, seeing that by the time his brother followed orders, the sharpness of their tics and the horror in their expressions had dulled along with the sounds coming from James, which got smaller, weaker with every foot that came down on him.

By the time the officer reached Anthony's rail, the fire was dying, and the thumb-sucker was long dead. Even so, they made every single boy step on what was left of James. Anthony didn't want to but now understood the depths of LRA ruthlessness. Waiting his turn, he lost hearing altogether. His vision got blurrier and even more shadowed as he finally put his foot on the corpse's back and stood still while a soldier took his picture in the building morning light. He wiped his eyes with his forearm as he stepped off the kid and trudged back toward the rail.

When he passed Albert, he could see something had died inside his little brother. Anthony felt it, too, a withering and perishing inside. His innocence. His belief in himself. His childhood. Everything George and Acoko and his teachers had taught him about growing up to be a good human.

All of it felt gone in a single step.

Chapter Eight

As LRA soldiers began tying them together again, Anthony felt revolted, traumatized, and wanted to sob for the thumb-sucker. But outside, he stayed emotionless, jaw slack, staring dully past the scene.

Henry came forward and shouted at the unroped boys, "You are all murderers now. The pictures we took prove it. You can never go back. Your parents will hate you for what you have done. And if the government catches you, they will hang you for killing this boy. Your only chance at life now is with us and the Great Teacher."

Anthony felt each sentence like a blow to the head. He felt damned and doomed and more lost than he'd been in his entire life. He looked at the sky and said to himself, *Forgive me. Please forgive me for what I have done.*

But he felt no forgiveness, only a shame and guilt that deepened during the days that followed. They left the hill near Patiko that same night and moved west and then northwest into denser bush. Anthony walked in a haze, bitter at the LRA soldiers guarding them.

Why hadn't Patrick warned him?

He said it was going to be very bad. But the murder of a poor little kid?

Anthony longed to talk to his old friend, to make him explain, to ask him if he, too, had had to step on some boy who'd been unable to keep up. But Patrick did not come close to him, and when he was near his brother, Albert would not even look at him. Patrick had evidently warned him as well about the dangers of acknowledging family or friendship inside the LRA.

———

For eleven more nights, they seemed to zigzag through the bush in all directions. More boys and now girls were abducted and made part of the growing group wandering through the wilds.

The skies cleared in the early-morning hours of October 1, 1994, a little more than two weeks after Anthony was taken. They were moving through an area with enough of a horizon that he was able to locate his stars and knew they were traveling north again. They crossed a road, kept going for several kilometers, and then stopped marching around dawn in a clearing in dense bush just east of the upper Unyama River and as far north as they'd been so far on the journey. Campfires were started. The bean-and-green mush was being prepared in pots for the nearly two hundred abducted children under LRA control. They freed them from the rope lines.

The wind picked up shortly after sunrise, rattling the tree limbs and rustling the walls of broad green leaves growing around the clearing. The rush of the river, the wind, the clacking branches, and the rustling leaves drowned out almost all sound until it was too late.

One second, the bush was peaceful and Anthony was on the ground, nodding off while waiting to be fed. In the next moment, he heard a humming over the background noise that became the throb and thump of helicopters coming hard and fast.

He jumped to his feet. The LRA soldiers were all trying to scatter with their weapons and take cover. The first Ugandan army chopper came in right off the treetops. A soldier stood in the open bay behind a heavy machine gun mounted on a tripod.

Henry and two other of Kony's men spun around and shot at the bird with their light automatic weapons. The aerial gunner lit up a heavy machine gun. Bullets chewed up the ground, and cut down Henry and the two other LRA gunmen.

Seeing the evil Henry die made Anthony smile grimly and got him moving. He ran south a hundred meters to the tree line, seeing a second helicopter appear and begin to rake the forest along the river to the west. The second he was inside the forest, Anthony stopped and looked back, trying to spot Albert. But his younger brother was nowhere to be seen.

In his mind, he heard Patrick warning him, *Whatever you do, don't try to escape. They have expert trackers. They'll find you.*

But as the first helicopter circled back for another strafing run on the LRA camp, Anthony clearly heard the voices of his mother and father screaming, *Run, Anthony! Run!*

He took one more look for Albert, didn't see him, and took off into the trees, heading directly south toward that road they'd crossed in the dark. Sprinting, jumping logs, ignoring the vines grabbing at his ankles and the thorns tearing at his skin, he caught glimpses of other people running to either side of him. The shooting stopped. The helicopters swung away and headed southwest.

Already exhausted from a night of marching, Anthony slowed when the forest turned to scattered trees and he saw the road ahead. Then he noticed a boy running pell-mell to his right. Someone shot behind them.

I'm going to die!

———

Anthony went into another gear, sprinting toward the road, praying he'd see a truck or a car, anything. Climbing the embankment, he saw the other boy ahead of him. He was up on the empty road and running west toward the river.

Crossing the road, Anthony looked the other boy's way, saw him stop and grab a bicycle that was lying there in the ditch. The kid jumped on it and rode off with a farmer working a field on the other side yelling after him, "Thief! Thief!"

Anthony ignored him, slid down the opposite embankment, and focused on getting to the thicker trees beyond the crop field. He made it and fought through bramble until he found a game trail. Shoulders heaving, gasping for air, he realized he'd been breaking branches.

They'll see them! They'll see my tracks!

He did the only thing he could think of. He broke a big, leafy branch off a tree and started backward down the game trail, sweeping away his tracks as he'd seen the LRA soldiers do.

It was maddeningly slow going. And walking backward like that, he did not grasp that the trail was bending to the west and intersecting with other trails that went off it like spokes on a wheel. When he finally stopped moving after fifteen or twenty frantic minutes of sweeping his back trail, he looked all around in the shadows and up at the jungle canopy.

There were no landmarks to see, no stars with which to navigate. He heard men shouting behind him and ran blindly down a trail that soon narrowed and petered out to nothing. He stood there, trembling, trying to control himself.

But Anthony could not, and then he had to admit it: he was lost and had no idea of what direction he was moving in. There were more men shouting in the forest, not far at all. He panicked and started slashing and tearing his way forward through the foliage, getting more and more turned around with every minute that passed.

Soon he was drenched in sweat. Blood trickled down his arms and legs from all the cuts.

I should go back, he thought. *But where is back?*

Finally, after what felt like hours of bushwhacking his way through the forest, he came to a clearing. He stopped at the edge, peering out, seeing nothing at first. But then he heard the hushed roar of the river out in front of him somewhere.

On the far side of the clearing, near a bend in the river, he spotted a woman walking with a basket on her head. He found the path that she was on and ran toward her. Coming over a small rise, he saw she was headed toward a footbridge that crossed the river, and now he could see far, far beyond the bridge that there were rocky hills to his west.

The Kilaks, he thought, feeling wildly happy. *I can get to them! From there, I should be able to see the three big trees at Rwotobilo!*

Running up behind the woman, Anthony caught motion in a tree on the riverbank about forty meters ahead, to the right and above the footbridge. His stomach fell. There was an LRA soldier in the tree, late twenties, with a big afro, a brutal scar across his right cheek, and an AK-47 in his hands.

My life is gone, living is done, Anthony thought, figuring he'd be shot now.

But the soldier didn't move. The woman turned around, eyeing him suspiciously.

"Who are you?" she demanded. "What do you want here?"

"I . . . I was looking for the soldiers I was with," Anthony said, loud enough for the one in the tree to hear. "The helicopters shot at us, and I ran, and I've been trying to find them."

"There's no LRA here," she snapped. "Go away."

"I'm just going to cross the river. Maybe they are over there?"

"They're not. I was just there, and—"

The gunshot from the tree hit the ground between them. The woman screamed, dropped her basket, and bolted across the footbridge. Anthony froze and looked up, seeing the LRA gunman aiming down the barrel of a rifle at him.

"Don't move," he said. "Or I'll blow your head off."

Drawn by the shot, several other LRA soldiers appeared within minutes. The scar-faced one in the tree climbed down.

"Why were you running?" he demanded. "Why were you trying to escape?"

"I wasn't trying to escape. When the helicopters came, I just ran. I didn't know where to go, where everyone was."

"I don't believe you," he said, and kicked Anthony in the stomach.

Anthony went down on his knees, barely aware of the men tying his wrists behind him. They hauled him to his feet and told him to turn around and march away from the river, away from the Kilak hills and the three big trees of Rwotobilo and home.

I'm going to die. They're going to have me stomped to death now.

But when they finally reached that clearing where the gunships had attacked them, there was no one waiting. Walking north, they caught up with the main group in the late afternoon. The other abductees were all roped together again.

Anthony had no chance to look for Albert. His captors bound his ankles and tied a short rope from them to his wrists and made him kneel. Shortly before dark, they brought in two other boys, including the one he'd seen riding away on the stolen bicycle. They tied them up the same way and left them with Anthony, far from the other recruits.

The third boy was shaking uncontrollably. When the soldiers walked away, he said in a whiny whisper, "What is going to happen to us?"

"We're all going to die badly," the bicycle thief said in a dull tone. "It's what they do to people who try to escape."

Anthony went numb inside, telling himself that it was over, that he had gambled and lost, and now he would pay with his life. He knelt there long after dark, hyperaware of the other abductees eating their mush and drinking their water, and the shadows from the campfires flickering behind him. At some point, the fires died.

He heard the bicyclist and the other boy fall over and moan. He dozed off a few minutes later, hit the ground, and felt his shoulders, wrists, and ankles scream.

My last night, he thought, fighting back tears at how helpless and alone he felt. *My last night ever.*

———

Anthony slept fitfully, waking whenever one of the LRA men would come over with flashlights to inspect his bonds.

Dawn came amid men shouting to the other kidnapped children to get up. Anthony opened his eyes, understanding that it was the final time he would see the light of a new day. A soldier grabbed him beneath the armpit and hoisted him up on his knees.

Like a lot of Acholi people, Anthony had been raised a Catholic who also believed in the power of the spirits of his ancestors, but he didn't think of himself as very religious. Still, he began to pray to God and the spirits as the LRA prodded the abductees into a large circle around him and the two other boys who'd tried to escape. He realized there were far more than two hundred kidnapped kids now. Twice that number, easily. So many that he could not spot Albert.

He prayed that his little brother wasn't there. He didn't want Albert to see what fate had in store for him.

The LRA soldier who'd been in the tree, the one with the afro and the brutal scar across his right cheek, walked to the middle of the circle. Anthony could see now that the scar ended below the stump that had been his right ear. He was followed by a second soldier wearing a black hood with holes cut for his eyes. He carried an AK-47 with a fixed bayonet.

"There is no escaping the LRA," the scarred one said loudly. "If you try to escape . . ."

The hooded soldier strode across the circle, holding his rifle at port arms. He stopped in front of the first boy, who shook uncontrollably and stammered, "N . . . no. Please, I—"

The soldier drove his bayonet dead center through the boy's chest and out his back. He held him there as the life drained out of him. The boy sagged. The bayonet came free. The dead boy flopped face down in the grass.

Anthony was so shocked by the inhumanity of the moment it felt as if someone had set his heart and brain afire. The boy who'd stolen the bicycle vomited.

Scarface said, "If you see someone escaping and you do not alert your commander . . ."

The soldier with the hood took a long side step, squared himself, and Anthony looked away before he thrust. Spatters of the bicycle thief's blood hit the side of his face like burning embers that seemed to sear his skin and cause every muscle in his body to cramp and spasm after the second boy fell to the earth beside him.

Anthony heard Scarface as if from a long way off, saying, "And if you suspect or know someone is planning to escape and you do not alert your commanders, then . . ."

The executioner took a second long step sideways to stand directly in front of Anthony, who lifted his head. He suddenly wanted to look his killer right in the eyes.

"Forgive me," Anthony said.

"No," the soldier said, and drew his gun and bayonet back, ready to thrust.

"Stop! Don't!"

The executioner froze and turned to his right. Trembling, wide-eyed, Anthony looked over to see an LRA officer in his early thirties, wearing crisp military fatigues and an olive-green beret, getting up off a stool. He strode across the circle and said to Scarface, "Untie him, Sergeant Bacia."

"General, this recruit clearly tried to escape," Sergeant Bacia said.

"It's disputed," the general said. "Free him."

Someone came behind Anthony and cut the ties around his wrists and ankles. The executioner turned and left with Sergeant Bacia. Scarface looked enraged at this turn of events. The general stood in front of Anthony, who was still on his knees, his body numb, paralyzed, his brain unable to grasp what had just happened.

"Look up at me the way you looked at that soldier with the bayonet," the general said.

Shaking, feeling gutted inside, Anthony raised his head, seeing that the man had smooth skin and large, probing brown eyes that locked on his.

"I am Brigade General Charles Tabuley of the Lord's Resistance Army," he said. "I am your second God now. Understand?"

Anthony did not, but he managed to nod slightly through his daze.

"Where I step, you step," General Tabuley went on. "When I say carry my stool, you carry it. When I say anything, you do it. Clear?"

Anthony finally understood that he was not going to die. His mouth felt flooded with a metallic taste, and he fought not to puke as he nodded.

"Get up, then," Tabuley said.

"I . . . I don't know if I can, General."

Someone grabbed him from behind and hoisted him to his feet. Anthony felt like he'd been unplugged from life, weak, disoriented, with legs so rubbery he thought he'd go right back down. Whoever was behind him must have sensed it and held him upright.

"You are not a soldier of the LRA yet, so you may not address me as General," Tabuley said. "You will call me Teacher or Father. What is your name, Recruit?"

For the life of him, he couldn't remember. His mouth opened and flapped, but no words came out.

"Opoka," said the man keeping him on his feet.

"Get my stool over there, Opoka," the general said. "And from now on, every time I look behind me, I better see you there. Got it?"

"Yes, Teacher," Anthony said.

Tabuley strode off. Anthony felt himself shoved after him. He staggered a little, then got his legs under him. He started after the general, but then looked back over his shoulder, seeing it was Patrick who'd shoved him. His old friend was standing there, no expression on his face.

"Step where he steps," Patrick said. "Your life depends on it."

He wanted to run and hug his friend, but Patrick turned away.

"Opoka!" the general yelled.

Anthony hustled past the bodies of the bicycle thief and the other boy, aware that the rails were already marching. He grabbed Tabuley's stool and started watching the heels of the general's boots, putting his sandaled feet in the imprints the man left in the sandy soil.

For hours as they walked, he did not look up, putting his feet exactly where Tabuley had while telling himself that his former life was over, that he would never make another escape attempt. Anthony kept recalling the bayonet, kept telling himself that he would never see the three trees of Rwotobilo or his mother and father ever again.

His life was over. He would die in the bush.

It was his destiny.

Chapter Nine

The next five days passed in the same mental fog that had dulled Anthony's senses and slowed his brain during his close encounter with the bayonet. When they were on the rail, on the move, which was almost constantly, he saw nothing except the back of General Tabuley's boots. When people called to him, it sounded like they were underwater. The food he ate had no taste. His fingers and lips felt numb. The wind carried no odors save those of suffering and death.

Early on October 7, 1994, they reached the outskirts of the small town of Palaro, Uganda, roughly forty-five kilometers northeast of Gulu and an area where many Ugandan army encampments were located at the time.

They joined a big group of Lord's Resistance Army troops and more abducted boys and girls. Anthony watched Tabuley get on a radio and heard him say they were a recruit force of five thousand kidnapped kids now.

Anthony was tight behind General Tabuley late that morning when he saw a man with a widow's peak, short dreadlocks, and a small beard standing off the trail. He wore a long white tunic. He was surrounded by armed men and was talking on a shortwave radio before he called out to the general. Tabuley told Anthony to sit and went to talk with the man.

When he returned, the general divided the five thousand recruits into five rails separated by fifty meters, one thousand children to a line, with older soldiers walking the flanks, making sure no one tried to bolt. Anthony walked directly behind Tabuley, who led the center rail.

They looped around the town of Palaro and the army bases before heading north-northeast. They crossed the Achwa River around midday and reached the outskirts of the town of Palabek after dark, a grueling journey through the bush of almost sixty kilometers. The abducted children got no food. They slept in their place on the rail. Anthony passed out at the head of the center rail after General Tabuley told him to lie down and not move until he returned. When Tabuley did come back, he handed Anthony a cup of dried beans and a canteen of water.

Anthony took the beans, crunched them down raw, and drank greedily from the canteen. "Thank you, Teacher."

The general said nothing.

———

"Ssst, no talking today" was the first thing Anthony heard from LRA gunmen at dawn.

They sat there for almost two hours while soldiers went into the town and raided for food. When they returned, each child was given a cup of dried beans and water. Determined to survive, Anthony wolfed the beans down raw. Tabuley gave him a pack and a heavy sack of beans to carry. The march began again mid-morning, with the five lines pushing north into the roadless wildlands between Palabek and the border with Sudan.

They moved at a punishing pace through bush and deep grasslands, with the general issuing a high-toned whistle every few minutes to keep the leaders of the rails to Anthony's left and right all headed in the same direction. Multiple whistles from the flanks meant there was something wrong, and Anthony and the children behind him were ordered to sit in place until an all-clear whistle sounded and the lines of boys and girls began to march north again.

When they reached grass taller than the tallest man, Tabuley sent soldiers up trees to get their bearings. Any child who could not stay with the pace was dragged off and shot. All five thousand kids were told once again that the Ugandan government was now hunting them as murderers. Anthony and the other abductees walked in constant fear until the general ordered, "All stop," and they sat and ate or slept. It took them several days to reach the border.

"You have no plans in life but mine, Opoka," the general told him after they slipped across the frontier into southern Sudan in the dark of night. "You have no friends and no future unless I allow it. Do you understand?"

"Yes, Teacher," Anthony said, masking the despair that grew inside him.

But he had become excellent at staying directly behind Tabuley. And the fog from surviving the bayoneting continued to fade as they moved north into southern Sudan across vast, flat, roadless areas until they reached a village called Ludu, a hardscrabble place so small it did not exist on maps. Above the village loomed the Acholi range of the Imatong Mountains: steep, towering, and heavily forested, wreathed in clouds, the biggest Anthony had ever seen.

"Your training as a soldier is about to begin up there, Opoka," the general told him that afternoon. "But first you will meet the Great Teacher, so you begin to understand your place in the new and coming world."

Anthony did not grasp exactly what that meant, but he said, "Yes, Father. Thank you, Father. I look forward to that."

"Patrick will take you to see him."

Stiffening inside and wondering if this was some kind of test, Anthony said, "Patrick? Do I know him?"

"You've evidently never met, but he knows of you," Tabuley said. "Says you had a reputation for being very fast and very smart in your old life."

Anthony wanted to smile but kept a blank face and shrugged instead. "I don't know about that, Father."

The general studied him. "Not too long ago, Patrick walked in my boot tracks as you do, Opoka, and I came to trust him. He was the one who cut your bonds, who helped you stand up after we taught the recruits their lesson. Because of Patrick, and because of me, you are alive."

Anthony nodded vigorously, saying, "You *are* my second God. Thank you, Father. Thank you for your mercy and my life."

———

Patrick came for Anthony late the next afternoon, when General Tabuley was mired in logistics for the coming training camp for five thousand recruits set to unfold in the deepest part of the Imatong Mountains, in a remote canyon he kept referring to as Gong One.

Anthony and Patrick left Ludu and, in a blustery, hot, and humid wind, started climbing the steep and mostly bare flank of the mountain directly behind the village.

"Thank you for saving my life," Anthony said when they were out of earshot of the village. "Again."

"I owed you."

"We're even now."

"We are," Patrick agreed. "And you can't tell the general that we raced each other. I told him I'd only heard of you. I didn't know you."

"You don't know me," Anthony said, puffing from the steepness of the Imatongs. "And I don't know you. Not really."

"That's true enough," Patrick said. "And let's keep it that way."

"Where is the Great Teacher?"

"Higher up," he said. "You'll see. And he's not what you expect."

"Joseph Kony?"

"I did not know what was going on the first time I heard him speak, but I felt it, man, his energy, his connection, his power. It comes right out of him, moves right through you."

"I heard he can call in thunder-and-lightning storms," Anthony said as they climbed higher and higher above the village.

"I have seen him do it with my own eyes," Patrick said, somewhat in awe, before looking to the west where darker clouds boiled on the horizon. "Feels like he's doing it again."

Anthony felt a chill go up his spine. They climbed for several more minutes until a worry wormed its way into his mind. "I'm not going to be there alone with him, am I?"

Patrick laughed and stopped. "Alone? No. Never. Kony has his personal guards with him at all times. His wives are there most of the time. And there will be everyone else below us."

Anthony turned and looked back down the steep hillside, seeing at least five hundred recruits, boys and girls alike, beginning their ascent. Twenty minutes later, breathing even harder, he and Patrick reached a bench high above the village. There were sparse trees growing around a large, grassy opening at the back of the bench, with ledges and sheer rock faces at the very rear. The cliffs were slick with water seeping down from higher up the mountain, which Patrick said soared to almost twenty-five hundred meters, with higher peaks beyond and above.

Eight LRA soldiers flanked those weeping walls, looking back out at other gunmen positioned in the trees and at Patrick and Anthony as they approached the opening, which was oval-shaped and about ninety meters across at its widest.

Patrick nodded to them and then led Anthony to a small rise on the near side of the gathering place. "This is where I was standing the first time I saw Kony preach. You'll see best and understand what I've been talking about from here."

———

Over the course of an hour, as more storm clouds built and roiled toward the Imatong Mountains, more than five hundred abductees and LRA soldiers crammed into the opening and among the trees that grew around it. Then someone whistled, and others took up the whistling until the crowd went silent.

A tall, imperious, and handsome woman in her thirties, dressed in a bright-green fitted bodice and wraparound skirt with matching headdress, entered from the woods to the left of the opening. She walked with precision, as if she'd been balancing heavy pots on her head her entire life, and ignored the crowd as she went to sit on one of the dry ledges at the back where she held herself with a haughty, almost regal bearing.

"Who's that?" Anthony whispered over his shoulder.

"Fatima," Patrick muttered. "Kony's number-one wife. Never cross her. General Tabuley says she is more ruthless than he is."

Three more women entered, crossed the opening, nodding to Fatima as they passed.

"The other main wives," Patrick whispered. "Lily, Christin, and Nighty."

These three wives were younger than Fatima, likely in their twenties. Christin and Nighty appeared bored out of their minds. Only Lily, the prettiest of the four, looked at the recruits with any interest.

"How many wives does he have?" Anthony whispered.

"Changes all the time."

The last three wives had no sooner taken their seats than someone whistled twice. The LRA soldiers began prodding the abductees to their feet. From Anthony's position on the slight rise, he could see over the heads of the other children as two armed men entered the opening followed by the same man in the white tunic he'd seen days before, talking on the shortwave.

"The Great Teacher," Patrick whispered. "Supreme LRA commander. Joseph Kony."

Kony nodded to his wives, then turned to face the recruits with his shoulders rolled back, chin up, and eyes wide. To Anthony, he seemed all-seeing as he pressed the tips of his fingers together to form a steeple of sorts that he held up in front of his chest.

"Here I am," he began in Acholi in a firm, powerful voice. "This is me. You have made a great journey, and entered new lands, entered a new life to be with me."

Kony paused before continuing. "You were chosen as I was chosen, as a child, much like you, when a shaman in my village began to teach me about the spirit world, a world that I found existed even in the Catholic church, where I served as an altar boy before joining my cousin Lakwena, the Messenger, in her fight against Museveni's corrupt government and army."

He gazed all around. "The Messenger gave up far too early and ran to exile in Kenya. Soldiers of the Lord's Resistance Army never run. LRA soldiers fight and attack straight on because we are blessed by the spirits through the anointing of shea butter, which wards off all bullets and bombs."

He smiled for the first time. "It's true. Everyone here has witnessed it in combat."

Anthony saw members of Kony's personal guard nodding as well as his wives.

The LRA commander raised his voice, thundering, "But for the shea butter to work, you must believe in the power of the spirits and the Lord and me!"

He stood there, staring, passion flaming in his eyes. Anthony could feel some of the force that Patrick had described, as if something invisible and powerful was coming through the man. He'd no sooner had that thought than real thunder rolled in the distance to the west.

"Here we go," Patrick whispered, and Anthony felt wonder as he looked to the sky and saw darker clouds forming and blocking off all view of the upper mountain.

Kony raised his hands spread wide. "You recruits are here to do the Lord's work and overthrow Museveni's government. You recruits are here to train to fight to take back our country, Kampala, and begin a new Uganda, a better

Uganda, for all its people, not just the corrupt few who hunt us. This is your dream now, your vision for all that can be in your life of resistance for the Lord. Do you see it? Can you hear it? Smell it? Taste it?"

Anthony had no idea what Kampala, Uganda's capital, looked like or tasted like, no idea what a better Uganda might sound like, and no sense of a life spent in resistance for the Lord. But he swore he could feel Kony's energy like a second pulse at his temples, and he found himself nodding as many of the other abducted kids were doing.

Kony said, "The spirits say that four hundred of you are destined to follow me all the way and will join me at the top of my government."

More thunder rumbled to the west, closer now. The Great Teacher seemed aware of the approaching storm because he made a sweeping turn of his back to the recruits and went to a low ledge near the center of the rear wall, turned to them, and sat upon it. To the left and right of the ledge, water seeped down the sheer cliffs. Where Kony sat, it was perfectly dry.

"Have someone write down what they say," he told Fatima. "I won't remember."

Before she could answer, the LRA commander raised his palms spread wide again. This time, however, his eyes fluttered and rolled back in their sockets before they closed. He tilted his face toward the sky. Kony's fingers, hands, and arms began to quiver, and then jerk and tremble.

"Who will it be?" Patrick whispered behind Anthony. "What spirit speaks first?"

The trembling spread into Kony's shoulders and ran down his body, becoming a tremor that rippled his face and lips before it all settled into stillness. His hands traveled slowly to his thighs. He opened his eyelids halfway, revealing his eyes still rolled back in his head.

"I command the four spirits," the Great Teacher said, speaking English in a voice that was not his own. "I command all operations and training in the Lord's Resistance Army."

"Jumma Driscer," Patrick whispered. "He is from Sudan and a brilliant military mind."

The spirit of Driscer spoke through Kony for some time, warning the recruits that their training would be long and difficult, but if they took their lessons seriously and persevered, they would emerge from the experience unstoppable, a rebel force more than capable of overthrowing the Museveni government.

"When you resist for the Lord, when you fight for the Lord, he and all the spirits in the universe know and rush to your side," Driscer said. "They see you are anointed with the shea butter, and they protect us, we the holy, as long as we believe in its power. In belief, all soldiers of the LRA become invincible. In belief, all LRA soldiers are ready to fight and lead!"

Anthony felt a rush go through him. He wanted to know what it felt like to be unstoppable, invincible, ready to fight and lead. And then he realized it was a little like this sensation pulsing in him. He puffed his chest out, lifted his head, and threw his shoulders back as Kony had when first arriving.

"That's right," Patrick whispered. "Feel the power of belief."

Anthony nodded, felt it like a super strength building inside. The Great Teacher's eyes rolled back in his head again. Kony's arms rose and spread before beginning to quiver, tremble, and jerk once more. A few moments later, lightning flashed, followed almost immediately by a thunderclap so loud Anthony thought they'd been bombed and went down on the ground, hugging his head.

He felt strong hands grab him by the arm and haul him to his feet. "Never do that!" Patrick hissed. "Never show the slightest fear. Of anything. Fear means you are a suspicious person, and sometimes suspicions are all that's needed for you to die in the LRA."

Anthony was shaking but kept it together when two more flashes came, followed by explosive claps of thunder that got farther away.

The Great Teacher's twitches and spasms eased. When Kony's hands settled on his thighs, his eyelids opened completely. His eyes rolled down out of his head to glare around. Then he stood, slashed the air with his arm, pointed in accusation at all the children.

In wrath and righteous anger, he bellowed, *"Who are you? Who are you above the law?"*

Anthony felt like he'd been kicked in the gut and almost paralyzed by more fear than he'd ever known. "What spirit is this?" he whispered, hearing the shakiness in his voice.

"This is Who Are You," Patrick whispered. "Who Are You is the spirit of law in the LRA. He is the prosecutor, defense, and judge of all. Who Are You can save you or doom you."

In a hoarse, and yet almost reasonable voice, Who Are You went on, saying, "The holy are not barbarians. We in the Lord's Resistance Army are not savages. We have laws just as all great cultures do, but like the Ten Commandments in the Bible, and the Sharia in the Koran, our laws come from the Lord. Number one, never try to escape. The penalty is death. Number two, no alcohol. No drugs. Ever. The penalty is death."

In the world of Who Are You, a conviction for rape, even of enemies, came with a death penalty as well. Sex between the unmarried merited a whipping. So did sex between married men and single women or married women and single men. Stealing from other LRA members would result in a beating or the loss of a finger and then a hand if the practice continued. Raiding townships for food was important to the cause, but no one was allowed to steal money. Having money was forbidden except for commanders. Lying about a host of issues could get you killed. So could a refusal to fight. And losing your weapon got you put in front of a firing squad. No question.

"Who are you?" Kony roared again at the children, moving toward them as if he might smite them down. *"Who are you above the law?"*

Many of the kids in the front rows shrank back and fell against others as Kony glared at them, possessed by darker forces than they could imagine.

"No one is above the law!" he bellowed. *"No one is above the laws of the Lord and his resistance army!"*

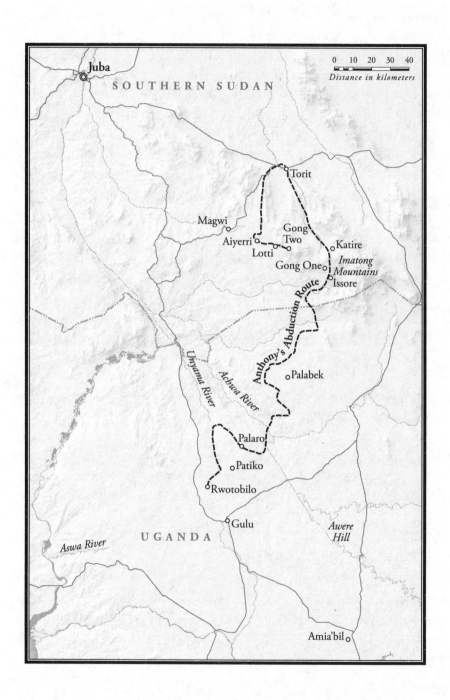

Chapter Ten

The spirit of Who Are You left the Great Teacher sweating, twitching, and exhausted.

When Kony finally opened his eyes, he smiled drowsily at the recruits.

"This body is okay," he said. "But I am not a human being like you. I am the body of four spirits. You? You are human, but you have a purpose, a purpose written by the four spirits. Your purpose now is to survive the next twenty days in the Imatongs."

The supreme commander of the LRA got up then, looking weakened by the channeling experience. He waited for his guards to surround him, and then left, followed by his quartet of wives. In the wake of their departure, Anthony felt the oddly aching absence of that energy that seemed to pulse out of the man. *But he isn't a man, is he? He is a body of four spirits.*

As he and Patrick climbed down the mountain in the rain and darkness, he asked about the other two spirits that spoke through Kony. Patrick said the third was named Cilindi, the spirit of a great doctor who treated the wounded and could heal pain. The fourth was named Jing Breking. He was from China and was a master of strategy and intrigue.

"Breking is why we are here in southern Sudan," Patrick said. "Breking is why Kony brought us here to forge an alliance with the Arab government, which is at war with the Sudanese People's Liberation Army, the SPLA, who are mostly Dinka people who want to break away from Sudan."

Anthony was thoroughly confused. "I don't get it."

"It's basically this. If we fight against the Dinka rebels in Sudan, the Arabs give us weapons, ammunition, and food we can eventually use to defeat Museveni at home in Uganda. Do you see? Very smart spirit, that Jing Breking."

Anthony did not quite grasp how smart the spirit was, but Patrick was certainly more knowledgeable about the LRA and this world than he was, so he accepted it as fact.

"Have you been to Gong One?" Anthony asked when they were close enough to see the village below them.

"No. It's something new that Jumma Driscer wants. A permanent training camp."

"Driscer is the commanding spirit?"

"That's right."

"Will you be going with me?" Anthony asked, hoping that was the case.

"No," he said. "I will stay and teach weapons to the other recruits until twenty days pass and it is their turn to go into the Imatongs. If you survive and come out, you'll learn to shoot."

In the morning, when General Tabuley got up in front of five hundred of the abductees, Anthony could still hear the echoes of Who Are You roaring in his head.

"You will all be given packs to carry on our march to Gong One, where you will be trained," Tabuley said, then gestured to a man Anthony knew all too well, with his afro, his scarred right cheek, and stump of an ear. "This is Sergeant Bacia, who will be assisting me during training. The sergeant is the best manhunter in the LRA, a tracker who actually enjoys killing those stupid enough to run."

Bacia stepped forward and gave them all a crooked smile. "Don't run, little ones. You can't outrun a dog like me. You can't trick me. I'll always find your tracks. You can't beat me, so don't even try."

The manhunter smiled again, and Anthony shuddered, thinking that the man's name suited him. In Acholi, *Bacia* meant family deaths ruined the home.

The pack Anthony was issued was soon filled with sacks of rice and beans for the general as well as a large cook pot, the folding stool, and a large tarp, the collective weight of which made it even more difficult to stay directly behind the man as they began to march into the Imatong Mountains. Behind them stretched a single rail of five hundred abductees who'd been released from their ropes and twenty armed LRA guards under Bacia's command, ten on each flank. They took a different route out of the village. Rather than scrambling straight up as they had the evening before, they climbed a trail that slanted to the west and quickly left the open face below that bench where Joseph Kony had summoned spirits and storms.

Anthony was disappointed and a little frightened at the prospect of not having Patrick along to tell him what to do as he followed General Tabuley's boots. They marched on a gentle incline beneath towering hardwoods with dark-green foliage and triple canopies with pale grasses and shrubs below. There were colorful birds everywhere, and blue monkeys, and they were constantly spooking unseen animals that crashed away to both sides of the trail.

After several hours, they reached a spot where the trail split. One continued along at that same reasonable pitch and slant they'd been following. The other went nearly straight uphill.

Bacia gestured up the steeper trail. "They climb up and over."

The general nodded, then said, "Opoka, you lead. Stay on the trail the entire way until you get to the very bottom of the other side, where we will be waiting."

Anthony felt a swell of pride, a rare, filling warmth at the idea that Tabuley trusted him enough to be at the front. But then, as he started up the rough, muddy trail, he felt guilty for enjoying the honor. The general had ordered the bayoneting of two innocent boys. If it hadn't been for Patrick, he would have watched Anthony killed as well.

They climbed for more than an hour. Anthony was having trouble getting his breath and was drenched in sweat when the leafed, high-canopy trees gave way to shorter ones with soft needles. He turned to look back and down, seeing the rail snaking behind him, and the nearest kids fighting to keep up. With every step higher, the pressure on his lungs increased. Another hour on, the path left those equatorial firs for a high alpine of lush heather and quartz rock and low trees stunted and gnarled by a chill wind that blew there.

The sky was mouse gray. The clouds lowered as they started across the mountaintop. Anthony was grateful they weren't climbing straight up anymore. His thighs and sandaled feet had begun to cramp from the near-vertical effort.

Forty minutes later, they crossed through a saddle and began to slowly drop off the east flank of the mountain. The wind slackened to a mild breeze. Then a dank fog rolled in, misty at first, and then suddenly so thick Anthony could barely see five meters ahead.

He took to moving forward in a crouch so he could get his hands on the wet rocks to either side of the trail, which turned slicker with each passing moment. After what seemed like an eternity, he reached the shadowed side of the mountain and peered over the edge.

The fog thinned slightly, revealing the way to the bottom as a series of short, whiplike switchbacks down a narrow, steep, rocky face. One of the LRA soldiers gestured with his rifle that he should start down first. He crept down the trail, using the hand closest to the mountain to steady himself. He could see that the downed trees, rocks, and even the trail in places were clad in thick, spongy moss. Anthony could not believe how good the wet moss felt on his feet after so many kilometers on the trail.

It began to rain as the alpine gave way to those soft-needled firs and more moss. At first, Anthony welcomed the rain and the brushing of the wet fir branches, which made his legs, shoulders, and his entire body feel better.

Then it began to pour.

The rain came down in a deluge. Anthony had to hold his arm in front of his face to shield his eyes. He didn't see where the terrain broke away again until it was too late. He stepped into a slurry of mud where the path was being undermined, lunged out one hand at some bamboo growing there, and missed.

He fell and flew off the trail, began to slide straight down the mountain. Bouncing, skidding, Anthony crossed the trail near the next switchback, and then plowed into a stand of soaking-wet ferns that tore away around and under him and served only to quicken his descent. He went across the switchback trail again and thought he would a third time when he caught on to a tree root with his left hand and finally stopped himself just above the path, pelted by rain and drenched by the runoff that flowed all around him.

He touched around his ribs and hands and legs. He would be sore in the morning, but nothing felt broken. Above him, he heard shouts and saw other boys and even a few LRA men sitting and sliding down the face, digging their heels in to control their speed.

Anthony waited for them, said nothing, as if what had happened had been his intention. After the LRA guards got down to him, he adjusted the straps of his pack and pressed on. He fell twice more but went nowhere near as far downhill as the first time. The rain eased when they finally reached the bottom of the canyon, where the hardwood canopy was thickest, and the light was as dim as dawn.

———

General Tabuley stood there waiting in knee-high forest grass at the intersection of two trails. He wore a poncho, hood up, as did Sergeant Bacia. A creek raged through the bottom of the canyon one hundred meters behind them.

"We'll set up here," Tabuley said.

Anthony looked all around, seeing no huts, no structures of any kind.

"Bring my tarp, Opoka," the general said. "Then get wood for a fire."

More LRA soldiers appeared as Anthony dug in his pack for the tarp. He heard Tabuley order them to tell the recruits to find a place to spend the night. Permanent shelters would be built in the morning.

Anthony helped the general suspend the tarp beside Bacia's and was able to find enough semidry wood to start a small fire for them. He boiled water and cooked rice and beans, and then stood off to the side as they ate by the light of a small lantern.

"Is there more?" Tabuley asked when he'd finished.

"Yes, Father," Anthony said.

"Eat it. You'll need your strength."

"Thank you, Father," he said, bowing his head, but taking up the cooking pot before Tabuley could change his mind.

He turned his back on the general and the manhunter and wolfed down the food, tasting it as the best pork chop he'd ever had, feeling it fill and warm his belly until he knew he could sleep. He saw other kids trying to find shelter from the rain in the roots and overhangs of upended trees and others lying down in the wide open after being given only a handful of dried beans to eat.

Tabuley told Anthony to sleep at his feet, under the protection of the tarp. He lay down perpendicular to and with his back to the general's feet, and using his muddy, soaking-wet pack as his pillow, he fell unconscious, blissfully unaware of what was to come.

———

In the middle of the night, the storm intensified. Rain pelted and tore at the hardwood canopy high overhead. More rain reached the canyon floor. Anthony awoke to the panicked voices of boys who'd been sleeping in the grass in the wide open, now up, now shouting for light, for help, and for shelter from the rain. Winds came whistling down the canyon walls, swirled in the bottom, tore two corners of the general's tarp free.

Tabuley held the flashlight on Anthony as he lashed the corners back in place. He tried to sleep again, tried to ignore the pleas from some of the recruits still wandering in the darkness of the storm that went on past dawn and into the day, when all across the flat ground he saw boys huddled three-deep and tightly together around the bases of trees.

Around noon, the rain broke, and some sun came through big gaps high in the canopy. Groups of abductees stood in the sun until the general ordered them to begin building huts.

"I know how," Anthony said. "I have built many with my father."

Tabuley softened a little. "I used to build them with my father, too."

"Is he alive, Teacher? Your father?"

He clouded. "My father somehow survived Idi Amin, but then died fighting Museveni."

Anthony took that in, then set about finding a slightly higher place that would drain well on which to build the hut. When he did, he used a downed tree limb to scratch out the circular base as his father had taught him to do.

He paused at one point, realizing that he'd thought little of his father, mother, brothers, and sisters in recent days. He hadn't even thought of Albert, though he knew his younger brother was not with this group of trainees. It made him sad that he could go that long a time and not even think of his family.

What would it be like in a month? A year? Ten? Would he even know his mother or father if he met them walking down the road one day?

Anthony got so upset he told himself to stop asking questions with unknowable answers. Instead, he went to the creek bank and found clay there and gravel at the bottom. He mixed both in a mound, added dead grass, and then began to shape large bricks that he carried over and placed in the sun with a warning to the kids there not to touch them.

After a while, he realized he was doing all the work and asked the general to give him ten boys and girls to help. He showed them how to mix the clay and gravel with grass and how to shape them and where to set them.

It was near dusk when Anthony set the fiftieth brick by the others, and then had the recruits gather wood for fires he wanted built by the bricks so they would dry through the night. He'd only just seen wood piles set ablaze among the bricks and was going back to cook Tabuley's meal when the dark skies opened up and the rains came again, a downpour worse than the night before, snuffing out the infant fires, melting all the bricks.

———

It rained nonstop for five days. At night, the temperatures dropped, becoming so cold Anthony could not sleep long without getting up to do calisthenics and to dream of a fire.

Worse, over the course of those five days, and repeated exposures, the rain spoiled much of the rice-and-bean supply. Sergeant Bacia had insisted on moving the sacks Anthony had packed in. On the fourth day of rain, a bank of saturated soil up the hill and behind the tarps let loose, slid down, and covered the sacks of food in mud. In the aftermath, he felt sure the general was going to beat the manhunter, but Tabuley seemed to think better of it and checked his anger.

After the fifth day of straight rain, there were several one-to-two-hour intervals when it stopped. But it was not time enough to build shelters, and not time enough to gather food. Many kids had begun to starve. Due to poor sanitation measures brought on by the incessant rain, others began to suffer from diarrhea.

On the seventh morning, three girls and two boys were found dead. Come the tenth dawn, there were fifteen cold bodies in the grass of Gong One, five girls and ten boys. Anthony was within earshot when General Tabuley called Kony on the shortwave to explain the situation.

"Six Bravo, this is Two Victor," he said at one point. "I'm killing children here, not making soldiers. Permission to abandon Gong One. Over."

The response was swift. "Two Victor, this is Six Bravo. Permission denied. Figure out a way for them to survive. Over."

The eleventh morning brought more rain and twenty-two bodies. Despite having but a handful of food from the supply they'd been able to rescue from the mud, Anthony spent most of the day digging with trenching tools and burying bodies in shallow graves. On the twelfth morning, nineteen more corpses showed up and they ran out of food completely.

With the rain falling in sheets, General Tabuley left the camp later that same morning and, with Anthony hungry and trudging behind him, walked to Issore, the nearest village, some ten kilometers away. There Tabuley traded extra clothes and ammunition for cooking oil and fifteen kilos of beans and maize.

On the way back, they got in under a rock overhang, built a fire, and fried the raw beans and corn in the general's pot. They were scorched when Anthony got his share at the bottom, but he didn't care and crunched them down eagerly. Before they reached Gong One, the general gave him ten cups of the raw food and told him to guard it and ration it well.

"Thank you, Father," Anthony said, and meant it. He knew that he was staying alive because of Tabuley.

Fifteen kilos of food among hundreds of starving children did not go far. Most kids got less than ten spoonfuls before it was all gone.

On the fifteenth day, more than thirty children died, and the general was back on the radio, frantically pleading his case to the Great Teacher.

"Six Bravo, this is Two Victor," he said. "Entire recruit group is threatened. Repeat, we either move or we attack the nearest village and loot it, which I do not think you wish me to do, given negotiations with Juba."

There was a long silence before Kony came back. "Two Victor, this is Six Bravo. Negotiations are complete. You are to abandon Gong One and proceed to Torit, where Sudanese army forces have supplies waiting for you. Over."

———

More than one hundred of the five hundred children who had climbed into Gong One on October 20, 1994, were dead and buried on November 5 when General Tabuley led the survivors downhill and out to the village of Katire, where they again traded ammunition for food.

From there, the general marched them as hard as he dared fifty kilometers north to the southern Sudan city of Torit. They arrived on November 7 and received a large supply of food, ammunition, clothes, and weapons, which Anthony and the other children carried fifty-five kilometers southwest to the village of Magwi over the course of that day and the next. Joseph Kony was there with his personal bodyguards and wives when they arrived.

The fewer than four hundred kids who'd survived Gong One were fed and rested for a day, given uniforms including new T-shirts and underwear, and then made to march the supplies to the village of Aiyerri, where they were joined by another hundred children from the camp at Ludu. On the morning of November 10, the reconstituted training group of five hundred were told to pick up their packs and to start marching east-southeast toward the forest village of Lotti, which sat on the west flank of the mighty and cruel Imatong Mountains.

When Anthony realized General Tabuley meant to lead them back into the Imatong, he felt sick to his stomach and, for the first time in weeks, seriously considered running for his life. There were enough groans and moans among the children in line that the general moved ten gunmen onto the roads whenever they crossed one to prevent escape attempts.

"If you try, Sergeant Bacia will hunt you," Tabuley announced before they skirted the village of Lotti and began to climb. "You will be found and shot."

Six hours later, they reached a canyon broader than the one at Gong One and stopped, as before, near quick, rushing, cold water fed by springs in the mountains above them. Tabuley and Bacia ordered Anthony and others to build four houses for the officers at Gong Two.

The kids had no hoes, no machetes, and they were told there would be no food until the job was done. Anthony and the others ripped grass with their hands and made bundles for the roofs. They broke bamboo for support poles while others wove rope from vines. Tabuley seemed pleased with their efforts before dark, but still he would not feed them. Not even the boy who put his feet where the general did.

It was the same story the following morning: no food until they were done.

The four huts were completed later that afternoon. Another commander, named Oryang Mixon, came and showed them a wild leafy plant called adyebo, which was edible and plentiful in the canyon. He said whole brigades of the

LRA had survived on adyebo during long combat battles. They needed to learn to survive on it as well.

Anthony picked some and put it in his mouth, finding it mildly bitter and difficult to chew. Mixon told them to boil it for broth, which they did, and it made the taste blander. Seeing that Tabuley was no longer a reliable food source, Anthony decided to eat as much of the adyebo as he could while stealing from the general's cook pot.

After a restless sleep due to the cold, training resumed at dawn. Boys and girls were broken up into teams of fifty, told to strip naked, and made to sprint through the forest to another stream with deeper pools than the one close to the Gong Two camp. They were ordered into the cold water up to their chins despite protests from many of the kids that they could not swim.

The water was the coldest Anthony had ever experienced, and he was quickly the coldest he'd ever been. From the moment he entered the pool, his system went into a form of shock. His blood raced. His teeth chattered. His body began to shake and tremble.

Frightened, realizing he could not last like this, not long, anyway, he did the only thing he could think of to warm up and began to run in place, pumping his arms and legs, and then closed his eyes to slits, imagining himself back on the hot, dusty red road between school and Rwotobilo, running all the way there with not a care in the world other than his desire to beat Patrick one on one.

After an hour in the water, he could keep his arms and legs going, but he could no longer retain that vision of the road home in the hazy, humid heat. He started looking around, seeing some of the other kids were moving as he was, out of sheer fear. But others were just standing there with stunned, glazed expressions on their faces. And three were floating face down.

Five had died by the end of the second hour, when they were finally ordered up out of the water and made to run the entire way back to Gong Two and their clothes. After meals of adyebo, they ran and climbed the steep hillsides before breaking into smaller groups to learn weaponry from Oryang Mixon, who was a veteran of the Ugandan Civil War.

Mixon taught them first how to disassemble, clean, and reassemble an AK-47, and then all the other variations of the Kalashnikov rifle that the LRA used. Each lesson began with precision parade marching, which Mixon believed was a necessary part of military training, along with his shouting.

"The village of Lotti is less than ten kilometers from here," Mixon bellowed at them the first day as they marched. "If you go there, you will die. If you take food from a villager you meet in the woods, you will die. Stay focused on your training. If you survive and when you are done here, you will be among the toughest soldiers on the planet."

When Mixon was convinced that they could assemble and reassemble the guns in the dark, he let them shoot.

Anthony, who had always loved math, especially geometry, caught on to the science of marksmanship quickly, starting with single shots at long range to learn about the forces of elevation and windage, then progressing to short bursts to mimic close-quarter combat and then longer sprays to understand how to control the gun when the barrel wanted to rise.

When the older, physically bigger recruits, including Anthony, proved they could shoot automatic rifles and not waste ammunition, Mixon taught them to load, maintain, and operate the rocket-propelled grenade guns. The rockets had fins that helped the missiles stabilize in flight. Though the smaller kids were not able to use them at that point, they were taught and tested on the firing sequences. Mixon also taught them about the use of bombs, how to aim and fire mortars, and finally the mechanics of the heavier machine guns.

The training at Gong Two often occurred in the rain, the fog, and the chill, with every morning beginning with the naked run and the cold-water bath. The ability to close his eyes to slits and imagine himself running in the heat while in the water usually evaporated when a body bumped up against Anthony. They came from upstream, where other recruits were suffering just as badly. The first time it happened, Anthony panicked and tried to get out of the water, only to be forced back in.

He suffered until he realized he could take his attention away from his pain and his panic by silently making fun of the LRA soldiers watching over them, including General Tabuley. In his mind, the general shit his pants or suffered some equal embarrassment. Other days, he imagined Sergeant Bacia taking Tabuley over his knee and spanking the general so hard he made squawking noises like a chicken. That one could usually get Anthony smiling, almost laughing in the frigid stream.

And when that did not work, he allowed himself thoughts of home, of his mother and father and the entire family and the fun times they had all had.

How Acoko had loved to dance before the sadness took her. How George had loved to sing, especially if he had a beer or two in him. How in Rwotobilo, he had never felt alone. How the love of family was always present. How there had always been someone to talk and laugh with.

Even on the worst of days.

———

But talking and laughter were forbidden at Gong Two. And the longer they were there, subsisting wholly on adyebo leaf, the more recruits began to sicken and die of hunger, diarrhea, and disease.

The LRA commanders did not care and intensified the training to the point where Anthony realized they wanted you to be either dead or crazy tough, able to handle anything the world might throw at you. By the fourth week, he found he could ignore it if a body floated past him in the water, but he had no doubt that he was weakening from the lack of real food.

Then midway through that week, the general gave him money and told him to walk to the village of Lotti to buy maize and rice, a kilo each, and that he wanted exact change. Anthony had a thought and grabbed the second T-shirt and briefs he'd been given by the Arabs before he left and walked the ten kilometers with no thought of escaping. Not only was he confused about his exact location, but he did not have the strength to make the attempt.

In the village, he bought the corn and rice and then traded the T-shirt and briefs for a half kilo of roasted maize, which he crunched and ate all the way back. While the food made him feel better, an oily inner voice that had been quiet for a long while came back.

You're going to die, Anthony. Why not? Everyone else is dying. There's no reason to think you will survive. One day soon, someone else will be burying you in a shallow grave.

Anthony tried to silence the voice of doom by thinking of home. But though he could summon up the compounds of Rwotobilo, they all seemed to be as empty as his mother's hut had been when he was kidnapped. And when he tried to see himself there, he appeared not as a human, but as some filthy, greasy, wild animal from the bush, a murderous hyena sniffing about.

That image stopped Anthony in his tracks. Not too long ago, he had been head boy, a top student, a leader, a revered son and brother, a running champion, a young man with a bright future in front of him. And now, he was a hyena, a nasty scavenger, a hunted thing, with no one to turn to.

That thought crushed him. The weeks of stoically watching other boys and girls his age dying or being murdered gave way. He staggered, broke down, and collapsed into the wet grass by the trail back to the training camp, sobbing for everything and everyone taken from him on the whim of some insane man twisted by spirits like Who Are You.

As he cried, his belief that Joseph Kony was some kind of chosen leader in communion with the Lord and the four spirits evaporated, replaced by something he'd never really felt before in his young life—bitterness. It was bitterness and rancor that his youth and promise had been stolen by a man who ruled by merciless fear, killing children or turning children into killers for his own insane ideas.

When Anthony finally sat up and wiped the tears from his eyes, he knew that he did not admire Joseph Kony; he hated him from the bottom of his heart and soul. No matter what Patrick said about the Great Teacher. On this subject, he decided, he would think for himself.

He began walking again, nurturing that hatred, realizing that this was a survival game and he was a player whether he liked it or not, and understanding that if he meant to survive and escape someday, he had to think differently, act differently, and slyly, never letting on to another what he was really up to.

And he would not be a hyena. As Anthony neared Gong Two with rice and maize for General Tabuley and the other officers, and with his own cache of roasted corn hidden in the woods nearby, he imagined himself not as a scavenger out looking for a dead animal but as a big cat hunting, a leopard on the prowl.

———

That attitude changed Anthony. Rather than timidly trying to please Tabuley, he began to take risks. Every time he prepared meals for the officers, he stole raw rice and corn, and he always made sure there was enough cooked food left at the bottom of the pots for him to scrape and wolf down later.

It was a smart move. As the weather worsened, more children succumbed to the hardships. Every kid who died deepened Anthony's hatred of the LRA, of Joseph Kony, and even of General Tabuley. But he was careful not to show anything but deference to the general, the manhunter, the other officers, and indeed every LRA soldier he encountered.

The concealed bitterness and rage fueled Anthony as much as the additional food. He began surging to the front of the pack whenever they were forced to run somewhere, no longer trying to keep pace, but trying to set the pace. When they were brought to steep walls in the canyon and taught to climb with ropes, he was the first to volunteer. And when they were told to get out of the icy water in the morning, he waited to be the last to leave.

Torrential rains returned in mid-December. There was a flash flood. Many of the huts and children and sources of food were washed away in the middle of the night. Anthony wondered if the training would ever end or if they would be stuck in the madness of the Imatongs until they were all taken by one catastrophe or another.

Given the level of devastation at Gong Two, Tabuley called again and again over the shortwave, asking Kony to end the camp. Finally, on December 20, 1994, Kony ordered the general to retreat from the mountains.

Five hundred boys and girls had gone back into the Imatong highlands forty days before. Three hundred and forty-five walked out along with Anthony, who finally realized that somewhere in the wilds, back during the Gong One camp, he had turned fifteen.

Chapter Eleven

December 25, 1994
Amia'bil, Uganda

Eleven-year-old Florence Okori went to church twice that Christmas Day, once with her born-again mother, Josca, and once with her Catholic father, Constantine. She'd long ago had her First Communion in the Catholic church, but she loved the story of the young pregnant mother and her husband finding no room at the inn and being forced to birth and lay their infant in a manger in a stable. She loved the story so much that she wanted to hear it told twice.

Flo adored the Christmas hymns, too, and sang them at the top of her lungs, so loud her mother had to settle her down, which only made Florence laugh later when she told her oldest and dearest brother, Owen, about it. She still put her mother above all others, but said, "Does Josca think I won't go to heaven if I sing so loud?"

Owen laughed. "I would think it was the other way around."

"Exactly," Florence said, grinning. "I'm telling God how much I care."

Josca's concern about being overly boisterous in church, however, was the only part of the day when Florence felt the slightest bit hampered. Constantine had sold his newest cotton crop and most of the herbal medicine he'd gathered in the bush and bought two small goats and plenty of Nile beer for the holiday feast.

By noon, much of the Okori clan was there, twenty people in all, and everyone was drinking, laughing, and singing. Florence's mother abstained from the beer, of course, and did a masterful job preparing the goats with oil, garlic, and salt, roasting them on wood frames over hot coals. Flo and her younger sister, Margaret, helped. As she did, she remembered her fifth Christmas.

"Why are you grinning?" Jasper asked her when he came over, carrying his prize possession, a small transistor radio he'd found on the road and gotten to work.

"I was thinking about one of the best days of my life," Florence said as Josca pulled the goats off the fire and got ready to cut them. "When Mama carried me home from the hospital."

Her cousin softened. "I remember that. Little spider legs."

"I'm bigger than you now!" she said, and playfully tried to slap him.

Jasper dodged her, and she chased him a bit before stopping when her father called for quiet.

"What is important is that we are all together on this day of days," Constantine announced, raising his second beer of the afternoon. "We need to bow our heads and give thanks for that and for this wonderful food Josca has prepared, and for the drink, and for all the blessings we've had since we were together for last Christmas dinner."

Florence had grown to love her father. He was still a man of few words—except when the beer was flowing—but ever since her recovery from the measles, he'd taken her on many forays into the bush, gathering herbs and plants and gently explaining what each did so she'd remember one day when she was a nurse. She figured that real nurses used pills but told herself the knowledge of folk remedies could only help her.

She bowed her head and gave thanks for Constantine and for her continued good fortune in the classroom, where she was still getting top grades some twenty months after she'd seen the Karimojong raiders burn the school and her book of dreams. The school had been rebuilt, and the teachers, including Mr. Alonsius, had gotten over their humiliation and were once again making her believe that becoming a nurse was possible, that anything in life was possible.

Constantine carved the roast goat on a big board and served steaming slices of it to everyone who stood in line with tin bowls and plates. Josca scooped out rice and beans she served with a spicy okra sauce while Florence gave everyone fresh tomatoes and cucumbers sprinkled with dill and rock salt.

"This is so good, Mama," Owen said, his mouth half-full.

Jasper said, "You should open a restaurant, Auntie. There will be lines out the door."

"I already kind of run a restaurant, Jasper," Josca said, smiling, pleased by the compliment.

"The best restaurant in or near Lira," Constantine said, and cracked his third beer.

"Josca's House of Love," Jasper cried. "That's what we'll name it! I can hear the ads on the radio already."

Everyone started laughing, except Josca, who frowned. "They'll think I'm a prostitute!"

That shocked Florence and Jasper, but made everyone else laugh harder, especially Constantine, who said, "No one who knows you would ever think that, Josca, but I see what you're saying. How about Josca's Table of Love?"

Her mother shrugged.

"Or Josca's Fine Fine Food?" Owen said.

"Getting there."

"How about Josca's Love Café of Fine Food?" Florence said.

Josca beamed. "Now, that's a name I could live with."

Jasper said, "Auntie, I swear you'll be turning people away."

"Maybe so," Josca said, before getting up and asking the children to wash the dishes so a treat could be served.

Florence shepherded the younger kids and soon had all the plates and cups cleaned, dried, and stacked in her mother's hut. When they came back, Josca was serving warm mangoes that she'd sprinkled with gingersnap crumbles. Flo could not believe how good the combo tasted and told her mother so later while everyone was starting to dance to music coming over Jasper's little transistor radio.

"Sometimes you have to use your imagination," Josca said. "But I think the ginger crisp might have been better with a little molasses glaze."

"Next year," Florence said as her father, who was on his fifth beer, jumped to the center of a dance circle and unloaded a series of fancy step moves that provoked the crowd to cheering.

She thought her mother might disapprove of his antics, but when she looked over, Josca had her hand over her mouth, trying to cover how hard she was laughing.

Florence raised an eyebrow, and Josca caught it. "What? Once or twice a year, he's funny. Why not enjoy it?"

"He's funny more than that," Florence said, getting up.

"Not by much," Josca said. "Where are you going?"

"To get your Christmas present."

She got a small present wrapped in tissue from her hut. When she returned, she saw that Josca had retrieved something rectangular wrapped in brown paper with twine she'd stained red with pomegranate juice.

"You first," Florence said, and handed her mother her gift, a beaded necklace.

"Oh, so pretty. How could you afford this?" her mother said, putting it on.

"The soap I made," Florence said.

"Then I thank you," Josca said. "I love it. And now yours."

Florence oohed over the stained twine, then tore it open and found two notebooks, just like the ones that had gone up in the fire.

"These are for your dreams," Josca said. "I never want to hear you don't have them."

Florence was so touched she cried and hugged her mother tight. "Thank you. I promise I will always have them. No matter what."

She gave Constantine a small hand spade he could take with him in the forest, and he gave her a small booklet illustrated with many of the medicinal plants found in various regions of Uganda. She loved it and told him so.

But the empty notebooks were what she turned to later that night by lantern light.

She got her pencil and began to write.

I am Florence Okori, and these are my dreams. No one can take them from me. Only I can let them go or hold them tight. Only I can write them down. Only I can say them out loud or hold them secret in my heart. Only I and God can make them come true.

Florence read what she'd written and smiled. *Thank you,* she added before shutting the notebook. *I had such a wonderful day. One of the best ever.*

Rwotobilo, Uganda

George Opoka's heart ached as he stared up at the moon and the dome of the Christmas night sky from that rocky high point near the village. He scanned the heavens from that single star in the east to that cluster of three in the west, took a swig of beer after too many beers, and felt a hot, raw ball of emotion come up his throat.

George struggled against the sorrow. He grunted in pain, swallowed, and shook his head.

"What is it, Papa?" eleven-year-old Charles asked behind him.

George sighed hoarsely, spoke a little drunkenly. "I taught your brothers to find their way at night, Charles, but I did not give them a way out of darkness. I didn't protect . . . I should have been home . . . and we don't know if Anthony or Albert is still alive. And they were . . . such good young . . . such . . ." His throat constricted again, and he hung his head. "Good young humans."

"They still are good young humans," Charles said, coming over to his tall father and hugging him around the waist. "And they're alive, Dad. I know it. I feel it. Anthony is so strong and smart, and Albert is always clever. They have to be alive."

George hugged the boy back but said nothing.

Charles said, "Anthony saved me, Dad. He took my place."

"I know. Your mother told me all about it."

"Well, then, he has to be alive."

His father took a deep breath and let it out slowly. "We just have to believe it, I guess. It's the only way to keep going, isn't it?"

He felt Charles's head nod, and he rubbed his youngest son's shoulders.

"Should we go back?" Charles asked.

George took one last look at the mysteries of the night sky. "Show me the way home."

Charles liked that and guided them through the darkness to the Opoka family compound. It was late, and Albert's and Charles's mothers had already gone to sleep after their Christmas dinner of roast guinea fowl. George said good night to his son and was about to go to his own hut when he noticed the flicker of fire through the thicket and back toward the road.

He walked that way, realizing that the fire was burning in front of Acoko's old hut. George's brother, Paul, had talked about using it to store their farming tools, so George went that way assuming he'd find his older sibling.

But when he broke free of the thicket, Anthony's mother stood there, looking unsure of herself and as beautiful as ever.

"Merry Christmas, George," Acoko said softly. "I feel better now. I want to come home."

For the first time in many months, George's heart rang not with hurt but with hope.

"Are you sure, Acoko?"

"It is all I have thought of since Anthony was taken," she said, taking a step toward him. "His kidnapping, it made me realize that I'd had no real reason to be sad before that day, and then I realized that I could not live through this without you. This morning, I decided it was time to tell you that I am better, and I want to come home and be your wife again."

George saw the longing in her eyes, felt the pain she'd caused him fall away, and opened his arms. Acoko came to him, crying, kissed him, and hugged him tight.

"Thank you," she whispered. "I could not do this without you."

Her husband hugged her back, kissed the top of her head. "And I don't want to do this without you, Acoko. I love you. I always have."

"I love you, too, though I haven't always, and I don't know why," she said, pulling back to look him in the eyes. "But I do now. Being away made me understand that you truly are a good man, *Omera*. Better than any other I know."

Anthony's father smiled. "Well, thank you."

"No, thank you," Acoko said, and hugged George tight again. "I miss him. Anthony."

"Every day. Sometimes every hour. And Albert, too."

"It's Christmas, George, and they're not here. They're with some blood-thirsty lunatic."

"I know. But we have to believe they're going to come home someday soon."

"If we don't believe," Acoko said, "we've already lost them."

———

Southern Sudan

Two hundred and twenty kilometers to the northeast, Anthony lay awake that same Christmas night, looking at the embers from the fire glowing in the breeze that blew over the windbreak behind him. For most of the day, he'd had no idea that it was Christmas, which had always been a time of great joy and fun in his family. But then he and the other 345 survivors of the Imatong Mountains had been called to a meeting place not far from where they were camped in the bush at the much-lower-altitude terrain west of Aiyerri, near one of the main routes south to the Ugandan border.

Joseph Kony had appeared without his wives, informing the recruits that it was Christmas, and therefore a day to give thanks to the Lord. He led them through a disjointed ceremony that was mostly based on the conventional story of the Nativity, but also began and ended with them all going down in supplication, praying in the Islamic style. He dismissed them after promising that several of the new recruits were about to get a "gift."

On the walk back to camp, Anthony had wondered what the gift was and who would get it and if he would be one of those favored few, when someone tapped him on the shoulder.

Looking back, he'd found Patrick grinning behind him. "Good to see you made it. And Merry Christmas."

Anthony smiled. "Thanks. And to you, too."

"I knew you'd make it out of the Gong," Patrick said, falling in beside him. "What spirits appeared tonight?"

"None, but he made us pray like Muslims. Putting our foreheads on the ground. What's that about? On Christmas of all days?"

Patrick gave him a playful swat. "Not so loud, idiot. He's just trying to impress the Arabs so they give us more weapons, ammo, and supplies."

"I guess," Anthony said. "But I didn't see any Arabs there."

"What's with the questions?"

"More like observations."

"Well, knock it off, especially around people you can't trust, which is everyone but me."

Anthony sighed and nodded. "Aren't you sad it's Christmas?"

"Not when I have a gift to give you. You've heard that, right? That it's better to give than receive on Christmas?"

Anthony looked up at Patrick's wild tangle of hair and beard. "You got me a present?"

"I'm delivering a gift from the Great Teacher," Patrick said. "Based on how you handled yourself in the training, he and the top commanders decided you and a few others are battle ready. You'll be in combat in three days."

Anthony felt a pit yawn open in his stomach. "Three days? Where?"

"Koromush, the Dinka barracks north of Magwi."

That rattled Anthony. "When will they give us guns?"

Patrick sobered. "Didn't they tell you? No guns for first-timers."

"What? How am I supposed to fight?"

"First-timers are not there to fight. They are there to show their courage and belief in the four spirits of Joseph Kony."

———

Lying there near General Tabuley, trying to sleep a few hours later, Anthony heard Patrick's voice over and over again: *You'll be in combat in three days. No guns for first-timers. First-timers are not there to fight. They are there to show their courage and belief in the four spirits of Joseph Kony.*

But I don't believe in them, he thought, and that provoked an inner voice that sounded like Kony's spirit Who Are You, hoarse and raspy: *Then you are going to die, Anthony Opoka. You are going to die in three days' time.*

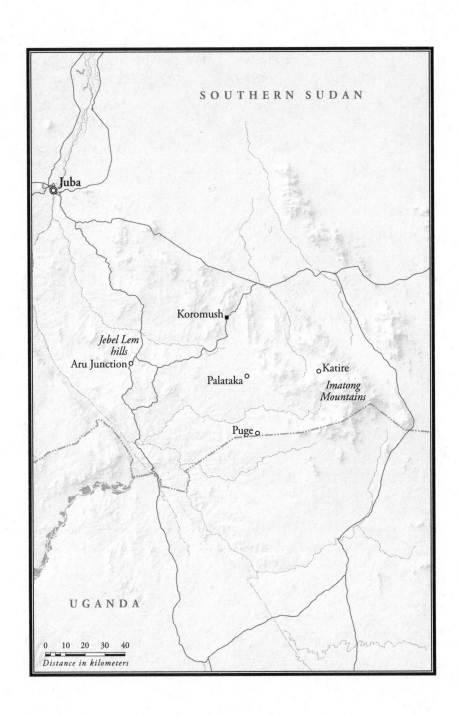

SOUTHERN SUDAN

Juba

Koromush ■

Jebel Lem
hills
Aru Junction ○

Palataka ○

○ Katire

Imatong
Mountains

Puge ○

UGANDA

0   10   20   30   40
Distance in kilometers

Chapter Twelve

December 27, 1994

Anthony, nineteen other boys from the training camps in the Imatong Mountains, and forty armed LRA soldiers, including Patrick and Sergeant Bacia, marched behind Charles Tabuley for two days to get within striking range of the Koromush barracks of the Sudanese People's Liberation Army.

During the long walk, he'd learned more about the SPLA from Patrick. They were mostly members of the Dinka tribe, tall, lean, and fierce.

"To become a man, they have to kill a lion with a spear," Patrick told Anthony when they were hiking through the bush on the second day.

The general had gone ahead of them on the trail with his radioman.

"Really?" Anthony said.

"That's what I heard."

"That would be an awful lot of lions, wouldn't it?"

Patrick gave him a good-natured punch. "You think too much, anybody told you that?"

"My mother," he said, thinking of Acoko, and for a few moments wondered where she was and how she was feeling. "She believes life is all about survival."

"She got that right. Which is why you better have your head on straight tomorrow."

It was nearing dark when the general stopped their march a little more than five kilometers from the Koromush barracks. They lit small fires to cook small meals. According to Patrick, they would not eat again until after the attack.

When night had fully fallen, General Tabuley ordered his radioman to call Joseph Kony. Anthony was watching from five meters away when the signaler clicked his mic and said, "Six Bravo, Six Bravo, this is Two Victor, over."

The radio crackled back almost immediately. "Six Bravo for Two Victor. Stand by. Over."

"On standby. Over."

The signaler took the radio and placed it on the stump of a tree, where they could all hear.

A few moments later, Kony's voice came over the speaker. "To all of you holy listening tonight, commanders and soldiers, I wish you blessings of the Lord, especially the strongest from the Imatongs, and now the first to face the bullets."

At that, Anthony's heart slammed in his chest. *I am going to die tomorrow!*

Kony went on. "You who will be in the front must take off your shirts and smear yourselves with shea butter I have personally blessed. Cover your skin with it and let it glisten with water before you attack. In the high grass, the enemy will think you are invisible, and their bullets will not hit you. Your weapons tomorrow are your voices and your hands. You must sing and clap for joy as you attack because it will break their will to fight, and victory will be yours, easily and unharmed."

Singing and clapping are my weapons? The shea butter will protect me?

Panic fountained in Anthony's stomach and weakened him so much he had to sit down.

As if he had heard Anthony's doubts echoing over the radio waves from eighty kilometers away, Kony said, "You must believe in the power of the four spirits and the blessed shea butter. If you do not believe with all your heart, their bullets will find you. But if you follow the spirits and the Lord, you will walk untouched.

"Two Victor? Here is the latest from our scouts: Hill east of the barracks is fortified with trenches and communications. Recommend 82 mm mortar barrage. Coordinates to follow. The Dinka commander sleeps in a grass hut dead center of the others, west of that hill. Coordinates to follow. Do not hit the cornfields between the hill and barracks. Recover all corn, all food, and any weapons and ammunition. Confirm. Over."

General Tabuley took the microphone from his signaler, said, "Six Bravo, this is Two Victor. Confirm fortification positions, trenches, coordinates to follow, need for mortars, corn protection and retrieval, commander location, and ammo and weapons. Over."

Kony said, "If you have followed my orders, you will live to hear my voice again. Over and out."

———

The radio connection died. The general ordered that everyone in the war party be smeared with the blessed shea butter. They had plastic tubs of it that they opened and held out to the recruits.

"Remove your clothes," Tabuley said. "Do not miss a spot."

Anthony felt awkward and did not move quickly enough for Patrick, who appeared behind him and whispered, "Do it. Everywhere. And believe. It's your only chance."

"Will it work?"

"I'm standing here, aren't I?"

Finally, Anthony took off his shirt, dipped his hands into the butter, and began to paint his arms with it. He'd eaten his share of shea butter. The shea oil nuts grew on trees all over the central highlands of Africa. His mother had often rendered the butter and cooked with it. Now it just made his skin slippery and gave it a dull gray tint. Still, under Patrick's watchful eye, he rubbed the shea butter all over his chest and down his legs.

Patrick slapped it on his back while singing, *"Polo, polo, yesu Lara."*

Other LRA soldiers around him picked up the song. *"Polo, polo, yesu Lara.* Heaven, heaven, Jesus save me."

"Sing," Patrick said.

"I don't know the words."

"You sing, *'Polo, polo, yesu Lara,'* in Acholi, then again in English. Then 'Heaven should come to rescue us in our lives! And we shall never leave the way to heaven! *Polo, polo, yesu Lara!* Heaven, heaven, Jesus save me.'"

"And it's my weapon?" Anthony asked. "I don't get that."

"You will," Patrick said. "Works every time. If you believe."

Anthony tried desperately to believe when he lay down near General Tabuley, shut his eyes, and longed for sleep. But he could not sleep and wanted his father and his mother and his family to tell him what to do. He prayed for their advice, and heard nothing but the wind, the tree limbs moving, the grass washing, and then the general snoring and farting.

He sat up with his back to a tree trunk and looked for his navigational stars but could not find them because of the dense foliage overhead.

I'm going to die tomorrow, he thought, and fought back tears. *I'm really going to die in the morning, and I can't even see my stars.*

———

Anthony felt someone nudge his hip. He cracked his eyelids, not knowing where he was for several moments, then saw General Tabuley standing over him, silhouetted in the moonlight.

"It's time to believe or die, Opoka," Tabuley said. "What will it be?"

He got to his feet, tried to appear confident, and said, "Believe, Teacher."

"I hope so," Tabuley said. "If not, I will have to find another boy to walk where I walk."

They were soon assembled, with scouts and the bare-chested recruits up front, followed by veteran LRA soldiers with automatic rifles and rocket-propelled grenade launchers, followed by the general, Sergeant Bacia, the other commanders, the signalers, and two mortar teams.

They walked in silence beneath a crescent moon for almost an hour before the scouts called a halt in a sea of high grass. They were reassembled into the battle formation that the Great Teacher preferred: recruits spread horizontally across the front of the main assault force, followed by three groups of ten soldiers, each led by a field commander. General Tabuley would remain high and back with his signaler and the mortar teams.

"You sing and clap at 6:00 a.m.," Tabuley told Anthony and the other recruits. "And if you don't sing and clap, the bullets will come from behind you."

Anthony watched the shapes of the general, his radioman, and the mortar teams head toward a low ridge about one hundred meters off. At the same time, the three scouts—boys sixteen and seventeen—scattered and slipped ahead to call out coordinates for the mortar attack.

For close to fifteen minutes, there was no talking, and for a good part of it, Anthony was overcome by paralyzing fear. He wanted to run but knew his legs would not carry him far.

Then Sergeant Bacia whispered, "There is no retreat. There is only attack. Recruits, keep the moon off your left shoulders, and move forward now, slowly, quietly."

Anthony glanced at the sliver of a moon before pushing aside tall stalks of grass and stepping forward. As he did, he felt his brain go foggy, as if this were a bad dream, but he kept going deeper into the sea of grass, hearing the soldiers behind him as he had after the bayoneting, as if they were underwater somehow. His other senses, however, especially sight and smell, became acute. Everything around him seemed sharper, even the shadows. He caught the acrid odor of the veteran soldiers behind him, the clean smell of breaking grass, and the musty odor of the equatorial dirt it grew in.

He almost forgot where he was until someone behind him tapped his back. He looked over his shoulder, seeing the first warm glow in the sky to the east, and an LRA soldier who whispered, "Link arms, Recruit. Start clapping. Start singing when we do."

Anthony remembered the general's admonition about the direction of bullets and linked his arms with the boys to his left and his right. Both of them were shaking. He saw dread in the whites of their eyes and noticed a harsh chemical taste in his mouth before the twenty battle virgins started clapping and moving forward as one.

I am going to die now unless I believe, Anthony thought. *I am going to die unless I sing.*

Behind him and the other recruits, the soldiers began to sing.

"*Polo, polo, yesu Lara!* Heaven, heaven, Jesus save me!"

The recruits joined them, high-toned, like a boys' choir.

"*Polo, polo, yesu Lara!* Heaven, heaven, Jesus save me!"

Anthony caught sight of the top of the hill ahead of him, knew guns were up there, aimed at him from trenches, and sang along.

"Heaven should come to rescue us in our lives!"

"And we shall never leave the way to heaven!"

"*Polo, polo, yesu Lara!* Heaven, heaven, Jesus save me!"

The chant-like song started over, and Anthony went with it full force. Though fear still curdled his stomach, singing "Heaven, heaven, Jesus save me" in the two languages prevented thoughts of doom from dominating his mind. The soldiers sang louder now, and so did the other recruits, and with every step forward, more of the outline of the rise was revealed. Within moments, Anthony could see through the screen of the last tall grass stalks to the entire hill.

"Polo, polo, yesu Lara! Heaven, heaven, Jesus save me!"

When he breathed deep to sing again, he caught the odor of a burn before stepping free of the elephant grass into a semicircle of blackened earth that surrounded the base of the hill some sixty meters away.

Whoomph!

A flare shot off the hill, arced high in the air above Anthony and the other recruits before bursting in a silver flash, lighting the savanna like a glary, black-and-white photograph.

Behind him and to either side, LRA soldiers opened up with AK-47s, strafing the upper hillside. The sudden barrage caused Anthony and many of the other recruits to startle, stumble, break locked arms, and then run farther out into that ring of burnt ground. In the last light of the flare and the growing light of dawn, the Dinka soldiers in the high trenches returned fire.

Anthony saw tracers ripping their way, hot orange in the low light. A recruit down the line fell.

"Move forward!" Sergeant Bacia shouted at them as he and his soldiers charged from the grass. "Sing! Clap! Believe!"

"Polo, polo, yesu Lara!" Anthony sang as more shots rang out from the trenches below the hillcrest and two more recruits dropped. "Heaven, heaven, Jesus save me!"

"Louder! Faster!" Bacia roared as he sprinted past Anthony, cutting off at an angle toward the base of the hill with four or five of his men right behind him.

Anthony broke into a run after them, clapping, singing, aware of all the shooting, but no longer flinching at every round. Other weaponless boys were ahead of him, almost to the base of the hill. He could make out their shadows before they vanished into a blast of light and energy that almost knocked Anthony off his feet.

He staggered, caught his footing woozily, seeing things in slower motion and mildly distorted. Not far to his right, a land mine was triggered. The second blast buffeted Anthony yet again, threw him farther off course, rang in his ears so loud he could not hear himself singing, but he knew he was, and somehow clapping.

"Polo, polo, yesu Lara!"

Sergeant Bacia was hit in the leg. A medic was working on the manhunter. Someone pushed Anthony in another direction. Even rocked by the two blasts, he understood he was now going into the minefield toward the bottom of the hill.

"Heaven, heaven, Jesus save me!"

Twenty meters. Fifteen. Ten meters to where the ground began to climb.

"Heaven should come to rescue us in our lives!"

Every step he took filled him with renewed dread, but still he sang.

"And we shall never leave the way to heaven!"

Anthony never had the chance to feel relief when he reached the base of the hill alive and in one piece. In the growing daylight and from the east, he heard a deep thump over the ringing in his ears and then another.

"Get down, idiot!" Patrick yelled, and pushed Anthony from behind, sent him sprawling just before the two mortar bombs exploded on the hillside high above them, sending down a shower of rock and dirt.

Thump! Thump!

Anthony saw these mortars streak across the early-morning sky and detonate even higher up the hill. He ducked and held his head with both hands as debris rained down on them. Even over the ringing in his ears, he could tell there was suddenly less shooting from above.

Thump! Thump!

These rounds hit at the same altitude but farther south along the flank of the hill.

Thump! Thump!

The seventh and eighth explosions were farther north, followed by even fewer shots from above. Patrick tapped him on the back, screamed, "Get up! They're retreating! Sing!"

Anthony pushed himself to his feet, feeling some of his balance return, and sang and clapped as he climbed the hillside along with the other surviving recruits, straight into the field of fire, bullets zinging past him.

Thump! Thump!

The LRA's ninth and tenth mortars soared over the hill, exploding somewhere on the other side. So did the next four before Anthony reached the rim of the trench—singing, clapping—and found that section empty, abandoned. Then a heavier machine gun opened up to their left across the hillside.

Three more recruits fell. Thirty LRA soldiers spread out across the face of the slope and returned fire. Anthony jumped down into the trench and stood there, singing and clapping, until the shooting stopped. He saw a boombox lying there, left behind.

Patrick appeared and motioned to him to climb out the other side and go to the very top of the hill. Anthony grabbed the boombox and carried it as he and the other recruits sang and clapped their way to the crest, which was being hit by the first strong rays of sunlight.

Thump! Thump!

The last two LRA mortars sailed right over the top of them, cleared the cornfields at the bottom of the backside of the hill, and exploded near the center of the twenty-five grass huts beyond. The thatch roofs of many of the huts were already ablaze.

Fifteen or twenty men in camouflage were running west away from the barracks and the hillside and the incoming bombs. Another forty were retreating in the backs of two dump trucks.

Anthony put the boombox down and just stood there, stunned by the entire experience, still mouthing the words of the song until Patrick, wild-eyed and laughing, grabbed him and hugged him hard.

"You made it, Recruit!"

Anthony started laughing, too, feeling crazy the way the joy burst up out of him.

"We're alive!" Anthony screamed as he pounded on Patrick's back. "Alive!"

His old friend spun away, threw his hands and weapon overhead, and shouted, "The greatest feeling there is, Opoka! Victory!"

Chapter Thirteen

The rest of the attack group reached the crest with the sun fully on them, and like Patrick and Anthony, they threw their arms and guns overhead, jumping up and down and screaming after the Dinka, who were in full retreat.

Anthony had never felt like this before, surging with a thrilling energy that seemed boundless. He saw himself and the other recruits in a whole new light. They had survived the battle with no other weapons but their voices and their hands. They were brothers bonded through an experience that could never be forgotten. They had faced death together, believed, and they had survived!

As the cheering and jeering went on around him, a grinning Anthony picked up the boombox, noticing an old cassette tape in the player with the words *Me Movin List* scrawled on it in blue ink. Not realizing the volume was turned all the way up, on a whim, he pressed play.

Out rifled a wicked machine-gun backbeat and snare that made the LRA boys and recruits cheer and pump their fists and guns over their heads all over again.

He set the boombox down. Eerie organ music came in over that wicked percussion. The tune was so catchy and the drumming so intense and uplifting, Anthony, still elated, still surging on adrenaline, suddenly, strangely, wanted to move his body to it.

Patrick and several of the other LRA regulars were looking over at him and the booming boombox, still caught up in their own fiery emotions of victory, but listening to the weird, beckoning music with puzzled smiles and interested expressions.

A guy on the recording began to softly chant over the drumbeat and the organ music.

The tempo picked up, turned funky as the chanter began to sing in English, so fast that Anthony could not catch the lyric. But the tune and the wicked drumming kept making him want to move. And then the chorus came, suddenly, strangely, and delivered in a mad wail that made him want to dance to it.

A roar went up. Anthony looked over to find Patrick grinning, bouncing up and down, dancing with his AK-47 held high overhead, and singing along in a deep voice.

Some of the LRA boys who'd been cheering the Dinka retreat were now watching Patrick and howling with laughter. A few of them started dancing with him as the singer returned to the second stanza in that rapid English that blew right past Anthony. But that infectious tune wormed its way deeper into his body and into the bodies of more soldiers and recruits, and soon got all of them singing and dancing. The music connected them all, and they became one full-throated, victorious, and joyful voice celebrating on the backside of combat.

Anthony felt almost delirious with happiness, innocent and carefree again. The terror of the battle was forgotten. His kidnapping was forgotten. His childhood, memories of family, of school, all forgotten. He got so caught up in the moment and the music and the thrill of victory that as they all started to sing the chorus for the third time, he felt a new life beginning, an existence as a small part of a mysterious whole, of something far bigger than himself.

General Tabuley reached the hilltop and started shouting, *"What the hell is going on here? Turn that goddamned thing off now!"*

———

Anthony panicked, stabbed at the stop button, but hit eject. The music stopped. The cassette door popped open. The general stormed toward them, shouting. "There's no goddamned dancing in the LRA! No singing like that!"

The cassette tape was right there. Anthony took it and pocketed it.

Tabuley came in with his hand on the grip of his sidearm, glaring at Patrick and Anthony.

"Explain," he said, his voice thick with anger.

"An accident, General," Patrick said. "The thing just kind of started."

Anthony said, "And we were all so happy to see the Dinka running for their lives, we just started dancing and singing along to the music."

The general looked like he wanted to shoot them. Instead, he took a breath and said, "No dancing. No singing songs. The Great Teacher has killed for less."

Anthony had been stepping in the man's footsteps for months now. He could tell when Tabuley was being dead serious.

"No dancing, no singing, sir," Anthony said.

"Nothing like that, sir," Patrick said.

The general glared at them another moment, then ordered half of the force to climb down to pick and haul the ripe corn and the other half, including Anthony and Patrick, to help search the barracks. In the first hut he searched, Anthony found three camouflage uniforms, a Chinese Type 56—an AK-47 knockoff with iron sights—and two detachable magazines with five rounds each in 7.62 mm.

"That's your gun now," Patrick said when Anthony showed him. "Keep it close, always. If you lose your gun, Who Are You will know."

"Firing squad?"

"The worst sin you can commit in the LRA."

He went to put the spare clip in his pocket and felt the cassette tape. He looked over at his old friend and handed it to him. "How did you know that song? I never heard it before."

Patrick shrugged, laughed, and tossed the tape. "I don't know. On the radio at my uncle's store, I think. The only thing I ever understood was the chorus, but all my cousins and stuff, we used to love to dance to it whenever it came on."

"What's it called? Who sings it?"

"No idea, Opoka. Focus here for a second. You have your gun now. Act like it."

Anthony picked up the gun, dropped the clip, opened the action the way he had been taught in the training camps, and found the weapon clean and well oiled. He liked the way it felt in his hands, too, balanced with the weight slightly forward. When he threw it to his shoulder, his right eye came naturally behind the rear peep sight.

"Like it?"

"It already feels like an old friend," Anthony said, grinning as he lowered the weapon, closed the action, and checked the safety before loading the clip.

They spent two hours searching the barracks and the armory, collecting more rifles and submachine guns, uniforms, ammunition, recoilless rifles, 82 mm mortar pipes and bombs. They carried all of it and the corn out on their backs. Two men and a stretcher carried Sergeant Bacia, who was racked with pain. The recruits who'd survived without a scratch took turns helping three of the boys who'd been wounded in that first assault.

For Anthony, the march away from the Koromush barracks was far different from the one coming in. He'd been plodding on the way there with almost no weight in his pack, and now he moved quick and sure with his pack stuffed full and the rifle over his shoulder. And he joked and laughed with some of the other recruits, who were also armed for the first time.

They passed their camp from the previous evening and pressed on. In the late afternoon, they passed a village. Several of the LRA soldiers went in and traded some of the corn for four chickens, which they later cooked over an open fire.

"In the LRA, if you have not faced the bullets, you do not deserve to eat meat," Tabuley explained. "But now you have been cleansed and blessed by the bullets passing you. You must eat meat now to build yourself up."

It had been more than two months since Anthony had eaten anything but rice, beans, and adyebo leaf. He tore into a chicken leg. It tasted so good he moaned. And when they were done feasting, he fell into the deepest sleep since his abduction.

The return trip to where Joseph Kony was camped took three days because they were carrying so much weight. When they finally arrived, the older soldiers took the heavy arms and left the lighter weapons to the recruits who'd survived.

None of the four spirits spoke through the Great Teacher that night. Kony spoke for himself when he made Anthony and the others stand in front of the three hundred boys and girls who had yet to face combat.

"See them?" the LRA commander in chief said. "They had strong hearts full of belief, and the bullets missed them. And now they can eat meat and carry their own rifles. You will be tested as they were in the coming weeks, and I expect all of you to be as courageous as these soldiers."

Soldiers!

It was the first time anyone had referred to them that way. Despite the fact that his father had told him that the worst thing a young man could become was a soldier, despite the fact that he still hated Kony, Anthony felt himself swell with inner pride, and that rare warmth that surprised him. But then again, he and the others had done something of weight, something that had changed them, certainly in the eyes of the Great Teacher, his commanders, and the other LRA soldiers. Anthony could feel that change for good and for bad.

He was one of them now.

———

Over the next ten days, Patrick talked about all the supplies pouring north over the Ugandan border into southern Sudan, all for the Sudanese People's Liberation Army, the Dinka, who'd cut a deal with President Museveni to fight not only the Sudanese Armed Forces, but Joseph Kony's private army. In response, the Arab government decided to give the LRA even more weapons and ammunition, along with new uniforms and proper combat boots.

Kony was thrilled. Anthony heard the Great Teacher telling Tabuley that they were close to having the kind of force that could defeat the Dinka and then the entire Ugandan army.

The spirit of Jumma Driscer spoke through the LRA's supreme commander that same day, deciding that they needed to cut the Dinka supply line by attacking a larger barracks near the town of Pajok, on the road coming north from the Ugandan border some twenty kilometers away. Kony waited until he had one thousand LRA soldiers assembled before he okayed the assault.

On January 9, 1995, the entire force attacked the Pajok barracks and supply depot at dawn with one hundred recruits up front, unarmed and singing.

There were roughly one hundred Dinka soldiers living in the barracks and protecting supply warehouses there. Seeing the odds stacked so heavily against them, the SPLA soldiers ran away just as they had run at Koromush.

Kony's plan called for them to block and hold the road, while looting the warehouses and waiting for more supplies to come north from Uganda. But the barracks and warehouses were booby-trapped with land mines, making them deadly to search. Then the Dinka returned and started shelling the barracks and the roadblock with mortar rounds.

Anthony was sent south along the highway with two other LRA soldiers and took possession of a three-story building that faced south down the road to Uganda. He spent three days at the observation post, listening to the two sides exchanging mortar fire and calling on a handheld radio anytime a vehicle appeared.

The radio battery died on the third evening.

At four in the morning on the fourth day, he awoke, hearing the sounds of motors. He used a pair of binoculars to search the road and made out dozens of lorries, an entire convoy coming at them. Anthony and the others took off running, made it to the barracks, and warned General Tabuley, Joseph Kony, and his chief of staff, General Lagony, who demanded not only that they stay and defend the barracks but that they take the fight to the Dinka.

"We came here because we had no food," Lagony said. "Now we have food and are ready to fight. Let's finish them. Go straight at them."

Anthony was at General Tabuley's side, watching as the LRA fought the SPLA forces from 5:00 a.m. to noon, ultimately driving the Dinka back despite heavy losses among the recruits who faced the bullets unarmed.

That night, Kony came again to talk to them. "You have strong hearts, and because you do, you won again today. You have come to know that you are special. You can look around yourself and say, 'This is our house now. We fought for it with strong morals and strong hearts.' You survived this fight, and you survived the Imatongs. Know that you will survive Pajok, too."

Strong morals? Anthony thought. *Is he kidding?*

———

Most of the original assault force, including Anthony, stayed at Pajok as the Dinka continued to bomb the town and the roadblock from afar. But Kony and his wives and personal bodyguards retreated to the camp near Lotti so he could better commune with his spirits about the next strategic move. At least, that was the way Anthony heard it while serving General Tabuley and General Matata, who was now commander of Patrick's brigade.

"Jumma Driscer came to him and said it is time to push the Dinka south, drive them back into Uganda so the Arabs are free of them," said Matata, a squat, powerfully built man in his forties who liked to chop the air with his hands as he talked. "If we do this, the government will arm us to take Uganda for ourselves."

Tabuley lowered his voice, said, "Did Jumma Driscer tell him to wear a woman's wig and dress when he left here? Because I don't think it was Who Are You."

Matata snorted. "Did he? Again?"

Anthony tried not to show surprise that the Great Teacher dressed in drag, or that the generals would dare laugh about it. The senior officers ignored him as he cleared their plates.

Tabuley said, "He says it's for security, allows him to move about where he's needed. But I think a part of him enjoys dressing as a woman, even the bras."

The other general chortled, then looked at Anthony, said, "You heard none of that."

"None of what, General?"

"Exactly," Tabuley said. "Good boy."

———

The Dinka rebels intensified the night shelling as the month went on. Anthony tried to sleep in a hole he'd dug close to General Tabuley's quarters. But every time he heard *thump!* he came wide awake and listened for the whistle and the explosion. Everyone did. Even the most battle-hardened LRA soldiers got testy and on edge.

Then, in the first week of February 1995, LRA scouts discovered that the Dinka rebels were now receiving and storing supplies from Uganda in the hamlet of Puge, well south of Pajok, closer to the border. Anthony was with Tabuley when Chief of Staff Lagony radioed Kony and asked for permission to attack.

"They have more mortars coming over the border every day," Lagony said. "They will finish us if we stay here. Our only chance is to fight and destroy their last barracks down there, cut off their supplies, and force them back into Uganda."

"Agreed," Kony said. "I have more weapons coming to you from the Arabs: 60 mm mortars, RPGs, and ammunition."

Three days later, the supplies arrived. Two hundred soldiers were ordered to prepare for the attack with Patrick's leader, General Matata, in command and Tabuley his second.

Anthony and the other soldiers smeared themselves with shea butter, put on the camouflage uniforms, and left after midnight on February 7, 1995, circling out of range of the mortars the Dinka were firing from high points east of Pajok. At dawn, the LRA took control of the highway, effectively severing the SPLA's supply of fresh mortar rounds from Uganda.

General Matata left twenty men to hold the road. Anthony, Tabuley, and 180 other LRA boys moved with Matata closer to Puge. The commanding general went with the mortar teams. Tabuley, who would lead the charge, Anthony, and one hundred others waited for the order to attack in the wooded hills northeast of the hamlet.

At Koromush, Anthony had dealt with his fear by singing and clapping. When the Dinka counterattacked at Pajok, he'd been largely out of the fight. Now in full uniform and armed, Anthony would be back on the front lines of combat. He lay there in a low spot he'd dug out beside a mahogany tree, cradling his rifle, trying to rehearse his reloading ritual while singing under his breath.

"*Polo, polo, yesu Lara!* Heaven, heaven, Jesus save me!"

But before he could continue the hymn, a question wormed its way into his head.

What if I have to shoot someone?

The thought had not entered Anthony's mind before. Within seconds, however, it dominated his being. He remembered his father always saying that violence was wrong, and surely there was nothing more violent than killing a man. But he had already crossed that line, hadn't he? When he was forced to step on James's body?

No, Anthony decided, this was different. If he aimed at and shot a Dinka soldier, he would be the one actually killing. Ending another person's life on purpose.

The idea shook him deep in his core. Who would he be if he did it? Who would he become? Still Anthony Opoka? Or the killer who used to be Anthony Opoka?

Thump!

Thump! Thump!

Three 82 mm mortar rounds came whistling up out of the barracks at Puge, exploded several hundred meters to the west. He could hear screaming. LRA soldiers had been hit.

Thump! Thump! Thump!

The next three erupted above and behind him two hundred meters. Debris rained down. He curled up in a fetal position and covered his head. The shelling from the Dinka barracks went on sporadically through the night, making it impossible to sleep. Anthony wondered why General Matata wasn't firing his mortars back at them until General Tabuley told him that the LRA mortars would be launched at 5:30 a.m. with the frontal attack to follow fifteen minutes later.

"I want you on the spearhead," the general told him. "Right out in front of me."

Anthony felt nauseous but slept briefly before the first LRA mortar went off behind him, sailed south, and blew up deep in the Dinka barracks. *Thump! Thump! Thump!* It went on, twelve shells in the first barrage, followed by another twelve, and then a third.

The veteran LRA soldiers around Anthony began to sing, "*Polo, polo, yesu Lara!* Heaven, heaven, Jesus save me!"

He joined in, singing even as some of the combat veterans began to shout and hoot. Their war cries picked up and carried through the rest of the attackers, who, on General Tabuley's signal, moved downhill out of the trees. A fourth barrage began from behind them, whistling over the advancing forces and throwing brilliant flares in the low light around the hamlet atop a smaller hill some two hundred meters away.

They hit a short flat between those two hills and started to move toward the silhouette of the village. Someone to his far right opened up with a short burst of gunfire. Then the battle spread and engulfed him, with guns barking from all sides.

He saw shadows running high on the hill in front of him, flipped the selector to full auto, threw up his rifle, and rattled an entire magazine at them. He had no idea whether he'd hit anyone, but he went to his knee, methodically extracted the spent magazine, pocketed it, and rammed a fresh one into the gun exactly as he'd practiced.

Anthony started forward again, aware of General Tabuley yelling orders behind him and noting LRA soldiers diagonally ahead of him and uphill some forty meters. The angle of shooting from the Dinka suddenly changed, coming from higher than before, from the second stories of the village buildings. Hot orange tracers ripped down on them, followed by heavy machine-gun fire that chewed up the hillside. He shouldered his gun, aimed at the origin of the tracers, and emptied his second clip.

Much faster at reloading the second time, Anthony jumped back up into withering machine-gun fire, peering ahead, seeing an LRA soldier diagonally above him and to his right about thirty meters. Another one to his left was higher up the hill and firing at the upper floors of the village houses.

Anthony took five fast steps uphill, wanting to flatten the bubble in the line of attack, when he heard a *whoosh!*

High at his two o'clock, he registered the flame of a rocket-propelled grenade, saw it hit something uphill and explode before white-hot metal stabilizer fins came spinning. They slashed and cleaved into his right shoulder like whirling, scalding hatchets.

The impact hurled him in a backward spiral through the early-morning air, and he hit the ground hard, chin first, and lost consciousness.

———

Anthony came around in a wavering daze and managed to drunkenly lift his head and open his eyes, finding that it was much lighter out and the battle on the hill above him had turned even more ferocious.

Mortars from both armies were exploding all around him. The rifle and machine-gun fire was constant. He was aware of bodies above him. When he looked down the hill, he saw Charles Tabuley bleeding heavily from his thigh and being dragged away by one of several LRA medics working on the wounded.

It was only then that he remembered he'd been hit. He tried to move his arms, to push himself up, but could not feel anything in his right arm, hand, or fingers. He pushed with his left hand, rolled awkwardly, grabbed his right arm with his left, sat up, and looked down at the shoulder. The superheated stabilizer fins from the RPG had cut into him raggedly and deep. Bones stuck out of the charred wound. Dark blood slicked that entire side of his body.

I'm going to die now, he thought. *I'm going to bleed to death now.*

Staring at the gash, he noticed there wasn't blood pouring out of him. Then he pushed at the underside of his dangling arm, releasing the tension against the side of his body, and blood started spurting from where his armpit had been.

He immediately grabbed the arm and pulled it tight, still so in shock he wasn't feeling pain.

Got to get out of here, he thought, and saw his gun lying there on the hillside, not far to his left, and realized he could not leave it. *The worst thing an LRA soldier could ever do!* He stretched out on his left side and got a grip on the stock, only to lose his purchase on the hillside. He began to roll and then tumbled but did not let go of the rifle. When he stopped, he was wedged in low brush and could not free himself.

This is it, he thought, and started to close his eyes, not caring anymore about the bullets and the bombs. *Too much blood is coming out. There's no hope for—*

Patrick appeared above him. "Anthony!"

"Hit," Anthony said. "Bad."

Patrick saw the wound, lost color, but then cut off the left sleeve of his own uniform blouse and used it with a stick to tourniquet Anthony's shoulder above the worst of it. He cut off more of the shirt and strapped the arm to Anthony's torso. When he did, some of Anthony's shock wore off, and the pain came, bursting hot and radiating through the right side of his body. His head swirled.

"Too much blood," he mumbled. "I'm dying."

"Not here, you're not," Patrick said, taking Anthony's gun, slinging it with his own.

Then he pulled Anthony to his feet and threw him over his shoulder in a fireman's carry. Patrick began to go downhill fast, each step jarring Anthony's broken ribs and wrenching what was left of his right arm, sending lightning bolts of agony through him that were finally too much for the fifteen-year-old to handle.

He saw black dots rushing into his vision, knew this was the end, and surrendered to it.

Chapter Fourteen

For the longest time, there was no consciousness, no awareness, only darkness, only emptiness, like the deepest of sleeps. Then, he stirred, and the void was replaced by a vast, comforting stillness that felt everywhere. The boy realized he was in the stillness and part of it, and that alone was peaceful, blissful even.

Then a voice came as if from the far end of a tunnel: "Leave him. He's dead. No one can take a hit like that and live."

Dead?

That dread word became a comforting stream that washed over the boy, and the bliss returned. There was the definite feel of lift then, of things separating, of things tearing away. In a flash, he knew himself as Anthony again, and understood that his spirit was leaving his heart for his head, the top of which felt like it was yawning open.

A force below pushed him then. A force above pulled him then.

The darkness, the emptiness, the stillness now erupted like a fountain of many shimmering blues that ran off him like raindrops and intensified into a radiance that beckoned him to float upward through translucent golden drapes. Anthony was taken with wonder, had never been anywhere so beautiful, so comforting.

He rose. He slipped through some cosmic vent in the last fabric of an existence that trailed behind and below him, already a fading memory, and emerged up to the waist of his spirit. Before him, around him, inside him, Anthony confronted a deep, dimensionless, black tranquility beyond time, beyond space, beyond the constraints of mere mortality. He knew himself then as part of the eternal and was in awe.

He became aware of distant lights, stars in the blackness. Some part of his consciousness swept back to childhood. He became certain that his soul was going back to the stars and felt comforted and pained about it.

Beyond the stars, deep, deep into the fathomless stillness, he saw a golden ball glowing. He realized the stillness was not completely quiet. The orb hummed softly and low toned, like some elder's breath and voice. He wanted to go to the ball, the voice, the hum, which rose and fell ever so softly, rose and fell like slow-sung air.

He gazed at the orb. *Can I go back if I come there?*

The answer came as a knowing. *You can go anywhere you want.*

He was suddenly in the three trees above his family's compound in Rwotobilo, seeing the cornfield where he'd worked the morning of his abduction and, to his happy surprise, his mother there, laughing with his father, but then putting her hand to her brow and looking up his way, as if she'd caught sight of a bird or sensed his spirit there.

"He's not dead."

In a flash, Anthony was back in that vent between and beyond, hearing the elder's breath, listening for the voice.

He heard, "He's got a pulse."

Anthony looked down then, down through the vent and the radiance, down through the shimmering see-through fabrics of time and space to a cinder-block building transformed into a makeshift hospital north of Pajok. There were at least fifty child soldiers wounded there. Patrick stood by Anthony's body, imploring a medic to work on him before it was too late.

Anthony's consciousness lifted again, left the vent up to his navel again, peered out into the hum and the darkness, felt mercy, felt grace, and knew that if he left this last vestige of existence and went to the orb he could never return. Not as Anthony anyway. Not as the boy he knew.

"C'mon, Opoka," Patrick called below him. "Stay with me, runner. Stay with me. You can't leave me like this. You can't leave Albert or your parents like this."

Straddling life and death, Anthony felt the insistent tug of Patrick's voice, fell back into the radiance, then plunged with some sorrow and some loss back into his body, where the pain howled and flared, all consuming, like windblown fire.

"Ahhhh," he moaned, and fluttered open his eyes. "Ahhhh."

"See!" Patrick cried. "He's alive! You said he was dead, told us to bury him, and now he's alive!"

The medic sprang into action, said, "He was dead an hour ago."

"And now he's not!" Patrick said, and laughed and shook his head. "Now he's not. What a tough kid!"

Anthony began to tremble and shake. "Cold," he whispered.

The medic looked at him. "Yeah, you're a cold, tough kid. You lost a lot of blood, but I got the artery to your arm sewed back last night before your heart stopped."

"Stopped?" he whispered.

"Stopped," the medic said.

"Can't feel my arm," Anthony said, cocking his chin to look at the wound, and again seeing several exposed bones and charred flaps of skin around a gaping hole.

Horrified, he fought not to vomit, feeling the fire there all the worse.

"Hurts. Hurts," he said, trying not to cry, but weeping.

"I bet it does," said the medic. "Sorry I can't give you anything for the pain."

"C'mon," Patrick said.

The medic shook his head, pulled out a leather pouch. "Cilindi spoke through the Great Teacher and said no drugs. No antibiotics. We clean his wounds with cottonwood-root water, then stuff the wound with mushrooms and salt."

Anthony was dazed but caught that. "What?"

"Mushrooms?" Patrick said.

"They're magic ones that grow on cattle pies," the medic said. "With luck, they'll take the poison from him, make him dream, and let him heal."

"Or infect and kill him."

"The Great Teacher said Cilindi says it's his only chance."

"Do it," Anthony whispered. "I'm not afraid to die. Not anymore, Patrick."

———

The root water cooled and soothed the ragged wound the spinning rocket fin had hacked through his right shoulder. But when the medic ground the dried psilocybin mushrooms with coarse salt and then wet the mixture with more cottonwood-root water and began to stuff the searing paste up into the cavity of his wound, Anthony chomped into the stick they'd put in his mouth and screamed.

He caught a glimpse of the radiance he'd seen after being hit, heard the hum, and begged the elder's breath to take him. When the medic began tugging hard on the skin flaps, pulling them over the exposed bones, he blacked out from shock. Again, he plunged into that deep, still darkness.

It did not last long.

Anthony came around to find the medic about to start stitching the flaps shut with a large sewing needle and a length of twine soaked in rubbing alcohol, felt the first piercing, and passed out a third time. Fueled by the mushrooms percolating hallucinogens into his bloodstream, his mind lit up, fired, and whirled with brilliant colors and strange dreams.

He saw his parents again. They were dancing. So was Uncle Paul, who played a flute and led Anthony, Patrick, and every kid Anthony had ever known down the red dust road toward the Rwotobilo primary school. It soon became some kind of wedding procession with a band, and he was driving cattle and sheep and many goats into a cheering village he knew he had never been to before. But his bride was stunningly beautiful and full of light and love, and everyone was joyous, and they danced and sang.

Anthony became a bird then that soared on the singing, soared on thermals, floated silent and sharp-eyed above the savanna. He became a Nile perch, a giant fish of the greatest river on earth, barely moving in its lie out of the current, silent and still, longing for a bug or lesser fish. He became a leopard, shoulder gored by a cape buffalo's horn, slinking away into thorn thickets, panting at the pain of his shattered limb.

He swirled like this for more than two days, barely rousing for the sugar water and boiled beans Patrick gave him, before lapsing again, overtaken no longer by the mushrooms but by a swelling and heat that built in the shoulder and spread outward like fire rolling through dry grass. The fever that followed seized him as strongly as the psychedelics had, but turned his visions darker, more sinister.

Anthony was running in the bush now, pursued. He was that wounded leopard, trying to outrun wild dogs that were on his blood trail and scent. Spinning around to face the pack coming through the scattered trees behind him, he saw them morph and all become one, a huge spectral canine with the head of Sergeant Bacia, which became the head of Joseph Kony snarling in the voice of Who Are You.

"Who are you above the law?" bayed the hound with the Great Teacher's head. "Who are you to escape? Do you think death will come for you that easy, boy? Do you think you will not be punished for all you've done, sooner or later? We have the evidence. The picture. Stomped on that poor, thumb-sucking kid. And in battle, emptied your gun at men in the shadows. Not even brave enough to see their faces as they died. Who are you? Who are you above the laws of the Lord's Resistance Army?"

The dog bristled, became unhinged, lunged at Anthony, Kony's jaws wide, teeth long, bloody, and feral. The boy, the leopard, sprang and ran on three legs, dodging, twisting, through the bush, aware of the hound gaining. He caught a whiff of the stench of him, far fouler than the reek of death, the rot and ruin of the creature's soul.

The cat found its stride and cadence then, ran up into rocks and brush, found a vertical slit in a stone face, a narrow cave he backed into as far as he could. He heard the hellhound sniffing his tracks before he saw Kony's face appear, wild-eyed, lost in his spirits, with shoulders too broad to enter the leopard's lair, Anthony's position just out of reach. The Great Teacher bayed and spit foam and barked threats in the voice of Who Are You. But Anthony knew without a doubt he was safe there and settled down, the leopard's eyes half-slitted as he licked his wounded limb and waited for the beast to tire and leave him be.

A month would pass before the fevers and the infections subsided. Even then, Anthony slept and slept, and when he was upright, he could not move more than fifty meters without resting.

Joseph Kony came to the hospital early in the second month, wearing long white robes, his dreadlocks oiled, accompanied by his lead wife, Fatima, who seemed irked to be there. The Great Teacher appeared not to notice and acted overjoyed as he went from boy to boy, congratulating them.

"You are now true warriors, real soldiers!" Kony said, clapping his hands. "You are the ones who get wounded, recover, and fight again! You will all be famous someday. Your faces will be printed on money, and there will be statues of you put up in Kampala!"

When he came to Anthony's side, all the fifteen-year-old could think of was that dog creature from his nightmares. Part of him wanted to recoil and turn away from the Great Teacher. Instead, he remembered himself as that wounded leopard in the narrow cave and understood he could stay beyond the dog's reach by backing up deep into his mind.

"You are truly LRA now, one of us, young Opoka," Kony said. "Your courage will not be forgotten. I predict it will be written about in books someday!"

Anthony smiled at the kind words, felt weirdly guilty about doing so, but said, "Thank you, Teacher. I hope it is so."

"As it is spoken," the LRA leader said, pointing a finger at him, "so it will be."

When he walked away, Anthony could not decide whether the man was a prophet with vision or simply a man who had no problem changing from one moment to the next, acting kind and then murderous. He kept these thoughts to himself, of course, played the leopard in the cave, and gradually, over the second and third months, he began to feel his fingers, hand, and some of his right arm. But as the rest of his body recovered from the trauma and strengthened, the right shoulder muscles, bones, and ligaments remained weak, almost useless. He kept the arm strapped tight to his body while the length of his daily walks increased, and he began to stomach meat and enough rice to gain back the weight he'd lost.

In the second month, he concluded that his right arm would never be the same, and he turned anxious about his future because he had heard that people who were useless to the LRA or a burden to the cause were often shot. He tried to think of every skill he had and how it could be useful to Tabuley and Kony. His speed was a good thing. And he was smart. But so what?

Then Anthony remembered George telling him that if he could memorize the positions of stars in the sky, he would never be lost at night. He took to staying up at night, studying the dome until he swore he could draw the positions of certain clusters of stars with his eyes closed. The day after he left the hospital for good, nearly three months after his wounding, General Tabuley confirmed his worst fears and gave him a way around them.

"You won't be good to anyone with a gun in your hand now, Opoka," Tabuley said. "I've recommended, and the Great Teacher has agreed, that you are to be trained as a signaler."

Signalers were a special breed in the LRA, widely respected, always assigned to a top commander, always relied upon to communicate over the shortwave radios in special codes called TONFAS that required an agile mind capable of encrypting and decoding messages in a matter of seconds. It suited Anthony perfectly. He felt that in his gut the second Tabuley made his announcement.

"My, my, how the fallen have risen," Patrick said before Anthony was sent off to signaler's school. "From raw recruit to following in the general's tracks to blown up to radioman in less than eight months."

"It would not have happened if you had not carried me off that hill," Anthony said.

"Couldn't just leave you there, could I?"

"Most people would have."

Patrick shrugged. "Anyway, they're shipping me out, too. General Matata is taking us east to fight Dinka. Bunch of others like Sergeant Bacia are going south into Uganda."

"To abduct more innocent kids like us?"

His friend sobered. "To find new recruits, which is how you should say it if you want your life as a signaler to last."

Anthony knew he was right and nodded. "When will I see you again?"

"No idea. I'm infantry. High casualties. You are a signaler. High casualties. And besides, I tend to think of people as dead when I'm not actually with them."

"What? Why?"

He frowned as if it should have been obvious. "Because it makes seeing them alive again more than a nice surprise. Kind of a miracle."

"You have an odd way of thinking sometimes."

"Odd thinking lets you survive odd times," Patrick said, and laughed as he walked away.

———

Anthony was shipped to a small village at the north end of the Imatong Mountains, joining twenty-four others who'd been sent for signaler's training. To his joy, the other trainees included his younger brother Albert, still hampered by a bum ankle. The boys had not seen each other for months, had no idea if the other was alive, and now had to act like strangers except for a few emotional nods from a distance.

But Albert's alive! And I'm alive!

For the first time in months, Anthony felt fully connected to someone other than Patrick. He might not be able to talk with his brother in front of others, but Albert was family, close family, and his presence was as familiar and comforting to Anthony as a long hug and laugh.

The trainers were all senior signalers, many of them veterans of the Ugandan Civil War, who taught by the watch-listen-and-repeat method. Day one saw them explaining the components of three different shortwaves: the ten-kilo Racal radio, used mostly in Uganda and in tight-quarter combat because it rarely lost its lock on a specific frequency; the fifteen-kilo Cascina radio, with greater range for the mountainous expanses of southern Sudan; and the temperamental twenty-kilo Yaesu radio that could reach out as far as Nairobi and Tanzania if properly handled. Anthony found the devices fascinating and listened closely as the instructors explained how radios "speak in and listen to invisible waves" that you had to send and catch by means of the antennae, the shortwave itself, and the batteries and solar panels that powered the mobile charging systems.

Practical lesson number one that first day required them to learn how to connect the radio to the solar panels and the batteries, negatives and positives linked in a specific chain pattern designed to keep the system from burning out. He learned the chain pattern quickly but was frustrated by his right hand's lack of dexterity in assembling it. He finally got them all put together correctly on his own, the last candidate to do so. He glanced at Albert, seeing his brother watching with concern.

He's right, that won't do. I'll have to practice until I can do it in my sleep.

They were fed and separated to sleep in a way that made it impossible for Anthony to get close to Albert, to be alone with his brother even for just a few moments. But he closed his eyes, feeling grateful they were both alive. His last thought before drifting off to sleep was that it really was incredible that they'd both made it this far.

———

On day two of signaler's school, they learned how to properly operate the various radios. Anthony was glued to the instructors as they talked about the control panels and their dials, switches, and meters in light of what they did to the invisible waves going into and coming out of the box, learning about things like oscillation, megacycles, kilocycles, frequency, drift, gain, and modulation.

He finally understood when they began drawing pictures of the waves in relation to various adjustments on the panel. From that point forward, operating the radio felt easy to him, natural; he got that aspect of signaling and he got it fast.

Not so on day three when tasked with controlling a fifteen-meter antenna wire to get a clear signal. He was required to orient the wire in a line either straight north or straight south and to maintain a line of sight from the wire to the sky whenever possible. The ideal setup called for having the antenna wire rise from the radio at a forty-five-degree angle beneath an open canopy and attached to a tree branch or other stable anchor.

Given the weakness in his right hand, Anthony struggled to climb a tree and hang the wire. It took him twice as long as it did Albert, who, despite the limp, was surprisingly adept at tree climbing and clambering up the sides of hills. Anxiety began to build in Anthony; the LRA was not kind to useless soldiers.

I have to be able to put the antenna up and take it down at least as fast as Albert.

He kept telling himself that over and over as he ate and got ready to sleep. Having to urinate, he slipped off and into a dry creek bed that ran around the small village. There was no thought of running. It was simply too far, and he wasn't strong enough to try.

As he was finishing, a shadow moved up on the bank, then scrambled down toward him.

Anthony saw the limp and went fast to his now thirteen-year-old brother, who froze when they were centimeters apart.

"I don't want to hug you and hurt you," Albert whispered.

"It won't," Anthony whispered back.

Albert stepped forward and put his arms gingerly around his brother. "I'm so happy to see you alive, Anthony."

"Me, too, Albert," Anthony choked. "Me, too."

"It's been hard," Albert whispered, trembling.

"Yes."

"Someone said you were hit with an RPG."

"The fin of one. Almost took my arm off. Patrick saved me."

"He saved me, too, telling me not to say I know anyone and to follow every order. I am alive because of that advice."

"Then we keep listening to him. We have to keep ignoring each other."

"I know."

They heard a branch snap farther down the creek.

"Be safe, Albert."

"I will, Anthony. You'll do better tomorrow. I love you."

"I love you, too," Anthony whispered as he pulled Albert so tight it hurt his shoulder. "More than you know."

They reluctantly parted. Anthony left first, climbed the creek bank with ease, feeling lighter somehow and filled with hope for the first time in months. Albert was alive. He was strong, a survivor. Together they were more than allies. They were brothers. Like that mad dog in his nightmares, as a pair they were more than the sum of their parts.

He went to sleep smiling. He went to sleep feeling like he had some say in his life again.

———

Day four of signaler's training was all about radio discipline and a communication style designed to be efficient and coherent. They began by giving the novices radio handles, the names by which they'd be known on air at all times.

Albert became Fourteen Charley. They called Anthony Nine Whiskey.

Then they taught them the language of the radio waves. By the end of that day, Anthony was mimicking the instructors' patois and both sides of the conversation.

"All stations, all stations, this is Nine Whiskey calling Two Alpha."

"Roger."

"Two Alpha?"

"Roger."

"Stand by, stand by, I have a message from the Great Teacher for you."

The other boys laughed, but the instructors were not amused.

"You are not hearing it, Opoka," one of them said. "We don't speak fast. We speak clear, and evenly. We pause. We give time for our colleague to acknowledge and answer. We do not speak over the top of others already transmitting. Understand?"

The smile had evaporated from Anthony's face, and he nodded. "I do, sir."

That entire night, he kept waking up, thinking he'd blown his chance, that the things he could not do well were going to count more than the things he could. And then he'd be a "throwaway," as he'd heard other LRA members refer to recruits or other soldiers who were of no use to Kony or his mission of taking over Uganda.

But day five of signaler's school played right into Anthony's skill set once again. He'd always liked math, and he'd always liked words. When they began explaining the TONFAS, the clever encoding and decoding system the LRA relied on to keep communications regarding troop movement from falling into Dinka or Ugandan army hands, he grasped it almost immediately.

Laid out on a grid system, the TONFAS were a series of code words and numbers that were changed every month. As long as you knew those words and numerals, you could plug them into the grid to see what was really being communicated.

It's like a game, he thought, and was soon deciphering messages twice as fast as the other boys. The instructors made note of it, praised him for it, and Anthony finally figured he could relax. Someone else might hang an antenna or rig the power system quicker than he could. But no one could touch him when it came to the TONFAS. He was confident of that. And he kept staying up late, studying the stars.

On the last day of the course, the instructors gave them their new assignments. Most of the boys, including Albert, were being sent to frontline combat units, the typical posting for a novice signaler. But not Anthony.

He was being transferred back to General Charles Tabuley, whose most-recent radioman had been bitten by a cobra, developed sepsis, and died. It struck Anthony then that a lot of Tabuley's signalers died. There were three that he knew of, which made him resistant to becoming the general's second voice.

But orders were orders. He did not have the chance to say goodbye to Albert or even to catch his eye before they were sent off in different directions. He told himself to be grateful to have seen his little brother again, but he couldn't help but worry about Albert surviving combat with his weak ankle and the extra weight of the radio on his back.

When he arrived at a new encampment eight hours later and reported for duty, General Tabuley brought up the string of dead radiomen straightaway.

"Signalers have to be on their toes around me," Tabuley admitted. "But I have a strong feeling about you, Opoka. After what you've gone through, after what you've survived, after what we've survived together, I think you're supposed to be alive and fighting right beside me."

Anthony smiled and nodded. "It looks like that. Yes, sir."

"There's your radio, then," the general said, nodding to a pack on the floor. "A brand-new Cascina courtesy of the Sudan government. Set it up. I need to talk with Major Okaya."

"Sergeant Bacia?"

"He's been reassigned. He's in Uganda, overseeing new recruitment."

The thought of the manhunter far away made the new signaler happy as he hung the antenna outside facing due south, using a hook on a stick to get the wire high enough. Then he linked the radio to the wire and to the battery pack before turning it on and looking up Okaya's frequency on the cheat sheet he'd found in the pack.

As he turned the dials, hearing the radio waves oscillate, he closed his eyes halfway, like the leopard in his cave, and thought, *This is my life now. I hide where the dogs can't get me. I talk on the radio, tell them what they want to hear, and never what I think.*

Finding the correct frequency, Anthony keyed the microphone and said, "Seven Delta, Seven Delta, this is Nine Whiskey, over."

Chapter Fifteen

Late in the year, northern Uganda becomes a glorious place to be alive. The heat and humidity have ebbed. Cooling breezes blow across the high savannas like whispers of salvation in a time of harvest and abundance. Indeed, in that season, ripe fruits and vegetables normally flooded out of the lush countryside into the towns and the outdoor markets of the area. But not that year.

"Half the things you'd expect to see aren't there," Josca complained on return from the market in Lira. "No eggplant. No radishes. Rice is being rationed. When will it end?"

Florence looked up from her notebooks at her mother and said, "When the LRA stops kidnapping children and stealing people's food."

"Yes, but does Museveni have to have everyone leave their farms, their lands, and move into these camps? Doesn't he see that if people can't till the land, grow their crops, there'll be no food in the markets?"

"The LRA does not attack big places like around Lira. And I heard on the radio that the camps are for the safety of the people. Not to starve us."

A helicopter flew overhead. Soldiers with the Uganda Peoples' Defence Forces peered down at them. There were always army choppers in the air these days. Florence, for one, was glad they were up there, hunting the Lord's Resistance Army.

"Maybe the camps are designed to do a little of both," Josca complained. "They push people into the camps, which gives them an excuse for starving us."

"Oh God, Mama, what *did* you find at the market?"

Josca said, "Yams, okra, garlic, a plucked chicken, and four puny tomatoes. A quarter kilo of rice. A bottle of cooking oil. That's it."

Florence said, "We have plenty of fruit from our trees still to pick, and Owen's entire garden is ready to harvest tomorrow. We won't starve."

"Not today, anyway, I suppose," her mother said, her shoulders relaxing. "Can you give me a hand, or should you be studying?"

"I've been studying for two hours already," Florence said, and set her notebooks aside.

"But it's still tomorrow, isn't it?" her mother asked as they began chopping and dumping chicken parts and oil into an iron pot hanging over an open fire.

"The first one," Florence said, feeling excited and a little breathless as well.

"Like your father always says, 'Don't be nervous. Be prepared.'"

"I am prepared. No one has studied harder than me. I know that is true."

"I'm proud of you no matter what happens."

"I am ready, Mama," Florence insisted. "I will pass with high scores. All my teachers have said so after I took the practice tests."

"But you don't know what will be on the real test."

"It will be close enough. The same kind of questions and problems to solve. And tomorrow's math. My best subject."

"I just worry too much sometimes."

Florence leaned over and kissed her mother's cheek. "The curse of all mothers."

"I just want you to do well."

"I know," she said, and kissed her mother's cheek again, this time making a wet smacking noise, which caused Josca to giggle.

Florence went back to chopping, telling herself not to worry. She *was* better prepared than anyone at her school. But she understood her mother's concern.

She had been working hard for years to catch up to classmates of her age and to prepare for the test she would take in the morning, one of five exams given by the Ugandan government over the course of three weeks. Bundled together, the exams would determine the course of her academic future.

If she just passed the test, she would at least go on to secondary school and likely college to become a teacher or to enter the government ranks in one capacity or another. But if she passed with high marks, she would be on her way to a better secondary school, which would prepare her for a better college or even university, and her longed-for nursing degree.

As she cut celery from their garden, Florence imagined herself walking into a hospital wearing a crisp white uniform and cap like Miss Catherine's. She chuckled at the idea.

"Florence!" Josca said. "What are you doing? You almost cut your fingertip off."

"I was just imagining my life as a nurse," she said, and chuckled again, but paid more attention to the knife. "Mr. Alonsius says it is important to dream of who you want to become."

"Just don't become your sisters when you're this close to the dream."

Florence rolled her eyes. "Mama."

"Your sister was seventeen when she left school to marry."

"I'm not even fourteen!"

"You will be next week."

"Still. Nothing is getting in the way of me following my dream and becoming a nurse. I can see it, Mama. I know what it smells like, what it tastes like. I know the path ahead of me so clearly. It's like it has already happened, you know?"

Josca looked at her as if she did not know, but then smiled and shook her head.

"What?" Florence asked.

"You are out of the ordinary, Florence Okori. You always have been. And now look at you. So beautiful inside and out. And smart. And hardworking."

Josca had tears in her eyes.

"Why are you crying?"

"Everything's so much better than it could have been," her mother choked. "I mean, who would have thought the little girl who couldn't walk for a year, the little girl people told me to abandon, would be about to start such a great, adventurous life?"

Florence grinned. "I am, aren't I?"

"You are," Josca said, and wiped the tears from her eyes before turning back to her cooking preparations. "Oh, I need some dried peppers. Can you get some from Owen?"

Putting the knife down, Florence stood, saying, "On my way."

"No big hurry. They go in last."

———

Florence was hurrying anyway, past the mango grove and the bamboo thicket, heading toward her older brother's house, when Jasper appeared, carrying his most-cherished possession, a handheld transistor radio he used to listen to the Lira music station. He'd grown a bunch in the last year and was tall, gangly, and a little goofy as he danced along with the radio.

He saw Flo and danced toward her, singing about drinking alcohol.

"You better not sing that one around Josca," Florence laughed. "What is that?"

He grinned, turning the volume down. "'Tubthumping' by Chumbawamba. It's from the UK. My new favorite song."

"For now, anyway."

"Exactly. It will change next week," Jasper said.

"Okay," she laughed again, and pushed by him. "I have to be somewhere."

He followed her. "Somewhere good, I hope."

"To Owen's for peppers for Josca's chicken-and-okra stew."

"I love that stew," Jasper moaned, and rubbed his belly. "Enough for me?"

"I don't know who's eating, but I'll ask Mama," she said, rounding a corner and seeing Owen leaning over a hoe in his garden. He didn't look well.

"Hey, are you all right?" Florence asked.

Owen coughed and straightened. "Got tired for a second. Couldn't catch my breath."

Her older brother was in his late twenties and ordinarily as strong as an ox. She and Jasper both went to him. "You're sure?"

Owen smiled. "I'm sure, and I'm done now. Ready to start picking tomorrow."

"I'll come help you after my exam," Florence said.

"That's right! I forgot," Owen said. "A big day for you, Flo."

"I forgot, too," Jasper said. "Why aren't you studying or something?"

"Because I'm ready."

"Not worried?" Owen said.

"I think it's a good sign I'm not worried. Mama sent me to get some red peppers for her chicken-and-okra stew."

Owen got a dreamy look on his face. "I love that stew."

Jasper said, "Everyone loves that stew."

"How many peppers?"

Florence said, "Depends on the size. Four?"

Owen leaned his hoe against a tree before going into a hut and soon returned with four dried red peppers. "They're hot, but not hot-hot."

"I'll tell her, thanks," she said, taking them from him.

Owen hugged her. "Good luck tomorrow."

"She doesn't need luck," Jasper said. "She's ready."

"I am ready, and I'll take the good luck," Florence said, hugging Owen back.

When they parted, her oldest brother said, "If there's enough, tell Mama I wouldn't mind a half bowl."

"Tell Auntie J the same for me," Jasper said.

"I'll tell her, but she says there's not a lot of food in the market these days."

"That's not good," Owen said.

"Which is why we need your garden and your peppers."

"We'll be here picking all day."

"See you after lunch."

———

She waved goodbye and ran back to her mother with the peppers.

"Is four enough?" she asked.

"Perfect," Josca said, and rolled them in her hands to break them up over the pot, which now contained water and the rest of the ingredients.

"Already smells delicious, Mama."

It tasted even better two hours later when her mother ladled out steaming bowls of her famous chicken-and-okra stew to Florence, her father, and her three siblings still living at home.

"She takes her test tomorrow, Constantine," Josca said.

"She'll pass," her father said, tapping his temple. "She remembers things. All the plants I've shown her, she remembers. Even if she's only seen something once!"

Florence basked in Constantine's praise.

There was enough stew left for Owen and Jasper, who declared it one of Josca's best batches ever, the perfect blend of garlic, salt, cayenne, tomatoes, and okra. Florence thought so as well and wished there'd been enough for her to have seconds.

But then she remembered the exam first thing in the morning and figured it best not to take it on a heavy stomach, or after a poor night's sleep. Darkness was already falling. She planned on going to bed early.

Her father said, "When will you hear about these tests?"

Florence began picking up the bowls and spoons for cleaning. "Late February, early March, I think. It depends on how many take the tests."

"From the entire country," Jasper said. "I'm just happy mine aren't until next year."

"The whole country," her father said. "What scores do you need?"

"Ninetieth percentile or higher," Florence said.

Owen whistled. "Top ten percent. You're shooting for the stars, little sister."

"Always," Josca said.

"Every day," Florence said, and felt a little giddy.

That giddiness remained like butterflies flitting in her stomach as she finished cleaning the dishes and the cook pot, gathered her notebooks and a kerosene lantern, and went into her hut. She lay on her mat, pulled a blanket over herself, and gazed at her book of dreams, reading some of her favorites before blowing out the flame.

Closing her eyes, out of the blue and for the first time in days, Florence heard a voice of doubt whisper to her:

You're too confident. You haven't studied the equations enough. You started school too late. There were things you skipped along the way, things that will be on that exam. You can bet on it. That's how it works, Flo. They always ask you what you don't know. And you don't know because you are not enough to do this. And because you are not enough, you will never be a nurse, and no one will respect and love you. That's how it works.

She felt a tightness in her chest that turned to growing panic. *That* is *how it works, isn't it? They'll try to trick me, won't they?*

Her stomach roiled, and she thought she might be sick. Everyone was counting on her. Her mother. Her father. Her brothers and sisters. Her cousins.

They all expected her to ace the test and be the hero, the girl who leaves Amia'bil and becomes a nurse.

But what if I can't?

Florence tossed and turned for hours that night. The long and deep sleep she so desperately sought gave way to fitful snatches of unconsciousness and dreams of not waking up in time, of missing the exam altogether. She kept seeing Mr. Alonsius gathering the finished exams from the other students as she ran into the classroom to start.

———

In the early-morning hours, she finally fell into a deep sleep, so deep Josca had to shake her shoulder. "You're late getting up!"

Florence came awake, terrified. "What time is it?"

"A little past seven."

She'd wanted to be up by six! She dressed fast. "I can eat a little and make it. If someone can take my chores."

Jasper was outside, listening to his radio. "I'll do them for you."

Florence hugged her cousin, ran to get bread and coffee by the fire. Josca gave her a boiled egg and some avocado to take with her along with several refills of water. Stuffing it all into her book bag, she ran off with cries of good luck from her mother and cousin and sisters behind her.

Twice on the two-kilometer route, she slowed and yawned and felt her head ache a little.

The voice of doubt said, *You're too tired now. See? I said you're not enough, and here you are, proving me right.*

Something told her to eat the egg and the avocado and to drink more water, which she did all the way to school. The headache ebbed as she reached the yard and saw a dozen other nervous kids filing past Mr. Alonsius, who gave them high fives on the veranda outside the exam room. He grinned when he saw her.

"There you are!"

"I'm not late, am I?"

"You are just in time," he said. "Are you ready?"

You are nowhere near ready, the voice of doubt said.

Florence forced herself to ignore the voice, to straighten up, smile, and say, "I'm as ready as I'll ever be."

Her teacher winked at her and gave her a high five. "Then go in there and seize your future, Florence. It is right there for the taking!"

Chapter Sixteen

Nearly three years had passed since Anthony Opoka had become a signaler.

"Is that all, General?" Anthony asked.

It was late at night. They'd been working since before dawn.

"For now, Opoka," General Tabuley said. "But the Great Teacher is consulting with the spirit of Jumma Driscer tonight and plans to share his new battle strategy at 6:00 a.m."

"I'll have the radio ready, General."

"And my breakfast beforehand," Tabuley grunted, and turned away.

Anything else, General? Anthony thought bitterly as he walked off. *Without a new recruit to walk in your footsteps, it's all on me, like your slave again. Your one-handed slave.*

He was, wasn't he?

In everything but name, he thought, moving twenty meters away from Tabuley's grass hut and lying down on his mat by his radio pack beneath a bamboo structure with rushes woven tightly overhead to give him some shelter. Having learned the need to take sleep whenever it was offered, he pulled his blanket up and closed his eyes, thinking that he did not know who he was anymore. Just someone who followed orders and stayed quiet. The boy he'd been before his abduction had almost faded from memory.

He was eighteen by then and a hardened veteran of frequent battles with the Dinka and with the Ugandan army, which was now actively trying to intercept all Lord's Resistance Army raiding parties as they crossed the border. But enough of the older LRA soldiers, including Sergeant Bacia, were still getting through and bringing back new recruits. By Anthony's count, Joseph Kony now had thousands of children and teenagers fighting for him, and the Great Teacher was still leading through fear and brutality, goading his soldiers to retaliate against Ugandans who tried to stop the kidnappings with barbaric acts of mutilation.

I hate this, he thought, revolted by the mere idea. *I hate who I have to be. What I've become.*

Outwardly, the young radioman had done everything he could to follow and relay General Tabuley's orders to other LRA commanders swiftly using the TONFAS coding system. He enjoyed the intricacies of being a signaler even though it often put him in harm's way. He pushed himself to do everything as fast as his bum arm would let him, and as cheerfully as he could, smiling, laughing, telling jokes, and always projecting total dedication to the cause of taking Uganda for Joseph Kony.

Secretly, however, Anthony despised his life, hated Kony for stealing it, hated the Lord's Resistance Army with his whole being. He remained friends with and a confidant of Patrick Lumumba, but they saw each other infrequently these days. And though he heard Albert's voice often on the shortwave, he hadn't seen or spoken to his younger brother in person in more than two years.

He blamed it on the Great Teacher. He blamed everything on Kony and his loony ideas and spirits. Of late, that hatred had turned to bitterness like a thick chain wrapped tight around him head to toe. The weight was heaviest about his chest, where he seemed to suffer heartache on a daily basis. The weight made him angry and more aware than ever of the loneliness of the wounded leopard in his cave.

As he drifted off in exhaustion from a day that had begun at 4:00 a.m. and was ending at midnight, he thought yet again, *I hate this. Something has to change.*

The signaler woke up thinking pretty much the same thing.

Similar thoughts soiled his entire morning. Inside, Anthony became gloomier and more bitter than ever. Then, midafternoon, the general ordered him to go into Torit to purchase supplies. Because of Anthony's intricate knowledge of the TONFAS and the LRA's battle plans, the general sent two soldiers to accompany him. He did not want his radioman caught by the Dinka or making an impromptu escape.

Christopher was nineteen and a seven-year LRA veteran. David was also nineteen and had fought for Kony for more than five years. Anthony was friendly enough with them because they spoke a similar dialect of the Acholi language and they had survived several battles together. But he knew they considered themselves his superiors, no matter who his commander was.

A storm was brewing in the west when the trio hustled toward Torit, a seven-kilometer journey that took them just over an hour. They'd no sooner reached the edge of town than the storm hit with such strong winds and slanting rain that they took refuge in a large mercantile business where a song in Swahili was playing. The place smelled of spices and incense.

The silver-haired shopkeeper sat behind a counter, reading a book, wearing thick, black-framed glasses and a sand-colored tunic. He looked up when they entered. If he felt any fear of the weapons they carried, or of Christopher's and David's filthy clothes and dreadlocks, he did not show it. Indeed, the old man smiled at them and at Anthony, who kept his uniform clean and his hair cut short at the general's insistence.

"Welcome, welcome, young ones," the shopkeeper said in English, coming off his stool and toward them with his hands in a prayer pose and a broad smile on his face. "Welcome to Mabior's Bazaar. How can I be of service? What would you like to purchase today?"

With no other provocation, Christopher smashed the man in the face with the butt of his gun. Mabior went down with a cry and hit the floor hard, bleeding from his cheek. He lay there, stunned, making gasping noises. One of the lenses of his glasses was spiderwebbed.

"Why the hell did you do that?" Anthony demanded.

"He was saying something rotten to me, Opoka," said Christopher. "I could tell."

"He was not. Don't you speak English?"

"Why would I?"

Anthony felt disgusted. "He was only asking what we wanted."

"Tell him anything I feel like," Christopher said. "It's all mine for the taking."

"And mine," David said, walking down an aisle and scooping sacks of rice and pasta into his pack.

Anthony swore softly before he heard the shopkeeper moan and saw him struggling to get up. He set his gun down and helped the man up.

Anthony said, "I'm sorry he did that, Mr. Mabior. I'm sorry they're stealing from you. I'm sorry about your glasses. I will give you as much money as I was given."

Even though his cheek was swollen and bleeding, the old man nodded, said, "Thank you. There is a first-aid kit behind the counter. Can you get it for me, please?"

Anthony glanced at the two other LRA soldiers, who were now adding canned goods to their packs, then went behind the counter and found the kit on a lower shelf. He opened it, found some antiseptic and gauze.

As he started to clean Mr. Mabior's wound, Christopher called from the back of the store in Acholi, "What the hell are you doing, Opoka?"

"Cleaning up after you, asshole," Anthony said, turning from the shopkeeper to get bandages.

"Helping one of the unholy is more like it," Christopher said, sounding disgusted. "I'm reporting you to—"

Whoomph! Whistle! Anthony knew a mortar when he heard it and dove to the floor just before the first one exploded close enough to shake the building.

David and Christopher shouldered their bulging packs and charged at Anthony, the shopkeeper, and the front door.

"Dinka!" David cried. "They must have seen us come in here! C'mon, Opoka!"

———

David jerked open the door even as Anthony heard the second whoomph and whistle. David went out into the rain with Christopher right behind him a moment before the second mortar exploded in the road, not ten meters from them. The LRA boys were blown off their feet.

The third mortar hit just outside the entry, the blast big enough to take down the door frame and collapse part of the front wall inward. Debris flew through the store along with a cloud of dust that settled over Anthony.

More mortars flew. But these exploded deeper into the town. Perhaps the Dinka soldiers thought only two LRA soldiers had entered the store, and now they were just softening up Torit for some kind of attack later in the day.

Anthony got to his feet, looked out the gaping hole in the side of the shop, and saw Christopher and David sprawled on the ground, bleeding, unmoving. He heard moaning behind him, looked back, and found Mr. Mabior on the floor, still bleeding. The old shopkeeper was holding on to his left side, where a second plume of blood was forming on his tunic. Anthony saw blood misting the air from his left thigh and reacted instinctively.

He unbuckled his belt, took it off, went straight to the old man. He wrapped the upper thigh with the belt one-handed, put his boot above a large gash, and cinched the belt tight enough to stop the blood from misting.

"Mr. Mabior?" Anthony said, kneeling and pulling up the man's shirt, seeing dark blood seep from a small, jagged wound on his belly. "Can you hear me?"

"Just fine," he croaked. "Thank you."

"You're badly hit."

"I know."

"I'm going to get you to a hospital."

Mortars landed closer to the shop, shaking the building.

"No, you're not," Mabior said, and smiled softly.

"Maybe not right now," Anthony said as machine-gun fire began in the distance. "You're not about to pass out on me, are you?"

"No," he said in an airy voice. "Hurts, but not bad."

Anthony got bolts of fabric, cut strips of it for binding before pouring alcohol from the first-aid kit into both wounds. Mabior shuddered both times but did not cry out.

When Anthony was done wrapping the wounds, the shopkeeper said, "And you, Opoka? How do you feel today?"

Frowning, Anthony said, "Me? Uh, I'm okay, considering I just lost two men and survived a bombardment and I'm trying to help you."

"What is your first name?"

"Anthony."

"You haven't survived the bombardment yet, young Anthony," the old man said matter-of-factly. "And you might not, because I sense you do not love your life."

Anthony stared at him. "What's there to love?"

"Many things, if you look around."

Anthony felt angry. "Look around yourself, Mr. Mabior. Look in the mirror. Your shop is in ruins. You have shrapnel in you. The big artery in your thigh got nicked, and I'm pretty sure a piece of it is in your liver."

"Minor things in the greater scheme," he replied with a weak flick of his hand. "I have learned not to suffer. You have not."

"What?"

"You have not learned how to end your suffering," Mr. Mabior said in an insistent, raspy voice. "When you fail to end it, you imprison your spirit, cut yourself off from the power of the universe. And when you are separated long enough, you hate your life. And it becomes an endless downward spiral of woe. You do, don't you? Hate your life? It was everywhere about you before the bombs started falling."

Anthony gritted his teeth, feeling even angrier at the man. "Why shouldn't I hate my life? It has been stolen from me."

"No one can steal your spirit. Only you can give it away."

"I am not listening to you," Anthony said. "You might die if we don't get you to a hospital. You have to be in pain. You have to hate your life."

The shopkeeper stiffened and closed his eyes for several seconds before smiling softly and opening them. "I am in physical pain, but I am not suffering the way you are right now. You see, pain is physical. Suffering is mental. When you learn to end your suffering, when your eyes and your heart have truly opened, you see everything in life in a different light, even death."

Anthony did not want to believe that. He did not want to entertain such hope. "You have no idea what I've gone through."

"No, not the details. But as I said, they are everywhere about you. They cling to you and will cling to you as long as you suffer. Once you end the suffering, they will leave you, and in that void, the universe will flow in, and you will get your special gift, the thing you need the most right then, and your life will change, become a better version of itself."

"Yeah? Can it change this?" Anthony asked, unbuttoning his shirt to show his shoulder.

The old man stared a moment and shook his head with great compassion. "How terrible. For this you hate your life?"

"Yes!" he said, feeling like the man was willfully not understanding his plight. "For this and for everything else about it! I was kidnapped, taken from my family by insane people who change boys into killing machines and monsters. They made me walk hundreds of kilometers from my home with hundreds of abducted children. They made me step on a little dead boy who could not keep up and still sucked his thumb.

"We were forced to kill him. I tried to escape, and they captured me again, and they bayoneted two other boys who'd tried to escape. They made me a slave to a general. They sent me into battle without a gun, forced me to walk at machine guns while singing for Jesus's mercy. Then they took my arm from me. I can't tell others in the LRA how I think because I could be killed for it, and because of that, I have no real friends. I can't escape because, even if I managed it, they've sent pictures to the Ugandan police showing me with my foot on that boy. I can never go home again. None of us can. Twenty thousand of us. I am stuck here in a life I hate with nothing *but* suffering, after what I've been through."

Anthony had no idea when he'd begun to cry during his rant, but the tears were flowing so fast and hard he could barely see the old man reach out and put his hand on his good shoulder. For a long time, he was silent, just kept his hand there as Anthony sobbed and choked and snot gushed from his nose.

Finally, as his crying ebbed, Mr. Mabior said, "I am sorry for what happened to you at such a young age. It is beyond terrible."

The mortars, which had been thumping and exploding farther and farther away in the town, now seemed to have changed direction, coming closer again. So had the machine-gun fire.

The shopkeeper ignored the sounds of combat, gazed intently at Anthony. "To stop suffering from these things, you must learn to let them go, and to let them go, you have to stop listening to those voices in your head. You have them, don't you? The four voices that keep repeating themselves. Urging you to work harder to survive. Pointing out the injustice of the things done to you and the people who did them to you. Letting you know that no matter how hard you try, you will always be missing something, lacking something. And most of all, filling you with fear. Fear that you deserve what happened to you. Fear that things will never be better because you are cursed by the universe. Fear that you will forever be that boy captured and twisted into someone he never wanted to be. Isn't that right?"

Anthony was so stunned he did not know what to say or do. It was as if the old man could read his mind.

"Aren't those the four voices that won't shut up?" the shopkeeper said gently. Finally, he nodded. "And others."

"Yes. There are others. But there are four that are always loudest?"

He thought and then nodded again. "How did you know that?"

"Because everyone hears those same four voices. Everyone."

A mortar thumped. It whistled right over the top of the shop. Anthony ducked and cringed before hearing it explode a good half kilometer to the west. When he straightened up, the old man was lying there, his body shifting at the pain, but his eyes and face remained unruffled.

Anthony said, "You don't hear the voices anymore?"

"I do. You can't get away from them completely, but you can learn to recognize them for what they are and how they try to destroy your spirit. And when you learn to recognize the four voices by name, they quiet down, and for long periods of time, you don't hear them at all."

Anthony thought about that. "They have names?"

"They do. Rush. Violence. Lack. And Fear."

———

While the mortar attack and battle raged on around them, Anthony cared for the shopkeeper, who got weaker every time the tourniquet was loosened and more in pain when the dressing on his stomach wound was replaced.

But between spasms of physical agony, and over the course of an hour, the old man kept telling the signaler about the four voices and how they attempt to destroy your life from inside. As sunset approached, the mortars fell silent. The shooting stopped.

"Do you understand?" Mr. Mabior whispered. "Can you recognize the voices now?"

"I think so," Anthony said.

"Good," the shopkeeper said, closing his eyes with a little smile on his face. "I have ended this life with a good deed. My next one will be better."

"You're not dying," Anthony said. "We're getting you to a hospital."

"No," Mr. Mabior said. "I can taste death coming."

Before he could reply, he heard voices outside and recognized one immediately.

"Patrick!" he cried, and ran and crawled out over the debris at the front of the store.

There was his long-lost friend along with five other LRA men. They were standing around the bodies of Christopher and David.

Patrick looked hard at him. "You were supposed to be back in camp hours ago. The general sent us to find you, and we got into a hell of a firefight getting here."

"The Dinka," Anthony said. "They were shelling us. They were hit, so I hid inside."

"Not thinking of running?" said another, unfamiliar soldier.

"I was thinking of surviving," Anthony shot back. "And then getting the food the general asked for, and then going back to camp."

"We're taking you there now, along with the food," Patrick said.

"Wait," Anthony said. "My gun is inside, and my pack. And there's a wounded man."

"Get your gun and pack. Leave the wounded man."

Anthony wanted to argue, but Patrick said, "Now, Opoka. You have a new assignment. I'll tell you all about it on the way back."

He hesitated and then turned and crawled back into the ruins of the shop. "Mr. Mabior," he said as he came close to the old man. "I'm going to try to call for a—"

Anthony could tell by the slackness in the shopkeeper's jaw that he had died. He stared at the body for a long time before whispering, "Thank you."

He put on his pack, retrieved his rifle, and crawled back out to find Patrick waiting impatiently.

"You okay?"

Anthony shrugged. The other LRA men had taken the packs off David and Christopher.

Patrick turned and started walking back toward the encampment in the last good light of day. There was acrid smoke in the air from the bombs and the buildings burning in the town.

"What's my new assignment?" Anthony asked.

"The Great Teacher's signaler died yesterday morning," Patrick said. "He asked General Matata and several other officers to name the best radioman in the LRA. I was there. Matata said, 'Opoka.' So did several others."

Anthony felt uneasy. "Okay?"

"You are leaving General Tabuley to become Kony's personal signaler. That's why I was sent to find you. From this point on, Anthony, you will live at the Great Teacher's side."

Stunned at this sudden turn of events, Anthony felt worse than ever. He was to live with the man he hated most, the one who'd ruined his life, the one at the root of his suffering.

"Aren't you happy?" Patrick asked. "It's a tremendous honor."

He forced a smile. "I am just . . . I never expected it, that's all."

"Let's move fast, then. Kony wants you with him when he breaks camp at Palataka."

They reached the top of a rise. Anthony glanced back at the silhouette of the bombed and burning town, imagining Mr. Mabior, now completely deaf to the four voices of suffering that had only gotten louder and more crippling in the poor young man's fragile mind.

Chapter Seventeen

Early in the afternoon two days later, with the four voices of suffering still rampaging through his head, Anthony cradled his rifle in his left hand and trudged toward the perimeter of Joseph Kony's camp in a wooded area near a stream, feeling like the worst days of his life were still yet to come.

And why not? On the way back to General Tabuley's camp two evenings before, Patrick had finally admitted how Kony's most recent signaler had died. He had been executed after making a mistake with the TONFAS that had cost the LRA a battle earlier in the week. Then General Tabuley had gone out of his way to warn Anthony that any mistake in Kony's presence would result in a visit from Who Are You followed by a beating. Or worse.

"Be alert and be careful, Opoka," Tabuley told Anthony before he left. "Kony goes through more signalers than I do."

Because he beats and shoots them, Anthony thought morosely as he approached a sentry, who said he was to wait. Someone would come for him soon.

Anthony dropped his pack. It felt strange to have it so light after nearly three years carrying General Tabuley's radio. Beyond the sentry, in a clearing in the forest, he could see men moving between grass huts, and others working in a garden where corn grew. There was the smell of meat grilling on the breeze.

An hour later, a big, burly older man walked up. He wore a new uniform and a black harness, on the front of which hung two pistols in holsters positioned for a cross draw at either side of his lower ribcage.

The sentry seemed nervous at the man's arrival and snapped to attention. "Colonel Yango. I didn't expect you'd come yourself."

Yango ignored him and studied Anthony for several moments before saying, "Charles Tabuley says you are the best radioman he has ever had."

"The general is very kind."

"No, he's not," Yango grunted. "And neither am I. Do you know why?"

"No, Colonel."

"Because I am in charge of the Great Teacher's security," Yango said. "Since you will often be with him, you must conduct yourself in a specific way. So listen closely as we walk."

My life depends on it, Anthony thought, and tried to focus his entire attention on what the chief of security was telling him.

Yango started by showing him the position of the thousand members of the Trincol Brigade, Kony's personal brigade. The Trincol always camped and moved in a square formation, 250 battle-hardened combatants to each side, surrounding a second, smaller inner square. One hundred men formed the four walls of the inner square, all hand-selected bodyguards fanatically devoted to protecting Control Altar, the core of the Lord's Resistance Army: Kony, his wives, and his most senior and loyal officers.

"And me and now you, Opoka," Yango said.

The security chief stopped and with a stick drew a square in the soft soil. Inside the square, he scratched nine horizontal lines, three to a vertical row. Yango said these were the sleeping and walking arrangements, which were to be adhered to rigidly.

"Kony is always number two in the middle row," Yango said. "I sleep and walk here, top of row three. Another of my bodyguards takes the top of row one. A third bodyguard bottom of row two. Five of his wives sleep and walk here, at the bottom of row one. Five sleep and walk at the bottom of row three."

"How many wives does the Great Teacher have?" Anthony asked.

"Many, but only the senior wives travel with him, which brings us to the second positions in rows one and three. Middle of row three is the wife that the Great Teacher will sleep with that night. Middle of row one is the wife he will sleep with the following night. Always."

Anthony felt odd about that, not only because it was weird but because it was the exact opposite of his life as an unmarried soldier, where he was banned from any kind of relationship. And he was eighteen, after all. He had a strong interest in girls, but in the LRA, all abducted women were given to senior officers. And he was forbidden to seek companionship outside Kony's army.

Anthony said, "And me?"

Yango pointed his stick at the top of the second row. "You will walk and sleep here, never more than fifteen meters away from Kony, always ready with the radio."

"Fifteen meters?" Anthony said. "Even when he's with his wives?"

"Here, in a hut, you won't care. In the bush, just turn your back."

I knew my life was going to get worse.

They started walking again. Yango told him that Kony needed to be on the radio at 0900 and 1100 hours, again at 1300 and 1600 hours, and as needed in the evening and early morning. He handed Anthony a brand-new Casio digital watch.

"Make sure it is synced with the Great Teacher's watch every day."

Anthony took off his old watch and put it on. "Anything else?"

"Lose the watch, you lose your hand. Get separated from Kony or your gun, or your radio? You lose your life. Just like his last signaler."

———

There were other rules, so many that Anthony had trouble keeping them all straight.

You'll never remember them all. You're not up to it, Opoka.

The voice of Lack kept at him as the colonel led him into the inner square and introduced him to many of the bodyguards who surrounded Kony, all men in their twenties and thirties. Some of them had protected the Great Teacher for more than a decade. Anthony tried to smile, tried to remember their names, but now he heard Fear say, *One of them is going to kill you before long, just like the last radioman.*

That sense of dread only grew stronger when they moved into the very core of Control Altar, close to the stream and well shaded, a cluster of nine grass huts laid out in that three-rows-of-three pattern Yango had described earlier. The closest huts on rows one and three were larger than the others. Several women and teenage girls were busy cooking over fires in front of these bigger huts while a dozen young children ran about playing.

Anthony recognized two of the women—Fatima, the head wife, and Lily, who looked ten years her junior and was much prettier. They were dressed in new batik bodices, skirts, and headscarves and were mostly watching the younger, less-well-dressed girls work.

"Who have we here, Yango?" Fatima demanded when she caught sight of them.

"Opoka," Yango said. "The new signaler."

She eyed Anthony with disdain, then looked at Lily and laughed scornfully. "I hope he lasts longer than the last one!"

Lily said, "What's wrong with his arm?"

"It was almost shot off," Anthony said.

"Did we talk to you?" Fatima asked sharply.

Yango said, "RPG hit him."

"Well, then he won't be much help carrying loads for us, will he?" Fatima said.

The security chief acted as if this kind of discussion was all too common. "We didn't bring him here to be your donkey, Fatima. He's the best radioman in the LRA."

"The best radioman would do both," she shot back before laughing caustically and turning. "We'll see, won't we, Lily?"

"Soon enough," Lily said, smiling at Anthony.

Fatima said, "Five days, I'll give him. He won't make the Ugandan border."

Lily said, "I'm betting he'll last at least twenty, maybe more. Maybe he'll outlive us all."

"Fool," Fatima said.

"Aging bitch," Lily said, and winked at Anthony.

Yango shook his head and led Anthony deeper into Control Altar, past the hut of the bodyguard at the bottom of row two. An octagonal grass hut, Kony's hut, occupied the center of row two. The area around it was empty. They went to the hut beyond Anthony's new home, which put them well out of earshot of Fatima and Lily, who were still squabbling.

"The main wives are different," the security chief said in a low voice. "He treats the big four like his queens. In Uganda, Fatima, Lily, and the others had nothing. With Kony, they have everything. As much as you can, stay away from them, focus on your job, don't get caught up in their dramas."

Anthony nodded. "If I am fifteen meters from the Great Teacher at all times, I will not have to talk with them unless he is talking to them."

"There you go," Yango said, then pointed at the hut. "New radios are inside. One of my men will carry the bigger one for you."

Anthony entered, finding a fifteen-kilo Cascina radio, similar to the one he'd operated for General Tabuley, and the bigger twenty-kilo Yaesu radio. Battery packs, antenna wire, and hooks lay on the ground beside their carrying cases.

Yango tapped his watch. "Kony will be here soon for the transmission at sixteen hundred. Leave your things here and set up the Cascina."

The more-powerful Yaesu shortwave was notoriously temperamental, and Anthony had only limited experience with the model, so he was happy to be operating the familiar Cascina for the Great Teacher. At the thought of working at demanding Kony's side, he felt shaky as he set up the radio in front of the octagonal hut.

Voices of suffering began to goad and berate him.

It won't last long, Lack said. *You won't last long.*

Fear said, *Fatima thinks you're useless. And no matter what Lily thinks, you won't make the Ugandan border.*

Anthony became angry, wishing he could shut the voices up, but did not succeed until he spotted Kony and Yango entering Control Altar, surrounded by bodyguards. Clad in his white tunic and pants, the Great Teacher ignored Fatima and Lily and came straight for Anthony and the radio. His eyes seemed to bore right into the signaler, making him feel again as if the LRA leader could read his thoughts and probe his mind.

He knows you! He knows you can't cut it! And so do his wives!

It took everything in his power not to tremble as he bowed his head and said, "Teacher."

"You are Opoka?"

Keeping his head bowed, he said, "Anthony Opoka."

"Look at me, Signaler."

Anthony raised his head uncertainly, forced himself to look Kony in his wide, glistening eyes, aware of his crooked smile and trying not to think of that dog creature from his nightmares.

"They say you are gifted at the TONFAS," Kony said. "That no one is faster with the code. Why is that?"

Despite his feelings about the man, Anthony felt flattered. "I don't know, Teacher. It's like a puzzle I learned to play right away. It just made sense."

The Great Teacher's smile disappeared. "But that is not why."

Anthony didn't know what to say.

Kony said, "Last night, the spirit of Cilindi spoke through me. The doctor said you were gifted with the TONFAS because of what happened to your shoulder. It's like the hearing of a blinded man. It gets better after the eyesight is gone."

Anthony raised his eyebrows, considering that Cilindi had supposedly been the spirit who recommended the medic put magic mushrooms and salt in his wound before sewing him up. Could this also be true? That he'd been given his ability with the codes because of the accident? He didn't know, and then, he didn't care. If Kony's spirit thought it was true, it was.

"I can see that," Anthony said.

"I'm sure you can. Now." The LRA's supreme leader stepped closer. "Whose love did you crave as a child? Whose love did you miss and long for? Your mother's? Or your father's? Say the truth, Signaler!"

Anthony felt compelled to reply, "My mother, Teacher."

Kony seemed interested in that. "Why?"

"She was a sad person. She ended up leaving my father. Our family."

"Hmmm," Kony said, checking his watch. "Time to broadcast."

Relieved, Anthony said, "The radio is ready for you, Teacher."

"I should hope so," Kony said. "Raise Generals Tabuley, Matata, and Major Okaya."

Anthony was a little shaken by this introduction to the Great Teacher and Control Altar, and a little excited as he tuned the radio to one of the five frequencies the senior commanders regularly used to communicate. His brother Albert was signaler for General Matata these days and would learn on the air whom Anthony was working for now.

He triggered the microphone. "This is Nine Whiskey with Six Bravo. Nine Whiskey with Six Bravo calling Seven Delta, Two Victor, and Fourteen Charley, come back."

Anthony called three times before hearing Albert say, "This is Fourteen Charley, confirm Nine Whiskey with Six Bravo?"

"Affirmative," Anthony said, conflicted for feeling proud. "This is Nine Whiskey. Stand by for Six Bravo."

———

The following morning was foggy, chilly. Kony and the eleven hundred men who guarded him and his family broke camp and reassembled as a marching force in that square-within-a-square design. The leader of the LRA appeared from his hut not in his normal white tunic and pants but in a woman's wraparound skirt, matching embroidered top, and headscarf.

"You look lovely today, Teacher," said Fatima when he appeared from his hut and joined the formation.

Anthony moved fifteen meters in front of the Great Teacher, the Cascina radio on his back, his rifle over his left shoulder.

"And you look lucky," Kony said to his first wife. "Walking to my right today."

"And sleeping in your bed tonight," Fatima said, and laughed when he tickled her.

Lily strolled into her position as wife for the following night. She carried nothing. Neither did Fatima, or Christin, or Nighty, who were with the other main wives, all of whom had taken positions behind and to the Great Teacher's left and right.

"General Potent!" Kony said.

"Teacher!" cried a long, lanky man in a uniform diagonally forward of the LRA commander and fifty meters to Anthony's left.

"Yango!"

The head of security for Kony's inner circle, diagonally forward and to the right fifty meters, yelled back, "Ready to march, Teacher!"

"Move out!" Kony roared.

The call echoed from the inner square of one hundred bodyguards outward through the thousand troops assembled on four sides. They began to march south, staying in the bush as much as possible. Anthony kept his eyes darting from General Potent to Yango to the forward wall of twenty-five bodyguards, tracking their positions, using them to calibrate his line of travel, and therefore Kony's and his wives'.

For roughly two hours, they walked in silence, save the Great Teacher's teasing of his wives and them chortling as he described what he would do to Fatima later in the evening and to Lily the following night. Anthony had heard other boys whisper of such activities, of course, but he'd never heard adults speak so openly and graphically about them.

Indeed, after stopping for the 1100 radio call, Kony picked up the banter right where he'd left off. And Fatima and Lily went with him, urging the Great Teacher's fantasies to new heights. Anthony had no idea what he'd gotten himself into, and felt exposed, wildly in danger as the December sun rose high overhead. He tried to remember all the rules Yango had told him the day before, and all the actions General Tabuley and Patrick said were critical to his longevity as Kony's signaler.

The advice, the rules, the things he had to do to stay alive, they began to be slung about in his thoughts and quickly came to dominate them. He kept glancing at his watch, fearful he'd miss one of the designated radio calls. He wondered if there was enough time in one day to do everything that was being demanded of him.

A tightness built in his stomach that spread to his chest, which struggled to expand for breath. The Cascina radio on his back ordinarily did not slow him down. Or at least, it had not slowed him when he was following General Tabuley. But now he felt the radio as a far heavier load and struggled to prevent his breathing from going shallow.

In his mind, he heard Fatima and Lily laughing as they'd placed bets on how long he'd last as Kony's radioman. He couldn't go down the first day. He couldn't even ask for help with his burden. Instead, he imagined himself back in school, back at the districts, racing Patrick back when they had no idea what malice life had in store for them.

Anthony's breathing got more relaxed, deeper, but thoughts of all those rules, of how important it was to do everything exactly right, kept intruding, kept gnawing at him as he pushed his way through elephant grass and listened to Kony and his women laughing behind him.

I can't do it all. There's not enough . . .

"Time?" he muttered to himself. "That's one of them, isn't it?"

Since leaving Torit with Patrick several days before, Anthony had not thought of Mr. Mabior or the things the old shopkeeper had told him as he died, about silencing the voices of suffering. But now some of it came back, and he realized exactly which of the four voices had been dominating his thoughts ever since they'd started marching toward the border.

It's not Time, it's Rush, he thought. *It's the voice of Rush.*

Some of Mr. Mabior's dying words echoed in Anthony's head, reminding him that Rush was the voice of *there's not enough time,* the voice of *there is never enough time, you have so many things to do just to survive that you feel like a great monster is always chasing you and you can never stop running from it.*

"Do you know what that monster is, Anthony?" the old shopkeeper had asked.

Moving through a thicket, semiaware of Kony still joking with his wives, Anthony remembered how he'd thought of that dog creature with the face of the Great Teacher, but then shook his head.

"The monster is death," the shopkeeper said.

Mabior said it was because humans only live so long in this form, and they are constantly made aware of it. The clock. The wristwatch. The language. There's no time to lose. They're already late. Why are they so concerned? Because sooner or later, all humans are going to die. It's guaranteed but they have no idea when or how. So, the shopkeeper said, the voice of Rush rises, and the pace of your thoughts increases and repeats, getting faster and faster, and quickly a human is no longer living.

"You are being controlled," the old man said. "You are cut off from your true self, and therefore you cannot act. You are trapped by the idea that there is nothing more after death."

Anthony remembered feeling instinctively that a lot of what Mr. Mabior said rang true. Except for that last one.

"I've seen a lot of people die," he said. "There's nothing there anymore."

Mr. Mabior grimaced at the pain in his stomach, but then nodded. "The immortal part of them has departed, just as the immortal part of me will go on soon and someday yours will as well. Once you grasp this truth, Anthony, once you dwell on your immortal spirit during times of Rush, your suffering will begin to quiet."

The key to further slowing Rush, the shopkeeper said, was learning to breathe correctly.

"Breathe deep, use air to fill out your ribcage and swell your lower belly. As you do, think, 'There is stillness.' Hold your breath for a count of two and then slowly, slowly exhale. As you do, think, 'There is stillness.' Do this seven times, and Rush will quiet even more.

"For total silence from Rush, put your hand over your heart, take seven more deep, slow breaths, and say to yourself each time, 'I am you. You are me. We are one.'"

Anthony remembered asking why.

"You are acknowledging that your spirit is part of the universe," Mr. Mabior said. "You are acknowledging that the universe is part of your soul. And you are saying your soul and the universe are both the same: timeless, rushless, and one. When you do this, time will seem to slow and expand and there will be more than enough of it to do everything you need to do. With no Rush, there is one less suffering voice trying to run your mind."

———

"Hey, Signaler!" Lily hissed, jerking Anthony from his memories.

He startled and looked back, seeing Kony's second wife tapping on her wrist while the Great Teacher talked to Fatima.

He glanced at his watch and saw it was 1250. How was that possible?

He did not bother to look at Kony, just ran ahead two hundred meters and hung the antenna, attached the batteries, and fired up the radio with two minutes to spare. The Great Teacher communicated with his field commanders before telling his entire entourage to rest and eat. They'd been walking hard and fast for nearly four hours.

Several of the younger female recruits were called forward to cook for Kony and his family. The wives did little but criticize the girls loudly for their shortcomings.

Yango wandered by Anthony. As he did, the security chief muttered, "They do it to knock the girls down in Kony's eyes. They don't want him to take an interest in any of the young girls for fear they will be pushed out to make room."

Anthony felt restless at that, looked over at Kony, who was sitting on a log ten meters away, still dressed as a woman, and teasing his wives Christin and Nighty now. Did he ever pay attention to his army beyond the four scheduled radio calls a day?

After handing her husband a bowl of food, Lily brought one for Anthony.

He bobbed his head as he took it, said softly, "Thank you. For warning me."

Kony's second wife shrugged but smiled. "I don't want to give Fatima the satisfaction."

"Thank you anyway."

Lily studied him. "You're welcome, Signaler. I hope you stick around. I really do."

She walked away then, her hips swaying before she looked over her shoulder, saw him watching, and laughed before continuing on. Anthony felt flushed, confused by her attention. Hunger overtook everything, and he ate. As he did, the voice of Fear began to speak.

Fear told him not to talk with Lily. Or at least as little as possible. *Kony might not understand. The penalty is death.*

Then he knew he should take the chance to rest, but Rush woke up, telling him he should be inspecting the radio or making sure he could draw the latest TONFAS cipher in the dirt or in his notebook. He got frustrated, feeling like the voices would not let him be.

At last, he surrendered and decided to follow Mr. Mabior's advice. He sat against the base of a tree, the radio at his side, and closed his eyes. Instead of falling into a doze, he thought of himself as a spirit beyond his body, took seven deep belly breaths, silently saying, *There is stillness,* on each inhalation and exhalation. And then he put his hands on his chest and took seven more breaths, each while saying silently, *I am you. You are me. We are one.*

When Anthony opened his eyes, he felt strangely calm and undistracted, even when he noticed Kony gazing at him with what seemed like kindness. "Did you sleep, Opoka?"

"A short nap, Teacher," Anthony said, struggling to his feet. "Do you need the radio?"

"All I need is a signaler who will last. I'm glad you know how to take your sleep when you need it." His expression changed, became sterner, though not as stone-faced as he was when possessed by the spirit of Who Are You. "My last radioman did not understand, and he got sleepy, and he made mistakes. Unforgivable ones, Opoka."

In another time and place, Anthony might have been hugely intimidated by the comment. But after his breathing, he was very clearheaded and felt his best response was to nod humbly. "I will learn from his fatal mistakes, Teacher."

That seemed to please Kony. Indeed, after he'd called his personal battalion, bodyguards, and inner circle to their feet and they were on the march, the LRA leader stopped talking to his wives about their nighttime activities and focused on adding to what Anthony would come to call "The Great Teacher's Guide to Becoming a Big Person."

"You see Opoka here?" he said in a loud voice about an hour after they'd gotten underway. "He thinks."

"The new signaler?" Lily said.

Fatima scoffed. "What do you need him to think for, Teacher?"

In a low growl, Kony said, "There are times when I think you are the smartest woman alive, Fatima. And others when I think there couldn't be a dumber ass on the face of the earth."

Anthony's eyes widened. He wanted nothing more than to look over his right shoulder to see the head wife's reaction to that statement, but he wisely kept his attention straight ahead. For several moments, there was only the sound of their legs swishing in the grass.

He glanced over his left shoulder finally, seeing Lily there. She raised her brows and widened her eyes at him as if to say she was enjoying herself very much.

Then Kony went on as if there'd been no interruption. "As I said, Opoka thinks. And because he thinks, he is capable of becoming a big person. I need all of you, including you, Fatima, to start thinking like a big person. Opoka, what did you say when I told you that my last signaler made mistakes?"

Anthony hesitated, but then looked back over his right shoulder, seeing Fatima was staring red-hot tracer bullets at him before he shifted his gaze to Kony. "I said I would learn from those fatal mistakes."

"Exactly what a future big person does," the Great Teacher exclaimed. "A small person does not do this. A small person thinks about the last mistakes, how they symbolize failure and death, and not lessons to be learned from. Do you see?"

"I see, Teacher," Lily said. "You're saying, one arm or not, Opoka could become a very, very big person."

Anthony stole a glance at Fatima, who was now staring bullets at her sister wife.

"Why not?" Kony said. "There is no signaler in the LRA who can run the TONFAS like him. And he always thinks of how to be better, how to be a bigger person. You could be my minister of communications someday, Opoka."

Anthony stood taller and could not help beaming when he looked back. "If it will help you, Teacher."

"Of course, it will help me. What's a leader without communication? What is a big person without communication?"

"A tall deaf-mute?" Fatima said.

Kony shook a finger at her and laughed. "That's very funny. I knew there was at least one reason I liked you."

"Ha ha," his head wife said.

"But you get what I'm saying, don't you?" her husband went on. "Opoka could become my minister of communications. He could live in a fine home in Kampala and be driven to his offices in a black Mercedes. And he could have a fine wife and children and the best in life because of what he did here, in the bush, with us. Isn't that right, Opoka?"

"If you say so, Teacher," Anthony said, feeling seduced by the idea. "I'd be glad to try."

"See? A risk-taker as well," Kony said.

Lily said, "Someone with the potential to be a big person."

Anthony glanced back, and she did that thing with her brows and eyes again.

They stopped again at four. Anthony got the Cascina running. Kony handed him written orders he wanted broadcast.

The signaler rapidly encoded the orders with the TONFAS system and then read the message over the radio, letter for letter, number for number, once again ordering the LRA's best raiders south into Uganda in search of new recruits for the Great Teacher and his ever-expanding army.

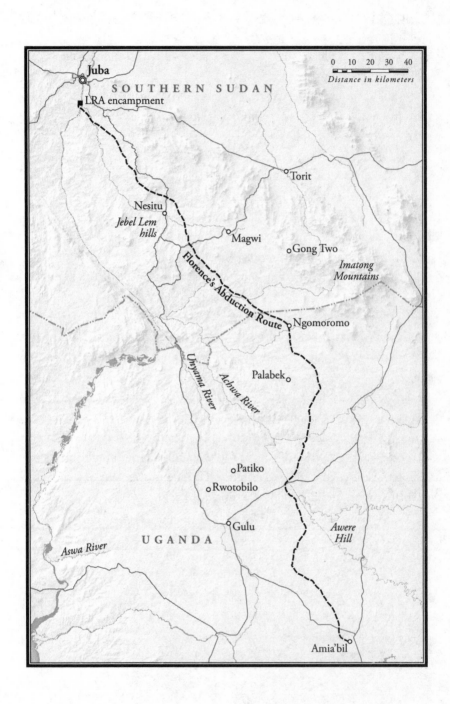

Chapter Eighteen

Like most of the friends and students she knew, fourteen-year-old Florence Okori was on a weeklong academic break, staying home and helping in the family gardens with her cousin Jasper and babysitting in the evening for her big brother Owen and his wife.

Twice a day—when she left the gardens for lunch, and again for dinner—she'd ask if they'd gotten any notification from Kampala yet about her test scores. And twice a day for more than a month, Josca had shaken her head no.

"But, Mama," Florence groaned that afternoon. "My friends at school say their cousins in the south have already received their results."

"You know as well as I do that the government works slower for Acholi people," Josca said. "Don't be surprised if you and your friends are the last to know."

"Last to know?" Florence felt sick to her stomach. "That's so unfair."

"Knowing last won't change your scores," her father said. "You came home from every single exam believing you'd known the answers to almost every question."

That was true. In her heart and in her mind, Florence had left all five of her exams feeling like she'd been in absolute control not only of the test but of her destiny. In the days immediately following the tests, she was confident she'd done it, that she'd aced the exams and would be going on to an excellent secondary school and then nursing school.

But as the days had turned into weeks and the weeks into months, doubt began to creep into her thoughts. Maybe she had it all wrong. Maybe she'd been unclear on the directions that accompanied the tests. Maybe she'd marked the answer sheets in the wrong manner, skipped one question and thrown off the entire sequence and logic of her answers.

And every time she asked her mother about her results and got no happy news in return, the feelings of doubt and anxiety grew.

"Keep praying, and good things will come of it," her mother said.

Florence did believe that. She'd believed it ever since she survived all those months in the hospital with the measles. But she also believed what her nurse, her angel at the hospital, had taught her: that if you wish God to hear your prayers, you must bow your head with a heart that is at peace. But her heart was not at peace. Every time she tried to make it so, she thought of her missing exam results, and she felt a dull ache in her chest.

"I hate this," Florence grumbled to Jasper after dinner that evening.

"Hold on," he said. "My new favorite's up next. Celine Dion's 'My Heart Will Go On.' It's number one on BBC again!"

Florence had heard the song and liked it, but she said, "Great. I'm babysitting."

"I'll come by when this is over."

"The results are taking forever," she told Owen a minute later when she arrived at his hut to take care of his little boy while he met his wife in town to shop at the night market.

Owen put both hands on her shoulders. "It sucks, getting stretched out, the waiting, but it will feel so good when you find out you passed with flying colors."

"You think?"

"I do," he said, giving her a hug. "Gotta go meet Ruth."

He broke into a jog, heading toward the front of the compound, but then slowed within ten strides, stopped, and bent over. Jasper put his radio down and ran to him with Florence right behind. "Owen, what's wrong?"

Florence's older brother was coughing and heaving for breath. "My chest and left arm are tight. Can't catch my breath."

"Sit him down," Florence said to Jasper, and then ran to her father.

Constantine grabbed his box of herbal medicines and raced after Florence back to his oldest son, who continued to labor for breath. Her father dug around, found a jar with dried willow bark. He put a chunk of it under Owen's tongue.

Within minutes, he began to breathe better and his color improved. The pain in his chest and arm eased as well.

"How did that work?" Jasper asked.

"Natural aspirin," Florence said.

Her father nodded. "Good for heart problems."

Owen said, "I'm only twenty-eight, Papa. I can't have a heart problem."

"Then you're very good at faking one," Constantine said.

His oldest son tried to get up. "I have to meet Ruth. I'll be late."

"You're not going anywhere," his father said. "You're going to rest, and in the morning, you are going to the hospital so they can listen to your heart."

"I've got a great heart," Owen protested. "A big one."

"You have a big one. Everyone who knows you knows that. I just want to make sure your big heart is not broken."

Florence ran to find Ruth, then stayed with her and helped with her son as Owen rested. She finally thought about sleep several hours later, told Ruth she'd be back at dawn, and walked down the familiar path past Jasper's hut to her father's part of the compound.

The moon overhead was in its final phase, barely throwing enough light for shadows. A hot, humid wind had been blowing for days, a harbinger of the rainy season to come. But the night was virtually windless and muggy. Mosquitoes were about. To get away from the bugs, she chose to sleep inside her hut with her twelve-year-old sister, Margaret, who was already snoring lightly when Florence kicked off her sandals, removed her shirt, and lay down on her mat in a pair of shorts she used for physical education at school.

She drifted into a deep sleep, barely rousing a few hours later when Margaret got up and went outside to relieve herself. Florence was falling away again when the shouting and screaming began.

———

She came around groggily. *Men are shouting. But who is screaming? A woman or a girl?* She came alert, thinking, *Margaret? No, that sounds like Ruth. Is that Owen's wife?*

Fearing the worst, Florence jumped up, got her sandals on, and was groping around for her shirt when the blanket door to her hut was torn off. Florence screamed when a flashlight found her, blinded her. A figure entered, grabbed her by the arm, and dragged her out.

"No!" Florence screamed. "What are you doing?"

"Shut up, or I'll make you shut up," he growled before shoving her down to her knees.

Florence tried to stop crying, realized she had no shirt on, and folded her arms across her chest. Outside, the night fires were still glowing enough for her to see him, or the silhouette of him, anyway, tall, muscular, dreadlocks, carrying an AK-47. He took a half step toward her. Florence kicked her way back from him, hearing Ruth screaming, *"No, you can't take him! You can't! He's sick!"*

There were other shouts. Other voices. *Jasper?*

"Florence!"

Her father ran into the compound with his own flashlight, and a machete. Before Constantine could raise his weapon, the big man who'd dragged her from her hut hit him in the chest with the butt of his gun. He was about to club her father in the head when men started shouting, "UPDF coming! UPDF patrol!"

"Stay down, old man," the big guy said, then grabbed Florence by the arm and yanked her to her feet. "Move! Say nothing!"

It had all happened so fast.

One minute she'd been asleep, and the next minute she was being dragged away from her family, then goaded forward into the darkness by a dreadlocked guy with a machine gun. She heard Ruth and Josca crying and screaming behind her. She stumbled.

He yanked her back to her feet and prodded her forward onto a trail that led not toward town, but down the bank to the stream where they got water. There were others there, but she had no idea how many. Some of them were armed men. Others were teenagers and younger whimpering with fear.

Of course Florence had heard about the LRA kidnapping kids, but it had always been a story told by someone who knew someone. The rebel group and the dangers it posed had always seemed like a distant problem, not hers, not when they lived so close to a town as big as Lira.

But now, hearing the whimpers and the trembling cries in the darkness, dread seized her. *Who else have they taken? Owen? Jasper? Are they here?*

The moon went behind a cloud. She barely made out her own shaking hand in front of her face. The dread became terror when the guy who'd grabbed her whispered harshly in her ear, "You cannot cry in the LRA. Keep quiet and keep up. Or die."

Behind them, she heard engines revving and people shouting, saw flashlight beams playing back toward her home. He pushed her to move. They walked quickly in a single-file line away from the stream and her father's compound. Someone up front used a flashlight now and then, but the rest of the walk unfolded in total darkness.

By first light, she was completely lost and had no idea how far they had come, or the direction they'd traveled. But Florence could soon see she was toward the front of a single-file line, which the LRA soldiers kept calling "the rail." Ahead of her on the rail were two men in their twenties and a third man, much older, and five or six kids she didn't recognize flanked on both sides by LRA soldiers.

Until then, she'd thought only her family had been attacked, and she wanted to look back to see how many others there were and who else was with her. Every time she tried, however, the guy who'd abducted her would rap her hard on the shoulder and tell her to keep her attention in front of her.

"The past is over," he whispered in her ear as they came to an opening where ten LRA soldiers stood guard over fifteen other terrified kids, some of them choking back tears. Seeing them, Florence wanted to cry as well.

But she had been warned that crying was not allowed, so she kept biting her lower lip and stayed quiet when they were ordered to sit. When she did, she looked around and saw Owen and Jasper about twenty meters away. Her older brother's face was swollen, and he looked exhausted, but he nodded at her in encouragement. Her cousin's right eye was bruised almost shut. A gash above it seeped blood.

Another band of LRA men came in with six more people. She was shocked to see one of them was her teacher, Mr. Alonsius, who was limping slightly.

Then she noticed one of the soldiers nearby was leering at her. She realized she didn't have a shirt on, flushed, and covered her breasts with her arm.

"No need to do that, little one," he said, grinning and winking at her.

"Back off, Phillip," the big guy with the dreads said. "You don't get to make that call."

Phillip, who was half her captor's size, lost the leer, said, "Okay, Oyet. Whatever."

Other soldiers came with a rope. They tied loops around every kid's waist and then tied them together in two rails of twenty, each rail guarded by five soldiers, who kept goading them to keep up the pace when they began to move. The rope soon began to chafe at Florence's bare waist. She kept having to uncover her breasts to move it with her fingers.

But she was happy she'd put her sandals on before Oyet had grabbed her. Some of the kids were barefoot; their feet had to be blistered and bleeding. When they slowed, one of the soldiers swatted at the culprit with a switch, especially when they had to cross a road swiftly and then drop downhill across a wide-open field and a river.

Partway across the field, she suddenly could see a helicopter flying in the distance. The LRA men saw it, too, and made them sprint until they'd reached the trees of the river bottom.

Women and girls were washing clothes there. When they spotted the LRA soldiers with their guns and the children tied in a line, they bolted, leaving their clothes spread and drying across bushes. Oyet walked over, snagged a T-shirt, and handed it to Florence.

"Put it on or I'll have a revolt on my hands," he said, and walked away.

Florence didn't know exactly what the soldier meant but felt better once she'd put the shirt on and got it tucked between her skin and the rope. They walked for several kilometers upstream along the bank. Mr. Alonsius was limping more and having trouble keeping up. The soldiers kept hitting him between his shoulder blades and telling him he was going to die if he didn't move faster. He grabbed a stick on the ground and used it like a crutch, but every time he put his left foot down, he would wince with pain.

They finally reached a spot where they could ford the Achwa River and take refuge in a large, roadless area on the other side. In the forest there, they stopped to cook food. Florence and ten other girls were told to fetch water. The boys were sent to gather firewood.

"If you try to run, you'll be shot," Oyet said. "So don't run."

Florence and the other girls took plastic water jugs to the river to fill them with Oyet watching, his submachine gun cradled in his massive arms. Behind him, Phillip, the soldier who'd leered at her, climbed a tree to take a look at the land beyond the river bottom.

As Florence hauled her full jug back toward the soldiers stacking wood for the fire, Phillip came scrambling back down the tree, hissing, "UPDF! UPDF!"

"How far?"

"Two, three hundred meters and coming our way, at least fifty of them!"

"Cut the girls loose," Oyet ordered. "They'll slow us down."

Oyet pulled a knife and came to Florence, cut her free, and said, "What's your name?"

She instinctively did not want him to know her real name, so she said, "Betty."

"It's your lucky day, Betty. Get back across the river. Run like hell to the road."

Florence felt adrenaline surge through her and joy at the thought of freedom a split second before the first mortar thumped from the east, whistled, and exploded in the trees about sixty meters away.

———

Florence had never heard a gunshot before, much less a bomb at close quarters. The force of the explosion pulsed through her, paralyzed her, rooted her to the spot.

Oyet spun away and began to run toward the other LRA soldiers, who were grabbing gear and stuffing it in packs. More mortars thumped, whistled, and exploded in the river bottom. The closest one landed right near Oyet and three of his men. She lost track of them all in a red, deafening flash.

Dumbfounded, befuddled, Florence didn't know what to do. Then she did. She turned to sprint for the river, seeing that Mr. Alonsius was already in the water and swimming downstream! She would do the same, get to the other side, and find her way back to that road and then home!

Thump! Thump! Thump! More mortars sailed overhead, struck closer to the river, and threw up a wall of fire down there. Feeling surrounded and hounded, she picked another direction and ran, only then thinking to look back for Owen and Jasper.

Bomb smoke spiraled and writhed through the woods. She could see other people running, but not her brother and not her cousin. Then she heard heavy machine-gun fire off to her right. She adjusted her direction left and sprinted, wanting to be out of the way of the guns and the bombs and the smoke. In the haze and the chaos of that first combat experience, Florence realized there was a girl about the same age running in the same direction she was, and so was one of the guys in his late twenties who'd been roped in front of her.

The ground sloped, turned swampy. Florence kicked off her sandals, held them, and went into the muck and the reeds with the other girl behind her and the guy ahead of them and off to the side. A fierce gun battle had erupted behind them, but it was getting farther and farther away and the shots more sporadic an hour later when they left the swamp and neared the edge of a sugarcane plantation.

The girl said her name was Palmer.

"Isn't that a boy's name?" Florence asked.

The girl looked irritated. "No. I mean, not necessarily. It was my mother's mother's name, too."

"When did they grab you?" Florence said, wanting to change the subject.

"Six days ago," she said, moving quicker. "I saw things. They will kill us all for running if they catch us."

"Not if they can't find us," said the man. "I'm Paul. And I know where I am now. I know the people who own this plantation. They're good people. They'll help us. We'll wait until it is almost dark and then go to the big house."

They pushed their way two hundred meters into the sugarcane. Paul found a rusty machete in the mud. He picked it up. They stood there, waiting, listening. The bombing stopped. Then the shooting died off.

For almost two hours, they waited and whispered. Paul said he had been taken the night before, dragged from his wife and children.

"After I hold them in my arms again, I'm moving them all south," he declared. "I'm done with Gulu until they get these LRA bastards under control."

An army helicopter chugged upriver. They crouched in the mud, not wanting to be spotted, not wanting to be thought of as LRA and shot at from above. It finally circled away.

Paul used the machete to cut and split sugarcane for them to eat. He said he knew the sons of the people who owned the plantation. They'd gone to secondary school together.

"I took the entrance exams for secondary," Florence said.

"I did, too," Palmer said. "How did you do?"

She felt herself tighten, and said, "I haven't gotten the results yet and it's been months!"

"I know! Me neither," Palmer said in soft squeals of indignation.

"Mine took forever, too," Paul said. "I think I got them in March."

"Who cares anyway?" Palmer said. "There are people close by who want to kill us."

Florence realized she was right and felt a little embarrassed that she'd fretted over her exam results after being held captive by lunatics.

Paul checked his watch. "It's close enough to sundown. Let's go find my friends."

He began to push and shove his way through the dense sugarcane, finding a trail at one point, and then following it for six or seven hundred meters until they reached a wider cart path that they followed into the yard of the plantation house, which had a long white front veranda.

On it sat fifteen LRA soldiers, including Phillip and Oyet, who had a bandage on his arm and another about his head. Nineteen or twenty abductees were sitting in the dirt by the porch. Jasper was there. So was Owen, who stared vacantly at the ground.

"Oh God," Palmer whispered. "They're going to kill us all."

Paul tossed the machete. "They've already seen us."

"You three!" Oyet shouted from the veranda. "Come here. Sit down or you'll be shot."

Florence couldn't believe it. They'd walked right into them.

"We're going to die now," Palmer said, head down, trudging toward the others.

Florence followed her, started to sit near Owen, who continued to stare at the ground.

"Move away, Flo," he whispered. "Don't let them see that you know me or Jasper. I was told it's dangerous."

She had so wanted to be next to her older brother and cousin, to be comforted by family. But she moved away and sat by Palmer, wondering what was to become of them. Was Palmer right? Were they going to be killed for running?

As darkness neared, two LRA soldiers came and asked them each their age. If you were twenty-six or older, they locked you in the plantation house. Owen was one of the first men asked. He didn't understand what was going on and told them the truth, that he was twenty-eight. Paul said he was twenty-nine and went willingly into the house along with four others.

Oyet came past her, looked at her with disgust. "I thought I told you to run, Betty."

"The bombs. I couldn't."

"Can't say I didn't try," he said, and moved on.

They were each given a pack to carry. Florence carried a radio. Palmer had a sack of rice on a frame on her back. Jasper and Owen were loaded down with boxes of ammunition. They started to walk at eight that evening and did not stop until four in the morning. The LRA soldiers cooked, ate, and napped in shifts in deep cover. The abductees were given no food or water.

A few times in her life, there had been blights and droughts and food had been scarce. Florence knew what it was like to go hungry. She told herself she could last a long time if she had to and tried to sleep. Around six thirty that morning, they were roused by the LRA, told to pick up their loads and to start marching again.

Midmorning it began to rain. They walked all day in a downpour and never crossed a road, sticking to game trails in the deep bush. The abductees were given no water. But the rain and the soaking-wet vegetation allowed Florence to wet her lips and keep going. More than once, she thought that if there had been a hot sun overhead, she would have dropped by noon.

Florence managed to stay on her feet until late afternoon when they reached a rendezvous point. Other bands of LRA soldiers were waiting in a secluded grassland of perhaps twenty acres, along with at least a hundred other abductees, mostly young teens, all roped. She collapsed into the wet grass, lay back, and opened her mouth. Owen lay back, too, letting the rain quench his thirst. Jasper just sat there, arms around his knobby knees, staring at the ground. Florence understood. She had never been so tired in her life.

As the rain abated, the soldiers ate again, and then Phillip came forward to announce that each recruit was to be "registered" that evening. The soldiers made a big deal out of the ritual. A bonfire was built. Lanterns were hung from branches to either side of a nearby tree.

The first candidate was a boy, who could not have been much older than ten. A soldier brought him before a tribunal of three LRA soldiers.

"Can this candidate be registered as a recruit?" the soldier asked.

The trio looked over the shaking boy. One of them said, "The registration fee is caning. Fifteen times."

"What?" the boy said. "No."

"Twenty, then," another of the trio said.

"Oh God," Florence whispered, and stared at the ground and the shadows thrown by the bonfire.

She heard them hit the kid twenty times, until he fell to his knees, sobbing, his back raised up in welts.

"There's no crying in the LRA!" Phillip said, and caned the boy a twenty-first time.

One by one, male and female, they were selected and brought forward to endure the same ritual. Florence could see that most males in their early teens got sixty canings. Older males got seventy-five. Older females received between thirty and sixty lashes. Girls like her, in their early teens, received forty-five canings.

Oyet took over before Jasper and Owen were brought up. Jasper was given fifty-five lashes and stayed on his feet even though his back was a bloody mess when Oyet finished.

Florence could not watch after her oldest brother was given a registration fee of eighty canings. She felt herself getting nauseous when the count passed sixty-five and each blow sounded like meat being pounded. At seventy-five, she had to look and saw her dear brother wobbling, holding on to the tree for dear life. How he survived the eighty canings, she would never know. But Owen did and staggered away from the tree on his own power, shaking off one LRA soldier's offer of assistance. Twenty meters later, he crumpled.

Phillip took the cane from Oyet. Two more young boys went up.

And then it was Florence's turn.

Chapter Nineteen

Until that point in her life, Florence had rarely been punished and never physically. Josca believed love was the best guidance a child could have. And Constantine had never had the heart to beat or spank his children.

So the first slash of the cane came as a complete shock to her system and psyche. She howled at the impact, gasped, and shuddered at the fire in her skin before the second slash came.

Every blow that followed made one part of her want to go down, unable to last, dragged into the darkness, and probably shot. But after the fortieth caning, there were only five slashes left. And then four. She stopped silently weeping with three left and didn't remember the forty-fifth at all. Something had shifted in her. She'd found a place of harsh comfort, one that she'd never known existed, a way of living called hatred.

After that last cut of the cane, the hatred built like fire, created invisible armor around her. She staggered away from the tree, glared murderously at Phillip, and then took several steps toward Owen and Jasper, feeling inhuman, like a lower form of life, cut off by the experience of the caning from everything she'd ever known, love certainly.

I am alone, the fourteen-year-old thought when she finally lay down in the wet grass by Palmer and some other moaning girls. *I am alone, and my life will never be good again.*

After the registration was complete, the LRA soldiers cooked and ate. The recruits were given no water and no food.

But Oyet came to them with rags and tubs of warm water. He ignored Florence's open loathing and told her and the others how to clean the wounds so they would not become infected.

When he was done, he said, "All of us have walked this same path. In the LRA, it's uncertain whether you will live on any day. So live for each day and do what the commanders tell you. Persevere, obey, and you have a chance of surviving until tomorrow."

He walked off. There was soap in the water, which savagely stung Florence's back when Palmer cleaned it. But the aspiring nurse knew Oyet was right: the greatest danger they faced now was infection. She had to keep her wounds clean, or she would succumb.

Flo cleaned Palmer's wounds and then draped her T-shirt over her own back, lay on her side, and closed her eyes. Her every sense was alert to the flares and aches crisscrossing her back, and she doubted she could sleep.

But it came for her.

Mercifully.

———

Something hit Florence softly in the face. She woke up, felt fabric over her head, and then the dull roar of her back. She sat up, slowly, painfully, the fabric falling, and saw dawn was coming. Oyet was walking away from her toward a campfire. In her lap lay a ratty, threadbare dress, but it was better than her T-shirt, which was now covered in stripes of dried blood.

Florence put on the dress and stuffed the bloody T-shirt in the radio pack. She would wash it later. When the word went out that they were getting ready to move on with no food and no water for the recruits again, she had to fight back tears. But shouldering the pack was worse.

She stood up, wondering how long she'd last with her wounds screaming at her under the weight of the radio. From the start, her legs ached, and different parts of her back flared at random. Her mouth was parched even before the sun had fully risen, and she was grateful there was a breeze blowing.

A kilometer into the march, however, they reached a vast expanse of elephant grass and headed directly into it. The grass was two meters high in places, so tall it blocked the breeze from making the building heat bearable.

I can't go on much longer like this, she thought.

But then she remembered her mother and how Josca had carried her everywhere when she was five and helpless and had to have weighed more than this radio. She could almost hear her mother's voice calling to her:

You are my daughter, Florence. I would carry you forever.

Those words echoed again and again through her mind, giving her strength and hope as she forged on in the infernal heat and humidity of the deep grassland.

They walked for four hours without rest.

I would carry you forever.

She got dizzy. She heard other voices behind and in front of her, but elongated and garbled, as if they were playing in slow motion.

I will carry you . . . I will . . .

The air felt scorched as she swooned and fell.

————

How long she lay there in the deep, hot grass, Florence had no idea. It wasn't until someone poured water on her that she roused, still hearing voices, slow and winding.

Palmer and another girl got her pack off and stripped the dress and shorts off her. They soaked her clothes in a nearby stream and put them on her body. Oyet gave her water and a bowl of rice. They drenched her clothes and reapplied them every two hours. They camped there by the stream, and Florence slept through the night.

At five thirty in the morning, they were roused. She went to put the radio on her back, but Oyet stopped her.

"More recruits arrived during the night," he said. "One of them will carry it, Betty."

"Thank you," she said, but still hated him. He had personally caned Owen eighty times and stood by while Phillip caned her forty-five times!

Florence looked around, seeing that Oyet was telling the truth. At least 150 new males and females between the ages of ten and twenty-five were sitting along the stream, roped together in groups of fifty.

She was not roped at first but allowed to walk between two rails of recruits as they headed north, again through the high grass. They finally broke free of it about two hours later and entered more of a classic savanna, with lower grass and far more trees scattered about.

A third troop of soldiers with abductees was waiting, the biggest Florence had seen so far, at least four hundred children, teens, and young adults, roped together in four rails. They finally tied Florence to a rail some twenty recruits in front of Jasper and Owen. They set off with the LRA prodding the seven hundred kidnappees to move faster and faster.

"Stay with the pace, Betty," Oyet said, sprinting past her toward the front of the line. "We're almost to the border with Sudan."

———

Three days later, they neared a town called Ngomoromo, hard by the border, which was obscured by trees and rocky outcroppings. They had to cross an open area twelve hundred meters from the frontier. The LRA soldiers began telling everyone to sprint.

But with the ropes, they crossed out into the open in what was, at best, a fast shuffle.

Thump! Thump! Thump! Thump!

Florence saw four flares spout from the rocky high ground to the northwest, heard the mortars whistling, and dove to the ground, pulling Palmer and the girl behind her before the missiles hit toward the fronts of the four rails. Debris rained down on them.

Oyet came running back down their rope line, cutting the girls free.

"That's UPDF," he shouted as he sliced the rope. "They will kill you for being with us."

He pointed northeast, away from the mortars. "Run there, Betty."

Florence wanted to run in the exact opposite direction, but then heavy machine guns opened up in front of them, and more mortars flew. Three missiles hit near a rail of boys still roped together about eighty meters in front of her.

"Go!" Oyet shouted.

Florence took off at an angle to the last blasts with Palmer and two other girls right behind her. She kept looking into the smoke of the mortars, seeing boys her age dead or bloodied and wandering in a daze. Horrified, she began to run even faster, aware that the LRA soldiers were returning fire at the same time more Ugandan army mortars sailed through the sky.

Florence jumped over a log, went down into a ditch, and scrambled up the other side, now less than two hundred meters from a grove of trees and real cover.

"Betty, wait!" Palmer yelled.

Florence slowed, looked back, and saw her friend was struggling to keep up. She took Palmer's hand and was turning back toward the trees when she spotted Phillip running toward the smoke and the wounded boys. A mortar round hit almost directly in front of him. The soldier who'd caned her died in an instant.

It shocked her enough to stop her cold. But not Palmer, who grabbed her wrist and dragged her forward. A minute later, they were into the trees and diagonally away from the center of the battle by almost four hundred meters. Dozens of other female abductees followed them into the forest. Florence slowed enough to look out where the majority of the mortars were hitting and saw nothing but carnage.

———

The battle of Ngomoromo went on for another three hours. Nine more LRA soldiers died in the fighting in addition to Phillip. Of the seven hundred abductees who tried to cross into Sudan under the mortar shelling, 350 survived. At least fifty of the survivors were wounded, some badly.

From a position on a hillside about a kilometer north of the border fence, Florence watched the battle and felt numb, cut off from everything she'd ever known or cherished as she watched the survivors limp and shuffle out of trees below them. Jasper appeared not long after she'd sat down. Her cousin had a nasty gash on his forehead and was pressing a rag to it as he trudged up the hill to her. Flo wanted to sob with relief but managed to keep silent as tears dripped down her cheeks.

Jasper paused by her as if he were going to sit.

"Don't," she whispered, and he moved on.

She had to wait an excruciating hour before Owen came out of the woods. Her older brother was filthy, cut up, and moving slow.

But he was alive! That cut through the numbness. That was a reason to have hope, wasn't it?

Oyet came out of the trees, jogged past Owen and then Florence. She and Palmer got up and followed him without being told. They left the ropes off her but gave her a pack again. Everyone carried a pack from then on.

The survivors walked all afternoon in the searing heat of southern Sudan, moving from well to well and finding them dry. The wounded began to collapse and die. Florence lost track of Jasper and Owen because she simply had only the energy to face forward, to keep up with Palmer, who was in front of her on the rail.

In her mind, Florence heard Miss Catherine, her nurse from the measles ward, telling her if she could find her way to peace in her heart, she could talk to God and ask for a way out of this hell she'd been dragged into. But try as she might, Flo could not find peace in her heart. Not after finding the harsh comfort of hatred to hide behind, not after the things she'd seen just that morning. All of it had been burned into her mind so deeply she doubted she'd ever feel true peace in her heart again.

That sense intensified later that day as they marched deeper and deeper into southern Sudan and a vast wilderness area.

"Gap in the rail!" someone shouted behind her. "Close that gap!"

Florence finally looked back, saw the gap some fifty people behind her, and saw who was responsible. Owen was struggling to catch up to Jasper, who had tied the rag around his head. Her older brother made it to her cousin, and they continued on.

Dusk was settling when she heard it again. "Gap. Close that gap in the rail!"

She looked back.

An LRA captain walked next to Owen, yelling, "Move, Recruit! Close that gap!"

Her brother looked at him blankly, but did not speed up, just kept on at a plodding pace. He seemed empty somehow, his jaw slack, his eyes vacantly focused ahead, his head wavering side to side as if he were unsure of his balance.

"Move!" the captain shouted.

Florence's brother tried but could not catch up to Jasper. The LRA officer lost it, hit Owen in the side with his rifle stock. Her brother fell to the ground, bent and groaning.

Florence and the rest of her rail stopped.

The captain shouted at the abductees behind Owen. "This recruit cannot keep up. As you pass, step on his head."

Florence whimpered, "What? No!"

"Shut up," Palmer hissed as Owen got to his hands and knees, tried to regain his feet.

The captain came over, put his boot on his caned back and pushed him down. He pointed to the first boy on the rail behind Owen. "You, step on his head. Hard! Now!"

Florence could not look. But she heard the sound of it and her brother's weak cry and every one after that as she stood there helpless, staring at the ground, ripped apart by sorrow.

She cried but did not weep. She stood there, trembling, grieving, begging God to have pity on the good soul Owen had always been to her, to everyone.

As if her silent plea had been heard, the LRA captain told someone to end it. A shot went off. She flinched, saw the despair in Palmer's face, and then Jasper's, and felt like her heart had been cut out of her whole.

Chapter Twenty

After seeing Joseph Kony leave a mosque and shake hands with a high-ranking official in the Sudanese military, Anthony grabbed his radio pack and rifle and sprinted to the white Hilux pickup truck parked across the street. He was up in the back of the pickup before Kony had crossed the street. Yango and three other armed bodyguards surrounded the Great Teacher, who was free of his women's travel clothes, back in a white tunic and pants.

After Kony climbed into the cab, Yango looked at Anthony and nodded. Anthony nodded back, feeling like his relationship with Kony's security chief and the other high-ranking officers inside Control Altar had changed. Not only had he defied the odds and survived his probation period as the Great Teacher's personal signaler, but he'd also proven his ability to keep a cool head under great pressure. Even the wives had noticed.

Yango took the wheel. The other bodyguards climbed into the truck bed with Anthony.

They drove through the bustle of Juba, weaving around small armies of motorcycles and jitneys jammed with passengers, goats and sheep tied to the roofs, all bound for outlying towns and villages. There were throngs of people everywhere—laughing, working, arguing—and music blaring from shops, and more smells than Anthony had ever encountered in one place. Then again, Juba was the biggest city he had ever seen.

He had told Kony that when they entered Juba earlier in the day. The Great Teacher had laughed and told him that Kampala was five times the size.

"You will see what a great city is when we rule it, Opoka," Kony said. "From there, we will travel the world and teach our philosophy to others. With you, my excellent future minister of communications!"

The LRA's supreme commander had been calling him that often now. Try as he might, Anthony could not help feeling filled, warmed by that idea and the praise behind it.

He had been the LRA leader's radioman for roughly three months at that point. In that time, he had learned to operate inside Control Altar, learning the unwritten rules and personal dynamics that surrounded Kony, his wives, and his closest aides, all while enduring the same physical training as the other soldiers in the Great Teacher's personal combat battalion. And he'd demonstrated again and again his uncanny ability to navigate at night by the stars.

Despite potholes in the road bouncing him around in the back of the pickup, Anthony yawned and shut his eyes. He could never remember being this tired, not even during the two training camps in the Imatong Mountains. Since joining Kony's inner circle, he had been on the move almost constantly, sometimes marching thirty to forty kilometers in a day, and never staying in any one place more than seventy-two hours.

In essence, they had made a giant loop, first south to the Ugandan border, where the Great Teacher abandoned plans to reenter and begin his fight for Kampala. The area turned out to be crawling with UPDF patrols, and Kony had grown paranoid, convinced that the Ugandan army was now actively pursuing him.

"We can't give them something to shoot at," Kony said repeatedly during the three months of roaming day and night that had led them back to Juba in search of more money, more weapons, more ammunition, and more supplies from the government. "I won't be a target."

But of course he's a target, Anthony thought, feeling sleepy. *Which makes me a target.*

His head bobbed. He dozed until they hit a big rut in the road and his chin slammed off his chest and he came awake, seeing they were almost to the new LRA encampment along the White Nile, southeast of Juba. They drove past LRA sentries and were soon in the shade of acacias and thorn trees. They parked near the inner square of security and got out.

Several of Kony's top men were waiting, including Anthony's old boss, Brigade General Charles Tabuley; Major Okaya, a savvy combat strategist; and General Otti Lagony, the LRA's chief of staff.

General Lagony was Kony's age. Major Okaya was seventy and had spent the better part of the past twenty-five years fighting before, during, and after the Ugandan Civil War. Fatima was there as well and got her husband's attention before his commanders did.

"What about food?" his head wife demanded. "We don't have much left, and our kids will go hungry if our stores are not refilled."

"Tomorrow," Kony said. "Government trucks will come."

"And the medicine? My ankle. It grows worse."

A thorn had recently punctured Fatima's foot just below her right ankle, and it had become infected. It was swollen now and oozing near the wound.

Kony reached into his pants pocket and came up with two small envelopes. "This one is an antibiotic," he said. "Take two now and then every morning and evening until they are gone. This one is for the pain. One every eight hours."

His head wife took the envelopes, looking relieved. "Thank you, Joseph."

"A man takes care of his wife."

Fatima bobbed her head before limping off, clutching the medicine like prizes. Anthony watched her go, feeling angry. When his arm had been almost blown off, he'd been given no antibiotics and no painkillers.

In fact, he'd been told multiple times that Kony forbade modern medicine in favor of treatments created by the spirit of Cilindi. It was true that Cilindi's prescription of cottonwood-root water, salt, and magic mushrooms had worked. But in the past three years, he had seen many wounded LRA soldiers die of infections that could have been beaten with antibiotics and others whose agony could have been eased by painkillers.

Everything is one way, everyone follows the rules except for the Great Teacher and his wives, he thought, feeling special contempt for Fatima, Christin, and Nighty, and conflicted over Lily. The Great Teacher's second wife liked to tease him good-naturedly and just the other day had outright praised him for his skills at night navigation and managing the radio and her husband.

But Lily aside, as far as he could tell, Kony's other top wives existed to do nothing except to bitch, to walk when they were told, and to show up when it was their turn to sleep with the Great Teacher. They carried no loads on the forced marches. They were waited on hand and foot by the younger wives and female recruits called *ting ting*, servants whom they treated horribly, especially in front of their husband. It was as Yango had told him the first day: the wives were queens scared of losing their thrones.

———

Kony beckoned to his commanders and took a seat in front of a grass hut erected the night before at the center of Control Altar's inner square. Anthony took his position fifteen meters from the Great Teacher and watched as Major Okaya and General Lagony greeted the LRA's supreme commander and took seats opposite him. Other bodyguards were finishing a grass hut for Lily, that evening's bed partner, and for Nighty, who would sleep with the LRA leader the following day.

"Did you come to an agreement with the Arabs, Teacher?" asked General Lagony, who spoke in a hoarse, low voice and had a habit of staring at people, dissecting them for their flaws.

"I sealed it with a trip to the mosque for noontime prayers," Kony said, and laughed.

Bald with a white beard and a creviced, scarred, and pocked face, Major Okaya said, "Is it enough, Teacher?"

Kony's expression hardened. "Twenty trucks' worth, Major. Mortars. Ammunition. Everything we asked for, including food, water filtration, and medicine. They're also giving Control Altar better housing at their barracks north of the city."

General Lagony said, "And in return?"

"We go at the Dinka twice as hard," Kony said. "Museveni has been send-ing the Sudanese People's Liberation Army more and more supplies up from Uganda, and the Sudanese government wants it stopped."

Okaya appeared disgusted. "As long as their troops don't have to do it."

"They have enough on their hands to the north. They want the Dinka gone from the south, and the holy running Uganda. That's enough reason for me. And it should be for you."

Lagony cleared his throat. "That is enough reason, Teacher. But we cannot be expected to attack now. We have lost too many men in the past six months. If we are to do this, we need more recruits than ever."

"Did I not send raiding parties south three weeks ago? Are they not coming north with seven hundred as we speak?"

Lagony nodded. "We need more yet, Teacher."

"I get it," Kony snapped. "But focus on what is on its way. All the twelve-to-sixteen-year-old boys. Brains not fully formed. Their weaknesses exposed, ready to be trained. I mean, if you've never had anything good in your entire life and suddenly you are one of our recruits who makes it through the march here and then the training and that first battle, you know that you are valued by me and by the LRA. You know that you are seen. You are rewarded for your actions. You are given a family and a vision of your future. It is enough, and they are ours. It was enough for you, wasn't it, Opoka? Coming here to Control Altar?"

Anthony had been unnerved by these comments, but he hid it and nodded.

"More than enough, Teacher," he said. "An honor."

"Exactly," the Great Teacher said, looking away from him and raising an index finger. "And so, we will be training these seven hundred, Lagony, and we will send more raiding parties south in the meantime. General Vincent, you will run multiple training cycles while Major Okaya keeps the Dinka harassed with skirmishes and ambushes. By the end of August, we will be at a full force of twenty brigades, and then we will wipe the Sudanese People's Liberation Army off the planet and begin our final march south to Kampala to drive Museveni from power."

The generals seemed pleased by this plan. Anthony stayed expressionless as he went around the back of the hut to rig the antenna wire for the 1600 radio call, but inside he was becoming more and more upset at Kony's comments about abducting twelve-to-sixteen-year-old boys because he could mold their minds by figuring out their weaknesses and using them, twisting them so they would do what he wanted.

You know that you are seen. You are rewarded for your actions. You are given a family and a vision of your future. It is enough, and they are ours.

Anthony stared darkly off into space, starting to wonder what weakness Kony had found in him and how he was using it against him.

Before he could give that his full attention, on the other side of the hut, he heard Major Okaya say, "Teacher, I promise we will be like a pack of howling dogs to the Dinka, but I ask one favor in return."

"Speak," the Great Teacher said.

"There are many females among the seven hundred on their way north?"

"More than one hundred among the three hundred and fifty who survived Ngomoromo."

"I ask for five of them as my wives, then. Young ones."

"Five?" Kony laughed. "You're seventy years old, and you already have eight wives!"

Okaya laughed. "I do. But what can I say? They keep me young."

"I can't argue, Major," the LRA's supreme leader said, and all four men laughed.

Anthony felt like spitting out the foul taste the talk left in his mouth as he attached the battery packs to the radio. Rape was forbidden in the LRA. But this giving of young, kidnapped girls as "wives" to old men was the same thing as far as he was concerned.

"Where is my future minister of communications?" Kony called.

He hurried back around the hut. "Here, Teacher."

The Great Teacher smiled at him. "Get the radio ready."

"Ten minutes, Teacher," Anthony said.

"See?" Kony said. "The best signaler in the LRA. A future minister in my government."

Despite himself, Anthony felt a weak version of the rare warmth at these comments. Lagony glared at him. Okaya regarded him suspiciously as Anthony went back around the hut to the radio.

As he started and tuned it, he thought about his father, who had always taught him to be the opposite kind of person from what Kony, Okaya, Lagony, and Vincent wanted and valued and were.

They want us like them. Monsters. Inhuman instead of human.

Anthony's eyes misted at an image of George that appeared in his mind. During his first three years with the LRA—when he was bent on surviving one day into the next—he had tried not to think of his father. But ever since his afternoon caring for the wounded old shopkeeper, he had been thinking almost daily about those evenings when he and his father had gone out to watch the stars and talk about what it meant to be a good human. He remembered how warm and filled up he felt, how seen and heard he felt, and how George seemed to understand everything about him and who he might become. There had been an incredible security in that, a total absence of fear.

Anthony realized that even though he lived now in near-constant fight-or-flight mode, he still remembered right from wrong, still knew what it was to be a good human. And he decided that everything about Kony and the LRA was wrong to the point of evil. No matter how he looked at it, the Great Teacher was a criminal, a murderer, and someone who promoted murder. Of children. By children. And now he was turning boys into monsters, machines, by preying on their weaknesses, and was giving old men young, kidnapped girls and laughing about it.

And how would he rule a country? The same damn way.

Anthony had seen all the death, the killings, caused by the man. He had been forced to participate in combat, and it still sickened him, made him angry inside. But he kept it bottled when Kony came behind the hut.

"Transmit this," the Great Teacher said. "I have to take a dump."

"Yes, Teacher," he said, and watched him hurry off.

Knowing this could take a while because Kony was prone to constipation, Anthony powered up the radio and then sat in the shade, his back against a nearby tree.

———

Lily came around, said, "Hello, Signaler."

"Hi, Lily," he said, brightening a little.

"Where is the Great Teacher?"

"Relieving himself."

"That could take a while," Lily said, and rolled her eyes.

Anthony could not help smiling. "Yes."

She studied him a moment. "You can be useful to me, Signaler."

Anthony did not like the sound of that, said, "I don't understand."

"You hear things that others don't," she said. "I want to know what you hear."

"I can't do that."

"Not about war or battle stuff," she said with a dismissive gesture. "I want to know what he says to Fatima, to Nighty, and to Christin. Can you do that for me?"

He felt cornered and said, "Why?"

Lily looked irritated, as if it should have been obvious, but said, "In case you haven't noticed, he has a lot of wives. We're replaceable. I don't want to be replaced."

Before he could reply to that, Anthony saw the Great Teacher emerge from the woods where the latrine had been dug. Lily saw him, too, and glided off, saying, "That was quick. I'm depending on you, Signaler."

Anthony did not reply but got up and went to the radio.

Kony hurried up with a piece of notebook paper in his hands. "Put them in the TONFAS and send them," he said, handing Anthony the paper. "I won't be far."

"Straightaway, Teacher," he said, taking the paper and watching Kony walk away.

Reading the orders, Anthony's anger returned in full force, and he feared he'd explode and chase down the LRA leader and attack him, which meant he would die. Instead, he chewed the inside of his lip and coded the order for six raiding parties to head south into Uganda in search of four thousand new recruits.

Four thousand kids like me.

This is wrong, he thought as he picked up the microphone. *You can't just get away with kidnapping thousands of kids and killing hundreds of them to keep the others in line. You just can't. And you can't kidnap girls and force them to marry old men.*

He tried to keep the building rage in check, but it made his voice quiver when he clicked the microphone twice and said, "This is Nine Whiskey with Six Bravo. Nine Whiskey with Six Bravo. Stand by."

———

When Anthony heard confirmation of the orders from the six commanders being sent south to find four thousand new recruits, he shut off the radio and repacked it. Sighing, he shouldered the radio, got his gun, and went to find Kony.

He was halfway around the hut when he heard soft laughter. He took another few steps and saw Kony there with Lily by the hut for that night's wife. It was almost done but for the thatch roof.

She was close to the Great Teacher, hand on his shoulder, laughing at whatever he'd said to her and shifting her hips slowly, side to side. She made a low humming noise when Kony ran a finger across her belly where it met the top of her colorful wraparound skirt and moved closer. He said something Anthony could not hear. Lowering his eyes, the signaler walked to within fifteen meters of Kony and his wife and sat down with his back to them, feeling humiliated, small, and worthless and despising everything they were now doing and saying to each other.

As if I am not here. As if I do not exist. The anger in him got so white hot at that point he swore he was going to pick up his rifle and unload it at them.

"Are you here, Opoka?" Kony called.

Anthony turned around and saw the Great Teacher facing Lily, his back turned. But she was peering over Kony's shoulder, gazing back at Anthony with great interest.

"Yes, Teacher."

"Excellent signaler," he said, and went back to tickling Lily. "Did you send the orders?"

"I did, and received confirmations. They are heading south as we speak, Teacher."

"The best signaler," the Great Teacher said.

Lily's gaze never left Anthony. "He is, isn't he?"

Anthony turned his back on them again. *Excellent signaler. The best signaler. Future minister in my government. And what is Lily doing? She's playing. She's playing, and I'm the toy.*

A metallic taste came up the back of his throat. He thought he was going to puke, and he wasn't sure why. Then he realized her toying could get him killed.

Kony called out, "Your mother would be proud of you, Opoka. Proud of who you have become, despite your hardships."

"Yes, Teacher," Anthony said, flushing with emotion. He remembered that first day inside Control Altar, when the Great Teacher had asked him whose love he'd craved as a child.

Then he was seized by a vivid memory of Acoko and saw his weakness, the one Kony was using against him. In his mind, he and Acoko were talking the night before his race against Patrick in the district finals. His mother was sad, negative, pointing out all the ways he could fail. He'd gotten angry at her.

I won't fail, he told her. *Everyone will know who I am.*

Acoko shook her head. *Sometimes I think you need people telling you how good you are, how special you are, all the time, Anthony.*

What's wrong with that?

You should know you're good without having to be told. It should come from inside you.

Sitting there, his back turned to Kony and his wife, Anthony remembered feeling deflated because he'd realized that his mother had rarely praised him and instead pointed out his shortcomings and invented ways his hopes could be dashed.

———

Anthony stared off into space, thinking, *My mom was right, and Kony figured it out. I need praise because she rarely gave me any. I need to be told I am special. Dad did, but she rarely told me anything like that. And the evil sonofabitch is using it to control me.*

He felt helpless at the idea that the Great Teacher had gotten inside his head so quickly, so deeply. As the giggling and joking went on behind him, he became almost paralyzed by his misery.

I'm weak, he thought. *Mom was right. Kony is right. I have always been weak.*

Lost, wanting to hold his head and curl up against the rage that suddenly seemed shot through him, Anthony realized he was suffering brutally. He thought again of the dying shopkeeper and how he'd described the four voices of suffering.

"Check your emotions," Mr. Mabior had said. "They will tell you which voice you're hearing in your head."

Barely aware of the Great Teacher and his wife now, Anthony forced himself to do it.

I keep feeling anger, injustice. I think it's Violence. I'm being controlled by it.

He realized he was right. The old man had described the voice of Violence perfectly. Anthony could remember almost every word he'd said.

"This voice is not the external violence of combat or the terrible things you may have witnessed in life, Anthony," the shopkeeper had said as he'd grown weaker. "It's the inner Violence that comes after some bad event happens to you."

It was the voice of anger, he said. Of rage. Of the injustice of the victim. The voice that constantly tells you that you've been wronged, treated unfairly by life. By events. And probably by a specific person.

"And out of that anger, hatred grows," Mr. Mabior said. "And in hatred, Violence sings loudest in your mind and cripples you."

Violence, it turned out, was capable of paralyzing you no matter its size or direction.

"Being frustrated or even sad about your life is Violence because you are engaging in an inner war between the universe and how you feel about life personally," he said.

Anthony said, "It's personal when you see a friend die right in front of you."

The dying shopkeeper had weakly held up his hands. "I understand. But again, the Violence I am talking about is not whatever unjust thing that has happened to you. The Violence is how you think and act after whatever unjust thing has happened to you."

Anthony had furrowed his brows. "Okay?"

"Think of it another way," the old man said. "When you listen to the voice of Violence, you are cut off from God, the universe, whatever higher power you believe in. When you are cut off, Anthony, you think poorly, you make bad decisions, and then you act in direct opposition to your true self. Take a jealous husband who hates that his wife is sleeping around and kills her. Is that man connected to the universe? Or his own pain?"

"His own pain."

"Yes, pain in the heart and injustice in the head are the two foods Violence always feeds on. They make the voice louder, and your actions more hurtful to you and to others."

Anthony had thought about that, and then said, "You don't hear that voice? You were never hurt badly? Or felt wronged?"

Mr. Mabior laughed and grimaced. "Of course I've been hurt badly. Of course I've known injustice. My own brother betrayed me with my fiancée a long time ago. I lived with hatred toward them for a long time, and it gradually became hatred against almost everything in my life. But eventually, I learned to quiet the voice of Violence by recognizing it and observing it."

"And by giving it a name?" Anthony said.

"By *calling* it by its name," the old man cautioned. "Violence. And just by closing your eyes and breathing deep, you will see how the voice is trying to keep the pain and anger boiling in your thoughts and body. Seeing that alone will begin to tamp down the flame below the anger, and as it cools, you will start to feel connected to goodness again. Less helpless, less paralyzed by events that have happened in your past."

Then the old man showed him that breathing sequence again. Eyes closed. Hands on thighs. Seven focused, full-belly breaths, but this time chanting, "There is peace in my heart" on every inhalation and exhalation. Then seven deep, full-belly breaths, chanting each time, "I am you. You are me. We are one."

———

Lily laughed, slow, like a cat purring. The noise broke Anthony from his thoughts before he could begin the breathing sequence.

Lily said, "Wait for my hut to be done. They're coming back with the rest of the thatch."

"Right," Kony said, paused. "In the meantime, I think I have to take another dump."

"That could take enough time," she said, and laughed.

"You're as funny as Fatima, sometimes," he said, and hurried off toward the latrine again.

"Signaler," Lily said.

Anthony felt weary as he stood to face her.

"You didn't like that, did you?"

He gazed at her from under half-lidded eyes. "It's not my business."

"Playing around makes him happy," she said. "And I like making him happy."

"As you said, Teacher has many wives."

"Exactly," she said as four boys came up, their arms laden with palm fronds for her roof. "Tell him I'll be back. I have a special outfit I want to wear for him."

Anthony nodded, then felt the anger flare up in him again when Lily walked away, swinging her hips provocatively before she looked over her shoulder at him and laughed.

She's playing with me. She keeps it up, she'll get us both killed.

That made him feel helpless and even angrier as he sat back down by the radio pack.

But he recognized the voice before it could sing and called it by its name.

You are Violence, and my heart won't let you control me, he thought, then closed his eyes and began to breathe deep and slow, telling himself:

There is peace in my heart.

There is peace in my heart.

There is peace . . .

Chapter Twenty-One

More than three weeks after being kidnapped, Florence, Palmer, Jasper, and the other survivors marched into a huge LRA encampment on the banks of the White Nile River, not far from the capital of southern Sudan.

"There have to be hundreds of LRA soldiers here," Palmer whispered. "Too many to escape from."

"I'm just happy to be alive and eating food and drinking water," Florence hissed back.

The rail stopped. She looked forward and saw Oyet speaking intensely with a smaller, older, wizened soldier. They were both waving their hands.

Palmer whispered, "I'm betting the old guy is asking how come Oyet started back from Uganda with so many kids and soldiers and only came in with us. He'll probably be shot or have his head stepped on."

Florence turned, looked her friend right in the eye, and whispered harshly, "That was my older brother that happened to."

"What?" Palmer said. "Oh my God, I'm so sorry, Betty. I had no idea."

"I know you didn't. It doesn't even seem real to me. None of it does."

Florence returned her attention to Oyet, trying not to think about her late brother, trying to enjoy the fact that the guy who'd dragged her from her home and caned Owen eighty times was getting chewed out by an old man half his size.

After ten minutes of this, Oyet saluted the older officer before stomping off along with the surviving LRA soldiers who'd guarded them during the march. Other soldiers appeared to flank the abductees.

"I am General Otti Vincent," the older man said in a loud, commanding voice. "I will be in charge of your training. You will be cut free of your ropes, and you will remain free of them. But do not attempt to escape. You will be shot. Or worse. But if you embrace the training, embrace the cause of the Great Teacher, your life will never be the same. Someday, you will be part of the ruling class of Uganda, the men and women who fought for our country's freedom."

Palmer whispered, "Yeah, but you had us kidnapped, asshole. We didn't sign up for this."

Florence had to bite her lip not to laugh.

General Vincent went on. "You will be divided, males and females. Males with me. Females will be taken to bathe, get clean clothes, eat, and then assemble to hear from the wife of the Great Teacher."

———

Guarded by armed female LRA soldiers, the girls were taken to a secluded part of the river, given bars of soap, told to strip and clean themselves. They were each given a bag with new undergarments, skirts, T-shirts, canvas boots and sandals, and basic toiletries. Then they were taken to an open-sided pavilion with wooden tables and benches, where they were fed two different kinds of stew with rice along with bottles of cold, flavored water.

"I could get used to this," Palmer whispered.

Florence shrugged. She was enjoying the food, especially the meat after having none for weeks. But aside from feeling physically good for the first time since her abduction, she could not get over the mental weight of being kidnapped and her brother being murdered.

"I'll never get used to this," Florence finally whispered back, and put her spoon in her empty tin bowl before a four-door Hilux SUV pulled up on the opposite side of the pavilion and one of the female LRA soldiers blew a whistle.

"On your feet," another shouted. "Fatima, your mother, the Great Teacher's wife, has come to speak to you."

Florence got up, annoyed to be interested in seeing this Great Teacher's wife. But she craned her neck to catch sight of her over the heads of the other girls. A big woman, Fatima climbed from the back of the SUV and swept into the pavilion, wearing a dark-blue batik-print outfit with a matching headdress. She wore big gold hoop earrings and many bracelets, which tinkled when she shook her finger, and looked down her nose at the abductees as if they were lesser forms of life.

"You all have been blessed by the Almighty and the spirits to be here," Fatima began, her head held high and haughty. "Someday, if you are lucky, you will be the wives of the holy, the soldiers who overthrew Uganda, the men who will lead our nation to greatness."

There was silence until several of the female LRA soldiers present started to clap. Palmer gave Florence a look of disgust before clapping along with her.

For her part, Fatima did not seem pleased by the weak applause. Her face hardened.

"You should tell yourself, you are never going back," she said. "You should tell yourself that your goal here is to survive, because that is the only hope you have."

Fatima paused for effect. "The way to survive is to follow the rules. There are rules for everyone in the LRA, and special rules for men and for women. Here are a few important ones. Number one, listen to the women who have been among the holy longer than you. They will teach you how to live among us. Number two, work hard. We do not tolerate laziness. If you are told to do something, do it immediately. Number three, if you are menstruating, isolate yourself. Number four, do not eat or use shea butter unless it has been blessed by Teacher. Number five, be loyal to your protector. Number six, do not fight with your sisters. And number seven, when you are called on to fight, forget you are a woman. Pick up your gun and fight."

Palmer whispered, "I don't know how to shoot a gun."

"Quiet," Florence hissed. "They'll teach us."

"What if I don't want to learn?"

Florence said nothing because Fatima seemed to be staring right at her and Palmer. Lowering her eyes, Florence was relieved when the Great Teacher's wife started talking again.

"Today, we will begin the process of distribution," Fatima said. "You will be given as someone's wife or given to an officer of the holy, who will protect you until a suitable husband is found for you. Do not complain about the man you are given to, not about him, not about his circumstances, not about his home. Do you understand?"

Florence was horrified at the idea she might be given as a wife. She was only fourteen, after all, and besides, she was supposed to become a nurse. She wanted to cry but nodded at Fatima's question.

So did Palmer, but under her breath, she said, "But what if he's pig ugly and smelly?"

Florence pinched the smaller girl's leg, whispered, "You are going to get us killed."

Fatima said, "You will leave here as a group and complete the first phase of distribution, which is the review period. Afterward, you will spend the night here and learn the results of the review in the morning. Later in the day, you will go to your new home among the holy. Welcome to the Lord's Resistance Army, ladies."

Without further ado, the Great Teacher's wife swept out of the pavilion and into the back seat of the Hilux, which quickly drove off.

"I don't like her," Palmer whispered. "I mean, she's our mother?"

"She's not my mother," Florence whispered back.

One of the female soldiers came over. "Shut up, the both of you. You're lucky the review is today, or I'd beat you senseless."

———

Palmer and Florence were separated for the walk through the camp. They felt the eyes of hundreds of LRA men on them as they passed, but no one said a word to them. The female soldiers led them to a secluded, grassy area right on the riverbank and told them to remove their T-shirts and bras. It was a hot day, but Florence felt uneasy about it.

Palmer took off her T-shirt and bra without further ado. For such a small, young woman, she had large breasts. She looked over at Florence and raised an eyebrow.

Florence sighed and removed her T-shirt and bra along with the other thirty-seven young women and girls. They stood there quiet, topless, unsure of what was going to happen.

After a few minutes, they heard men talking and laughing. About twenty of them appeared in uniform, all older men than Florence expected, much older. Most of them could have been her father. A few could have been her grandfather.

The men's eyes lit up when they saw the topless girls and began to circle them. The women started to bunch together, arms across their breasts, until one of the female soldiers told them, "Drop the arms and spread out so they can see you, talk to you."

Florence moved a meter away from the closest girl and just stood there as a string of men came close and ogled her up and down. Then the oldest of the men, a bald LRA major with a scruffy white beard and a scarred, wrinkled face, came at her with hunched shoulders and a smile of broken teeth.

"How old are you, child?" he asked in a voice like sand.

"Fourteen," Flo said, feeling her breath shorten and not wanting to look at him.

"Hmmm," he said, interested.

He took a step closer, and she smelled his foul body and mouth when he asked her name.

"Betty," she said, praying that he would not touch her as she'd seen some of the men do to the other girls already.

"Pleased to meet you, Betty. You may call me Okaya."

"Nice to meet you, too, Mr. Okaya."

"Just Okaya," he said, then inhaled sharply through his nose and walked away.

Florence let go her breath, and felt weak-kneed, as if she'd been circled and sniffed by a hyena. She watched Okaya go to Palmer and stare at her breasts. Her friend looked like she was fighting nausea as they spoke.

Okaya reached out for one of her breasts. Palmer knocked his hand aside.

"You're not doing that," she said, loudly. "No."

The old man stood there and chuckled. "I like spirit," he said, and left her.

The review went on for another twenty minutes, during which two other men asked Florence her name, age, and what skills she had.

She told them both the same thing: "I can read, write, and do algebra and geometry. I can cook. I can farm. I know a lot about natural medicine. The plants. The herbs."

One of the female guards called time on the review. The men left. Okaya had never looked at Florence again, which gave her some relief.

On the walk back to the pavilion, Palmer slipped up beside Florence. "Did you see that guy?" she whispered, and shuddered. "His face looks like it hit a truck, he's missing half his teeth, his breath is like a dog turd, and he's, like, seventy."

"You're lucky he didn't kill you," Florence whispered back.

"I'm sorry. I'm not letting some disgusting old man touch me. And you should have seen the way he smiled and laughed after I swatted his hand away."

"I saw," Florence said, feeling a building sense of dread for her friend.

———

That dread became real for both Florence and Palmer the next morning when they were told they were both being given to Major Okaya, who would be along to collect them soon.

When they were left alone, Palmer whispered, "I'm telling you, if that walking corpse touches me, I'm going to be sick all over him."

Feeling bitter and bewildered, Florence said, "I was supposed to be a nurse and find a good man to start a family with. Not this. I feel like I want to just run. Even if they shoot me, I just want to run."

"Shhhh," Palmer hushed. "No, don't say that, Betty. Don't ever say that out loud."

"It's what I feel," Florence whispered, and put her head on her knees. "Like I'm doomed, and I don't know why."

They were quiet for several beats.

"I know why," Palmer whispered. "It's Okaya's teeth. They look like the gates of doom!"

Florence looked up at her friend, wanted to cry, but broke into giggles.

"Those are the teeth of doom," she whispered, and choked back a snort of laughter. "I mean, what did we do to deserve this?"

Palmer started laughing, too. An old Land Rover turned down the lane and parked where Fatima's vehicle had stopped.

"That's Major Okaya's car," the guard called to them. "Get your things."

They got their bags reluctantly and started across the pavilion toward the vehicle as if they were walking to their own funerals. The driver's-side door opened, and a soldier in uniform got out. He went around and opened the passenger-side door. Recalling Okaya's teeth, breath, and face, Florence breathed through her mouth.

But the seventy-year-old major did not climb out of the back. Another man did. Midthirties, broad-shouldered, and tall, he was square-jawed and clean-shaven with close-cropped hair and a crisp new uniform. Florence didn't know him until she saw the name stenciled on the left breast pocket of his shirt.

"Oyet?" she said, shocked that his filthy clothes, dreadlocks, and beard were gone.

He looked at her evenly. "Captain Oyet now, Recruit Betty. I was promoted for getting you all here safely. Get in the car. Both of you."

"We weren't given to Major Okaya?" Palmer said with relief.

Florence had a moment of hope.

But then Oyet said, "Oh yes, you were. But the major has been sent south to engage the Dinka while you are trained. In the meantime, I have been assigned as your protector. You will live in my compound, under my direction, and be maintained in a virgin state until Major Okaya is ready to receive you as his wives."

"A virgin state?" Palmer said, looking sour. "God. So, uh, what are we talking here, Captain? Our time with you, I mean. Weeks? Months?"

"To get you through training and his return? Months, I'd think."

"Oh, well, that's better," Palmer said, went to the back door of the Land Rover, and opened it. She looked back at Florence, who was standing there feeling controlled, and helpless to do a thing about it. "You coming, Betty?"

Chapter Twenty-Two

Late August 1998

In the heat of the day, Florence dug hard with the hoe, hacking at weeds sprouting between low rows of corn in a newly cleared field by the river, not far from that secluded open spot where she'd been forced to engage in the topless review.

Although she'd been brutally sick in the prior six weeks, she liked having the garden tool in her hands again. If she closed her eyes and just kept turning over the soil, smelling it, listening to the wind in the trees around her, she could almost believe she was home in Amia'bil, working her own section of the Okori family garden, seeing her eggplants and tomatoes ripening with morning dew on their skin.

"Slow down, Betty," Palmer said, breaking Florence's wonderful imagining.

She looked back at her friend a couple of rows over and behind her a good fifteen meters. Palmer stared indignantly at her. "You just got back on your feet, and you're making me look bad here. I can't keep up."

"I didn't mean to get ahead," Florence said. "Working in the garden just reminds me of home, and I get happy."

Palmer's face fell. "Don't think about home, Betty. It doesn't exist anymore. At least, not the way we remembered it. And besides, as 'our mother' says, we're better off forgetting we even had a life before the LRA."

Florence knew that was what Fatima said. It was also what Oyet said to her and to Palmer a dozen times in the first month they lived in a hut in his compound. *That life? That person? Gone.*

She had tried to live that way throughout the course of their training, which lasted five hard weeks. She was taught to shoot, strip, and clean her rifle, a new

Russian AK-47 knockoff. And she was put through the most grueling physical training of her life.

At the end, however, because Florence had proved so strong and durable in the long hikes they took every day, she was chosen along with forty-nine other recruits, including Palmer, to be part of an ammunition train moving boxes of ammo from Juba to remote LRA positions. Throughout May and June, she had worked on six different munition trains, usually taking three days going out loaded and two days coming back.

Then Florence drank bad water and contracted cholera. So did Palmer. So did half the children hauling bullets and mortars to the field. Luckily, they had all fallen ill when they were at the main encampment near Juba, suffering debilitating bouts of diarrhea, fevers, and chills. She woke up one night so convinced she was back in the measles ward at the hospital in Lira that she cried out, *Miss Catherine! My angel! Please help me!*

Palmer had put her hand weakly on her shoulder. *There's no angel here, Betty. Go back to sleep.*

The LRA medics would not give them antibiotics, just told them to drink lots of clean water, bury their poop, and wash their hands constantly. Latrines were scrubbed down with bleach and water. The cholera outbreak died.

Though she was briefly as weak as she'd been with measles, Florence began to recover toward the third week in July. She'd started working in the gardens in early August. Palmer was strong enough to join Florence a week later.

"Do you realize we have never seen the Great Teacher?" Florence said.

"Seen his wife."

Florence nodded, hearing and then seeing a vehicle, a small pickup truck, coming down the lane toward Oyet's compound and the field. It stopped out of their view.

For some reason, despite Palmer's warning, as she returned to her hoeing, she thought of home again, of her old life. She remembered her beloved book of dreams left behind the night Oyet took her. She found herself longing for a pencil and paper to write down her hopes the way she used to, studying them, believing in them.

She thought about Kony. She hated the idea of him, a man so selfish he'd kidnap boys for his army and girls for his officers. She'd never seen the man, but she despised him, nonetheless. He had ruined her dreams, stolen her future, and for what?

She said a little bitterly, "You would think we would have seen him by now, Kony. They say he's gigantic."

"They also say spirits talk through him," Palmer said, hoeing as well.

"Four of them. How is that possible?"

Her friend shrugged. "I don't know. Maybe he got a four-for-one deal at the local witch doctor growing up."

Florence snorted, and then said, "Well, I heard he was trained by a shaman, supposedly, before he joined his crazy cousin, the Messenger or something like that."

"I know," Palmer said. "That's why I . . ."

Florence looked over at her friend, who had stopped hoeing and was now gazing intently back toward Captain Oyet's compound. She straightened up, turned, and saw their protector standing at the other end of the field. Seventy-year-old Major Okaya stood there beside him in filthy, battle-grimed clothes, his beard longer and scragglier than she remembered it.

"Betty, Palmer," Oyet called. "Your husband is back from the fight. It's time for you to leave me and join him."

———

The LRA battlefield commander watched them load their bags and things before climbing into the bed of his pickup. He looked at each of them before chuckling and climbing into the passenger seat. As the truck took them away from Oyet's compound, Florence felt her stomach souring. From the look on her face, Palmer was feeling the same way.

They drove no more than five kilometers before turning off and parking under a tree by a bamboo fence. Major Okaya's senior wife, Mariama, a very tall and stern woman, was waiting by an open gate in the fence. The major himself didn't give them a second glance, just got out and went into his compound.

Mariama looked at them with flared nostrils. "He doesn't need more wives."

Palmer said, "We agree."

Florence nodded.

"You're just extra mouths to feed," Okaya's wife said. "Taking it from our children."

Palmer got annoyed. "We didn't ask for this."

Mariama shot back, "That makes three of us."

"Tell us what to do," Florence said. "We're here to help you, Mariama."

She looked at her suspiciously. "Why would you say that?"

"We have to live together even if we don't like it, so we might as well be helping out as best we can in whatever way we can."

"Humph," Mariama said.

After showing them to their newly constructed hut, where they left their belongings, she put them to work hauling buckets of water from the well, which Florence actually enjoyed because it reminded her of going to the stream with her mother. More than five months had passed since Oyet tore her out of her old life in Amia'bil, five months since she'd been dragged away from Josca and Constantine and the rest of her brothers and sisters. Five months, but she could still see her parents fresh in her mind, the best of them, laughing, clapping, and singing the Christmas before. She wondered what they would say if they knew she'd been given to an old man as his wife.

I was supposed to be a nurse, she thought again during the third return trip from the well. She had to swallow hard at the emotion in her throat and blink back tears before going into the compound and pouring the water into big ceramic urns Mariama kept near the cooking area. They ate rice with curried goat that night, which was delicious, and they told the senior wife.

Mariama almost smiled before giving them a list of other chores that they set about doing immediately, washing dishes, scouring pots, and stacking firewood for the morning. It was long past dark when they finished and went to their hut.

Florence lay down, fell asleep in an instant, and did not move until she heard cocks crowing before dawn. Palmer stirred as well.

"We should be up first," Florence said. "Waiting for her."

Palmer groaned but nodded. They went out in the low light, shivering against the slight chill in the humid air, and dug around in the firepit to find coals that they fed into a flame. A few minutes later, Mariama emerged from her hut, saw the crackling little fire they had going, and almost smiled again.

They spent the day trying to fulfill Okaya's senior wife's desires as fast and as completely as possible. They had not seen the major since their arrival, and Palmer was quite pleased when they finished their chores that evening and returned to their hut.

"He's probably been called back into battle," she whispered by candlelight.

"Could be," Florence said. "It's not that big a compound."

She'd no sooner said that than someone rapped on the wall of the hut.

"Palmer," Mariama said.

She frowned. "Yes?"

"You are called to your husband's house. Bring your sleeping mat."

For the first time since she'd known Palmer, Florence saw pure desperation in her eyes.

Palmer said, "You know, Mariama. It's not a good time. If you know what I mean."

A pause, then Mariama replied, "If so, you are supposed to isolate. Those are the rules."

"I'm just on the verge, you know? My stomach's cramping."

"Betty, then," Mariama said. "Bring your sleeping mat."

Florence thought of Okaya, thought of his bad teeth and breath. "I'm in the same sort of time, Mariama. We thought we would isolate together."

There was a long silence before the first wife said, "Suit yourselves."

Palmer waited until she'd walked away to whisper, "Betty, I think I'm about to have the world's longest period."

Florence burst out laughing. "I heard it's contagious."

———

They were outside building the fire before dawn. Mariama came out of her hut, said, "You're supposed to isolate."

"Oh, right," Palmer said, and they returned to the hut.

They lay on the mats and whispered, congratulating themselves, telling each other that they were in control. After all, they weren't yet fifteen, and he was seventy.

"We can outwait him," Palmer said. "He'll get shot or he'll be clutching at his heart at some point."

A knock came at the door. "Come out, please," Mariama said.

The girls looked at each other, shrugged, then ducked through the blanket that served as their door.

"Your husband wishes a word," the first wife said, and gestured toward the main firepit, where Major Okaya was sitting on a chair, flanked by two soldiers wearing dark sunglasses despite the early hour. Okaya's other seven wives sat on the ground to one side of him.

Florence knew this was bad. She glanced at Palmer and saw that her friend had a glazed look about her as they followed Mariama until they were standing in front of Okaya, who nodded at his first wife.

She walked straight to Palmer, tore off her wraparound skirt, and put her hand between the fourteen-year-old's thighs.

"Hey!" Palmer shouted, and tried to push the first wife away.

Mariama slapped her, stunned her, and then walked to Florence. She glared at her.

"Are you? Or not?"

Florence knew better than to lie, and shook her head. "False alarm?"

"Idiot," Mariama said under her breath. "You brought this on yourselves."

Florence had no idea what was about to happen, but she began to tremble when the first wife walked over and sat with Okaya's other seven wives.

The major stared at them, wagged his right index finger. The men put down their weapons, took off their belts, and came toward them.

The major broke his silence. "If you run, if you squirm, if you scream, it will get worse."

Florence had thought the pain of her caning was the worst she'd ever felt. Okaya's men never touched their head, hands, or feet. But they whipped her and Palmer with their belts and beat them about the torso and back with their fists. Florence had no idea if she cried or tried to get away from the blows. It just went on and on until she lost consciousness. She did not remember being carried into her hut.

Hours later, she heard Palmer whimper, "What do you want?"

Mariama said, "To give you the same thing I was given when I made the same mistake you did."

Florence lifted her head, feeling the throb of every bruise and welt on her body, arms, and upper legs. She saw the senior wife standing there with a bucket and some rags.

"It's been boiled, and there is salt in it. It is going to sting, but you'll heal faster," Mariama said. "Help each other. I'll bring you food and water until you can fetch it yourselves."

"Thank you," Florence said.

"Yes, thank you," Palmer said.

"A word of advice," the woman said. "The next time your husband calls, answer, and surrender. It's your only hope."

Ten days later, they had recovered enough to leave their hut, walk stiffly, and stand before Major Okaya, who glowered at them before licking his broken upper teeth.

"I repulse you, don't I?" he said. "Well, it does not matter. The next time you try to work together against me, I will tell the Great Teacher that the two of you were shot trying to escape. Do you understand?"

Florence swallowed hard but nodded. So did Palmer.

Four days later, when Mariama knocked on the exterior of their hut and told Florence her husband was calling her, she did not look at Palmer, who had been called the night before and returned sobbing. Instead, Flo told herself it was better than a beating or dying. She picked up her mat and surrendered to her fate.

———

When Florence returned to her hut in the morning, she took one look at Palmer and burst into tears.

"What did he do?" Palmer said, rushing to her and hugging her.

"Whatever he wanted," she blubbered. "I did what Mariama said. I surrendered."

"It was our only hope," Palmer said, pulling her closer. "Our only hope."

For the next eight nights, they alternated going to Major Okaya's hut. But on the ninth night, the knock did not come. And when they got up before dawn to build the fire, Mariama was already up, the fire was lit, and water was boiling in the pot.

"Pack your things," she said. "Okaya has gone south with Captain Oyet to prepare for a battle to end the Dinka revolt for good. We are all being moved to help at the hospital at Nesitu. They're expecting many casualties."

The girls went back to their hut, feeling giddy.

"We're rid of that pig!" Palmer said. "At least for a while."

Florence grinned. "Not only that, but it sounds like I am going to get my wish after all. I'll be Betty the Nurse."

Chapter Twenty-Three

April 11, 1999
Nine Kilometers North of Moli, Southern Sudan

That morning, under a heavy barrage of mortar fire, nineteen-year-old Anthony Opoka crouched in a deep pit blown into the east side of one of what the LRA soldiers referred to as the Jebel Lem, or Two Rock Hills.

"Six Bravo, Six Bravo, this is Nine Whiskey, copy?" Anthony shouted into his Cascina radio as rock, gravel, and other bomb debris rained down on him.

He expected a junior radioman to answer and was surprised when Joseph Kony himself came back. "Nine Whiskey, this is Six Bravo."

"Six Bravo, Dinka shelling and gathering for an assault on the east side of Jebel Lem," Anthony said, not bothering with the TONFAS codes. "Seven Delta's men are taking heavy casualties. Need permission to return mortar fire."

They'd been rationing their mortars for almost a day now.

"Permission granted, Nine Whiskey," Kony replied. "Tell Seven Delta to keep that road. We haven't spent six months holding it to lose it now."

"Copy, Six Bravo," Anthony said, then changed radios, going to the lighter Racal shortwave because of its ability to hold precise frequencies during close-quarter combat. He altered the frequency. "Seven Delta, this is Nine Whiskey. Need coordinates. Over."

He got no reply. Before he could try again, two LRA soldiers dove into the pit. A mortar exploded uphill from their position. They all ducked and covered as they were pelted with debris.

There was a lull in the barrage.

"Opoka?" one of the soldiers said. "You're alive?"

Anthony looked up and saw Patrick lying there, bleeding from a small scalp wound and grinning like a fool. He did not recognize the other soldier sitting up beside him, filthy from combat, long, long dreads, and the beginnings of a beard.

He grinned at Patrick. "I'm alive. What are you doing here?"

"Matata's in the fight now," Patrick said. "Or will be. We've got four hundred men following us. They'll be here by morning."

"How did you find me?"

The other soldier said, "We just asked where we could find the famous Nine Whiskey we hear on the radio all the time, and they pointed up here."

Something in the inflection of his voice caught Anthony off guard, and he stared at the soldier, puzzled.

"Have I changed that much, Brother?" the soldier said.

Anthony's jaw went slack. "Albert?"

His brother grinned, crawled over, and hugged an astonished Anthony.

"Long time," Albert said. "Too long."

Anthony grinned and hugged him back. "Four years. You're grown up!"

"Nine Whiskey," the radio chattered. "Need Seven Delta's coordinates."

"Trying," he said, and again got no reply.

"Seven Delta," Albert said. "That's Okaya."

"His men are up front," Anthony said, nodding. "He's with them."

"Crazy old bastard, isn't he?" Patrick said.

"Always," Anthony said before repeating the call to Okaya's radioman a third time.

The mortars started again from the Dinka side of what some of the LRA holy had taken to calling the Tight Bend of Death.

Set between the Jebel Lem hills where the Torit road met the A43 highway from Uganda, the bend was like a kink in a hose, with the tightest spot the intersection critical to all north–south travel. The Uganda-backed Dinka rebels needed to control the Two Rock Hills so supplies and ammunition would continue to flow in their quest to seize control of southern Sudan, and the Sudanese government was paying the LRA to fight off the Dinka at all costs.

In the six months of savage combat that had unfolded around this critical north–south pinch point, Kony's army had lost more than a thousand combatants, most of them younger than eighteen. The rebels had suffered at least as many dead and wounded.

Many of Anthony's superiors in the signal corps had died at Jebel Lem. The Great Teacher had had no choice but to name his personal radioman as senior signals commander and director of all radios under combat.

The nineteen-year-old now reported directly to Kony and to General Vincent, who was in charge of the defense of the hills and the strategic intersection below them. But both of the LRA's top leaders were in Juba at the moment, pleading with the Sudan government for more weapons and ammunition, which had left Major Okaya in charge of combat operations.

"Seven Delta, Seven Delta, this is Nine Whiskey, over," Anthony called yet again into the smaller of the two radios in the pit.

Still, nothing but a hiss.

A man covered in dirt and blood jumped into the pit. Patrick swung his gun.

"Stop," Anthony said. "It's Oyet. Okaya's second."

The LRA captain dug in his pocket, saying, "Our signaler's dead, and our radio's down."

"C'mon," Anthony groaned. "We lost two last week."

"I know," Oyet said, handing Anthony a piece of paper with latitude and longitude coordinates. Turning the light radio to the mortar unit's frequency, he called in the coordinates. Within moments, the familiar thump of the 82 mm rockets began from their side and exploded downrange to the south.

"That should soften them up," Patrick said.

"Not for long," Captain Oyet grunted. "They've got reinforcements and armor, and they're moving. I can't keep running back and forth like this. Okaya needs a radioman up front to call out coordinates for the mortars in real time. He wants you."

"That puts me with no way to talk with Kony."

"You going to defy a direct order?"

"I answer to the Great Teacher and General Vincent."

"Not today, you don't. Or do you want to explain to them why we were overrun, why we lost the bend?"

Anthony hesitated. But then he imagined one of Kony's unfathomable rages as Who Are You should they lose the Two Rock Hills.

"I'll go," Albert said.

"No, you won't," Anthony said immediately. "Okaya is the commander, and he wants me. You and Patrick stay here with the Cascina. You'll be my relay if I need to send a longer-range transmission."

Anthony quickly packed the lighter radio, put it on his back. Then he picked up his rifle and waited with Oyet for another lull in the waves of mortar rounds being fired over their heads.

He glanced at Albert, still amazed at how different his younger brother looked, and smiled. "Talk to you soon."

"You're already dead to me," Patrick said.

"Gee, thanks."

The mortars stilled.

"Now," Oyet said.

They scrambled up out of the pit. They traversed the steep, bomb-pocked hillside, getting closer and closer to the sporadic machine-gun fire ahead.

As he had learned to do in situations like this, Anthony focused 100 percent on his job. He did not allow his brain to wander to Albert or to Patrick or to anything other than being a signaler who'd been given an order and a task.

"Lead on," Anthony said, crouching after the captain crouched. They moved in a low duckwalk to an opening in a trench that had been dug about a meter into the hillside.

Heads down, they kept moving forward in the trench toward the gunfire, reaching a T where the topography changed. They were now back from and above that kink in the highway where it met the road to Torit, on a sidehill above a ravine system some six hundred meters wide. The Dinka were massing and lobbing mortars from a hill on the other side of the ravine.

For a good hundred meters, Oyet led Anthony past scores of LRA soldiers positioned against the left wall of the trench and shooting at the SPLA forces. The captain climbed a staircase of sorts up and over the south wall of the trench, which had been reinforced with logs.

Anthony looked over, seeing Oyet hurry down the rude stairs ten meters to a fortified observation post where Major Okaya peered over boulders, scanning the enemy side of the ravine with binoculars. The dead signaler lay on the ground in back of the battle commander. Anthony felt sick. He'd trained the fifteen-year-old himself.

When Oyet made it safely into the forward position, the shooting from both sides quieted enough for Anthony to feel confident climbing the rude stairs to get over the trench wall.

A flash across the ravine. The thump of a mortar.

He put his right foot on the top of the stairs and was about to step over and start down the other side when he was punched hard in his right shoulder, just above the scarred mess of the rocket wound. The bullet impact spun him around to his right, knocking him off balance.

———

Anthony fell in a spiral, hearing the report of the rifle that shot him in midair before hitting the bottom of the trench hard enough to blow the wind out of his chest. He fought to breathe, feeling his shoulder burn in a way he'd forgotten, so hot it cut you off, made you . . .

Even wounded in the same shoulder for the second time in his young life and consumed with the all-too-familiar agony, Anthony was aware of the whistle of yet another mortar from the Dinka side and knew by the sound that this bomb wasn't sailing past him. This one was coming close.

He threw his good arm over his head a split second before the bomb exploded downhill on the other side of the trench wall, loud enough to cuff his ears, powerful enough to shake the ground beneath him, and close enough to throw a heavy shower of rock and dirt. Part of the trench wall behind him collapsed, burying his feet and shins.

Shocked by the intensity of the explosion and by being shot again, he got up slowly, dazed, trying to think of what to do. *Gun*, he thought. *Find your gun. Never leave your gun.*

In shock, he gaped around, finally spotting it a meter or so in front of him. He picked it up, blinked, and then shouldered it, trying to figure out what to do next.

Back to Patrick and Albert, he thought in slow motion. *They'll help you.*

He got himself oriented, headed back the way he'd come in the trench, took two steps in that direction, and looked to his right where the wall had collapsed, leaving a gaping hole. Downhill, the forward observation post was now a bomb crater. It had taken a direct hit. Okaya and Oyet were gone. So was the body of the dead signaler.

Then, over the ringing in his ears, he heard something else before catching motion across the ravine. Hundreds of Dinka soldiers were now charging down the far side. The LRA soldiers in the trench started firing furiously at them.

He looked at his shoulder, saw the spreading bloodstain, and knew through his daze that he had to move or die. Ignoring the battle now, Anthony slipped behind the soldiers shooting, made it to the T in the trench, and took a left. Soon, he was walking along that game trail that traversed the steep sidehill but feeling woozier by the minute.

The combat behind him intensified. A volley of mortars from the LRA battery thumped and whistled over his head, landing out in the ravine somewhere. He didn't care. He just wanted to get to that pit where he'd set up his signaling station and left his brother and old friend.

With one hundred meters to go, Anthony felt dizzy, nauseated. With fifty meters left, he had to use his rifle as a crutch to stay on his feet and shuffle to the edge of the pit. Familiar black spots were gathering before his eyes when he slid down into the hole, seeing Albert turn from the radio and Patrick gape at the blood all over the front of his uniform.

"What? Again?" Patrick said before Anthony lost consciousness.

April 13, 1999

Nesitu, Southern Sudan

Florence ran through the LRA field hospital, carrying bandages, antiseptic, and gauze to the medics working triage outside the two big tents, evaluating the latest round of the wounded being brought in from the Jebel Lem hills, south about seven kilometers.

They'd been coming around the clock for the last few days, more than she'd seen in the seven months she'd been living and working in Nesitu. And the wounds were more gruesome than ever due to the nonstop bombardment the Dinka had inflicted on the LRA.

Lost arms. Lost legs. Lost eyes. As Betty the Nurse, Florence had seen it all and listened to the boys moan and call for God and their mothers, just as she had as a little girl, lost and lonely in the measles ward, wondering why she'd been abandoned.

"Help me, Betty," one boy croaked as Florence passed.

She glanced down at him, no more than her age, saw he'd been peppered and slashed with shrapnel but wore no tourniquets. "We'll be back for you as soon as we can," she promised. "Just waiting for an operating room to get all that metal out of you, okay?"

"It hurts, Betty," he said. "It hurts everywhere."

Florence did not know what to say. For some reason, the Great Teacher did not believe in giving the wounded painkillers or antibiotics. Which meant the boy at her feet could die of infection even if the Arab surgeons who'd been sent to the hospital could get the steel out of him.

"We'll be back for you," she promised, and hurried and set the supplies before the medics.

"We need more sterile water," said one of the medics, a friend of Florence's named Joyce.

"I'll bring it," Florence promised the woman, who was twenty years her senior, and hurried back through the tent, seeing that boy with the shrapnel wounds still lying there.

"Will it help if I pray, Betty?" he said as she passed.

She flashed on herself at five, saying the same thing to Miss Catherine, and stopped. She knelt down by him and repeated what her nurse had told her. "Of course it will help. But if you wish God to hear your prayers, you must bow your head with a heart that is already at peace, even as painful as it is right now. Okay?"

Tears ran from the boy's eyes as he nodded.

"I'll be back," she promised, and got up.

Florence went out the back of the field hospital to where a fire burned under a twenty-liter pot of water. The man tending it pointed to a big plastic jerry can.

"Clean?" she asked.

"And hot," he said.

She grabbed the jerry can and went back through the hospital, seeing the shrapnel boy with his eyes closed, hands over his heart, the faintest of smiles on his lips. It made her feel better as she continued on with the sterile water and hoisted the can up on a folding table where Joyce and the other medics could get at it.

"More gauze, more pads, more bandages," Joyce said.

"I just brought them."

"More gauze, more pads, more bandages, Betty."

Florence set off once more back into and through the hospital toward the supply room. She glanced at the shrapnel boy on the floor, got a sinking feeling in her gut, and stopped. His head was lolled to one side, his mouth agape, blood trickling out the corner of his lips. She didn't need to take his pulse to know he was gone.

He knew, she thought. *He knew he was—*

"Betty!" someone behind her shrieked.

She startled, thinking it was Joyce, but then looked over and saw Palmer rushing toward her, grinning, and doing a little two-step move. Her friend threw her arms around her and hugged her. "Miss Betty!" she squealed. "It's time to celebrate!"

"My patient just died, Palmer."

"Oh," she said, taking a step back and looking down at the shrapnel boy. She spoke softer, more compassionately. "I'm sorry, Betty." The joy in her face would not be suppressed, though. "But Okaya and Oyet are dead!"

As bad as she felt about the shrapnel boy, Florence's heart soared. "No!"

"I heard it from an eyewitness just now! Opoka, the Great Teacher's signaler, he saw a mortar land right on top of them two mornings ago! Go ask him if you don't believe me!"

"No, I believe you!" Florence said, feeling giddy now and wanting to jump around and cheer and dance at the understanding that Okaya would never abuse her again. And as ambivalent as she was about Oyet, she would not miss him, either. They were both gone!

"Betty!" Joyce shouted from the doorway. "Supplies!"

"Coming!" she yelled, and turned and ran with Palmer right beside her as they crossed through the area where men recovered from surgeries.

"He's down there, south end, third cot on the right," Palmer said.

"Who?"

"Opoka. The signaler. The one who saw it."

"I don't really care who saw it as long as it's true," Florence said, going into the vestibule off the main tent where the supplies were kept and grabbing everything Joyce needed.

"Grab what I grab, bring it to Joyce," she said to Palmer, and ran.

Two orderlies were already carrying the body of the shrapnel boy out of the back hallway. She said a brief prayer for him as she went outside, arranging the gauze, bandages, and pads on the table where Joyce liked them. She helped Palmer with her load of supplies, checked the jerry can, and announced, "Getting more water."

Joyce had her back to them but waved. For the fifth time in twenty minutes, Florence walked through the holding area, meaning to cross through the main hospital, when an armed soldier appeared and stopped her and Palmer.

"What's going on?" Palmer said. "We work here. We're nurses."

"The Great Teacher," he grunted. "He's here to see the wounded of Jebel Lem."

———

The giant? Florence thought. *He's here?*

She tried to look around the bodyguard, tried to see the giant, and wondered if his head would touch the top of the tent.

Palmer said, "He's here to see Opoka. His signaler. We're Opoka's nurses and his dressing needs to be changed. So stand aside, please."

Florence was in awe of her friend's brazenness even before the gunman hesitated and then took a step back to let her pass.

"Thank you," Palmer said, and pushed by him into the main tent of the hospital.

Many of the wounded were sitting up in their beds, looking toward the south end of the tent, where a group of armed men stood around a grinning man of modest height wearing a white tunic, pants, and fez over a slight widow's peak. He raised his hands, palms out to the wounded, nodding, smiling, laughing.

"I have had a wonderful day," he announced, and laughed again. "One of those days when you know you are blessed by the spirits."

Florence was confused. "Who's he?" she whispered.

"Joseph Kony," Palmer whispered as if she were daft.

"Oh," Florence said, kind of disappointed because she'd expected someone huge enough to hold four spirits in him, not this guy laughing and clapping in a hospital for the wounded.

And what's that all about? Laughing and cheering for boys who've been shot or blown up for you?

Working in the hospital the past few months, Florence had found purpose and some degree of peace. But seeing Kony like this, up close, laughing, cheering, she felt the old bitterness flood through her.

"Let me tell you what happened, the miracle," Kony said, chuckling now. "Just this morning, I was back at our camp north of here, minding my own business and taking a bath in the river. I have soap in my hair, and out of the bush come three big, tall Dinka with guns. I look at them. They look at me. And do you know what happened? What they said?"

He paused for dramatic effect before deepening his voice: "Where is Joseph Kony? Where is the LRA?"

People in the room started laughing, and the Great Teacher laughed along with them.

"They had no idea it was me!" Kony cackled. "They had me dead to rights, but to them I was just some naked guy taking a bath in the river! I held up my bar of soap and pointed it downstream, and said, 'I was told that Kony is that way, down by the Torit road.' Stupid Dinka, they thanked me and walked away!"

The Great Teacher spun around, arms wide, still caught up in the thrill of the experience, before he stopped and went to a young wounded soldier lying on the third cot on the right, and said, "Can you believe it, Opoka?"

The soldier, a handsome young man whose shoulder was heavily bandaged, struggled to sit up, saying, "The spirits were protecting you, Teacher."

"And you, future communications minister of Uganda," Kony said, saluting, grinning, and looking around at everyone. "Anthony Opoka. My signals commander. The best there is."

Florence saw Opoka smile weakly. "Thank you, Teacher."

"The doctors say you will be at my side again in no time."

The signaler cleared his throat, winced. "I look forward to it, Teacher."

Kony patted him on the leg and went to the next man, talking to him, asking him the circumstances of his wounding, and becoming visibly moved by what he was hearing. The closer he came, the more Florence felt the energy pulsing off the man, so strong it shifted her anger at him to fright. He seemed one of those people who are capable of any evil, and she suddenly wanted a reason to get away from him. But then he paused about two meters from her, shifted his head, and gazed right into Flo's eyes. She would later say it was mesmerizing, like she was transfixed by a cobra that could peer inside her soul and understand its every weakness.

Kony smiled as if he knew her already and moved on, leaving her shaking inside. Then she remembered she was supposed to be hauling sterile water for the medics. She slipped away, left the tent, retrieved another fresh jerry can of water, and brought it around the entire field hospital, rather than cutting through again.

"He's in there," she told Joyce after she'd set the can on the table and removed the empty one. "The Great Teacher."

"I heard," Joyce said, drinking water while the other two medics worked on the latest victim to come in from the Jebel Lem battlefield.

"He's not a giant."

"Who said he was?"

"I don't know. Someone who saw him last year."

Palmer came skipping out of the holding area to the field hospital. "Did you hear?" she asked.

"Uh, no," Florence said.

"We're officially widows," Palmer said. "'The widows of Jebel Lem,' Kony called us, I mean, everyone whose husband died there. And he wants us all to go on a widows' walk."

"Widows' walk? What the heck is—?"

"Listen! He's so happy about escaping the Dinka this morning he decided that when we come back from our widows' walk, there won't be another distribution ceremony held for us, for any of the widows of Jebel Lem."

"Well, that's good."

"It's better. The Great Teacher is going to let us choose our own husbands, Betty."

Chapter Twenty-Four

Late in the afternoon, some eighteen days after he was shot in the Jebel Lem hills, Anthony's shoulder was less on fire than smoldering, better than it was, but liable to catch wind and flare up out of the blue.

He kept his right arm in a sling while the new wound healed. Because he'd already become so skilled at doing his job almost one-handed, he was soon able to hang antenna wires, link radio components, and solar charge the batteries. But he tired too easily to return to combat. The Great Teacher had told him to take at least two more weeks before rejoining Control Altar.

The camp at Nesitu was on a hill, with the field hospital low on the east side and closer to the highway to Juba. In the past few months, hundreds of LRA huts had been built up over the top of the hill and down its backside, where many of the officers were bivouacked in compounds. Anthony had moved to a hut on a treed flat about a kilometer north of the hospital. Patrick and Albert, who had controlled his bleeding and got him to the hospital, had lived there briefly before returning to Jebel Lem, where the fight raged on.

Even now, as he left his hut to go for a walk to improve his stamina and to charge his solar batteries while working on his radio, he could hear the distant booming of the mortars and wondered how long the LRA could last with the casualties mounting every day. Then he asked himself if he cared if Kony won or lost. Aside from not wanting to get killed in winning or losing and not wanting

Patrick or Albert to get killed in winning or losing, he decided he no longer cared one way or the other about the Great Teacher's cause.

The fact was he hadn't cared about much since waking up in the hospital after one of the Arab surgeons from Juba had repaired his collarbone and sewn the bullet wound shut. Even the Great Teacher's visit to the field hospital and being called out as the best signaler in the LRA had failed to cheer him; he knew the man's intent was to control him through praise.

And after Patrick and Albert left to fight again, he'd felt more alone and down than ever. He was nineteen and a half, and he had nothing in life that wasn't approved by Joseph Kony. No family. No girlfriend. No money. Nothing except his uniform, his boots, his radio pack, his rifle, and his mess kit. Oh, and the remnants of his right arm.

"Quite the fortune, Opoka," Anthony muttered to himself as he wandered toward the field hospital. It was time for the dressing on his shoulder to be checked again.

His mind began to whirl, giving him all the ways in which life had failed him. Being abducted. Having the rocket fin hack through his shoulder. Forced to live with Kony and his wives. Shot again, with nothing in life to show for it.

Then a list of all the things he did not have began to play again in his mind. This list and the loop of terrible events cycled over and over as he walked, making him feel more and more miserable. Halfway to the field hospital, he realized he'd made himself feel so bad he'd almost forgotten about the pain in his shoulder.

He was suffering so much mentally he wanted to sit down and cry. Then he remembered the old shopkeeper and his prescription to ease misery. Anthony thought about Mr. Mabior and the four voices, setting aside Rush and Violence. He was dealing with the third voice.

"You are the voice of Lack," he muttered to himself as he spread out his solar panels and batteries before sitting on a low boulder in the shade of an acacia tree.

———

Anthony closed his eyes, hearing the mortars still falling and the machine guns rattling, seeing the dying old man tell him that Lack always spoke of what was absent in life.

"Lack dwells on your belief in your own poverty," Mr. Mabior had said, taking short, shallow breaths. "Lack feeds on what you think you need to be happy in life, then shows you that you have not met that need, and therefore, you cannot be happy."

According to the dying shopkeeper, Lack whispered even to rich men, who could be some of the saddest people you'd ever meet because they spend their entire lives believing that if they can get a certain amount of money, they will find happiness.

Of course, they work and work and sacrifice and they get the money. But then, after a day or two, they realize they are still unhappy. So they set a new goal to fulfill, an even bigger number to amass, and Lack grows stronger.

Mr. Mabior said, "The voice gets so loud that eventually the rich man can't hear birds singing, can't see the sunrise or taste the best wine or touch the beauty and wonder of life all around him. And so, he has more money in the bank, but he never really lives, and so, he dies a rich man on paper but a pauper in spirit."

The shopkeeper had told him the same was true of many things in life, the belief, for example, that if Opoka's shoulder could be returned to normal, he'd be happy.

"It would sure help," he had replied sharply.

"Of course, it would help," Mr. Mabior said, his own voice getting rattly. "But would your suffering from Lack, from the voice of scarcity, end?"

"Would I stop hearing the voice?"

"That's right."

Anthony thought about that. "Probably not."

"That's right, probably not. Lack is one of the loudest voices. It barked at me for years. Never did me a bit of good. Can you get me water? Behind the counter."

Anthony left him, went behind the shop counter, and found a crock with fresh water in it and a cup. He brought both over next to Mr. Mabior, who sipped the water and closed his eyes against some internal agony for a moment.

When he opened his eyes, the dying man said, "Do you want to know how to silence Lack and to summon good things to yourself? To make them almost magically appear in your life?"

Anthony shrugged. He didn't believe in magic, but said, "Sure. Why not?"

Mr. Mabior laughed softly. "You begin by looking around for what you do have, things that allow you to live another day or have brought you moments of happiness. And you thank the stars for giving it to you. And then you look for something else, or somebody who is a gift in your life, and you give thanks for that, too."

The old man told him to give thanks for at least ten things, and then, with his heart aglow, Anthony was to shut his eyes and take seven deep breaths. On each slow inhalation and slow exhalation, he was to dwell on the good parts of his life and whisper, "There is abundance." And then he was to take seven more breaths. On the inhalation, he was to think, *I am you. You are me.* And on the exhalation, he was to whisper, "We are one."

———

Sitting there on the rock a few hundred meters from the field hospital, sick of listening to Lack, Anthony followed Mr. Mabior's prescription for silencing that voice of suffering. He gave thanks to the stars that he was alive. Then he thanked the surgeon who had operated on him. Then Patrick and Albert for saving him. The food he'd eaten that morning. The new uniform and canvas boots he'd been given. The breeze on his skin. It went on until he'd reached ten and eleven—the sun in the sky, the stars overhead—when he felt his heart physically warm. Then he began the breath and chant sequences.

When he finished, he followed the instructions the shopkeeper had given him to complete the ritual. He arranged his good arm and the arm in the sling so his hands covered his heart, left over right, thumbs entwined.

Then he whispered, "You have given me so many gifts, and now that I have looked at them, they have made me realize how blessed I am. Thank you for my life and for stopping my suffering."

Anthony opened his eyes a few minutes later, understanding that he did feel entirely different from when he'd sat down just twenty minutes before. Lighter somehow. And then he figured out it was because he wasn't hearing the gnawing voice of Lack at all.

Then he remembered Mr. Mabior saying something about the universe rushing in when the voice stopped and often giving a gift, the thing he needed most right now.

Anthony stood up from the rock, smiling, head held higher, and looked all around, keen to see if it was true.

———

Earlier that same day, on the backside of the hill at Nesitu, Florence had paced nervously inside the compound of Commander Ossinga, who had been acting as her protector since she, Palmer, and the twenty-two other widows of Jebel Lem had returned from an almost two-week hike down to the border of Uganda and back.

Ossinga, a short, brutishly built man in his forties, walked up to her.

"I'll open the gate in fifteen minutes, oh nine hundred. You ready to talk?"

Florence nodded uncertainly, and he walked away.

She remained torn by her predicament. On the one hand, she was only fifteen, and believed she was still too young to be married. On the other hand, she feared the idea that someone else would make the choice for her. And there was also the fear of humiliation, that no one good would want her at all.

Rather than worry, Florence found herself thinking about the widows' walk she'd been forced to take along with all the others who'd lost a husband at Jebel Lem. The ritual was supposed to have been taken in total silence and to represent some kind of rebirth. But Palmer had immediately started whispering and chatting, offering sharp commentary on whatever was happening at the time. Soon, some of the other women were whispering about how tired they were of life in the LRA and how they should make a run for it if they got close to the border.

In the evenings, when they'd stopped to rest and she was tired of Palmer's chatter, she'd lie down after eating, close her eyes, and remember her book of dreams and how she'd loved to look at the words she'd written every night before sleeping. The first few nights on the widows' walk had all ended with her feeling deeply sad at the loss of her notebooks.

Palmer had commented on her mood as they marched the fourth morning. *What are you so cranky about?*

Florence shrugged. *I used to have these two notebooks that I called my book of dreams. I used to write down everything in them that I could imagine happening in my life. I lost one when the crazy Karimojong men burned down our school and the second one when Oyet dragged me away from home.*

Oyet's dead. Okaya's dead. Be happy about that.

I am, she said. *I just miss my book of dreams.*

About an hour later, Palmer, who was walking behind Florence, said, *When you close your eyes, can you see your book of dreams?*

I don't have to close my eyes. I can see it right now.

Then what's stopping you from opening it and writing in it in your mind?

That idea floored Florence. She looked back at her friend. *Sometimes you are very smart.*

Sometimes?

Okay, most of the time.

All the time, Palmer said.

Florence laughed and kept marching. As she did, she saw a notebook in her mind and opened it. She saw clearly what she'd written there:

> *I am Florence Okori, and these are my dreams. No one can take them from me. Only I can let them go or hold them tight. Only I can write them down. Only I can say them out loud or hold them secret in my heart. Only I and God can make them come true.*

Then, smiling to herself, she turned to a blank page and watched as her imaginary pencil began to dance on the paper, spinning and looping out hopes and dreams for herself.

I will get away, she wrote. *I will go home. I will be with my parents. I will go back to school. I will become a nurse.*

She wrote on as she marched on, but oddly, she never wrote down anything about her impending choice of a husband. It was as if she'd erased that completely from her thoughts.

Florence did not tell Palmer, but as they approached the Ugandan border, she'd decided to try to escape even if the four LRA escorts who guarded them were likely to shoot at her. But when she had at last stood on a rocky ridge above the border crossing at Nimule and saw the guards there checking everyone for documents, she had realized she and the others were trapped and doomed to return north.

She'd tried to console herself by daydreaming about her book of dreams on the return hike, but renewed sadness kept blurring the image. When the walk had finally ended, Florence and Palmer were separated and sent off to different protectors. They'd both been upset. They had not been apart since the early hours of Florence's abduction. They'd come to rely on each other.

But Flo had had little time to think of her friend after Palmer was led away. Ossinga's wives had taken her out, cut off her hair, and shaved her head to tell everyone she was a widow. Then she bathed and anointed herself with shea butter blessed by Kony, who had decreed publicly by then that the widows of Jebel Lem were going to be free to choose a husband.

The Great Teacher had given the widows one week to make a choice among the available suitors. If the widow could not decide in seven days, they would repeat the distribution ritual that had gotten them their first husband, the option of choice removed from their hands.

———

Precisely at nine the first day of the week, the gate had opened and a fat sergeant in his twenties with a fake left leg came waddling and limping in. His name was Samuel. His lower leg had been blown off by a land mine three years before, and he now worked cooking for the hospital workers.

Florence thanked him for his time and told him she'd get in touch if she was interested.

The next day, Colonel Joseph, an artillery commander in his fifties and a friend of Ossinga's, came to call on her. She noticed quickly that he was missing two fingers on his left hand and was virtually deaf from his years around cannons. She'd had to shout at him to make herself heard.

She thanked him for his time and said she'd get in touch if she wanted to talk more. Ossinga was irritated with her, but she said, *I don't want to spend my life yelling. And the Great Teacher said it was my choice. Not yours, Commander Ossinga.*

The third day, a jungle rat in his twenties who hadn't bathed in weeks was waiting when the gate opened at 9:00 a.m. She took one look at him, was reminded of Captain Oyet the day he kidnapped her, and thanked the rat for his time.

Her protector got angry. "You didn't even ask his name!"

"I didn't need his name," Florence said. "I already had everything I needed to know."

Ossinga got spitting mad later in the day when she passed on candidates four and five, both of whom were almost as old as Okaya and had multiple wives.

"I would have been the bottom wife of both of them," she told Ossinga. "I would have been mistreated and been forced into all the work. And they're twice as old as you!"

"Look, I didn't ask for you to live here, and now you have four days left to find someone," her assigned protector said, clenching and unclenching his fists. "In the meantime, I am forcing you into work. Go to the big water hole near the hospital. Fill those two jerry cans."

The water hole near the hospital was far, on the other side of the hill, and there was a perfectly adequate one much closer. Ossinga was punishing her for wasting his time.

But she went and got the two twenty-liter jerry cans, and left the compound.

———

Knowing that Ossinga was probably watching her, Florence climbed up and over the hill, ignoring the appraising looks she was getting from some of the LRA soldiers who were also camped in the area.

The big water hole was a deep wide pool in a stream that crossed a flat about 150 meters south of the field hospital. As she climbed down the hill toward that flat, she could hear the rumble of the ongoing battle at Jebel Lem. And now she could see several men and women walking toward the water hole with buckets or jerry cans in their hands or balanced on their heads.

To her pleasant surprise, one of them was Joyce, her friend the medic, whom she had not seen since returning from the widows' walk. She hurried down the hill, hoping to intercept her.

Just after Joyce had filled a jerry can of her own and turned away from the stream, Florence caught up to her, almost out of breath. At first, Joyce did not recognize her with her head shaved, but then did, and they hugged and caught up on their lives during the past few weeks, including her need to find a husband.

Joyce said, "Do you have your eye on anyone, Betty?"

"No," Florence said. "And I don't like the eyes that are on me."

"Four more days to decide?"

"That's what Commander Ossinga keeps telling me," she said, feeling anxious. "He made me come all the way here for water when there's water one hundred meters from his compound."

"And a long, heavy haul back from here."

"Uphill," Florence sighed.

"Let me know what you decide," Joyce said, and went off lugging her jerry can.

When Florence turned, she found no one else around the water hole and went to it. She began filling Ossinga's jerry cans.

She was topping off the second one when she heard footsteps approach and then a pleasant, oddly familiar voice say, "Hello there. How are you today?"

———

Ten minutes before, Anthony had left the field hospital after a nurse changed the dressing on his shoulder. He'd headed south, meaning to spread out his solar collectors on a rise there that got sun all day long and then work on his radio. He was in a good mood. No suffering. And as he walked, he continued to be alert to his surroundings, fully expecting the gift he needed most to appear in front of him.

And here came Joyce, the medic who'd helped Patrick and Albert lift Anthony out of the back of a pickup and got him stabilized before he was moved to an operating room.

"Joyce!" he cried. "How are you?"

The medic seemed taken aback by his enthusiasm, but then smiled. "I'm fine, Signal Commander Opoka. How is your shoulder?"

"Better every day."

"That's good. Where are you off to?"

"Ahh," Anthony said. "I am in search of a gift!"

"Okay," she said, puzzled. "Let me know if you find it."

"I will do that, my good friend!" he said, grinning, and hurried off toward the water hole and the rise beyond it where he wanted to lay out his solar panels.

As he came through the scattered trees there, Anthony saw a young woman facing almost completely away from him, squatting in the water, filling a jerry can. The sun was on her. He realized her head was shaved.

She's a widow, he thought. *One of the Jebel Lem widows.*

When she turned to put the jerry can on the stream bank, her face was cast in sunlight, and he saw just how beautiful she was. In that instant, the signaler became happier than he could remember being, maybe as far back as the time he beat Patrick in the race.

She's the gift, he thought, feeling breathless. *The one I need most right now.*

Before Fear's voice could rise up and talk him out of it, Anthony walked right up to her and said, "Hello there. How are you today?"

———

Still in the water, Florence looked up into glary light, seeing a man backlit, standing at a respectful distance. She stepped up out of the water hole, shielded her eyes from the sun, and saw that he was a young, handsome guy, sharply dressed in a crisp uniform and new boots, right arm in a sling, and grinning stupidly at her.

"I am fine," she said, recognizing him now. "And you?"

"Like a gift has been given to me!" he said. "What is your name?"

"Betty."

"Betty," he said, and smiled. "I am—"

"Opoka, the Great Teacher's signaler. You told my friend Palmer about the death of our husband, Okaya, and Captain Oyet."

"Ahhhh, I see now. Yes, I know Palmer. A nurse. Are you a nurse, Betty?"

"Kind of," she said, and smiled.

Opoka's eyes struck her as deeply kind, and his smile was brilliant and real. She liked his voice, too, soft, knowing, humble. She felt a surging attraction to him and, slightly embarrassed at the sensation, looked down.

"Where do you stay, Betty the Nurse?" he asked.

"With Commander Ossinga," she said, still not looking up at him.

"Commander of the recoilless rifles. Two Foxtrot. Very good."

And then she heard the crunch of his boots.

Florence's brows knitted, and she raised her head, seeing that the radioman had turned his back on her and was walking away.

And he never looked back!

Chapter Twenty-Five

What? Florence thought as Kony's signaler disappeared into the trees south of the water hole. *"Commander of the recoilless rifles. Two Foxtrot. Very good."* *You had nothing else to say to me?*

She felt a little indignant, and then more than a little hurt as she started back toward Ossinga's compound. By the top of the hill, the hurt had turned to anger. At Opoka. And then at life.

Everything about her existence felt unfair, unjust, and by the time she'd reached her protector's compound, she had forced herself to see and open her book of dreams and to begin writing down terrible fantasies about her future.

I will not find a good husband because I don't want one. But then they will give me one.

He'll probably be eighty, face like dried cow pie.

Florence was morose when she finally put down the full jerry cans by the cooking area in Ossinga's yard. Her mood steadily worsened throughout the evening and was not eased by sleep. It got fouler when the nine o'clock hour came on day four and there was no one at the gate.

———

Anthony hurried to the field hospital around eleven that morning, happy to find Joyce at her normal post, working triage.

"Opoka," she said when she saw him. "Did you find that gift?"

He grinned. "Maybe. What do you think about Betty, the nurse? She works here, right?"

Joyce seemed amused, said, "She did before her husband died. And she's not only beautiful, Opoka, she's a very hard worker. And smart, too. She was studying to be a real nurse back in the real world."

Anthony liked the idea of a smart woman. "Can you talk to her about me? See if it's worth going to speak with her at Ossinga's?"

He could tell she was trying not to smile, but then she did. "I see so much that's not good, Opoka. This feels good. So for you, Signaler, I will."

———

Shortly before dark that evening, Joyce appeared at Ossinga's gate and found Florence in a deep funk.

"Hello, Betty," Joyce said. "We miss you at the hospital."

"They won't let me go back to work until I choose a husband," Florence said, her voice wavering slightly. "And today, no one came to talk to me."

"I know someone who wants to come talk to you," Joyce said.

"Yeah, who's that? An eighty-year-old?"

"Opoka. The one they call Commander Tony."

Florence whipped her head around, surprised at how her spirits had risen. But then again, he'd walked away from her. And never looked back.

"What about him?" she said, trying to sound cool, uninterested.

"He is a signal commander in the LRA, Kony's personal radioman, and he is not yet twenty," Joyce said. "He got there because he is smart, hardworking, humble, and a good man. He would be a fine husband to have, Betty."

Florence waited a moment before saying, "I guess you can tell him to come around."

Joyce clapped her hands and laughed. "This is the most fun I've had in a long time."

———

But the fifth day of the seven Florence had been given to find a suitable husband again saw no one at the gate at 9:00 a.m. She could not believe it and was two cycles into working herself into a tizzy when Opoka came smartly through the gate, wearing a freshly cleaned and pressed uniform. His right arm was out of the sling and held at his side.

The signal commander scanned the compound, saw her, smiled, and then went straight to Ossinga, who was sitting in the shade and greeted him.

"Commander," Anthony said. "It has been a while."

"First month at Jebel Lem," Ossinga said. "I was glad to hear you survived the latest hit."

"I am, too," Anthony said. "I wasn't for a while. But now I am, which brings me here. I believe I am in love with your daughter, Betty, the nurse. I have inquired about her character and have great admiration for her."

Ossinga smiled with relief. "She is a good young woman. I have seen five men come to see her, and all five she sent home. I want to give her to you right now, but there are rules. I'm saying if I see you here in my compound, unannounced, it's okay."

Anthony bobbed his head. "Thank you, sir."

The commander of the recoilless rifles waved to Florence. She got up, wearing an outfit one of Ossinga's wives had lent her. She walked over.

"Betty," Ossinga said. "You remember Signal Commander Opoka. He says you met the other day at the water hole."

Florence smiled brilliantly at him, reminded him of just how beautiful she was, and said, "I remember the radioman."

Then she turned her back on him and walked away.

She never looked back before disappearing out the gate.

———

One second, Anthony had been basking in Betty's dazzling smile, feeling like anything was possible again in life, and the next, he was watching her leave.

He looked back at Ossinga, stunned. "Uh, why would she just leave like that?"

Florence's protector looked like he wanted to break something. "Who knows? She's a woman. She probably doesn't even know why."

Feeling rejected, dejected, and confused, Anthony left, thinking, *Why would she smile at me like that and then leave?*

He went and told Joyce what had happened. She laughed and explained that he'd done the same to Florence the day at the water hole.

"I did? Oh. I didn't mean to. I mean, I was probably all over the place because of how pretty she was and how she made me feel happy the second I saw her."

"Go back and see her in the morning. Apologize for walking away at the water hole and tell her how you feel."

"Just tell her?"

"Women like to know. It helps."

———

Opoka was standing at the gate on the sixth morning at 9:00 a.m. He waved to Ossinga and went straight to Betty the Nurse, who was helping one of the wives with the laundry.

"I am sorry I walked off at the water hole," he said, looking at the ground. "You're just so beautiful and so unexpected. I got confused."

Florence could not help but smile.

Still, she spoke from her heart. "Okaya. He . . . he abused me and Palmer. I know you are a good person, Signal Commander Opoka, but I'm only fifteen. I'm not ready for a man. Ossinga and his wives care for me. I fetch wood and carry water for them, and I hope I can go back to the hospital, but I'm just not interested in becoming your wife or anyone's wife right now."

She saw the signaler's hopes go crashing down and turned away from him, unwilling to watch him leave.

———

Crestfallen, Anthony began to detach from the idea that Betty was the gift he needed most right now. Every time he'd seen her since the water hole, she'd managed to leave him feeling crushed, unwanted, and alone all over again.

The second Joyce saw him trudging back toward the hospital, she put down what she was doing and came to his side.

"No?"

"She said she's not interested in becoming anyone's wife right now because of what Okaya did to her."

"Things are rarely easy," Joyce sighed. "I'll talk to her when I'm done here."

———

Florence hoed in Ossinga's garden for the rest of the day, glancing toward the gate, seeing no one there, and wondering if she was making the right decision putting Opoka off like this. She was almost relieved when Joyce came into the compound around six that evening.

"How old do you think I am?" Joyce asked by way of greeting.

She shrugged. "I don't know."

"Thirty-five," Joyce said. "I was taken by the LRA when I was twenty-three. They killed my husband and gave me to an older man, just like Okaya. He had me for a lot longer than Okaya had you and Palmer. When he died in battle, leaving me with no children after three years, I was believed barren, and no one wanted me. To keep Kony from killing me, I told him I would work the rest of my life as a medic, saving the lives of the holy. He let me live."

Florence did not know what to say and stayed silent.

Joyce went on. "Don't you see, Betty? I had no choice. But you do. If you feel any attraction to Opoka, you should act. You won't get another chance like this again with the LRA. If you have not chosen by tomorrow sundown, I promise you they will come collect you and you will be devastated to learn you have again become the wife of a seventy-year-old. Or worse."

———

At nine o'clock on the seventh morning, Anthony adjusted the cuffs of his freshly pressed uniform, swallowed his pride, and again went through the gate of Ossinga's compound.

"Hello, Betty the Nurse," he said when she saw him, got up, and came over.

"Hello, Commander Tony," she said softly.

"I need you to decide. Even if it is not me, make it so you have some say in your life."

She seemed surprised by that last bit. *Some say in my life.*

With her eyes cast down, she said, "I have had trauma."

"I see it in you," he said.

Florence raised her head to look at him. "You do?"

He nodded and smiled. "But I still think you are the most beautiful girl I have ever met."

Betty smiled shyly, said, "The trauma was why I wished to stay here longer, but because of my attraction to you, Opoka, I will agree to be your wife."

"Your attraction?"

She giggled. "You are very handsome."

He felt baffled by this but deliriously happy. "Are you sure?"

She laughed. "That you are very handsome? Yes, I am sure."

"A gift, then!" he said, and laughed with her. "You are a gift, Betty! The gift I needed most right now in my life!"

Florence wasn't expecting that, but she liked that idea. "Well, of course, I am," she said.

"So I can tell Ossinga?"

"No, I will tell him. You are *my* choice, Commander Tony."

"Thank you for that, Betty the Nurse," he said, grinning and bowing to her. "And I think you can call me Anthony from now on."

———

Normally, in Acholi culture, the days leading up to a wedding are filled with great preparation, and the rituals and celebrations are grand, multiday affairs. But in the LRA and especially during the battle at Jebel Lem, the long sequence of normal events was trimmed to a handful.

As soon as Anthony left the compound, Florence went to Commander Ossinga and told him she had chosen Opoka as her husband. Ossinga took the news with relief and told her she had chosen well and to prepare herself to move within the week.

Anthony went to Joseph Kony at his camp north of Nesitu and found him sitting on a bench by his hut, having a heated discussion with General Lagony, his chief of staff. Once he realized they were in an argument, he'd stayed respectfully back, hearing only a few words like *casualties*; *our reason for being!*; and *the danger of shifting purposes.*

"Enough!" the Great Teacher roared. "I can't listen to you anymore, Lagony."

His chief of staff looked ready to ignore him and argue more, but Kony glared at him and said something low enough that Anthony did not catch it. General Lagony got the message, however, stiffened, spun on his heels, and marched past Anthony, fixing the radioman with one of his trademark stares as he did.

After waiting a few minutes for Kony to settle, Anthony adopted a humble posture and walked toward the Great Teacher. When Kony saw his signaler, he frowned and said, "I told you two more weeks' rest, Opoka."

"Yes, Teacher, this is about something else. I intend to marry. Her name is Betty. She is a nurse in the hospital. I wanted your blessing."

"You? Married? No."

Anthony felt his stomach plunge. "No, Teacher?"

"You'll be distracted. I can't have my signaler distracted."

Kony began to turn away as if the matter were settled.

Anthony blurted after him, "But Betty is one of the Jebel Lem widows. She chose me."

The Great Teacher looked back at him, his features softening a little. "I did not know she was a Jebel Lem widow. You should have said so. Who was her husband?"

"Major Okaya," Anthony said, praying he would change his mind.

"Okaya," Kony said, his face screwing up a little during a long pause. "Well, I expect you'd treat her better than he did."

"Yes, Teacher. She is a gift."

"A gift?" he said, and snorted. "You saying you are in love, Opoka?"

"I guess I am, Teacher," Anthony said anxiously.

The LRA's supreme commander said nothing for several moments.

"Who is this Betty's protector?"

"Two Foxtrot. Commander Ossinga. Recoilless rifles."

After another prolonged silence, Kony said, "Do you have money to buy food and gifts for Ossinga? For a honeymoon?"

Anthony feared it was a trick question because having cash was considered an offense.

"No, Teacher."

"Then I will give you the money. Consider it my wedding present to you."

Bobbing his head, grinning from ear to ear, Anthony said, "You are most kind, Teacher."

Kony made a dismissive gesture. "On second thought, having you married is a good thing. Makes you much less likely to think foolish thoughts and try to leave me. You're not having foolish thoughts, are you, Commander Tony?"

"Never, Teacher," he said, looking the LRA leader in the eyes. "I am your signaler. I belong at your side."

———

Anthony and Florence were kept separated for the rest of the week.

The signaler accepted the money Kony gave him and took a jitney north to Juba to buy food and gifts to give to Betty and to Ossinga, her "father" in the LRA. He also took a Sudan-mandated blood test for sexually transmitted diseases, including HIV, before returning to Nesitu.

Florence felt excited, caught up in forces beyond herself. Ossinga had one of his wives buy her a beautiful new batik outfit in blues and reds the same day she took her blood test.

Both of their tests came back negative. On that Sunday, in the pavilion at the LRA camp on the White Nile south of Juba, Kony himself married the twenty-four widows of Jebel Lem, including Palmer, who had chosen a major in his late thirties.

Anthony fully expected Kony to wear white robes and to channel the spirit of Cilindi during the ceremony, but the Great Teacher wore his uniform, seemed distracted, and married them all by himself in a shea-butter-based ritual, calling the widows "the heroes of the LRA today." Fatima was there and rolled her eyes. But she seemed on edge as well.

Lily came by, looked at Florence, and smiled at Anthony. "Well done, Commander Tony."

Anthony grinned broadly. "Thank you."

Talking with his old boss, General Tabuley, after the ceremony, Anthony learned why Fatima and Kony appeared agitated. The Dinka's supply lines were growing stronger, and they were pouring men into the fight. There had been so many casualties during the four days of Anthony and Florence's brief engagement that the LRA was barely holding on.

Tabuley lowered his voice, said, "General Lagony thinks the hills are already lost. He thinks it may be time to talk truce with Museveni."

Anthony was thrown by that. His focus had been on his marriage to Florence, and here the general was treating him like an equal, sharing information.

"Does Teacher know this?"

"Lagony has been trying to make him come to that conclusion himself," Tabuley said.

"What do you think?"

"Never. Not in a million years. One thing I know about Joseph Kony. That man has no quit in him, never has, never will."

———

Because so many widows were married that day, the Great Teacher allowed a rare celebration among the holy. A reception was held for all the married couples at the pavilion, with three goats roasted over an open pit fire, fresh root vegetables, and punch made from grape and lemon juice. People ate politely, constantly taking glances at Kony, who had stayed for the reception with Fatima and Lily, both of whom seemed put out to have the attention off them.

Anthony only had eyes for Betty. He could not believe his luck after having none for so long. She was the most beautiful girl ever, inside and outside.

I am easily the luckiest man alive, he thought, mooning at her from across a table while she gabbed and laughed with her friend Palmer.

It turned out that Palmer's new husband, Major Thomas, was in the same battalion as Anthony's brother Albert. Since no one in the LRA knew they were brothers, he asked Palmer's husband about Albert in passing.

"Very sharp," Thomas said. "Very good with the TONFAS. Like you, Opoka."

"We trained together to be signalers," Anthony said. "He was very good, even then."

Beyond that, Anthony knew better than to dig deeper, to show he had any interest beyond the fate of a casual acquaintance.

———

Across the table, Florence was reveling in Palmer's take on the day.

"If we could just get rid of Kony and his wives, we'd have a shot at getting people up and dancing," Palmer muttered.

Florence chuckled. "Is dancing allowed in the LRA?"

"Oh, nothing's allowed in the LRA," Palmer said, disgusted. "Except killing people or kidnapping them or gifting them like slaves."

"Keep your voice down," Florence said.

Palmer was quiet a moment, fidgeted with her fingers.

"What's the matter?"

"I'm worried. About, you know, what we went through with Okaya."

"I don't think it's always supposed to be like that."

"You don't know that."

"I asked Joyce, and she said it's absolutely not supposed to be like with Okaya. She said it can be, well, nice sometimes."

"Sometimes nice," Palmer sniffed, unconvinced. "Well, one thing I've got going for me is he's got two other wives, which means those chores are split three ways. But you, Betty, you've got that all to yourself. Then again, when you're a minister's first wife in Kampala, you'll get to abuse younger wives like me."

"No younger wives. I am the only wife."

She threw back her head and laughed. "Good luck with that!"

Florence didn't reply, focused now on a Land Rover pulling up by the pavilion.

Yango, Kony's head of security, got out.

———

Anthony saw Yango arrive as well and stopped talking, along with Palmer's new husband.

General Lagony, the LRA's chief of staff, exited the Land Rover and waited by it as the security chief went to the Great Teacher and whispered something in his ear. Then Yango reached into his pocket and handed Kony several pieces of paper. The LRA's leader scanned them, turned each page over slowly. He looked at the pages all over again, folded them, and held them a moment before leaning over and saying something to Fatima. She stiffened, but nodded. She said something to Lily. The two wives got up and left the pavilion on the side opposite the Land Rover.

Yango moved toward the vehicle and General Lagony, with the Great Teacher trailing. Something had changed in Lagony, just in the moments since his arrival. Ordinarily, Kony's chief of staff was quiet in his body and words, and he had that unnerving tendency to stare at people for a long period of time without saying a thing. But now, Anthony noticed that the man was moving back and forth on the balls of his feet and chewing the air.

"What's happening?" Betty asked, appearing at his side.

"I don't know," Anthony said, taking her hand. "I've never . . ."

Kony shook the papers and shouted at Lagony, "You left these notes of your treachery right out in the open where Yango could find them!"

Every voice in the pavilion fell silent. Every eye at the wedding reception turned to the drama unfolding outside, to General Lagony backed up against the Land Rover and the Great Teacher a couple of meters away, shaking the papers high over his head.

Kony's chief of staff said, "They were an exercise, Teacher. A scenario that I felt should be considered by—"

"Surrender and go home?!" Kony thundered. "That's the scenario? Talk to Museveni? Pray for his mercy when you know there will be none? Who are you? Who are you above the laws of the Lord's Resistance Army?"

"Teacher, I have followed you from the beginning," Lagony said in a shaky voice, loud enough to be heard throughout the pavilion. "I have been there through the difficult times before, but we have lost nearly fifteen hundred men at Jebel Lem, and another seven hundred wounded."

The Great Teacher handed Yango the papers. "Who Are You does not care. What you have written down is a strategy of surrender, which makes you a traitor to the cause of the LRA. You are hereby found guilty"—Anthony sensed what was coming, grabbed Betty with his good arm, and pulled her to him, shielding her eyes—"and sentenced to death."

Anthony nuzzled his head against hers, said, "Don't look, Betty."

A pistol shot went off. And then another.

When Anthony finally allowed himself to look, Kony was holstering his sidearm and Lagony was dead on the ground. The thing that upset him most about the scene was the silence. No one cried. No one was shocked enough to even whimper.

He's made us all into unfeeling monsters, Anthony thought.

"Thank you," Betty whispered, pulling back from his grasp with a grateful smile on her face. "For thinking of me."

"You still have feelings."

"And so do you," she said.

He grinned a little. "I guess I do."

———

Yango came up to Anthony shortly after the general's corpse had been removed and Kony had left the camp. For a moment, Anthony was sure the security chief was going to ask if General Tabuley had told him about Lagony's plan to surrender. But the security chief told him that the top commanders had decided he and Betty deserved a honeymoon. They were giving them the use of a small house on the Sudanese Armed Forces base outside Juba.

"It's yours for ten days," Yango said, acting as if the murder of Lagony was an event already long forgotten.

Anthony gaped at him. He had never considered a honeymoon. Especially when there was still fighting going on in the Jebel Lem hills.

"Ten days," he said in wonder.

"Unless the Great Teacher needs you sooner."

He told Betty, who had never been to Juba, and she got excited. Yango arranged for a pickup to take them and gave Anthony an envelope with cash in it, a gift from the senior officers.

They sat by themselves in the back of the truck on the way. Anthony said, "We're going to eat like kings and queens!"

Betty laughed and told him what Palmer had said about it not being right to have no dancing at a wedding.

"She's right," Anthony said, trying to remember the last time he'd danced, and then saw himself singing and dancing on the hill above the Koromush barracks after he'd survived his first combat. He was going to tell her about it, but then decided not to.

"What was a wedding like in your family growing up?" he asked instead.

"Oh, a big, big party," she said. "Lots of people coming and going and dancing and eating and drinking and singing for three whole days!"

"Wow," he said. "Three days?"

She held up her hands and said, "I swear. My mother is born again and does not drink. My father is Catholic and drinks. After both my older sisters' weddings, he couldn't stay on his feet for a week."

They went through a gate being guarded by Sudanese and LRA sentries, and soon pulled up in front of the small cottage. Across the dirt road in a group of huts were several of Kony's other commanders living with their wives and children. They watched as Anthony thanked the driver, got out, and ran around to open Betty's door.

She giggled as she climbed out, saying, "Thank you, Commander Tony."

"You are welcome, Betty the Nurse," Anthony said before offering her his elbow.

She took it, and they walked to the front door. Betty looked at him, and he read fear in her eyes.

"Not until you're ready," he said. "Okay?"

Betty smiled. "Okay."

"And one more thing you should know before we go inside?"

"Yes?"

"Today was not a proper wedding or a proper celebration. But I promise you someday, when Kony and the LRA and all of this is behind us, we will get married for real and we'll dance and sing and feast and party for three days straight."

Anthony said it all with such conviction in his voice and love in his goofy smile and mooning eyes that her eyes began to well up.

"I don't know why, but I believe you," she said. "One more thing you should know about me before we go inside?"

"Yes?" he said, wiping a tear from her cheek.

"Betty isn't my real name," she said softly. "It's Florence."

Now Anthony's eyes welled up. "Florence. That is my mother's name. Acoko Florence."

"No, it's not."

"I swear," he said, and opened the door. "It's like we were fated to be together."

Chapter Twenty-Six

Florence entered the little house deeply happy for the first time since her abduction. Not only was Anthony a decent person, but she had also chosen him. She had not been forced into it, and that made all the difference in her mind.

And while Okaya had not wanted to talk, the signaler seemed genuinely interested in her.

"But what's your favorite memory from before the LRA?" he asked as she made a spicy chicken-and-rice dish for dinner.

She thought about that and then described the Christmas Eve when Josca rescued her from the measles ward and carried her home.

"I told her to put me down and take a rest. She said, 'You are my daughter, Florence. I love you with all my heart and soul. And love is the strongest force there is. If I had to, I would carry you forever.' That is my favorite memory."

"It's a great memory, and she sounds like a wonderful mother."

She barely noticed his expression had saddened a little; the past fourteen months of keeping her emotions bottled up, of keeping silent about everything, all caved in, and Florence broke down sobbing. "I miss her. I miss all of them, just everything about my life."

Anthony rubbed her back while she cried and told her how much he missed his old life as well. He described his father and how he taught him as a young boy to navigate at night by the silver stars, and he told her about his mother, Acoko Florence, who was as troubled as she was beautiful.

"Did she ever come back?"

"Not that I know of," he said. "But she had asked to see me after months of not hearing from her. That happened the day before I was taken."

"So there was hope?"

"I guess there was that day."

"Is that your favorite memory?"

He thought about that. "I guess it is one of my favorites. I mean, the same day I found out she wanted to see me, I was voted head boy at my school."

At the mention of school, Florence brightened and told him about wanting to be a nurse and, for some reason, the story of the Karimojong raiders coming to her school.

"They just walked into the schoolyard naked?" Anthony roared with laughter.

"Naked with guns," she laughed. "It was scary. They burned the school down."

"Oh," he said. "How far did you go? In school?"

"I took my level two entrance exams, but I was kidnapped before I got the results," Florence said, feeling angry all over again at Joseph Kony and the LRA.

"Could have been worse."

"How? I know in my heart I did well on those tests. I know in my heart I did well enough to someday go to university and become a nurse. But then I got taken. So how could it have been worse?"

"I never even got to take my level twos," Anthony said. "I was studying for them when I was kidnapped three months before the exams."

Florence had not expected that. "You're right. That is worse. I'm sorry."

"So am I, but I would never admit that to Kony or to anyone else in the LRA."

"You keep secrets, too?"

"If I didn't, I'd probably be insane by now."

She studied his face. "Can I trust you, Commander Tony?"

"I told you to call me Anthony, and not yet, you can't, Betty the Nurse. Trust is something gained. My father taught me that."

"I think that's true. But how do you gain trust?"

"I just shared a secret I wouldn't tell anyone else in the LRA. I gave you trust. You gained it. Now you share a secret you wouldn't tell anyone else in the LRA. You'll give trust. I'll gain it."

Florence hesitated. She'd heard stories about LRA commanders denouncing their wives to Kony and Who Are You for admitting that they hated their lives and wanted to escape.

Anthony said, "It doesn't have to be a big secret."

He was so sincere she said, "On the march north, after my abduction, there was a young man who kept falling behind on the rail. They kept warning him, and finally they . . ."

Anthony saw the horror on her face and knew. "They made other recruits step on him."

She nodded and wept, saying, "It was my older brother, Owen. He had a heart condition, and he couldn't keep up. And I couldn't cry. I couldn't say anything. I couldn't watch."

Anthony again rubbed her back until Florence stopped crying; then he told her the story of the thumb-sucker and then the bayoneting.

"Right next to you?" Florence said. "Oh my God, you must have gone crazy."

"For almost a week," Anthony admitted as she served dinner.

He took a bite and moaned. "It's so good! Where did you learn to cook like this?"

"Josca's Love Café of Fine Food," she said, grinning.

"Love Café?" he said, laughing.

"The Love Café. That's what Jasper called it."

"Perfect," Anthony said, taking another bite. "Food fresh from the Love Café. Who's Jasper?"

"My cousin," she said. "He was taken the same night I was. He could tell you the name of every song he heard on the radio and who sang it."

"What happened to him?"

"I don't know," she said. "They took him away to training, and I haven't seen him since."

"I have a brother in the LRA," Anthony said. "I can't talk to him."

"Definitely not. They'd use it against the both of you."

They stayed up deep into the night, talking, sharing more of their histories, their favorite foods, favorite music, and a dozen other subjects. Florence told him about her book of dreams and how she wrote in it in her mind. He told her about his race against Patrick. When they were finally too tired to go on, Anthony laid down two mats a respectful distance apart and immediately got under his sheet and blanket before kicking off his pants and shirt.

Florence did the same. "Good night, Commander Tony . . . sorry, Anthony."

"Good night, Betty the Nurse . . . sorry, Florence."

Flo giggled and then closed her eyes, thinking that she had never known anyone like him.

On the other side of the same little room, Anthony was thinking much the same thing. A feeling in his heart triggered a memory of leaving Patrick after rescuing him from the river, of thinking that he'd just made a close friend, someone who would be important in his life.

As he drifted off to sleep, he realized he felt exactly the same way about Florence.

———

Those feelings only deepened in the days that followed as more stories of their early lives and dreams spilled out. The war and their captivity in the LRA were largely forgotten.

Florence had never met anyone so easy to talk to. Anthony respected her, didn't talk over her. *He sees me,* she thought multiple times that first week together. *He hears me, too.*

Anthony loved the way she listened intently to his stories, then asked him questions so she made sure she understood. She was fascinated by the strange inner world of Control Altar and the Great Teacher.

"Do you believe Kony is possessed by spirits?" she asked quietly one day as they walked back from the market, with a couple of LRA soldiers from the base trailing behind them as they always did whenever they left the Sudanese army base.

He glanced over his shoulder at the soldiers talking to each other. "You can't repeat this."

"We're building trust."

After describing how the thunderstorm had struck the first night he'd seen Kony possessed by the spirits, he told her how the Great Teacher liked to listen to weather reports on the shortwave all the time.

"Supposedly to anticipate battle conditions," Anthony said. "But then I noticed that whenever there were thunderstorms predicted, he would suddenly call for a gathering where he would relay some important message from the spirit world."

"And everyone would think Kony called the storm in."

"Every time. I think he's as much a con man as he is a murderer."

This time Florence looked over her shoulder at their minders, still lost in their own conversation, before turning back to Anthony.

"I definitely won't repeat that to anyone else in the LRA," Florence said.

"Please don't, or we'll both be dead."

———

Near the end of the first week, they learned that the Jebel Lem hills had been lost. It was the biggest defeat in the LRA's long fight with the Dinka, and Kony was evidently in a foul mood and in seclusion.

By then, Anthony and Florence hated to be out of the other's presence for longer than a few minutes. And when they would come back together, they'd almost immediately start laughing and smiling.

One evening, as they sat outside late at night, looking up at the stars, Anthony told her about his father's lessons, about celestial navigation and how a medicine man had told him that our spirits come from and return to the stars.

"So it's like we're looking up at the souls of our ancestors and our children shining back at us."

Flo smiled. "I like that. And I think I would like your father."

"You would love him the same way I do," Anthony said. "When Omera George said he loved you, he showed it, made you feel as if you were the only other person in the world. And he didn't want you to be a better man. He wanted you to be a better human, to really think about who you were and who you were going to become. He thought it was important to have values and rules to guide you through life. And he taught me to try to look for the humanity in another person, even an enemy. He always said, 'You never know what another person is going through inside, so treat them as a fellow human, and you'll never go wrong.' He also told me that whenever I was confused about what to do, I should ask myself a simple question—What would a good human do?"

Florence liked that and said so. "My mother and father had rules, too. But there was one rule above all. 'There is nothing stronger than the power of love.' Josca used to say that whatever your problem was, it could be solved by turning to love as the answer."

For reasons they didn't quite understand, they kept calling up other lessons from their childhoods, looking for the ones that they remembered and used in times of difficulty. He told her about meeting Mr. Mabior and the four voices of suffering. He explained them so clearly Florence got the point immediately. When they went inside, by lantern light, Florence started to write down the lessons on a piece of paper but stopped after writing, *Avoid voices of Fear, Lack—*

She looked at him with concern. "When was the last time that dressing on your wound was changed?"

Anthony frowned. "I don't know. Last week?"

"Last week! What were you thinking?"

He blinked. "Uh, I guess I was thinking about you?"

"Oh. Well then, understandable. Take the shirt off. I saw bandages and tape in the cupboard in the bathroom."

Florence left the room and came back to find Anthony standing there awkwardly.

"What's the matter?" she said. "Take the shirt off. It's not like I haven't seen bullet wounds before."

"But you probably haven't seen a wound from an RPG fin before," he said. "I didn't want you to see it and . . . you know."

"I'll be fine," Florence said. "Really, let Betty the Nurse help you."

"Commander Tony can do it himself," he said, sighing, and unbuttoned his uniform shirt and then pulled off his undershirt.

Flo was shocked when she saw the extent of the scarring and broken bones that had never healed and the much smaller wound bandaged above it.

"My God, how did you live through that?" she asked, coming closer.

He told her how Patrick had carried him off the battlefield and how the spirit of Cilindi prescribed magic mushrooms and salt be put into the wound and sewn up.

"Really?"

"No painkillers. No antibiotics. He doesn't believe in them for us, but he sure believes in them for himself and the wives."

He said this with more than a little rancor in his voice.

Florence finished removing the old dressing and inspected the wound.

"No redness. No swelling. This will probably be the last bandage you'll need."

She put the new dressing on, taped it in place. She was about to tell him to put his shirt back on when she thought of Anthony's father talking about never knowing what another person was going through, and so to treat them like a fellow human above all.

Florence could feel how sensitive Anthony was about his disfigurement.

Treat him how you'd want to be treated, Flo.

She reached out and put her hands softly on the damaged and scarred area, feeling him tense and almost get up.

"It's all right," she whispered, and kept moving her fingers lightly over the skin, feeling the muscles and bones out of place.

Then she came around the front of him, hands still on him, and looked at the wound from that side.

"It's beautiful," she said at last.

"It's not beautiful," he said. "You are beautiful."

"It has made you who you are, and I think you are beautiful and handsome, and so your shoulder is beautiful and handsome."

She could see just how desperate he was to believe her, and felt she had to show him.

Florence leaned in and kissed Anthony.

The feeling started in his breathlessness, spread down into his chest, filled his lungs and stomach, buzzed in his mind.

When they parted, he said, "I . . ."

"What?"

"When I was seven, my father was teaching me about the stars, and he told me I was special, and I got filled with this—this rare warmth that I only felt with him. When I look at you, Florence, I feel that same rare warmth everywhere, inside and out."

"Because this rare warmth you're feeling is true love, Signaler," she said, and kissed him again.

Chapter Twenty-Seven

August 22, 1999
Amia'bil, Uganda

By then, Florence had been gone from her mother eighteen months. The women in the village had reminded Josca time and again that kids taken by the Lord's Resistance Army rarely came home. And when they did, they were damaged goods, beyond help or repair.

Forget Florence, they told her. *Forget Owen and Jasper, too. You should just consider them all dead and move on.*

But Josca could not move on, and neither could Constantine. Their oldest son, their precocious daughter, and their favorite nephew still lived in their hearts.

When Josca closed her eyes, she could feel them there. And when she did, she tried to envision them alive, desperate to return home, and coming down the road from Lira to greet her with arms wide open.

She tried to see that scene in vivid colors, with music behind the ululations and screams of relief, happiness, and welcome home. With the vision at its sharpest, when it had filled her with joy, she would bow her head and pray that she would see her dream realized, that she would hold Owen, Florence, and Jasper in her arms again someday soon.

Josca did the ritual twice a day and three times on Sunday, when she attended evangelical services and prayed hardest for her vision to come true.

When she found Constantine outside church that Sunday morning, waiting to walk her home, she said, "Florence is almost sixteen. I asked Jesus to send her home before her birthday."

Florence's father looked at his wife a little oddly, but then said, "She would like that."

"I would like it, too."

"Wouldn't we all?" he said, starting to walk through the throng leaving church. "I miss her eagerness."

Josca nodded and went with him. "She just loved life and was looking forward to the next new thing. Do you think there's time if she gets back before her birthday?"

"Time for what?"

"To go to university. To become a nurse. She's missed eighteen months already."

"She missed the first two years of primary school, and look what she did after that."

"That's true. Once she puts her mind to something, she's capable of anything."

"Anything you can imagine," Constantine said. "Florence is a very special girl."

Josca choked. Her shoulders trembled, and she started weeping right there in the street.

"What's the matter?" her husband said, coming close.

"I miss her so much," Josca blubbered. "And I just hate that this has happened to her. To us. After all her hard work, she was stolen, Constantine. And God knows what's been stolen from her since then."

"It's unfair," Constantine said. "But life is unfair, Josca."

"I know it is," she said finally, wiping at her tears and looking around to see if any of the village women had seen her break down. "The important thing is to never give up. Isn't that what you always told Florence?"

He nodded. "I know that girl as well as I know you. And she will never give up."

Josca sniffed, and then smiled. "Then I won't, either."

———

Rwotobilo

In the evening twilight that same Sunday, George Opoka walked the dusty red road toward the family compound, carrying a knapsack. He saw no one else and was not surprised.

Due to the increasing severity of the clashes between the Lord's Resistance Army and the Uganda Peoples' Defence Forces, most of his neighbors had given up and moved to one of dozens of internally displaced persons camps the government had set up near Gulu and other cities in the north.

Anthony's father had resisted the move as long as he could. Two days before, however, he'd been told by government soldiers that evacuation from that part of rural Acholi land was going to be mandatory by the end of the month.

To make matters worse, George was being harassed by the police, who accused him of wanting to stay in his village because he was somehow getting money from Anthony!

His oldest son had been gone close to five years, and he had not heard a whisper of him anywhere. The idea that Anthony was bringing him money was simply, well, stupid.

And painful, George admitted to himself as he turned down the path toward Acoko Florence's old hut. In the past year or so, he had had days in a row when he didn't think of Anthony or Albert. But the recent police harassment had changed that, made him relive the loss of his sons all over again. He was so caught up in his thoughts that he did not smell the woodsmoke or the garlic in the air.

Anthony's mother was sitting on a bench outside her old hut, tending a fire beneath a cast-iron pot. George's fifty-seven-year-old father, John, sat beside her, smoking a cigarette.

"The last holdouts," George said, and grinned at them. His other two wives had already moved to one of the IDP camps along with his brother Paul's family.

"I'll be going on to Gulu in the morning," John said. "Just getting the last of your mother's things organized."

George's mother had died of pneumonia a few months before. His father seemed lost without her.

"I'll leave with you, George," Acoko said.

"I'm harvesting the yams, and then we'll go," George said. "Day after tomorrow. Wednesday at the latest."

"I'll help you. It will go quicker."

"What's cooking?"

"One of the neighbor's guinea hens," John said, and laughed hoarsely.

Acoko laughed with him. "They just left a flock of them running around when they went to town. We figured this was better than having some animals get them."

"Which they will," John said.

George couldn't argue with the logic, especially when the logic smelled as delicious as the guinea hen did.

"I think these will go great with it," he said, and opened the knapsack and got out six large Nile lagers that were still somewhat cold. "Last beer at the last store. They're all closing down."

He opened one and handed it to Acoko, who said, "What a perfect idea."

"I have them now and then," George said, and winked at her.

He opened another for his father, who said, "Last beer at the last store for my last night."

"Cheers," George said, and they clinked bottles and drank.

After all the hard, physical labor and after the long walk to and from the last local store open in the area, the beer hit the spot, and George took several big gulps before sighing.

"Dinner's ready," Acoko said, getting up to retrieve three metal bowls and spoons.

She ladled steaming chunks of guinea hen in garlic-and-tomato sauce into the bowls and handed them to George and his father before serving herself.

George took a bite and moaned. "It tastes better than it smells, and it smells unbelievable."

Acoko smiled. "I basically just used whatever we had left."

The three of them ate until they could not eat another bite. Acoko put on another pot to boil water to clean the dishes. John finished his beer and opened another.

When he was halfway done, John started to nod off. George shook his arm. Anthony's grandfather startled.

"Dad, go to sleep before you fall off the bench and hurt yourself."

John nodded sleepily, then headed off toward the hut he used when he was visiting his son's family.

George helped Acoko wash the dishes and pots, and then sat with her and opened one of the remaining beers to share while the fire burned down to embers.

"I was thinking about Anthony again today," Acoko said wistfully.

"I was, too, walking home. Five years."

"Almost six for me," she said, her voice cracking. "He must be a man now, if he's alive."

"He's alive," George said immediately. "And so is Albert. I just feel it."

His wife drank from the beer. "I hope so. I feel a lot of guilt for not seeing Anthony before he was taken."

"And I feel a lot of guilt for not waking up early enough to be here when the LRA came."

Acoko looked at the flames. "He's my only boy, George."

He put his arm around her. "I know."

"I try not to get sad about it, but I do."

"I do, too," he said, and hugged her tight.

From over by the hut where his father slept, they suddenly heard a shout of surprise, a crash, and then a groan of pain.

"What was that?" Acoko said, pulling away in alarm.

"Sounded like someone who hasn't had beer in a while tripping and falling over something," he said, taking his arm away and standing up. "I'll go check and then sleep."

Acoko looked at him. "You could always come back and sleep here."

"I'd like that."

"See you soon," she said, and smiled.

He picked up a flashlight, turned it on, and started toward his father's hut, calling out, "Dad? Are you okay?"

George heard nothing but the night birds and the rustle of wind in the leaves. He took a trail to his right, took ten steps, and shone the light toward the hut.

His father was on the ground. An LRA soldier with short little dreads jutting off his head stood with his boot on John's back, squinting at the glare. He raised his rifle toward George.

George ducked and spun, thumbing off the light just before the shot, which went wide. He took off, nearly blind.

"Runner!" he heard the man shout behind him.

"No!" Acoko screamed ahead of him.

George felt the path give way to a heavier trail, took a left, and went sprinting toward Acoko's hut. In the last glow of the fire, he saw his somewhat drunk and terrified wife holding one of their hoes and swinging it at a second LRA soldier, a big muscular guy with an afro and a wicked scar across his right cheek.

"What have you done with my son!" she screamed.

The soldier laughed. "Who?"

"Anthony! Anthony Opoka!"

He stared at her a moment, frowning before he noticed George coming. Acoko swung and hit him in the face below his left eye, opening up a gash there. But rather than stun him, the blow enraged him. When Acoko swung again, he parried it with the barrel of his weapon, stepped in, and clubbed her forehead viciously with the butt of the gun.

George watched his wife go down in a heap. He skidded to a stop. The soldier swung his gun at him and said, "Hands where I can see them, or you die right now."

"Please, let me help her."

The LRA guy snorted. "No. We're leaving. Now."

The guy with the tiny dreads came up behind George. "Gimme the flashlight. Hands in front of you. No funny business."

"Aren't I too old?"

"We're scraping the bottom of the barrel, aren't we, Sergeant Bacia?" Tiny Dreads said, and laughed.

"Nah, that bitch was the bottom of the barrel," the scarred and bleeding one said. "Flashlight. Hands."

With two guns on him, George gave him the flashlight and held out his hands. Tiny Dreads stepped up with a length of twine and tied George's wrists tight.

"Move," Bacia said, gesturing with his gun and the flashlight beam not south toward the road but north toward the edge of the bluff and that outcropping where he'd taught seven-year-old Anthony the intricacies of the African night sky.

George took one last look at Acoko lying there motionless and then headed north with Sergeant Bacia and Tiny Dreads following. Anthony's father took trails he knew by heart, hearing the dead leaves crunching under his feet and knowing how dry it had been lately. Dry and dusty.

Remembering that there was a decent drop-off just ahead near the outcropping, a plan formed in his head. George faked tripping and sprawling and then scrambling to push himself up with his bound hands.

Tiny Dreads grabbed him by the back of his shirt and yanked him to his feet.

"Move," he said. "We have people to meet."

George waited until he could see the outcropping to his right before hesitating.

"What's the matter?" Bacia said.

"It gets really steep here, and I can't see the way down. Can you bring the light?"

He stood there until the flashlight went on. He squinted so he was barely seeing the beam and waited for the scarred one to come around him to play the light down the bank.

George took a deferential step back when Bacia moved around to his right, holding his rifle in his left hand, flashlight in the right, his left cheek bleeding, his left eye almost swollen shut from Acoko's blow. Just as George had hoped.

The scarred LRA soldier aimed the flashlight over the bank. The second he did, George threw up both hands, hurling crushed leaves, gravel, and dust right into Bacia's eyes.

The soldier bellowed in surprise and rage. George jumped over the edge of the bluff and sprinted downhill into the darkness.

He heard Tiny Dreads yell something, and then there were two shots, which only spurred George on. He hit a log across his ankle, tumbled forward, and struck something with his ribs.

Gasping, he ignored the pain, lurched back to his feet, and kept going. Only when he'd reached one of the neighbor's fields at the bottom of the bluff did he stop to look and listen. He did not see anyone following or any light playing back up toward the outcropping.

But he did hear them arguing. That was enough to send him straight west across the field to a line of trees about two hundred meters away. He got into the woods, turned, and stood there, peering back across the field, hoping to catch sight of them in the pale moonlight.

George stayed there unmoving until the sky started to brighten. Then he found a rock with enough of an edge to cut the twine binding his wrists. He took another route back up onto the bluff and circled toward the family compound slowly, taking a step beneath the three big trees, listening, looking, and then taking another step.

He found his father face down and dead by the hut he'd gone to sleep in. Grief-stricken, he forced himself to go check Acoko. Fully expecting her to be gone as well, he was shocked to see that despite being unconscious and bleeding out her right ear, his wife was still breathing.

George squatted, grunted at the pain in his ribs, but got his arms under her neck and the backs of her knees before hoisting her up. Her eyelids opened. Her eyes traveled out of sync.

"Happen?" Acoko said in a slurred voice.

"The LRA guy you tried to kill hit you," he said, heading toward the road. "I'm taking you to the hospital in Gulu."

Chapter Twenty-Eight

September 12, 1999
Nesitu, Southern Sudan

Anthony checked in at the field hospital. Learning that Florence had already gone home, he ran the kilometer north to their hut, still flooded with the rare warmth of true love and feeling yet again like he was the luckiest young man alive.

He spotted Florence hanging wet clothes on the line he'd tied between two acacia trees.

"Betty!" he cried. "I have very good news!"

Florence turned and gave him a wan smile. "What is your good news?"

"Kony is going north with Control Altar to a town called Rubangatek," he said. "Because of the pain in my shoulder, I don't have to go! They're sending another radioman. We can stay here! Isn't that great?"

She nodded without conviction.

He grew concerned. "You okay?"

Florence swallowed at the metallic taste at the back of her throat and forced herself to nod. "Just feel like I ate something bad. Maybe the eggs last night."

"I'll hang the rest," he said. "Sit over there in the shade, and I will finish for you."

Looking relieved, Florence went to sit under a thorn tree, while Anthony got the rest of their clothes from the basket and hung them over the line, feeling odd for reasons he did not grasp at first. Then he realized that for the first time he could remember, the LRA was at peace, or at least not actively seeking combat.

After their devastating defeat at the Jebel Lem hills, giving the Dinka control over the intersection of the two north–south roads in southern Sudan, there were rumors that the spirits had left the Great Teacher, who had become withdrawn and paranoid. The Arab government in Khartoum had lost confidence in his ability to defeat the SPLA and were withholding arms and supplies, which was why Kony was going to Rubangatek, closer to Juba, in hopes he could renegotiate their deal.

When Anthony finished, he looked over at Florence, and immediately a smile appeared on his face and hers.

"You are a good human, Betty the Nurse."

"And you are a good human, Commander Tony," she said.

"I'm grateful for you."

In the short time they'd been married, Anthony and Florence had not only fallen deeply in love, they had also learned and kept each other's deepest secrets and dreams. Trust between them had grown and deepened into an unshakable bond. They'd created a world inside and around their little home that made Anthony feel more settled and rooted than he had in five years. It wasn't just that they were now able to stay in one place for the foreseeable future; as they'd told each other the stories of their early lives, they'd been continually surprised at the parallels in the ways they were raised.

Family was a vital thing. The family supported each other, fought for each other. You were to be kind to each other. You were to be polite and welcoming. You were to treat others the way you wanted to be treated. You did your work without argument. You tried your best. You believed in the power of love. You were humble in victory and gracious in defeat. You were thankful to God and the universe for all you were given.

This last common lesson had proved to be the stable core of their relationship. One night in the second week of married life, they talked about how George and Josca had consistently told them to be thankful for their lives, their health, their food, the roof over their head.

"And they made us feel warm inside doing it, didn't they?"

Florence thought of her mother carrying her from the measles ward as a little girl, and how deeply loved Josca made her feel. "Yes, they did. Like I was wrapped up in love with no limit."

Now giving thanks and expressing love had become a daily part of their lives.

"Why are you grateful for me?" Florence teased.

"For the way you don't make me feel bad about my shoulder. For your smile. For your smarts. For your beauty. For the way you think I'm funny."

"I think you're funny?"

"As much as I think you're funny."

"Well, I'm thankful for that. And for the way you fought for me. And the kind way you have treated me, and how you've made sure I felt taken care of."

Anthony took the empty basket and put it inside their hut. When he came back out, Florence was on her feet and leaning against the tree with her head down.

Then she bent over and vomited violently. He ran to her.

Florence was dry heaving and trembling. She looked at him with fright in her eyes. "Something's wrong, Anthony. I don't feel right."

"We're going to the hospital right now. The Arab doctor is there today. I saw him."

———

Palmer was working intake at the field hospital, which was slow now that there was a lull in combat.

"I feel like I have cholera again," Florence told her. "Or dysentery. I'm weak. Chills. Can't keep anything down."

She told the doctor the same thing. He ordered a blood test and had her lie on a cot and drink electrolyte salts dissolved in water. They made her want to gag all over again.

Anthony sat at her side, holding her hand, while she tried to close her eyes.

Two hours later, Palmer and the doctor returned, laughing.

Palmer said, "You don't have cholera, dysentery, or giardia."

The doctor said, "You are pregnant, young lady."

"Pregnant?" Florence said, feeling like a distant door had suddenly slammed shut.

"I'm going to be a father?" Anthony said.

"That's usually how it works when your wife's pregnant," Palmer said, and clapped and laughed again.

Anthony ignored the wisecrack, squeezed his good hand into a fist, and threw it overhead. "I am going to be a father! The Opoka line goes on!"

Palmer went to Florence's side. "Betty, you're going to be a mommy."

Florence smiled, but knew it was halfhearted. "I kind of wanted to be a real nurse first."

"You can still work here if you're pregnant," Palmer said.

"That's right," Florence said, getting to a sitting position. "I forgot. We should go, Anthony. I've got dinner to make."

Anthony felt like his chest was going to burst open with pride, and then overwhelmed with concern for Florence's well-being. He helped her to her feet and held her elbow as they thanked Palmer and the doctor, and then left.

On the walk back to their home, Florence was quiet.

"You're not happy?" Anthony asked.

"I'm not *not* happy," she said.

"What does that mean?"

"It means I don't know how I feel right now, Anthony. I had been hoping that since the shooting stopped, we might get sent on a mission to bring food back from Uganda, and then we could have escaped and gone home."

"I know," he said quietly.

They had discussed the idea the other night, one of the few times they'd really talked about running since their marriage.

"That's over now," she said. "They won't let a pregnant woman go on a food convoy."

She began to cry.

Anthony knew she was right and put his arms around her. Now that he had the chance to think about it, they had a baby on the way, and he did not want that baby growing up in the Lord's Resistance Army.

"We'll figure another way out," he whispered. "I don't know how. I don't know when. But I promise you, we will go home."

Florence clung to him tighter. "Thank you, Anthony."

———

Florence and Anthony stayed in Nesitu for the entire pregnancy. The bouts of morning sickness had stopped in her second trimester, and Florence continued to work at the hospital with Palmer and Joyce, learning how to splint broken bones, suture wounds, and clean burns, until her water broke the evening of May 1, 2000.

For all the time she'd spent in the hospital and even in her life back in Amia'bil, she had never seen a baby born. She had no idea what she was about to endure.

The pain began in her hips, dull and heavy at first. Then the contractions began, and Florence was terrified. The labor pain turned brutal. She could not take it lying down. It felt like someone was stabbing her in the spine every time a contraction came. She spent the night walking around their yard by lantern light. Anthony, Palmer, and Joyce took shifts supporting her. With Florence suffering and her strength fading around dawn, they took her to the field hospital.

The doctor examined her and found that the baby was presenting breech, which made the birth difficult and Florence weaker. Even so, at eleven o'clock that morning, a son slid out of her and tears poured from her eyes.

They cleaned him and laid him on Florence's chest. His eyes were open, and he seemed to look directly into hers. In that moment, she felt the overwhelming power of love and pure connection in a way she never knew imaginable, and she began to sob with sheer joy.

"Can you see how beautiful our baby is, Anthony?"

"I see how handsome our son is!" Anthony said, tears rolling down his cheeks, too. "He looks just like me!"

Florence laughed before going into the worst contraction yet.

"I thought it was over," she gasped when it passed.

"That's the placenta," Joyce said. "You need to get that out of you, Betty."

Palmer said, "She's right. You're losing a lot of blood. You need to push."

Florence pushed for two more hours. For a time, the doctor feared she was going to become infected. But at last, she was able to deliver the placenta and passed out cold.

Anthony sat at her side, holding the baby and watching Florence, who finally opened her eyes an hour later when the baby started fussing and crying.

"I think he needs to eat," Joyce said, and showed her how to hold the baby so he could find her breast. He clamped onto her nipple so hard she winced. But then the pain stopped, and she found it far more pleasant than she ever expected, a continuation and expansion of that feeling of instant connection she'd had at their first touch.

"You have a name yet?" Palmer asked.

"No," Anthony said.

"Kenneth," Florence said.

"Kenneth?"

"When I was a girl, we had a friend named Kenneth. He helped our family a lot. He was a good human, Anthony."

He smiled. "What better reason for a name?"

"Kenneth," Florence said, stroking the baby's back. "Welcome to the world."

"Kenneth Opoka," Anthony said, touching his head. "We are so grateful for you."

———

Around five that evening, Patrick came into the hospital in a rush.

"There you are," he said to Anthony, who had his back to him, sitting in a chair by Florence's bed. "I've been looking everywhere for you."

"We've been here," Anthony said, getting up with Kenneth in his arms. "Having a son."

In all the time Anthony had known Patrick, he'd almost never seen him nervous. But the sight of Kenneth swaddled in his friend's arms was enough to make him take a step back.

"I don't do babies," he said.

"But he looks like me."

"Don't care," Patrick said. "The Dinka are massing again. Our scouts saw multiple convoys come up out of Uganda to rearm the SPLA. The Arabs want us back in the fight. Kony wants us all to move to Rubangatek. Now."

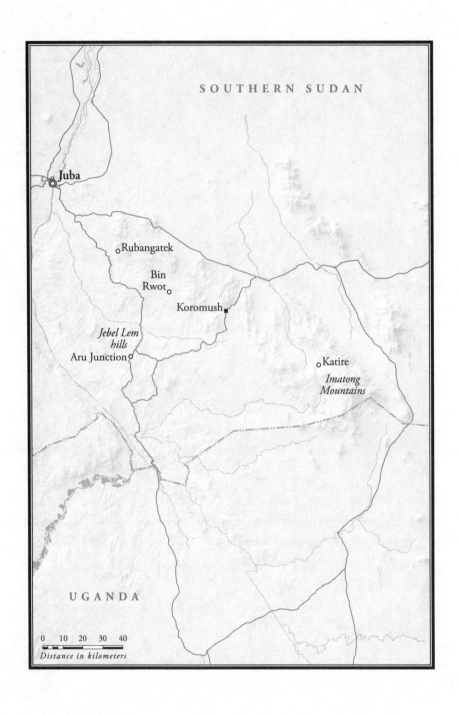

SOUTHERN SUDAN

Juba

Rubangatek

Bin
Rwot

Koromush

Jebel Lem
hills
Aru Junction

Katire

Imatong
Mountains

UGANDA

0   10   20   30   40
Distance in kilometers

Chapter Twenty-Nine

May 30, 2000
Rubangatek, Southern Sudan

Florence felt jittery, unprotected with Kenneth drowsing in her arms as she paced back and forth outside the hut Anthony had built for them as soon as they arrived at this new, smaller LRA base outside Juba.

"I don't understand why I can't go with you," she said when Anthony came out of the hut with his radio pack and a second pack with his gear and clothes.

"Because we're about to train for war again," Anthony said. "And they don't want our wives with us."

"But I want you with us," she said, hearing the fear in her voice.

Anthony heard it, too. "Remember what the old shopkeeper told me about Fear?"

Florence shrugged. "That it was just some voice of suffering."

"That's right. It's in our head, trying to convince us we are not enough to handle whatever we have to—"

Before he could finish, he heard Fatima start to yell at her children, demanding to know who had broken her clay pot and threatening hell, damnation, and a visit from Who Are You if someone didn't come forward and admit to it. Fatima, Nighty, and Christin lived no more than 150 meters away, on the other side of a boggy creek bottom, up against a dry, grassy hillside. Lily had hurt her leg and had remained behind with her children in Nesitu.

"It's always something with her," Florence said as Fatima raged on. "She'll stay on this even if one of the kids confesses. For hours. How do you stop *that* voice of suffering?"

Anthony chuckled. "I have no clue. Mr. Mabior didn't mention Fatima."

A pickup truck pulled up. Patrick was in the passenger seat.

"My ride," Anthony said.

Florence tried not to, but tears began to roll down her cheeks. "We'll miss you."

"You have no idea," Anthony said, tuning out Fatima, who'd taken her ranting to a whole other level. "I love you. I am grateful for you. And I promise I will send money for clothes for the baby."

Patrick called, "Sometime this year, Opoka!"

Anthony kissed Florence and Kenneth on the forehead.

"Stay alive," she said when he picked up his packs and tossed them in the back of the pickup. "I don't know what I'd do without you."

"You won't have to," he said, climbing into the back. "Now smile so that's the memory I'll take with me."

"You, too," Florence said, and adjusted her hold on Kenneth, who started fussing again. She looked down at the baby. "Say goodbye to Daddy!"

Then she did her best to smile at Anthony and to hold his gaze as the pickup pulled away.

When he and the truck were gone from her sight and all she could hear was Fatima picking up speed again, she fought back the emotion in her throat and looked down at her son, who did look so much like Anthony it made her heart ache.

"Just you and me now, little man," she said. "You and Mommy against the world."

———

For several months, Anthony and the signalers for three full battalions of LRA soldiers trained daily under combat conditions in the wilds southwest of Juba. The best part was that Albert was there. When he learned that Anthony was married and had a son, he was stunned.

"I'm an uncle?" Albert asked.

"You are."

"When do I meet him?"

"The sooner the better," Anthony said before hustling off to serve as Kony's signaler.

At the end of each day, when his fellow signalers were having their dinner and relaxing, Anthony retrieved an axe with a handle he had shortened and modified so he could swing it mostly one-handed, with his bad right hand helping to guide the direction of the blade. Albert came, too. Every night, they chopped wood, gathered it, and sold it to a merchant in the local market.

He and Albert told each other about their lives in the LRA. General Matata, Albert said, was a decent-enough leader.

"Patrick has always liked him," Anthony said.

"And thank God he's not as crazy as Brigade Commander Ongwen."

"I don't know him."

"That man is not a good human."

"Are we?"

Albert stopped chopping and stared into the distance. "I've tried to be."

"I have, too," Anthony said. "It has been easier since Florence, and definitely since Kenneth. It changes how you think."

"I hope so. Sometimes I don't think very well."

During those chopping sessions, Anthony told Albert about the things that the dying shopkeeper had taught him about suffering, and they seemed to help his younger brother. He delivered the money he earned to Florence once a month when he was given a two-day leave to visit her and the baby. There were two wonderful reunions and two terrible goodbyes in the months that followed. Each time he was forced to separate from Florence and Kenneth, he left more convinced than ever that he was a lucky, lucky man.

———

He did not see his family for almost six months before Kony showed heart and let Anthony return to Rubangatek with him for Christmas 2000.

But the night before they left for the LRA encampment and their wives, Kony had once again warned him about running.

"You know too much, Opoka," he said. "The TONFAS. Me. Our methods. If you ever tried to run, we'd have to hunt you down, Signaler. No matter where you went. We'd have to shut you up forever."

"I have no reason to run, Teacher," Anthony replied. "My family is here."

Anthony arrived in the encampment filthy, thirsty, and hungry, but most of all grateful to see Florence.

"You stink," she said when he tried to hug her. "I'll heat you up some water, get you a washbasin and some soap."

"But not before I see Kenneth."

Florence smiled, kissed him again. "But you have to be quiet."

"Like the smallest mouse," he whispered.

They walked over to the entrance. Florence carefully raised the blanket, and Anthony crouched to look inside, seeing Kenneth sleeping on his back.

"Wow," he said out loud. "He's big!"

Florence swatted him on the arm, put her finger to her lips while Kenneth squirmed for a new position and then settled. She lowered the blanket, and she waved Anthony to follow her.

"How did he get that big?" he whispered after her.

"They grow fast at this age," she whispered back. "And you've been gone a long time."

"Too long," he said, and tried to kiss her again.

Florence held him off, said, "You stink."

"I think you're going to have to boil this uniform."

"Twice," she said, and laughed.

———

Anthony went down into the creek bottom close to the hut, carrying a bucket of heated water, a towel, his second uniform, a razor, and soap in a washbasin. He set it all by the stream, stripped, and got down into the water up to his thighs. After dropping under, he took the bar of soap, dipped it in the hot water, and lathered every centimeter of skin before dunking again. Then he scooped out hot water with his hands and splashed his face enough to wilt his sparse whiskers. He shaved, dunked again. He climbed out and poured the rest of the bucket of hot water all over him.

After drying off, he got dressed, left his used uniform, and picked up the bucket and basin. Coming out of the creek bottom and rounding the hut, he saw Florence and was seized by the fact that after what had seemed an eternity, he was back with the girl he loved.

"You look better," Florence said when she saw him. "So handsome."

Anthony grinned. "And you are the most beautiful, funny, smart woman I know."

"You don't get around much."

The baby started squawking.

"I'm going to need you to stir that pot while I feed and change him," she said.

"I can do that one-handed."

"Ha ha," Florence replied, and retrieved Kenneth.

"Here's our big boy," she said as he snuggled into her neck. "You see Daddy, Kenneth?"

Anthony was delighted and fascinated as he came around to see his baby boy up close. Kenneth saw him and retreated slightly.

"It's okay," she soothed.

Kenneth kept taking glances at his father, who put his finger in his little hand.

"You are so big," he whispered. "I bet you can walk."

"We're not even crawling yet," she said. "Close, but not quite."

Kenneth began to squirm in her arms.

"You want to get down?" she said, turning him and putting him down on all fours.

He started rocking back and forth and giggling.

"That's all he does!" Florence said, laughing. "He wants to go, but he just does this rocking thing."

"Let me try," Anthony said, getting down on the mat on all fours with Kenneth.

The baby did not know what to make of that and stopped rocking.

"No, the rocking is good," Anthony said, and mimicked the motion.

Kenneth grinned and rocked again. Then Anthony crawled around, which stopped the rocking and caused the boy to look at him closely.

"You see?" Anthony said, turning to face him about a meter away. Then he sat back on his legs, grinned, and held out his good hand. "Come to Daddy."

Kenneth pushed himself up and tried again, back to giggling at every unsteady move.

"Come to Mommy and Daddy, Kenneth," Florence said, getting down beside Anthony.

The baby got excited seeing their arms stretched out. He moved one hand forward, then the opposite knee, then the opposite hand, and had raised his second knee when he collapsed and started crying.

"That was a crawl!" Florence said, moving to pick him up. "You did it! You moved forward for Daddy for Christmas!"

Seeing such a milestone in Kenneth's life after not being there for so many, Anthony threw back his head and crowed softly, feeling so much joy it surprised him.

He reached out, took Florence's hand, and placed it over his heart, knowing that tears were welling in his eyes and not caring.

"What?" she said.

"See my happiness?" he whispered.

Flo cocked her head and then nodded, emotion swelling. "I see it." Then she took his bad hand and put it over her heart. "See my happiness?"

"I see it, I feel it, I do," he said. "It's like a miracle, isn't it? All of us together like this?"

"The best present I could imagine," Florence said.

Alone in their hut after eating, they held each other and softly sang Christmas songs that Anthony barely remembered from church. But Florence remembered them all and coached him.

She told the story of her favorite Christmas. She was five. It was the day after Josca had come to bring her home from the measles ward.

"I thought I'd never be home again," she said, tears welling in her eyes as she smiled at the memory. "But my mother did not forget me."

"That was the Christmas she told you she would carry you forever."

"That's right," Florence said, and hugged him. "Thank you, Anthony."

"For what?"

"Remembering. For caring about me, about my life."

"I do."

"What was your favorite Christmas?"

Anthony closed his eyes and thought about that for a while.

"It's funny," he said. "When the LRA took me, they kept telling me to forget my life before. That the only thing that mattered was the Great Teacher's mission. I guess it's worked a little. I can't say one Christmas sticks out. But I remember it always being a day when we all went to church first. Then we went home, and there was singing and dancing and a feast where they butchered a goat and barbecued it. I remember the smell of that, the sounds of it."

"You'll smell and hear it all again."

"We will," Anthony said, and hugged her tight. "Someday."

Chapter Thirty

Ever mercurial, Joseph Kony changed plans overnight. He ordered all members of Control Altar, including Anthony, to move closer to the formidable Imatong Mountains.

"Why?" Florence asked.

"I heard him tell General Vincent and General Tabuley he doesn't trust the Arab leaders," Anthony said. "He thinks they're talking to Museveni about letting the UPDF come into Sudan to hunt us. If they do, he's going deep."

"Is that true? The UPDF is coming into Sudan?"

"I don't know. But he believes it."

"Why is he moving me and Kenneth, too? I thought it was safer here."

"Don't argue, Flo," Anthony said. "We'll be together for at least a month while we build a new barracks in a remote area called Bin Rwot. No one will know we are there. It will be safer for us. And we'll keep this hut in case we need to return."

Florence looked around, feeling a pang at the good memories she and her baby had shared there. But she also acknowledged that even the best moments had been soured by Anthony's absence.

"Okay," she said, happy at the idea of another month with him. "When do we leave?"

Anthony, Florence, Kenneth, and the inner core of Control Altar slipped out of the encampment at Rubangatek early the following morning. None of the thousand-man battalion that usually surrounded Kony went with them. The hundred bodyguards did.

Still, they were an armed force of nearly three hundred moving east-south-east through the bush toward the Imatongs. Even Florence carried an AK-47 knockoff, the first time since she'd been put to work in the hospital at Nesitu two years before. Marching well back on the middle of the three rails, she also carried a heavy pack and Kenneth strapped to her chest.

At the head of the middle rail, Anthony walked out in front of Joseph Kony between Yango leading the far-right rail and Brigade Commander Dominic Ongwen leading the far left. The Great Teacher's bodyguards shadowed them from the flanks and scouted the route ahead.

They reached Bin Rwot, or "Come God," shortly after dark. General Vincent had sent men ahead to build quarters for Kony and the wife who would sleep with him that night and the wife who would sleep with him the following night. Florence and Kenneth slept with Anthony fifteen meters from the back of the LRA supreme commander's hut. They were so tired they barely heard Kony laughing and one of his senior wives giggling.

The next day, Anthony and Florence began building themselves a home outside Control Altar, but inside the area being patrolled by the bodyguards. They were done within a week and had even erected a bamboo fence around it with a gate that swung open on ropes.

The Great Teacher decided that he liked using two radiomen in shifts. Anthony would spend a week shadowing Kony, and then he'd be replaced for a week by his boss, Signal Commander in Chief Charles Joura.

Anthony spent his first two weeks off with Florence and Kenneth, and they would both long remember those fourteen days in January 2001 as some of the happiest of their lives in the LRA. Florence's friend Palmer was there as well and took a photograph of the three of them and Kenneth beaming at her husband's camera. When Palmer's husband went to Juba, he had the photograph developed and two copies made.

"For when we are apart," Anthony told Florence when he gave her a copy. "So you remember how handsome I am."

"And you remember how beautiful I am?"

"I don't need a photograph to remember that. Your beauty is burned in my brain."

"Good answer."

"I thought so," he said, laughed, and kissed her.

Anthony was assigned to other top LRA battle commanders during the off weeks that followed, which were spent training for hit-and-run, constant-movement, guerrilla-style warfare with Kony's personal battalion, which moved to the area at the end of January. More battalions arrived in February, all of them put through the same training and then moved to other remote locations so the Great Teacher's current standing army of twenty thousand child soldiers would never be caught in one place.

Kony was growing ever more suspicious of government officials in Juba and Khartoum. In a fit of paranoia, he decided to leave Bin Rwot with his wives and children and head deep into the Imatong Mountains until he was more certain of his situation. Anthony dreaded having to go with him, but then found out that he would be rotated in and out of Kony's camp on one-month intervals.

Charles Joura went into the Imatongs first with the Great Teacher, his wives and children, a hundred bodyguards, and everything they could carry on their backs. When Anthony asked Kony where exactly they were headed, he pointed to one of the highest peaks on the map.

"I'll be able to think up there," he said. "Hear the spirits better."

In March, Anthony was assigned to Dominic Ongwen and to Anthony's old boss, Charles Tabuley, traveling between their encampments to train junior signalers. Or at least, that was the idea.

But then Commander Ongwen was attacked by Dinka forces in April. And in a development that shocked everyone, General Tabuley's battalion came under fire a good eighty kilometers inside Sudan by Ugandan army soldiers supported by helicopter gunships in May.

At the time, Anthony was with Tabuley's forces, which managed to slip away from the attack without sustaining heavy losses. But he knew what it meant. The UPDF was no longer respecting the border. With or without permission, the Ugandan army was now hunting Kony and the LRA wherever they were hiding.

The rebel group's intelligence officers quickly picked up word of hundreds of soldiers streaming north out of Uganda. The guards at the border were waving them through.

On the shortwave, Anthony heard Kony having a meltdown, calling the Sudanese government "a bunch of Arab traitors who will not even get on the wire with me to tell me why they have done this. Zero communication."

"What are your orders, Teacher?" General Tabuley asked.

"Fight," Kony said. "Make them pay."

———

What followed was the most difficult time Anthony and Florence had ever faced. They were separated for the better part of seven months. With the pace of attacks building, it was decided to keep Anthony out of the Imatong Mountains. As head of all battlefield signaling, Anthony was in or near combat on a daily basis.

He was also on the move almost constantly and never knew where he'd sleep. His only contact with Florence for three months was one brief call on the wire. He went to Commander Ongwen to ask for a week's leave in June and was denied.

By July, it seemed that Kony's efforts to engage the Sudan government were starting to work. They were getting more shipments of food and equipment.

In late August, Anthony was shot for the fourth time fighting the Dinka. The bullet went through his right thigh, just missing his femur and femoral artery.

The wound was bad enough, however, that he was sent to the LRA field hospital, which had moved to Bin Rwot. Florence and Kenneth stayed at his bedside as he recovered.

The attacks from Uganda slowed to a trickle as September came on. But various LRA groups were still engaged in battle with the Dinka near the border. Anthony listened to the radio chatter from the south because he often heard his younger brother Albert, now full-time signaler to General Matata, the same commander Patrick fought under most often.

Then, in the wake of the attacks on the United States on September 11, 2001, Anthony heard that the United States of America had named the Lord's Resistance Army a "terrorist organization," and because of that, the Sudan government had vowed to cut off all ties with Kony. The Great Teacher went ballistic. With his men quickly going hungry, he ordered multiple attacks on villages around the Imatong Mountains, where food and grains were looted and brought back.

In the tense months that followed, a rumor kept circling through the encampment at Bin Rwot. They were going to receive an important visitor soon. Anthony and Florence were told to clean their guns and keep them handy. And yet, they had a quiet Christmas, and New Year's Day 2002 passed with no important visitors and little word of combat.

That was about to change.

By the middle of January 2002, Kony's intelligence operators in northern Uganda were reporting a huge buildup of UPDF soldiers and equipment along the border. The Great Teacher came to Bin Rwot on January 20. To Anthony's surprise, he saw Lily with him. He almost did not recognize her at first. She'd been sick after a compound leg fracture and had aged.

Kony warned them they were about to be attacked without mercy by as many as one hundred thousand men.

"They will come here, and they will come to Rubangatek to try to annihilate us," Kony said, dressed in his combat fatigues. "But I have consulted with the spirits on the mountain. Jumma Driscer has advised that I empty this camp and Rubangatek, and that we should go on the offensive long before they get here.

"We are going to attack the Sudanese government today because they are joining the UPDF to fight us. We are going to have to fight the Sudanese, the Dinka, and the Ugandan army. All at once, all of us, alone. Anyone you will see on the battlefield besides the LRA will be your enemy. Any human besides the holy will be your foe."

Anthony looked around, seeing that there were roughly five hundred LRA soldiers there that day. The rest of the Great Teacher's troops were scattered through the Imatongs and east. How were they going to fight one hundred thousand soldiers?

It turned out they weren't.

Kony's plan called for all five hundred soldiers in Bin Rwot to go on standby in three groups. Two hundred would go with General Vincent. General Tabuley was given 150 men. So was General Bunyi.

The Great Teacher assigned three signalers to each group. Anthony would go with General Tabuley. The commander of all signalers, Charles Joura, would go with Bunyi. The strategy called for the three groups to attack the Jebel Lem hills, the small southern Sudan army barracks at Aru Junction, and the larger barracks at Moli in rapid succession and from three different directions.

Vincent and his men would come in from the northwest. Tabuley would attack from the north. Bunyi would march from the east and go straight to the critical junction of the supply routes before heading straight south to Moli. Kony would get up high where he could see the entire battlefield and call for adjustments.

"You will be attacking along a ten-kilometer battle line," Kony said. "But surprise will be with us. The spirits have said the Lord is on our side and we will prevail."

Before they left the camp, they were ordered to take what food they had and hide it in caves. Then the women and children were sent closer to the relative safety of the Imatongs.

"I will come find you," Anthony told Florence as he rushed about, packing.

Florence was worried. "One hundred thousand soldiers are hunting us?"

"Not today," he said. "And when they do come, you'll be hiding with Kenneth."

His little boy was up walking around, a toddler getting into mischief.

Anthony kissed Florence goodbye, then scooped up his son and tickled and hugged him.

As he walked away, heading for General Tabuley's camp, Anthony wondered when and for how long they'd be together again.

I already miss them. I've only just seen Flo and Kenneth, and I already miss them.

"How is your wound, Opoka?" Tabuley asked when he got there.

"It's tight, General, but it will loosen as we march."

The general seemed upset but said nothing for several minutes.

Finally, Tabuley said in a low voice, "I don't like this plan of the Great Teacher's."

Anthony frowned, glanced over, thinking that the general rarely disagreed with Kony.

"Sir?"

"We don't know how many Sudanese there are at Aru Junction, and we don't know how many UPDF there are already in the country and the area. We were given no time for proper reconnaissance."

The general's instincts were spot on. While the five hundred Lord's Resistance Army soldiers vastly outnumbered the Sudanese forces at Aru Junction, they were ill prepared to face the full brigade of UPDF already encamped at Moli and preparing to move north.

The Ugandan army soldiers and the Sudanese at Moli heard the fighting nine kilometers north at Aru Junction and were ready when the attack on their position came. The combat was brutal, with both sides using mortars, heavy machine guns, and recoilless rifles. The Ugandans also had antitank missiles that they shot at the LRA.

Anthony, who had been in the fight with Tabuley for much of the day, was wounded yet again. This time shrapnel flayed open his skin and skittered across the left side of his ribcage for almost twenty millimeters.

After hours of intense battle, the hardened LRA forced the Sudanese and Ugandan soldiers to retreat from Moli after sustaining heavy casualties. They took the barracks there, but at their own high cost. One hundred and thirty child soldiers died.

Five of the Great Teacher's most veteran field commanders also perished in the fighting, including Anthony's superior, Charles Joura, who died in an explosion, leaving the signal corps without a commander. Joura was the only loss of life among the radiomen that day, but strangely, five other signalers were taken out of combat by lower-leg wounds.

Kony's original plan called for the LRA to hold Aru Junction and Moli and blow six bridges in between the towns in an effort to slow the UPDF's supply lines north. But after hearing the number of casualties, the Great Teacher reversed himself and ordered retreat.

"We are going to regroup and then send forces into Uganda," he said. "We will take the attack to them, make them suffer for coming after us here."

Kony sent General Bunyi and his men down into northern Uganda to begin wreaking havoc in retaliation for what was being called Operation Iron Fist on the Juba FM radio station. He also ordered Anthony to rejoin Control Altar, not as his personal radioman, but as commander of all signalers in the LRA.

"You are now a real senior commander, Commander Tony," Kony said, beaming and clapping Anthony on the back. "I knew you would be the one to lead our communications. Here and in Kampala!"

———

Anthony felt that same rare warmth he always got when someone commended him or predicted a rosy future for him. But he also knew Kony had an ulterior motive of controlling him, and did everything he could to extinguish the warmth by telling himself he was being dragged deeper and deeper into the Great Teacher's nightmare.

If there was any consolation, it was that Kony decided in late February 2002 that he and his wives would accompany the women, children, and wounded, which meant Anthony would get to move ahead of, but not far from, Florence and Kenneth. And he would get to sleep with and keep watch over them at night.

"Where are we going, Teacher?" Anthony asked at the end of the first day's march.

"Safety," he said.

When he went to Florence and Kenneth, she was sleeping with their little boy in her arms. Florence roused when Kenneth woke and wanted to get into his father's arms.

"How was the hike?"

"Long," she said with a sour face. "I got sick twice."

"You okay?"

She whispered. "I think I'm pregnant again, Anthony."

Anthony grinned. "Really?"

"It's not good, Anthony."

His face fell.

Florence said, "No, no, I mean, I'm glad it will be our child. I really am. But this means we are going to have another baby in the LRA, which means another target for Kony's enemies."

Anthony felt it, too, the instant threat that arose when their daily way of life was considered. They were constant moving targets. Through no fault of their own. But there was no denying what Florence was saying.

"I hear you," he whispered. "I do. But for you and me to try to run now? From deep in here? There is no saying you or Kenneth would survive. Or me. Let's wait until we get to Uganda."

"If we get to Uganda."

Sensing Kony was on the run, Museveni sent more troops, more helicopters, and more rockets and ammunition north into Sudan. Sensing Museveni was leaving his rear guard open, Kony sent hundreds of LRA soldiers into Uganda ahead of the main group, including Dominic Ongwen, and told them to start killing civilians.

Hunted, under regular attack from above, it took the main group almost a month to get close to the Ugandan border. They marched in three rails. Luckily, Anthony was assigned to the front of Florence's rail, "the rail of pregnant women," as she called it, and he was able to sleep with her and Kenneth at night. They began and ended each day as a family, happy to have lived, and happy to be headed toward home.

But then ghoulish and barbaric reports started to circulate on the LRA shortwave radios. Soldiers under Brigade Commander Ongwen's control had forged ahead of the main group. They encountered a funeral with sixty mourners. One of the mourners stole an LRA soldier's gun. When Ongwen heard, he sent the soldier back to get his weapon. When no one came forward, the soldier demanded the sixty attendants cook and eat the corpse. Believing they would be spared, the mourners agreed and did so only to be executed after the fact. The gun was eventually found and Ongwen expressed his approval. So did Kony.

In late April, they rendezvoused with troops led by General Tabuley and headed straight south under moonlit skies. Kony believed he had to take the war into Uganda if he was to counter Museveni's strategy.

As the rails traveled across the savannas, Florence honestly did not know how she'd made it this far pregnant. But then sleeping Kenneth shifted in her arms and she knew.

Love, Florence thought, and kissed her little boy on the head. *We made it because of love, and we will survive and escape because of love.*

For almost two weeks, Florence wrote those words again and again in her mental book of dreams as they repeatedly tried to cross into Uganda only to be thwarted by the presence of UPDF patrols along the border at night and helicopters searching for them during the day while they were holed up out of sight. By the fourth failed attempt to leave southern Sudan, she'd begun to doubt whether a crossing was possible.

Then, deep in a wilderness area, Patrick slipped off by himself during the day and returned a few hours later with word that the border about two kilometers away was high barbed wire with dirt roads on both sides. A gate there allowed truck traffic to and from the countries. It was guarded on both sides by soldiers in small tin-roofed shacks. There were barracks on both sides as well, full of Ugandan and Sudanese soldiers. But about 250 meters west of the gate, Patrick had spotted an almost-blind spot where he thought they might get through the fence unnoticed.

"If there was the right kind of action east of the gate," he cautioned. "Like a diversionary force attacking the barracks in broad daylight when they won't expect it."

Kony, Tabuley, Vincent, and Ongwen listened to him. Around four that afternoon, they ordered the rails forward, and the women were told to pray along with the Great Teacher. Flo refused to pray with him. She just kept telling herself she was protected.

They moved quietly through the dense underbrush until reaching a ridge with the border fence below them several hundred meters. Anthony, Patrick, and two other fighters slipped ahead to watch while other LRA boys moved into position.

Florence sat on the forested hillside with Kenneth in her lap, knowing she was on her own now, knowing she was supposed to get up and run when she heard the shooting, and telling herself over and over that they would survive and thrive because of the power of love.

She was sure of it.

Moments later, from above the forest canopy, she heard a tremendous crack she feared was another missile. But then it became thunder and lightning and gale winds driving rain as torrential as she had ever seen.

———

The rain came so swift and so hard it caught Anthony, Patrick, and the guards on both sides of the border crossing by surprise. The rain intensified, fell in billowing drapes. The lightning and thunder turned violent enough that the border guards abandoned their posts in the shacks and ran for the shelter of the barracks.

"Go," Patrick said, tapping Anthony on the shoulder.

They went to the fence and had it clipped open in seconds.

During the hour that followed, as the storm went on and on, they kept a lookout for activity at the barracks as hundreds and then more than a thousand in the retreating LRA convoy slipped through the fence and into Uganda.

Florence hurried through early, holding a blanket over Kenneth, and smiling at Anthony as she passed, saying, "After everything, we just walk right through."

"Sometimes we get lucky," he replied, grinning back at her.

During the night, they marched south and deeper into Uganda. It was the first time Anthony had been in his homeland in almost eight years, and he kept focused on that happy thought. Florence did, too, writing in her mental book of dreams that she was almost home now. They halted after dawn, some ten kilometers from the border. The boys and men found dry wood and brought water. The girls and women lit fires and prepared to cook.

Florence helped while keeping an eye on Kenneth, who played with another little boy. They'd no sooner set pots on the fires than they heard the chug of gunships coming yet again.

"Run!" Anthony yelled at her.

Florence snatched up her pack, her gun, and Kenneth and dashed after her husband deeper into the forest, hearing machine-gun fire behind them.

Despite being hounded all day by the helicopters and ground troops trying to intercept them, they managed to cross the Achwa River at dusk and head cross-country. Kony seemed shaken after hearing how many of his kidnapped boys and girls had died in this most recent attack, and he ordered no fires be lit.

Forced to move in daylight by Ugandan army patrols, they were assaulted twice more the following day and slept in deep cover overnight. In the morning, the Great Teacher finally owned up to the danger posed to anyone who continued to follow him, as well as to the burden of feeding such a large group.

"Any woman with two or more children and any woman with one child whose husband has died in battle can leave," he declared. "There is no one to protect you here. You are set free."

At the time, in early May of 2002, Florence was more than three months pregnant. Anthony immediately went to General Tabuley and argued that she should be set free.

"She has two children," he said. "One in and one out."

"Nice argument, Opoka," the general replied. "But Teacher and General Vincent and I believe if we release Betty, then you will try to follow her. As a matter of fact, we've decided to give you a minder who will keep an eye on you from now on."

Anthony swallowed his rage, said, "I have done nothing to make you suspicious of me, General. I have been nothing but a loyal soldier of the LRA. I just want Betty and—"

"The spirits that dwell in Kony disagree," Tabuley said, and turned away.

He went and found the Great Teacher with his wife Evelyn, who was begging him unsuccessfully to free her because she had two of his children. Anthony waited until she'd stomped off, told him the situation, and asked why Florence would not be released with the other women when she was clearly with her second child.

The LRA leader smiled at him. "She cannot go because you are important to me, to the cause, Opoka. And because you know too much. About me. The TONFAS. How I conduct war."

"I promise you, Teacher, I am going nowhere except where you tell me to go," Anthony insisted with his head bowed. "Please, I beg the good in—"

Kony grew angry, yelled, "Are you the one who ordered Betty's abduction? Were you the one who decided she could find her own husband? You? No. I did all this, and I decide if and when your wife is released. Now get out of my sight. You and your wife shall be separated. And you retain your rank, but consider yourself permanently assigned to Tabuley, Commander Tony."

Chapter Thirty-One

October 9, 2002
North of Aringa, Northern Uganda

Late in the day and fully into her pregnancy, Florence fast-waddled more than trotted as she and Kenneth and a hundred other moms, children, and LRA boys moved quickly and quietly along a secluded game trail favored by elephants, cape buffalo, lions, and leopards. She was on edge, unable to shake the pressure of the situation. They'd spooked several very, very big animals in the bush just a few minutes earlier. Two times since dawn, they'd been shot at by gunships. And behind them, a Ugandan army patrol was hunting them on the ground. She'd been assigned as a combat medic. Three times since dawn, she'd patched up wounded men, which was exhausting.

Kenneth, now a two-year-old, pulled on her hand.

"Mama, where we go?" he asked.

"I don't know, baby," she said. "I'm never told."

That was true. For almost five months now, since shortly after Kony ordered her separated from Anthony, she'd been marching blindly behind one abusive and uncommunicative LRA commander after another.

She'd known exactly where she was at the beginning of the ordeal. Her original group, which numbered five hundred, had been led by General Vincent. They'd crossed two more rivers the day after she and Anthony were separated. Kony's boys attacked a displaced persons camp, got food, and then they all melted back into the bush.

But from that point on, things got fuzzy for her. The looted food had run out in days, and they'd been forced to get by on adyebo leaf, wild yams, and red chili plants. They'd attacked a tribe called the Madi for food. And then they'd stayed for almost two weeks near the Ayugi River, a tributary of the White Nile. Florence was made a field medic, which forced her to carry medical supplies as well as food and Kenneth when he was too tired to walk.

But then she heard that Kony had ordered other LRA groups to the displaced persons camps his violence had helped create in Uganda. Those attacks had brought the UPDF back to the area in force, and they had been flushed out of the Ayugi River bottom and on the run ever since.

In August, she'd heard that the town of Torit in southern Sudan had been taken by the Dinka rebels and that there was talk of the LRA being allowed back into the country to fight them. More recently, she'd listened to an FM radio news report that said the Ugandan government had ordered all civilians north of Gulu into camps while the LRA was hunted down.

One by one, Museveni said in a recording. *We will hunt them down one by one until they are gone.*

With the Ugandan army harassing them almost constantly, Florence had lost track of days, of time and place. But as they hurried along the game path that day, they passed an opening that gave her a view of a smaller river flowing into a large one.

That has to be the Ayugi again, she thought. *The big one's the White Nile.*

Though it was not raining at that moment, late September and early October storms had caused both rivers to flood and blow their banks. The lower Ayugi had been eighty meters wide the last time she'd crossed it. Now it was double that size. The same was true of the White Nile, one hundred meters across and relatively lazy when she'd last walked beside it, now a raging, flooded beast, at least two hundred meters across, with a churning, frothing center.

An hour before sunset, they reached the west bank of the Ayugi River bottom. A helicopter came for them, the third one that day. Florence grabbed Kenneth, ran to a ditch where someone had been dumping and burning trash. She pushed him down and covered him as best she could before the shooting started—strafing machine-gun fire from the chopper in repeated passes and then light arms from the LRA and from the UPDF patrol atop the bluff. As dusk began to settle, the gunship departed, and the patrol got reinforcements.

Florence heard people yelling that they had to move toward the White Nile.

She got Kenneth up into a crouch, noticing they'd been lying on five or six large, empty plastic bottles amid full plastic bags and other loose trash that had not yet been burned.

"Mama?" Kenneth whined. "I no like guns."

"Mama doesn't like them, either," Florence said. "But we've both got to be brave now, okay? You Mama's brave little boy?"

He nodded. She took him by the hand, not noticing Kenneth had picked up one of the smaller plastic bottles. They ran through the scattered trees near the flooding along the Ayugi River until they'd passed a line of LRA boys assembling logs and limbs to fight behind and reached the main group. She learned the plan was to cross the Ayugi. It was their only chance.

Cross it? she thought in an instant panic. *I can't swim. Kenneth can't swim. How in God's name are we going to get across the Ayugi?*

She walked away, feeling like she was in her first trimester again, ready to heave her guts out at any minute.

I can't do this. I can't, and I'm going to die and so is my boy and my baby!

Looking out in the fading light at the confluence of the raging, roiling rivers, Florence shook her head at the impossibility of what they were asking. *But what about those boys out there already?* She put her hand to her brow, seeing the vague shapes of soldiers swimming above the confluence, where the Ayugi split around an island of sorts with a few trees and many tangles of grasses, brush, and rushes. The boys in the water had ropes made of several ropes tied together trailing behind them.

The idea was that they'd rig a lifeline from the west bank to the island, and then a second from the island to the east bank of the river. Each person would tie themselves to the lifeline and drag themselves sideways along the rope for eighty meters to the island, where they'd untie from the first rope and move to the second.

But what about Kenneth? If she was tied to the rope and lifeline, and holding on to the lifeline as well, she had to have him tied to her, right? Florence would insist on that when the time came, but how was she going to keep her little boy's head above water if she was using her hands to pull them along the rope?

If she couldn't use her hands, she couldn't cross, because Kenneth would probably drown on the way. And if she couldn't cross, they were probably going to be shot by the UPDF like so many other women and girls unlucky enough to be slaves to the LRA and the Great Teacher.

A dread unlike any other seized Florence. East, west, in both directions lay not only her death and her unborn baby's, but Kenneth's. And then she noticed her son sitting in the wet leaves, oblivious to their peril, playing with the plastic bottle. She remembered the larger bottles back there in the trash ditch.

An idea hit her.

"Kenneth, Mama wants you to stay right here. Do not move until I get back, okay?"

He didn't like it, but he nodded. Florence turned around and took off in her rapid waddle. An LRA soldier tried to stop her from going beyond the barricade, but she ignored him and kept going despite the steady shooting coming from high on the bluff. Keeping to the shadows in the river bottom, Florence made it back to where she thought they'd taken cover. She couldn't find the ditch until she smelled the burnt odor of it and tracked the trash pit on the wind. She emptied two of the larger trash bags and put as many plastic bottles in them as she could find before putting each of them inside other trash bags, then waddled and skipped back to the barricades in the last dim light.

Rigging the ropes across the Ayugi River took more than two hours. The first to go, an LRA boy, tied himself to the lifeline under the glow of a red lamp around six thirty that evening.

Florence watched him wade out into the floodwaters. He faded almost immediately into dark shadows. The clouds had parted a bit, revealing the moon in its waxing crescent, barely giving enough light to see his silhouette going deeper, seeming to struggle with his footing before he disappeared into the blackness of the river and the night.

The UPDF patrol left the bluff and attacked about the time the tenth person got on the lifeline. The Ugandans began lobbing mortar rounds into the trees. Flashes and detonations. Fire and destruction. Florence held Kenneth tight through the bombardment, soothing him, waiting their turn, and desperately hoping that love was enough to conquer her inability to swim and that her idea would get them both safely to the other side.

Around nine that night, she was told they would likely go into the river around midnight. She saw that Kenneth was fed and put the only little blanket she had on his shoulders and got to work in the light of a small flashlight

Anthony had given her as a present. She blew air into the crushed plastic bottles until they straightened and screwed the lids on tight. There were six large bottles and four small bottles. Dividing the large bottles evenly, Florence put them inside and to either wall of one of the trash bags before tying off the top and cinching the bag down the middle with twine to create two wings filled with air bottles. She put the four small bottles in a second trash bag and tied it the same way. Finished, thinking it just might work, Florence set her invention aside and shut off the flashlight, meaning to close her eyes until they were called.

And then the first contraction hit.

It was short, and she gritted her way through the sensation, believing it was like others she'd suffered intermittently over the past month. She felt another about thirty minutes later, and a third a half hour after that before her water broke and she groaned at the impossibility of her situation, knowing for sure now that she was in active labor.

———

Near midnight, Florence lay beside Kenneth, panting after the longest contraction yet. They were still coming fairly far apart, twenty minutes by her last rough count. Mortars were still falling, and the battle was getting closer when one of the other women came with a big flashlight and shook her, saying it was their turn to cross soon. Or she could wait until the end.

She figured she had fifteen, maybe eighteen minutes before the next contraction hit. Florence said, "We'll go now."

Before she could second-guess herself, she woke Kenneth, put his blanket in her pack, strapped her rifle to the pack, and put it on her back. Then she picked up her invention and held her hand out to Kenneth.

"Where we go, Mama?" Kenneth yawned even as the gunfire behind them quickened.

"To a safe place," she said, and squeezed his hand. "Somewhere the bullets can't find us."

At the edge of the floodwater, there were more flashlights, and she was able to show the soldiers there what she wanted them to do. In short order, they put Kenneth into the third and fourth trash bags and tied them tight under his armpits. They held up Florence's big, improvised flotation device and tied him to it with rope, belly down, then linked a second piece about a meter long from his chest to the rope tied around Florence's upper back. A last length of rope connected her to the overhead line. Then they tied the smaller float under Kenneth's chest and chin to keep his face out of the water.

"Where we go, Mama?" Kenneth asked, the fear palpable in his voice.

"On an adventure."

"What that?"

"This."

"Ready?" one of the LRA boys asked.

"No, but we're going anyway. Can you lift him to me?"

He nodded. Florence held her son below the floats and waded him out into the floodwater and the darkness, feeling the tug of the rope that connected her to the lifeline, telling herself she could do this. She promptly went knee deep in a muck of mud, cattails, and reeds. Twice she almost keeled over trying to free herself. Three times she almost dropped Kenneth.

But after almost thirty meters of the floodwaters, she heard the rushing water in the channel in front of her and felt the fear build inside her. Rather than succumb to it, she remembered what Anthony had learned from the dying shopkeeper, that there were four main voices of suffering and that Fear was the worst, the one that cut you off from God, from the universe, the misery that said you did not trust powers beyond yourself, that you did not believe.

"I believe," she whispered to herself. "I do."

"Mama," Kenneth began.

"You hold on to that rope and keep your head up, now," Florence said, setting him belly down in the water, feeling more than seeing that she was right, her boy was floating shy of the current. "If you go underwater, you hold your breath. Mama will bring you up."

All of a sudden, from an angle she didn't expect, off toward the Nile, a heavy machine gun opened up. White-hot tracers ripped through the trees.

"Mama!"

"Hold on to that rope. Mama's got you."

The LRA boys returned fire. Quickly it was all-out war, unfolding not two hundred meters away. Bullets whizzed past their heads.

"I believe," she said, holding tight to the lifeline with her right hand and to the rope that tethered her to Kenneth with the left. She waded into the full flow of the river.

Her feet went out from under her almost immediately, and she fought not to scream as her feet, legs, and lower body rose up on the raging current that was trying to drag her downstream toward the confluence with the Nile. Florence dangled from the lifeline by her right hand. Her feet and lower legs found the wings of Kenneth's big float. She pressed her calves tightly against the sides of it, and shouted, "Kenneth, are you all right?"

"I scared!" he shouted.

"Don't be, Mama's got you," Florence said, taking her left hand off his tether and grabbing the lifeline. She slid her left hand along the line and then her right, pulling them farther out into the main channel of the river.

It began to rain. Twice in the next seventy meters, she ran into a standing wave in the river. Water rushed over her shoulders and then over her face, forcing her to hold her breath and pull wildly to get free and come up sputtering for air.

"Kenneth!"

"I here!" he yelled from between her legs.

The second time it happened, she was more surprised than the first. The current twisted her shoulders, submerged her, and her feet almost came free of the wings of Kenneth's float. She almost let go of the lifeline, but then did the right thing and slid her hands and hauled them sideways again and again.

"Oh God, please," she gasped when she came free of the second wave. "No more."

With two more pulls, she felt they had moved into some kind of eddy and tried to put her feet down. She immediately sank in mud above her knees. "We made it!"

"Quiet!" a male voice hushed in the darkness.

She wanted to scream and shout but did as she was told. She kept moving along with the line, floating Kenneth until she had to pick him up, fighting against the muck and the reeds and the night and the close-quarter combat playing out behind her. She felt dry land. A hand reached out to help her up.

"You did good," the boy no older than thirteen said, holding a flashlight in his teeth and untying her rope from the lifeline. "Let's get you to the second line. The water's faster, but it's not as far to the other side."

"Faster?" Florence said, and wanted to cry.

The current was so swift that the moment she stepped off the opposite side of the island, it grabbed her lower body and Kenneth and his float and popped them up on the surface, the action yanking hard at her hands and shoulder sockets as she clung to the lifeline. But it *was* a shorter distance, less than seventy meters. Through the rain, she could see the charcoal smudge of the east bank of the river right there in front of her, and once she had Kenneth stabilized with her feet, she began pulling and hauling herself sideways with more confidence. A little more than halfway across the channel, the contraction hit her like a knee to her gut, a blow that radiated into her spine and down her legs. She couldn't help it. She pulled back her legs, lost control of Kenneth, and screamed through the worst of it as they both dangled there in the raging water.

The contraction faded at last.

She gasped for air, then yelled, "Kenneth?"

"Mama! I hold breath. Can we get out of water?"

Florence wanted to throw her head back and cry for joy, but instead found the sides of the float's wings again, pressed her feet into them, felt Kenneth's body there, and yanked herself sideways again and again and again, saying, "Yes, we can get out of the water. Yes, we can."

A flashlight with a red filter came on several meters away. "You're almost here," a woman said. "Two more pulls and reach out for my hand."

Florence did, saw the woman's hand extended, and reached for it at the same time the knot that secured her to the lifeline unraveled. The woman's fingers slipped through hers. They broke away.

"No!" Florence screamed and threw both hands toward the bank before she went under. Her fingers found thick roots. She held on to them like the last things keeping her alive and then clawed up, finding more roots, and hauling herself to the surface.

"Kenneth!"

She heard no answer. "Kenneth!"

The woman reached down, got hold of Florence's rope, and pulled her up onto the bank, Kenneth along with her. The toddler had gone under, breathed in water, but almost immediately started coughing and hacking.

She got them both up against a massive tree trunk facing away from the river and the ongoing combat.

"He's going to be okay," the woman said. "Just a scare."

"I'm in labor."

"Let me check you."

"Are you a nurse?"

"As close as you're going to get."

"Do you know Joyce?"

"I do."

"I worked for Joyce in Nesitu."

"I'm Ellen, and I worked with Joyce back in Uganda."

Ellen checked Florence's cervix and said, "Not tonight. You're only two centimeters dilated. Maybe midday tomorrow. Rest a while. I'll come back to help you move farther away from here."

Sighing with relief, Florence continued to soothe Kenneth until he'd coughed all the river water out and clung to her, shivering. She clung back, happy that she wasn't having this baby anytime soon. They both fell asleep.

———

It felt like forever to her but was probably more like twenty minutes when heavy machine-gun fire began again, from the west bank of the river, shooting at the island and the east side of the Ayugi where she lay. Odd bullets began whacking the enormous tree they were hiding behind and taking down leaves and branches all around them.

"Mama!" Kenneth cried.

"You'll be fine," she said in a shaky voice, holding him tight. "You've got Mama."

The rain stopped. The shooting lessened.

She peeked around the tree, saw lights back on the west bank where she'd built Kenneth's float. The machine gun started up again. Tracers tore through the island's vegetation. The LRA soldiers still stacked up there, waiting to cross the last channel, were returning fire. So were the soldiers who'd already crossed. Almost every one of them ran by, either not seeing her or ignoring her as they got into a new battle position.

When Florence drew back behind the tree, she felt something shift inside her before she was hit by a monumental contraction that locked her up, unable to hear her son crying, the rattle of gunfire, or the smack of bullets against trees all around her. As it faded, she collapsed in a pool of sweat.

"Mama?" Kenneth whimpered. "What wrong?"

"I don't care what that woman said, this baby's coming tonight, little man," she gasped as the combat behind her turned ferocious and another contraction began.

The contraction passed. She used the little flashlight to show him a low spot against the massive tree where he'd be protected by the ridges of the roots.

"You get down in there and keep your head low. Mama's going to scream every once in a while, but she's going to be fine. You just stay down there until I tell you it's okay to come up."

"Okay," he said, but when she shone the light on his face, he was crying.

The poor little kid looked awful—so frightened, hungry, and exhausted that it made Florence feel helpless about their situation. But she kept the light on until he'd burrowed his head into the little pocket between the tree roots and curled up fetal.

"I love you, Kenneth," she said.

"Love you, Mama," he said, sniffling.

Florence shut off the light, set it down, rolled over on her knees, and got to her feet. She held on to the tree with both hands, rested her head against the trunk, waiting for the contraction she knew was coming sooner than later.

It's just new love coming into your life, Flo tried to tell herself. *That's all this is, and what could be better?*

The pain that surged next was so shocking she felt like she was going to lose consciousness. But then it plateaued, and she managed to hang on to the ancient tree and slowly squat into the rest of the contraction. When it ended, she stood up, leaning against the trunk, sweat pouring off her until the next round began and she squatted once more. This time, she pushed and screamed her way through it.

Time seemed to evaporate.

The battle seemed to vanish.

There was only Florence and the night and the giving of new life. The fourteenth time she squatted and pushed, she felt the baby's head crowning at the end of the contraction.

It began to rain again, which cooled her body and wet her lips.

"Okay, okay, okay," she whispered to herself as she rested her head and arms against the tree, odd bullets still smacking the opposite side of the trunk and gouging the dirt around the base. "You can do this, Flo. Just one more now."

At the first sense of a contraction, Florence held her breath and dropped into her squat. She pushed as hard as she could, yelling as the baby's head came out. Grunting, panting, she forced herself to take another big breath and push until she couldn't take it anymore and screamed and screamed until she felt the shoulders pass.

Head against the tree, she reached between her legs and guided the baby fully out and up into her arms.

"Oh my," she croaked, feeling gigantic relief. "You're a slippery one, aren't you?"

Then she heard a slight cough. She slapped the newborn's bum twice and was rewarded with a squawk and crying that put a huge grin on Florence's face.

"What that, Mama?" Kenneth asked in the darkness.

Florence felt around as the baby cried, and laughed. "You have a baby brother."

———

Another contraction hit her, weaker than before, but it still wobbled her, made her turn around and slide her back down the trunk, her second son squawking again, announcing himself to the world in the middle of a battle that continued to sputter and rage around her. She knew enough from delivering Kenneth that she wasn't finished, and she wasn't out of danger.

As before, the placenta did not deliver quickly. Between contractions, she found the little flashlight, turned it on, admired her baby for a second, still covered in blood, before putting the light in her mouth and groping in her pack for her medic's kit. She found scissors, alcohol swabs, and surgical thread, which she used to clean and tie off the umbilical cord in two places before cutting down the middle.

An LRA soldier came up the bank to her left, turned, and opened fire at the opposite side of the river before running off. The shots, so close, caused the baby to startle and cry again.

"There, there," she said, shaken as well and trying to soothe the infant. "Mama's here."

Another contraction hit. She dug her heels into the soil on the riverbank and pushed and pushed until she felt the entire placenta come free. Florence fell back against the tree in total relief and total exhaustion. The pace of shooting had fallen off again, this time almost to an irregular shot now and then, and then nothing.

She did not know why. She did not care why.

In the blessed silence, the baby fussed. She turned on the flashlight and saw his mouth trying to find her breast. She moved him to her nipple, feeling him latch on almost immediately. Florence wondered how that was possible in the middle of a gunfight.

But it was. He was sucking.

And in that moment, she was overcome with a rush of emotion that left her knowing that even though he was less than an hour old, even though he was born under the most vicious of circumstances, she already loved her second son as much as she loved her first.

Florence fell asleep a few minutes later with Kenneth beside her, hiding in the roots of the tree, and her new son lying on her chest, protected in her arms.

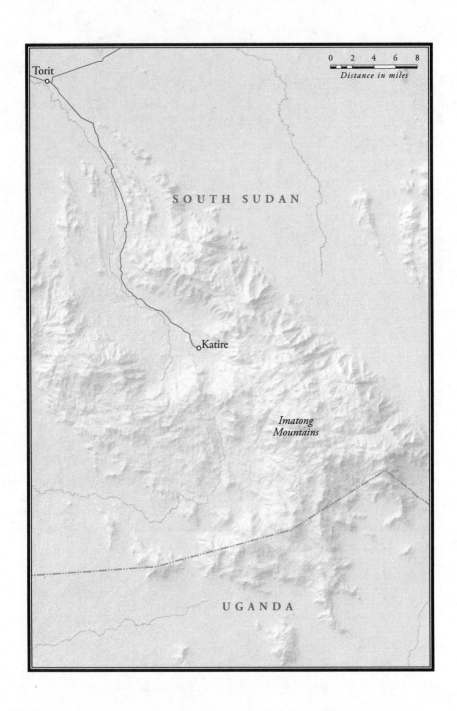

Chapter Thirty-Two

The lull in combat and the break in the rain lasted several hours, and Florence slept deeply. But as dawn came on, the shooting from the far bank of the river started again.

When she peeked around the tree, she saw that the last few LRA soldiers were coming across the channel on the lifeline. A boy came up the bank, carrying a pack and rifle. She recognized him as the thirteen-year-old who'd helped her across the island the night before. There were other LRA soldiers shouting in the forest now, telling everyone to fall back.

The baby began squawking. The boy looked over and saw Florence there, trying to get him to nurse again.

"He's a young one!" he said, his eyes lighting up as he came over and crouched by them.

"Last night," she said, smiling weakly. "Or this morning, actually."

"A boy," he said approvingly. "What's his name?"

"I don't know yet."

"You should call him Boniface."

"Boniface?"

"It means someone who does good things," he said, then smiled.

"Oh."

"You should get out of here. UPDF's coming."

"I don't know if I can move yet," she said.

Someone yelled, "Boniface, fall back!"

The boy laughed. "It's also my name."

He stood up then and took two steps beyond the tree before a heavy machine gun opened fire from the island, not seventy meters away. The heavy bullets strafed Boniface side to side, then whizzed past her and ripped into the trunks of trees facing the river. Florence gaped in horror at what remained of the boy, one minute delighted by a newborn's presence in the middle of combat, the next gone.

LRA soldiers opened fire from deeper in the cover. Their bullets whizzed right by her, going the other way. She was caught in a cross fire.

"Mama!" Kenneth screamed.

Florence slid them down until she lay flat on her back, her head cradled in the tree roots, holding on to her infant as he tried to find her breast.

We're going to die right here. All of us.

Despite her ragged state, despite the fear paralyzing her, she knew she had to get out of there. She had to save her boys.

My boys! Anthony's boys! Our boys!

But she honestly did not know if she had the strength to get to her feet, much less run, carrying two little ones through a combat zone. The heavy machine gun swept back her way again, gnawing at the far side of the trunk before continuing laterally along the bank toward the confluence with the Nile. She felt the impact of the heavy bullets smashing the tree, refilling her with fear. For her sons. For herself.

But gazing at her nursing newborn, and then at little Kenneth curled up under the roots, arms over his head, something changed in Florence. Her love for them triggered instincts deep in her genes, mother instincts that took the fear coursing through her every cell and transformed it into raw, burning rage.

Flo sat up, wild-eyed, held her newborn with one arm, and unstrapped her AK-47 from her pack before emptying the pack on the ground. She took the two loaded banana clips for the rifle, set them by the gun, and found two lengths of cloth she used as extra skirts, one to tie the baby to her chest. The other she folded and tucked to cradle his head. She put two packets of cooked rice and beans back in the pack along with her canteen and medic's kit and left the rest in the dirt.

"Kenneth!" she shouted when the machine gun went quiet to reload. "Crawl out!"

Her oldest son hesitated until she pulled on his foot. "Now!"

He wiggled backward out of the tree roots, sat up, and looked at the baby, then over her shoulder at the dead boy, with a ghastly expression.

"Don't look there," Florence said. "You're going to get in the pack now."

"In?"

"In."

Kenneth nodded. The machine gun started up, raked back their way. She grabbed him and pressed him to the tree as the bullets slammed into the trunk.

The bullets continued downriver. She picked up Kenneth and put him in the pack.

"Crouch down," she said, sitting in front of the pack with her back to it so she could get her arms through the shoulder straps and buckle it. "Hold tight."

Florence buckled the waist belt loosely, slid the banana clips between her hips and the belt, and then snugged it. She picked up the gun and used it to slowly stand.

It was agony every centimeter of the way. Her belly, her legs, her insides, her entire body felt battered and shaky. But when the machine-gun fire started sweeping back upriver, that mother instinct possessed her once more. As the bullets slashed the opposite side of her tree yet again, Florence fed her maternal rage with her love for her sons until she burned head to toe with full-blown bloodlust.

Prior to this moment in her life, Florence had only been a witness to combat. She had never fired her gun except in training. But now the training kicked in.

Thumbing down the safety lever, Florence shouldered the AK-47. The instant the machine-gun bullets swept upstream beyond her, she stepped out from behind the tree that had given shelter and sanctuary to her and her family.

"I've had enough!" she screamed.

Flo yanked on the trigger, firing most of the thirty-two-round banana clip in short bursts at the flash and fire coming out the muzzle of the heavy machine gun on the island now. When her action clanked open, smoke curling from the barrel, the big gun had gone silent.

From the bottom of her soul, Florence screeched at the reeds where the machine gunner had been firing from, releasing every bit of her fury and victory.

"I am their mother! I would carry them forever!"

She heard the chug of a helicopter coming. Other guns on the island started barking.

Florence turned and ran with her sons, bullets pinging at her heels.

———

The leaden skies opened up yet again, spewed a deluge that made it even harder to see in the dense bush as Florence clawed at vines and ran forward wildly, ignoring Kenneth's frightened squeals, trying to get her boys far from the riverbank and combat. When she finally slowed, she realized she had no idea where she was.

"I wet, Mama," Kenneth said.

"Mama is, too," she said, covering her newborn's head with the folded skirt.

"I hungry, Mama."

"I'll bet you are," she said. "Reach in the bottom of the pack. There's food and water."

A moment later, he said, "I find."

"Good. Don't eat all of it."

"Okay."

Florence shielded her brow, trying to get a visual sense of where she was and in what direction she should move. But the rain was falling in sheets, and the jungle canopy was so thick she saw no bearing point whatsoever. She closed her eyes to listen for the rivers, but the rain's drumming deafened all other sound.

Pick a direction and go. As long as it's not back.

She flashed on vivid memories of the night before—crossing the river, giving birth, fighting her way out with one son on her back and a newborn on her chest—and knew she was 100 percent done with the LRA, with Kony, with all of it.

Someone had once told her that the only time people risk change is when they get fed up with the pain of their current life. They know change is going to hurt, but they believe it will hurt less than staying the same. Florence was more than fed up, more than ready for change. Standing there in the drenching rain deep in the bush, she decided she was taking her sons and she was going home. Now.

Let them hunt me. Let them shoot at me. I don't care. I am getting my boys out of here.

Once she made the decision, Florence felt a strange calm fall with the rain. She heard Anthony's voice in her head, telling her to think carefully before she acted.

Based on where they'd crossed the Ayugi River, she figured it would take her four days to figure out a way across the White Nile and then to walk south out of the wilderness. She'd find a road, someone to help her.

But was she moving south? Toward the Nile? It felt that way, so she decided to just keep plowing on in the direction she'd been following since fleeing the battle.

"Let's go home," she said to herself, and pushed her way forward through the jungle.

She came after a time to an opening in the sopping vegetation, which looked as if it had burned sometime in the past year. Peering out through the pouring rain, she saw a path winding past a charred little hill near the far edge of the burn.

If I get up there, I should be able to see where the rivers are, she thought. Instead of the direct route across the burn, Florence stuck to the edge and stayed just inside the tree line until she crossed the path that led to the rise in elevation.

Head down into the rain, she plodded along the path across the burn and reached the base of the hill at the same time that two women and three armed men came out of the bush on the other side of the clearing. One of the women was Ellen, the medic. One of the three LRA soldiers was Florence's commander, David Lakwall.

A part of her wanted to break down crying at the injustice of it all. Another part of her wanted to give in to maternal rage again and kill Lakwall, the other two LRA boys, and, if need be, Ellen and continue her way back to Amia'bil and home. But the biggest part of her told her to stay calm, to stay committed to escape. Rather than wallow in her bad luck, she would focus on taking care of the boys until she had another chance to run.

But in Florence's mind and in her heart, she was already gone.

———

Anthony huddled under a tarp that same evening, feeling as low as he'd been in a long time. Because of the onslaught the Ugandan army had unleashed on the LRA, the Great Teacher had been forced into peace negotiations three times. Just a few minutes before, Anthony had sent a message from Kony to the Sudanese and Ugandan governments, breaking off the third series of truce talks. There would be no peace, no surrender, no free passage home.

Only more war, Anthony thought numbly. *Only more dying. He just can't give it up. He is like a dog that way. Except no one would keep a mad dog like that around. They'd shoot him.*

Looking out into the gloaming, he fantasized yet again about putting a gun to the back of Kony's head and ending his reign of—

"Time to put that radio to sleep for the night, don't you think, Commander Tony?"

Anthony looked over his shoulder at Corporal Leonard, his minder, taller, more muscular, ten years older, with half the rank and a sneering, condescending attitude that told you that while he believed he was acting below his station in life, he would make sure the LRA's top signaler and TONFAS coder was not tempted to make a run for freedom. After all, Leonard came with a reputation. For years, he had been one of Kony's better trackers. Like Sergeant Bacia, he hunted the holy who tried to escape.

"You don't know a thing about radios, Corporal," Anthony said. "If you want them to last, you have to let them cool a little before you shut them off."

That was nonsense, of course, but Anthony was feeling little urgency now that Kony had ditched the most recent peace proposals. In the morning, they would hurry and hide somewhere else, then hurry and hide the next day and the next until they ran into the Ugandan army, and the shooting and the chaos would start all over again. Once that happened, he would have five hundred days under fire. He'd been counting since the first time at the Koromush barracks. Four hundred and ninety-nine times since his kidnapping, Anthony Opoka had gone into battle.

Five hundred times. What does that do to you? Turn you into a mad dog like—?

His radio crackled.

"Nine Whiskey, Nine Whiskey, this is Two Bravo, come back, over."

Anthony almost smiled. Two Bravo was the call sign of the signaler for David Lakwall, Florence's new commander. He had not seen his wife in nearly five months and desperately wanted to know how she and Kenneth were doing.

"Two Bravo, this is Nine Whiskey, over."

"Nine Whiskey, you have a new baby boy."

Feeling his grin go wall to wall, Anthony threw back his head and howled. "A son! I have another son!"

Corporal Leonard said, "And how is that a good thing?"

"Nine Whiskey?"

Anthony ignored his minder, brought the mic back to his mouth. "Nine Whiskey, here. What is his name?"

"Boniface."

He frowned. "Boniface?"

"Boniface?" Leonard said, and snorted.

Two Bravo said, "Betty says it means someone who does good things."

"Someone who does good things," Anthony said, ignoring his minder's rolling eyes. "Boniface."

He keyed the mic. "Tell her I like his name very much. Can I speak with Betty, Two Bravo?"

"Negative, Nine Whiskey. Baby is fine, but Betty and son number one had a difficult time. Both are in sick bay, resting, getting their strength back. Over."

Anthony was concerned and disappointed. "Copy. Tell Betty that Nine Whiskey wishes she could see his happiness."

"Roger that, Nine Whiskey. Two Bravo out."

"See your happiness?" Leonard said, and snorted again.

"Corporal?" Anthony said, picking up his rifle. "You may be a man tracker, and I may shoot with one and a half arms, but I will not miss your knees if you continue with the remarks about my private life."

Leonard's eyes shifted left and right. "You wouldn't."

"No, but Commander Tony would, and Commander Tony has known the Great Teacher a long time. Kony will accept his reason for crippling you as a matter of honor. Tracker or not."

He didn't wait for a response, shut off the radio, repacked it, and spread his mat to sleep there. Leonard said nothing for several moments, then left the cover of the tarp for another he had set up about ten meters away.

Glad to be somewhat alone at last, Anthony lay down in the gathering darkness, thinking about his mother and father, trying to see them the way they were the last time they were together, and wanting to tell them that they had another grandson. *A boy I can teach to grow up to be a good human who fits his name. Boniface.*

Anthony sighed and shut his eyes, admitting that these were all just dreams for now, dreams that started with him being back with his own family again, holding Florence, Kenneth, and now Boniface in his arms.

Commander Tony drifted off believing that once that vision became real, everything else he needed in life would start to fall into place.

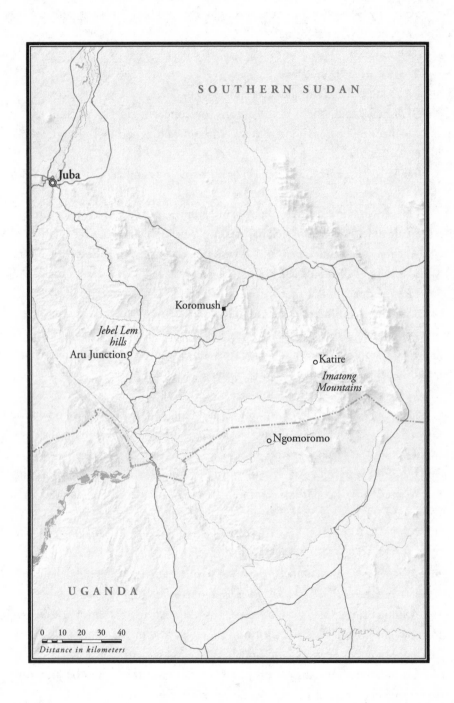

Chapter Thirty-Three

But in the weeks that followed, nothing fell into place for Anthony or the LRA.

Incensed by the Great Teacher's refusal to surrender, the president of Uganda doubled down. With the vast majority of his country's rural north empty and its populace living in displaced persons camps, Museveni ordered that anyone in the zone other than his soldiers be shot on sight.

Kony dressed as a woman almost constantly now and split off from General Tabuley's group, heading north, trying to convince the Sudanese that in return for ammunition and supplies, LRA boys hiding in southern Sudan could help regain control of Torit.

As he left, the Great Teacher ordered Dominic Ongwen to remain in Uganda and to attack more refugee camps, kill more civilians, and kidnap more new recruits. Hundreds of innocents died at Ongwen's hands. And nine hundred more children found themselves dragged off into the nightmare life of the Lord's Resistance Army.

Over the shortwave, Anthony listened to Kony, still sounding bellicose in messages to the troops, still declaring that one day his "growing" army would seize Kampala.

But the signal commander knew that the LRA was not growing. The Great Teacher still had as many as fifteen thousand boys under arms, but the Ugandan army's relentless air and ground assaults were killing more of his child soldiers than he was kidnapping. In an effort to avoid the casualties caused by being spotted and bombed from the sky, he ordered all large groups traveling together to break up into smaller bands.

The strategy did not work. Anthony had stayed with General Tabuley and fifty of his best boys, moving almost constantly in the vast roadless areas of northern Uganda. Yet they were encountering and engaging in battle with the Ugandan army on an almost daily basis.

Then Kony reported over the radio that he had once again been visited by the spirit of Jumma Driscer, the Sudanese strategist, who decreed that any attack in close cover be repelled by ruthless counterattack. There would be no defensive positions taken. Counterattack and fade away were the orders of battle.

Anthony's number of days in combat had climbed to 520 by early December when General Vincent and fifty of his seasoned veterans rendezvoused with Tabuley's group. Vincent told Tabuley that LRA soldiers helped the Sudanese army retake the town of Torit and that the Great Teacher was coming south with ammunition and supplies as his reward. They were all to march two days north and meet him at the border.

Dreading the idea that they might be going back into Sudan, Anthony wanted to run the entire first day of the march. But Corporal Leonard was there behind him when Vincent's and Tabuley's forces bumped into two UPDF patrols, which provoked brief, intense counterattacks before they retreated and moved into the thickest cover they could find.

Anthony hardly slept and felt uneasy and on edge when they rose and set off the second day. Both generals seemed especially wary as well.

Around nine that morning, they broke out of deep jungle into a transition area before full savanna, with scattered pocket openings of high grass amid the trees. He heard General Tabuley say, "I can't shake the feeling we're being watched."

"Or they're using heat sensors to locate us," General Vincent said, "which makes it easier to ambush us."

"They do seem to know right where we—"

Three quick rifle shots went off at the back of one of those pockets of grass to their right. The two soldiers ahead of Anthony spun, went to their knees, and fired at the spot. Bursts from automatic weapons came back at them.

"Attack!" General Vincent shouted.

Anthony pinned his SMG to his left hip and began blazing along with all of the LRA soldiers with him, mowing down grass and saplings alike. The return fire was equally savage. One of General Vincent's boys took a round to the throat right next to Anthony, who stopped shooting when he heard his battlefield radio squawk.

"Nine Whiskey, Nine Whiskey, come back!"

He dove on the ground, got his pack off, and got out the short-range radio. "Nine Whiskey. Identify yourself."

"Two Bravo. We are under UPDF attack. Request support. Over."

"Negative, Two Bravo. We are under UPDF attack also. Over."

The shooting around him was intensifying. Then the next transmission began, "Nine Whiskey . . ."

Anthony wasn't listening to the words coming over the radio after that. He was listening to the background noise.

"Cease fire!" he shouted suddenly at the backs of General Vincent and General Tabuley.

Tabuley looked back. "What?"

Anthony keyed the microphone, shouted, "Friendly fire, Two Bravo! Cease fire, Two Bravo! Repeat, friendly fire! Repeat, friendly fire! Cease fire!"

Tabuley started shouting, "Cease fire! Friendly fire!"

The shooting slowed and then stopped. Anthony, panting at the adrenaline flooding his system, had figured out that they were in a battle with another LRA band when he heard the same rhythm of shots over the radio. But it wasn't until then that it registered in his brain that Two Bravo was the handle of the signaler for Florence's commander.

"Florence?" he whispered, horrified at the sheer number of bullets they'd just sent downrange in her direction, and Kenneth's and Boniface's.

Lurching to his feet, he shouldered his pack and rifle and ran, yelling, "Betty! Betty!"

He pushed through bullet-chopped vegetation at the other end of the pocket opening, saw two LRA soldiers he recognized lying dead in the trees, and others standing there looking stunned. Beyond them, he could make out a group of women offering comfort to another woman, who was down on her hands and knees, wailing over a small dead child. She had her face turned from Anthony, and for a single, heart-stopping moment, he thought it was Florence.

"Betty!" he yelled. "Betty!"

The woman on the ground did not turn to his calling, but a woman toward the back of the group did. She looked dazed, confused as she searched for the voice calling her name. But then Florence saw Anthony, and she began to cry.

For the first time since Patrick told him years before never to show emotion in front of other LRA soldiers, Anthony had tears in his eyes as he ran to Florence. When he saw that she was holding the baby and that his tiny arms were moving and that little Kenneth was standing there holding tight to his mother's knees, he realized how close to death they'd all come. He might have shot them himself. The weight of what might have been broke Anthony's heart, and he went sobbing into Florence's arms.

They stood there holding each other, both crying, for the longest time. Anthony finally slowed and gently pulled back. Seeing Boniface, his heart seemed to instantly heal and grow, and he started crying all over again, which set her off all over again. The same thing happened when he picked up Kenneth and Florence lifted Anthony's bad arm and put it around her shoulder. Only this time, first Florence and then Anthony started laughing through their tears.

"Opoka!" General Tabuley shouted in the trees behind him. "Where's my signaler? We're moving out!"

"Coming, General!" Anthony shouted back, putting Kenneth down, then whispering to Florence, "See my happiness?"

"See my happiness?" Florence replied, smiling and putting her hand on his cheek. "Now go. We'll be back here, waiting for you."

"I have a lot to tell you."

"So do I."

———

Anthony walked on clouds when the rails started marching again. They left the transition zone for more-open savanna country. The signal commander should have been on high alert for the sound of gunships in the air. But he wasn't. He was marching along in front of General Tabuley and General Vincent, daydreaming about Florence and how she filled him with such joy every time he saw her. And how Kenneth had grown! And how Boniface had batted the air with his tiny hands!

I am a lucky, lucky man. That could have been it. The end of my life.

He knew the second he had that last thought that it was true. Florence was not just the only person who still connected him to threads of normalcy; she was the mother of his children and the love of his life. *Without her, without the boys, I would be nothing.*

But luckily, he did not have to think that way any longer. Florence was more than alive. She was on the rail somewhere behind him. And so were his sons.

The rest of the day passed in a pleasant blur that turned even more pleasant when they reached the rendezvous point and found Kony in a secluded grove of trees with several of his younger wives, including Evelyn, and more than two hundred LRA boys waiting with crates of ammunition and supplies, including sacks of rice and boxes filled with sardine cans. The men and boys began gathering wood. The women and girls prepared to cook. General Tabuley told Anthony he and General Vincent needed to talk alone with Kony. He wasn't needed for the time being.

Leaving Control Altar when Corporal Leonard's back was turned, Anthony searched among the trees and the women and children until he saw Florence crouched down, using a flint and steel to light a fire. The baby was swaddled and lying on the ground next to Kenneth, who was curled up, sleeping after the long day walking and the trauma of the firefight. When Florence stood up and saw him standing there, she looked a little embarrassed as she smiled.

"How long have you been standing there?" she asked.

"Long enough to know you are the most beautiful girl I have ever seen."

She laughed. "Listen to you."

"Listen to me, Betty the Nurse."

"I am, Commander Tony."

They stood there mooning at each other for several moments. Anthony was about to go to her, but stopped when he heard a voice say, "Flo? Is that you?"

Both Florence and Anthony looked at the tall, skinny guy with the short dreadlocks and beard coming at them, AK-47 over his shoulders, one leg heavily bandaged, and balancing on a rude crutch. He was staring at Florence, who was puzzled.

"My name is Betty," she said.

"Whatever you call yourself in this godforsaken army, it's me, Jasper."

Florence gasped. Her hand flew to her mouth. "Jasper, is that really you?"

He nodded, and they almost moved to hug each other, then stopped. Anthony got puffed up until Florence looked at him and whispered, "He's my cousin! You know, the one who always listened to the latest music on the radio!"

"And one of her closest friends, a long, long time ago," Jasper said, smiling.

Anthony felt the tension drain from his chest as Florence said, "This is Signal Commander Opoka, my husband, and very best friend."

Jasper looked at Anthony with respect. "Commander Tony."

Anthony smiled. "She says you knew all the music."

"Once upon a time," Florence's cousin said.

For some reason, Anthony thought back to that first battle, when he'd sung his way into combat and found the boombox, and how they'd all sung and danced.

He told them about that, then said, "But I didn't know the song or who sang it."

"How'd it go?"

Anthony sang the chorus as he remembered it.

Jasper laughed. "That's 'Somebody's Watching Me' by Rockwell. Big hit. That's what you danced to? In the LRA?"

"First song on the mixtape," Anthony said, laughing.

Florence grinned at Anthony. "I told you he knew all the songs. And now two of my favorite people have come back into my life on the same day. How lucky am I?"

Anthony heard a low tone in the distance. He held up his hand to listen. They stopped talking, and he made out the sound amplifying and then changing to soft thudding.

Jasper shouted, "Gunship!"

Anthony grabbed his pack, rifle, and Kenneth. Florence got Boniface and her gun.

"Where?" she asked in a panic.

"Follow me," Anthony said, and took off toward the thickest cover he could see. They tore into it, with Jasper hobbling after them.

Three Ugandan army helicopters roared in over the grove of scattered trees. Until then, the UPDF had been using machine guns mounted behind the pilots in the open doors of the gunships. But now the pilots fired their own weapons mounted to the landing skids: twin-barreled, 20 mm autocannons, a devastating weapon meant to lay waste to armored cars, not kidnapped humans running for their lives.

The autocannons made a terrifying, rapid thump-boom, thump-boom noise that boxed their ears over and over, made them stumble and grope their way into the dense bush and keep going. Anthony put Kenneth down, got in front of Florence, and began tearing a way forward away from the aerial assault.

"I'm staying here," Jasper said, out of breath. "Can't go."

Florence looked at Anthony.

"A little more," he said.

She nodded, but then called to her cousin. "We won't be far, Jasper. I promise."

———

When they at last sat down and caught their breath, they could still hear the ongoing attack and LRA boys returning fire. Boniface started fussing. Florence fed him. Kenneth lay down to sleep next to her. Anthony watched it all with a gentle smile.

Florence looked at him. Her lip twisted a little. She tried to speak, but the tremor in her voice got the best of her. She closed her eyes. Tears streamed down her cheeks. Finally, she cleared her throat and looked at him with a piteous expression.

"I can't take it anymore, Anthony," Flo whispered. "I tell myself I can, but I can't. Life is not supposed to be like this. You aren't supposed to run from soldiers three times a day. You aren't supposed to give birth while someone's trying to cut you in half with a machine gun."

Anthony's smile had long since vanished. Softly, he said, "Is that what happened?"

She nodded, crying again, and then told him about that night, how she'd gone into labor before they'd had to cross a swollen river on a rope line at night, how they'd taken refuge behind a huge tree, and how she'd given birth there alone on the riverbank.

"There were bullets flying everywhere," she said. "And Kenneth was crying, and I had no one to help me, and nothing except my love for you and for Kenneth to get me through."

Stunned at her inner strength, Anthony listened in awe as Florence described the entire birth in detail, how dawn had come and with it a young teenage boy soldier touched by the presence of her newborn amid so much death, only to be cut down when the Ugandan army moved their heavy machine gun to the island.

"His name was Boniface," she said. "He wanted our baby to have his name because it meant someone who does good things. Isn't that just so sweet and sad?"

"It's not just sad, it's wrong."

"He was thirteen. Will Boniface live to thirteen? Will Kenneth? Will you live to see them turn thirteen? Will I?"

Anthony took each question like blows to his head and heart. "I can't tell you."

"I can. If we stay here, the answer to every one of those questions is no."

As it had after the friendly-fire incident earlier in the day, Anthony's heart broke again because he knew she was right. The way things were going, it was only a matter of time before a bullet, or a bomb, or a missile, or an autocannon round caught up to Florence, to Kenneth, to Boniface, to himself. If they continued on this way, they were all doomed to die in the bush.

"What do you want to do?"

Florence swallowed. "I want to end this. I want to escape and run. Right now."

Anthony closed his eyes, then opened them. "Do you believe I am a brave man?"

"Yes, but—"

"Do you believe I love you?"

"I do, but—"

"I am not afraid to run. But I am terrified of losing you. And Kenneth. And Boniface."

"Which I am telling you will happen if we do not run."

"And I am telling you that if the Great Teacher survived this attack and discovers me and you are gone, he will hunt us. He will send his best trackers. Leonard and probably Bacia."

"Why would he?"

"I could give you ten reasons. The TONFAS. What I know about everything. But most of all, he'll do it for spite, to see us dragged in front of Who Are You and executed."

Florence sat there silently for a long time before saying, "Find me a way out. I am not afraid to go if I know the way out."

Anthony thought again, and then listened to his heart. "I will do you one better. I will find someone I can trust to lead you out. When you are safe, I'll wait for my chance and follow."

She appeared unconvinced. "Who in the LRA can you trust enough to do that?"

"There's just two."

Chapter Thirty-Four

Like a cat on its thirteenth life, Joseph Kony did indeed survive the autocannon attack the UPDF had hoped would destroy the leadership of the LRA. Instead, it forced the Great Teacher to change tactics and splinter his army permanently.

Gone would be the days when rails of a thousand or more LRA soldiers marched brazenly across the savannas, possessed by the spirits, singing headlong into battle. They would become more of a traditional guerrilla army, slicing in and out of southern Sudan and northern Uganda, attacking brutally and often.

Anthony was only able to move with Florence, Jasper, and the boys for one day. On the second day, the Great Teacher ordered that the wounded be brought to a field hospital closer to southern Sudan, where they would recover instead of slowing down the rails. That meant Jasper would be leaving for that hospital.

"They need nurses," Anthony told Florence. "I think you should volunteer and go there."

"Absolutely not," she said. "I want to go home, not in the other direction."

"The UPDF is focused on us now. You'll keep the boys safe until I find you a guide."

"Unless I find one myself?"

He gazed at her and smiled a little sadly. "Unless you find one yourself."

Jasper said, "I'll make sure she's okay, Commander Tony."

There was none of the usual good-natured banter between him and Florence before they said their goodbyes. There was a heaviness in their parting. They both wondered whether it was the last time they would ever see each other.

———

Once more Anthony was assigned to walk with the Great Teacher as his sig-naler. Kony was behind him on the rail when he was told to turn due north and head back into Sudan. The radioman felt like he'd been gut-punched when he learned they were going all the way back to Rubangatek. Now that he was back in Sudanese graces, the Great Teacher wanted to spend Christmas with Fatima and the other senior wives and children.

They moved through the wilds on the rails again, five lines of twenty to forty men, women, boys, girls, and little children. Anthony and Kony—once more dressed as a woman—and his wives marched well back from the front of the third rail. Evelyn, the young wife with the baby and the toddler, dislocated her knee and had to be helped along, slowing their progress.

They camped for a total of four nights to let Evelyn's knee recover and then headed north again. After having already marched for more than three months, Anthony felt exhausted and began having doubts he could make it all the way back to Rubangatek.

Then he realized that he was listening to a voice of suffering again, Fear this time, which he kept at bay with the breathing and chants Mr. Mabior had taught him. At the end of each cycle, he'd see his wife and sons in his mind, waiting for him, and that would be enough for him to keep putting one foot in front of the other.

As they marched, Anthony noticed how dry the grasslands south and west of the Imatong Mountains had become, and he realized it hadn't rained in weeks. Kony noticed it, too. He said drought was a bad omen. Then he said at night the spirits were telling him he was about to have a severe loss.

Even though some people claimed that the spirits had stopped visiting the Great Teacher, Anthony had learned to at least listen to Kony's sense of what was to come. The LRA's supreme commander had foretold victory before Anthony's first battle at the Koromush barracks. He'd also described having "dark visions" before the combat at Puge, where Anthony was hit by the RPG fin. And the spirits had evidently foretold Kony's defeat at Jebel Lem.

The farther north they marched, the more drought-stricken the land became. They were hiking through stands of tall, dry elephant grass, which chafed at their passing, lingered in the air, and caused them to itch, sneeze, and cough. Kony's mood turned foul because the Sudanese government had cut off his funding again. Yango told Anthony that the LRA leader was sleeping very little and racked by nightmares he could not stop.

On December 19 and 20, they were ambushed by bands of Dinka rebels. Almost twenty child soldiers died. Oddly, that seemed to cheer Kony up.

"I believe that is the bad luck that has been foretold to me," he told Anthony. "And now I will sleep well."

The Great Teacher slept so well the nights of December 22 and 23, he ordered the rails to move even faster. On Christmas Eve, they broke camp and set out at a blistering pace. Tired and still not feeling well, Anthony kept up by continually reminding himself that they were closer to Rubangatek with every step. Around noon that day, they began to see black clouds rising and billowing to the north. The wind switched. They could smell smoke.

When they stopped to eat and rest for the night, Anthony climbed a nearby hill and looked north, seeing a line of fire about ten kilometers away, and moving north on a south wind.

"I think we're going to want to head east before we go north to get around it," he told Kony as he set up the wire to make an evening radio call.

"How big is it?"

"Biggest fire I've ever seen, Teacher," Anthony said.

Kony had him raise the Rubangatek signaler and ask him to bring his wife Fatima to the radio and to call back. About fifteen minutes later, she did.

"Where are you?" she asked. "The children keep asking, and they're very excited to see you. I can't wait to see you."

"I'd hoped we'd be there by midday," Kony said. "But there's a big wildfire north of us and west of you. We're going to have to work around it."

"Call when you're close so we can start cooking," Fatima said.

Kony promised he would, and Anthony signed off. The Great Teacher stood there afterward, staring north toward the glow of the fire before walking away without a word.

———

The wind picked up during the night, blowing from the southwest now, and driving the fire northeast. At dawn, the winds turned erratic, going back to south and then to southeast, sending the flames in a new direction with each switch.

They were up and moving in the low light. Every person on every rail knew they were close to a long and well-deserved rest, and the pace was fast from the beginning.

As they crossed several hills, Anthony could make out the flames belching smoke into the sky as the wind changed yet again, out of the southwest now, pushing the fire northeast once more. He kept watching it, calculating, and deciding that, based on the maps he'd gone over with Kony the night before, the fire was going to pass well north of Rubangatek.

They took an unfamiliar route, nonetheless, heading east and then north, outflanking the blaze. They crossed a river and became turned around in the forest on the other side before finally emerging into savanna land again around half past noon.

Distant flames danced in and above the grass fire, sending dense smoke north, west, and southeast of them. Kony abruptly called a halt and had Anthony rig the wire. He called Fatima and told her it was too difficult to pass at the moment and they were going to wait until a clear path opened. Fatima said they had been nervous about the blaze until the wind shifted. The fire was currently several kilometers northwest of Rubangatek and burning away from them. She said she and the other wives would start cooking the Christmas feast in two hours.

"Tell the children we will be there soon," Kony said, and signed off.

The Great Teacher asked Evelyn and another wife to cook him some food while they waited, and then stood there while they did, staring north toward the flames and the smoke again.

Some time passed before he announced that he was no longer hungry and that he was going to take Evelyn's young daughter Bakita to meet Fatima. Evelyn started to argue, but he just walked away with the girl on his shoulders.

Anthony jumped up, grabbed his radio pack with his rifle strapped to it, and hurried after the Great Teacher, needing to stay close to him.

Fifteen minutes later, the wind shifted once more, turned out of the west-northwest, and began to blow and gust.

Chapter Thirty-Five

They were two kilometers from Rubangatek, climbing a low hill that blocked their view, when Anthony heard pots banging. Kony heard them, too. They hurried to the top of the hill, looked across the undulating valley to the village and then to the flames sweeping down the hillside above the flat where the Great Teacher's family lived.

"Fatima!" Kony shouted, then handed the young girl, Bakita, to Anthony and took off in a dead sprint down the hill.

The toddler started crying when Anthony tried to keep up with the Great Teacher. Anthony slowed enough to calm her and yet keep Kony in sight. For the first kilometer, all he could think was that the fire was going to cross the creek and take out the home he'd built for Florence long ago. But then, just as he was about to have their old hut in sight, the wind direction shifted almost 180 degrees.

He saw Kony run by a woman who'd been hitting the pot, sounding the alarm, heading toward a trail that crossed the creek bottom. He saw the flames climbing back up the hillside and the fire ebbing on the flat below.

"Here," he said to the woman with the pot. "Can you take her? Evelyn, the Teacher's wife, will be here soon."

He handed her the girl and turned away, heading after Kony.

"What are you doing? It's still burning over there," she called after him.

"It's my job to stay close to him," he said, and ran east toward the trail.

He reached the path and saw Kony sitting there on a tree stump, looking across the creek where the fire was all but out, reduced to smoke, ash, and heat.

The Great Teacher noticed Anthony, blinked dumbly, and then shook his head a little, as if at some worrisome insect.

"My wives and children," he said in a dazed voice. "I'm sure it's bad, Opoka, and I don't . . . Can you go and see if there's anything to be done for them? Here, take this." He held out a toothpaste tube. "Have them put it on their skin. Cilindi says it will help."

Anthony had never heard of such a thing, did not take the toothpaste, and started down the path, steeling himself for what was to come. Crossing the stream, he could feel the heat rising, growing stronger with every step.

Then he heard a boy crying in a garbled voice. "Mommy! Mommy, I can't see!"

Anthony moved faster. He climbed the far bank and entered a vision of hell.

———

Everything that had once stood on the flat had burned to charcoal and ash: the grass itself, which had been chest deep in places, and the grass-walled-and-roofed huts that Fatima, Nighty, and Christin preferred to sleep in with their children. There were clusters of bodies amid the charred ruins of the huts. Four of Fatima's kids were dead in a circle straight ahead. It looked like they'd all been taking refuge from the gusts and were caught unawares by the wind shift and the blaze roaring down the hill, engulfing the huts, and burning them all alive.

"Mommy!"

In shock, Anthony saw him then, one of Fatima's younger boys, which one he could not tell because the poor kid had been burned everywhere. He wandered in circles, arms out, groping.

"It hurts, Mommy."

Evelyn limped onto the scene, her baby on her back, clutching the tube of toothpaste. Other women, men, and children followed. She and several of them went to the boy to soothe him, but he could not be calmed.

Another one of Fatima's boys staggered up. He had minor burns on the backs of his legs and arms but appeared otherwise unscathed physically. Mentally was a different story; he was screaming that his mother was dead.

"Where is she?" Anthony said.

The kid pointed back at smoke curling from a body in a ditch on the far side of the flat. Anthony was so shocked at Fatima's horrific fate he just stood there, unable to fathom the extent of the tragedy and its random cause. A shift in the wind. The deaths of eight children, three wives, and a bodyguard.

They carried the blinded boy out on a sheet. When they reached the stream, they tried to put water and wet cloths on him. He began to shake violently before life gave out on him, and he died. Nine children were gone.

———

Anthony left then. There was nothing to do but bury the dead, and with his arm, he was not the man for that job.

Kony was still sitting on a stump. The Great Teacher looked him in the eye. "Tell me."

"Fatima, Nighty, and Christin are all dead. Five of your children by Fatima are dead, including Kony. Two of your children by Nighty. And two by Christin."

The LRA leader gazed at Anthony as if he had been speaking another language. Then he whispered, "How can that be?"

Anthony did not know what to say, so he just stood there as disbelief and grief rippled across Kony's face.

"Nine of the children?" the Great Teacher whispered.

"Yes."

He frowned. "I don't know how to live without Fatima. She——"

His jaw shifted slightly left and down, something Anthony had noticed when the spirit of Who Are You was taking control of him. Kony closed his eyes and began to tremble and sweat.

Anthony got nervous, knowing that the Great Teacher could easily be driven to murder by what had happened to his family. He did not want to be around Kony if that was to be the case.

But then the LRA leader opened his bloodshot eyes, got unsteadily to his feet. "Go see your wife and son. That's an order. If I need you, I will send someone."

Even though Florence was at the hospital in the northern Uganda bush, Anthony nodded, then lowered his head. "I am very sorry for what has happened to you, Teacher. No man should have to go through something like this."

"But I do, Opoka," he said, and walked away toward the small compound where he stayed when he was in Rubangatek.

Anthony watched him go for a moment before walking in the opposite direction. Two men were hurrying toward him. One was General Vincent. The other was Patrick Lumumba.

It had been months since he'd seen either of them, but there were no greetings.

"How bad?" Vincent asked. The LRA's second-in-command was gaunt, intense, but also pragmatic. Many times, Anthony had seen Vincent talk Kony down when he was getting frantic and proposing things like mass-suicide missions. He was one of the few people who could talk straight to the Great Teacher, and Anthony liked him for it.

Anthony gave them the same body count he'd given Kony.

The general was stunned. "Where is he?"

"In his compound," Anthony said, pointing through the trees on this side of the creek bed.

Patrick said, "Where he keeps his guns."

Vincent seemed unnerved by that idea. "You're right, Sergeant. A man who loses that many wives and children in one sweep cannot be right in the head. I will go talk to him, get him to walk with me. When we leave, remove his weapons. Put them in my compound."

"Straightaway," Patrick said. "Opoka will help me."

———

Kony was in the latrine when they entered Control Altar, went to his hut, and retrieved his weapons, including his beloved Beretta that he often wore as a sidearm. They slipped out without him knowing they'd even been there. Evelyn went in as they left.

Outside, Anthony whispered, "I shouldn't ask because I know you've already paid me back in full a bunch of times, but I need your help, Patrick."

"What's that?"

"Can you get Florence and my sons out? Help them escape?"

Patrick got irritated. "You're right. You shouldn't have asked. That kind of help could get me killed, and you and your wife and kids. So, no."

He walked away before Anthony could reply. He sat in the shade outside Control Altar, feeling like he should not have asked, that he'd threatened a friendship that went back to another lifetime. General Vincent and Yango went inside.

Anthony slept fitfully outside the compound that night, hearing Kony weeping, ranting, wailing. General Vincent woke him the next morning.

"We need you in there," Vincent said. "He trusts you, and I trust you to keep him calm."

Anthony remembered the bewildered expression on Kony's face when he was sitting on that stump by the trail that led to the burnt flat where Fatima and his children had died. He remembered him offering toothpaste as a burn salve.

"Okay," Anthony said, and sighed. "I'll go back in."

General Vincent cleared his throat. "There's more to this, Commander."

"Sir?"

"He keeps going into long periods of silence when he just stares. Then he asks for a pistol and gets very angry when we don't give him one. I want you to make sure he doesn't get one. At least not anytime soon."

"Me, sir?"

"Three senior wives are dead, Opoka. And Lily is very sick and can't come. He has Yango. He has me. He has Evelyn and the younger wives, and he has you. But of all of us, you are the one who will almost always be with him. You are in the most danger."

Anthony saw the truth of that and said, "No pistols. I'll make sure."

He went to the entrance to Control Altar.

The sentry recognized him, saluted, and said, "Commander Tony."

He returned the salute but did not think about how far and how fast he'd risen within the ranks of the Lord's Resistance Army. He was steeling himself to be in the presence of Kony at his most unpredictable.

Anthony had seen glimpses of sheer madness in the man before. He saw it the very first time Kony channeled the spirit of Who Are You. He'd witnessed it a dozen other times when the Great Teacher would learn of some setback and fly off the handle, threatening to kill scores in retaliation. Somehow, Anthony had always managed to stay under Kony's radar by simply and consistently doing his job right and not listening too closely when the Great Teacher showered him with praise. Now, the generals wanted Anthony to keep the supreme LRA commander on his radar at all times.

He found the inner sanctum of Control Altar laid out as it always was, with nine grass huts in three rows of three. But the huts in the third positions in the first and third rows were empty. They should have been filled with women and children.

Anthony did not see anyone until he saw Kony sitting on a stool outside his hut with Yango, General Vincent, and his young wife Evelyn, who was on her knees crying.

"Please, Teacher," Evelyn was saying. "Please. Please release me. Let me bring my babies home."

Kony's eyes were red, rheumy, and puffy and kept blinking slowly, like an old dog's, as he thumbed prayer beads with his left hand and said, "Our babies, Evelyn. So, no."

She raised her voice, deepened her pleas. "Do you want them to die like your nine children just died? Do you want me to die like your three wives?"

He looked at her with such hatred for a moment that Anthony feared Evelyn had gone too far, that he was going to stand up and strike her down, beat her at the very least.

But then he sagged, said, "I don't. Can someone please find me my Beretta?"

Evelyn shuddered, said, "Joseph, release me. Let me go home."

"No," he said firmly. "You're all I've got now, Evelyn. Don't you see? Can someone get me my pistol?"

Before Yango or General Vincent could reply, Anthony stepped forward, said, "Hello, Teacher. You asked for me?"

Kony seemed back in the haze of grief and little sleep again. He gazed at Anthony with a bemused and exhausted expression.

"The one-armed signaler returns," he said. "The only sane one in the bunch."

Anthony ignored that, said, "Teacher, will you broadcast at oh nine hundred?"

He thought about that before shaking his head. "General Vincent will do that today. And before and between transmissions, Commander Opoka, you will find me my pistol, the Beretta."

Anthony glanced at the security chief and the Great Teacher's chief of staff, both of whom shook their heads ever so slightly.

"I was told there were mechanical difficulties with it, Teacher," Anthony said.

"What mechanical difficulties?" he said skeptically. "It's a Beretta."

"Sand got in the action, Teacher. The sear broke. The firing pin was damaged, but they believe it can be fixed. It will just take time."

Evelyn said, "I throw myself on your mercy, Teacher. Please let me go."

Kony ignored her, stared at Anthony, getting angry. "Then get me another pistol, Opoka. Loaded. With extra clips."

Yango said, "I will look for you, Teacher."

General Vincent said, "But as you know, our armory is low on everything."

The LRA leader's eyes blinked slowly; then he said snidely, "I know that. It's why we are here. To get rearmed. What makes you think I didn't know that, General Vincent?"

Vincent looked like he wanted to be anywhere but there.

Anthony said, "Teacher? You need to sleep. The funeral for your wives and children is later this afternoon."

Kony said, "Before the sun sets."

"That's right. So sleep."

The Great Teacher nodded, got up, and went toward the entry to his hut.

Evelyn called after him, "Teacher, can you—"

Anthony grabbed her by the shoulder and squeezed with his good hand. Hard.

She yipped and then looked up at him and hissed, "You can't do that. I'm his wife."

"A wife who wants to be released," Anthony said quietly. "Leave him alone for now. Let him get through this. Help him get through this, and maybe he will grant your wish."

Evelyn looked ready to argue, but then surrendered and nodded.

Kony slept for several hours and seemed more clearheaded when he first emerged from his hut. But as it got closer to the funeral, the haze came over the Great Teacher again. Twice, he asked Anthony if he'd gotten him a replacement pistol yet.

At the ceremony by the graves, Kony seemed dull, separated. He gazed at the ground when the names of the dead were called. He showed no emotion until the names of Fatima and his favorite son, Kony, rang out. He choked, hung his head. His shoulders heaved several times before they stopped.

He got up, went to each grave in silence, blessing them with shea butter, sorrowful as he stood before Christin and Nighty and choking again at Fatima's final resting spot. But then he just walked away with two bodyguards and Anthony hustling along behind him.

"I don't deserve to live, Opoka," Kony said when they were safely inside Control Altar. "The spirits have left me. Even silly Cilindi won't talk to me anymore. Get me a pistol and let me end everyone's misery and mine."

Chapter Thirty-Six

For a moment, a really long moment, Anthony considered doing just that, going to one of the armories and finding a loaded pistol and slipping it to the Great Teacher. But he'd be defying a direct order from General Vincent, the man who would rule the LRA with Kony gone. Anthony knew he could rid the world of Jumma Driscer, Who Are You, Jing Breking, and even silly Cilindi, rid the world of the mad dog those spirits possessed, a hellhound that should have been put down ages ago.

But Anthony knew he would surely be killing himself, too. And where would that leave Florence, Kenneth, and Boniface?

"Opoka?" Kony said.

"Teacher," Anthony said finally. "You are suffering. I don't want to give a gun to someone who is in as much misery as you are."

The Great Teacher's eyes narrowed, and his features stiffened. Anthony thought he'd miscalculated. He'd spoken with compassion, but maybe Kony did not want compassion, maybe he'd lash out at it like a dog who's been beaten early in life.

"If I give you a direct order?" he asked.

Anthony swallowed, gazing back at the warlord. "Please don't, Teacher."

Kony finally broke eye contact, spit on the ground, and then sat on the bench outside his quarters. He put his head in his hands and moaned, "Then how do I stop this suffering, Opoka? It's everywhere and endless. Their loss is endless. There is no justice to this at all."

Harking back to his afternoon with Mr. Mabior, Anthony believed he understood the voices torturing the Great Teacher. Lack was goading him with the enormity of his loss, the finality of it. When Lack wasn't speaking, Violence was, confronting him with his own inability to change the unchangeable, to get justice against nature. And how wrong that was for a man who talked to spirits. And how unfair that was to a man who summoned thunderstorms.

The young signal commander stood there, watching the LRA's supreme commander agonize. He knew he could probably ease Kony's pain by teaching him how to recognize the four voices of suffering, the importance of naming them, and the simple methods the old shopkeeper had shown him to quiet them enough to think clearly.

But Anthony said nothing, did nothing to help the Great Teacher. Though he felt sorry for everyone who'd died in the flash fire, he felt cold indifference to what Kony was going through. After everything that had been done in his name—the kidnappings, the killings, the maimings—he felt as if the man was getting his due.

In the days that followed, Kony's moods swung wildly, from abject sorrow to outright rage. At the peaks and troughs of his emotions, he would demand a pistol to end the life of an invented enemy, or to snuff out his own. Each time, Anthony refused on the basis of suffering, which once provoked the Great Teacher to such anger that he stalked his signaler around Control Altar, his right hand and fingers configured like a pistol, like a kid playing.

"Bang," Kony said, poking the barrel of the imaginary gun against Anthony's forehead. "Bang, you're dead, Commander Tony. As soon as I get a pistol, bang, you're dead!"

"Yes, Teacher," Anthony said, waiting for him to stalk off and then letting his entire body tremble for a few seconds before composing himself and carrying on.

Between caring for her kids and working at the hospital where seriously wounded LRA soldiers convalesced, Florence barely had time to think or act for herself. And under orders from the Great Teacher himself, LRA guards watched her constantly.

She knew why Kony wanted her kept in close captivity. It weighed on her as she worked. As a result, with each passing day, she felt her will to go on dwindle. Her spirits always worsened when she heard Nine Whiskey transmitting on the morning and afternoon radio calls, describing one battle and retreat after another.

She wondered if Anthony had found someone to help her escape, or whether that was just something to cling to as the days in the bush became weeks and then months. She begged her commander, David Lakwall, multiple times, asking him to set her free. She had two children now. Kony should let her go.

But when Lakwall radioed Nine Whiskey to ask the Great Teacher's permission, she heard Anthony's grim voice come back, "Teacher denies permission. Betty is too important to the cause. Over."

I'm Anthony's chain, she thought bitterly that night. *I keep him at Kony's side.*

———

Every time Anthony had to relay the Great Teacher's negative verdict on his wife and sons' freedom, he could see Florence in his mind, sitting there by the radio, hoping, praying that this would be the day Kony decided to release her, only to have her dreams dashed again.

He had seen Kony do this with his wife Evelyn after Fatima's death. Making a promise, then breaking the promise. Holding out hope, then extinguishing it. At a deep level, he believed the Great Teacher enjoyed his cruelties, large and small.

His own relationship with Kony ebbed and flowed. One day he was still destined to be the minister of communications in his Kampala government. The next the Great Teacher would banish Anthony from his sight and disappear for days at a time.

For more than two months after the fire, Kony stayed in Rubangatek. But in late February, they were on the move again, heading south, slipping back into Uganda. To Anthony's surprise, once they were across the border, the Great Teacher announced that he was going to meet with Florence's commander at the hospital in the bush.

They reached the hospital encampment in the middle of March. Anthony took care of Kony's radio needs, then left to find Florence and the boys when a Hilux vehicle arrived and left with the Great Teacher.

———

At the same time, Florence was in a field about a kilometer away, weeding between rows of almost-pickable cabbage and cornstalks barely erupted from the dark soil. Kenneth, almost three, was playing in the dirt about sixty meters from her, by the two-track that led back to the camp and on to the banks of the river.

Five-month-old Boniface was strapped to her back, sleeping. She was enjoying the field work and how it reminded her of home when she heard a vehicle coming, a Hilux pickup truck bouncing down the rough track that led from the hospital to the fields. The truck bed held five LRA soldiers with rifles. A woman sat up front in the passenger seat. She had a white scarf pulled across her face.

The driver downshifted approaching a pothole filled with rainwater, then overgunned it coming out, which caused the truck's muffler to submerge and the engine to backfire. Florence jumped. Kenneth was much closer to the sound and started screaming with fear.

Before she could go to him, the truck stopped, and the woman got out. She went straight to Kenneth, let go the scarf across her face, and picked Florence's son up, causing him to wail all the more.

Florence ran toward them with her hoe, hearing the woman say in a deep, strangely familiar voice, "It's okay, good boy. There's nothing to be afraid of here."

Florence stopped in her tracks, seeing it was Joseph Kony in disguise. The Great Teacher seemed oblivious to her, his entire focus on Kenneth.

"I've had little boys your age," he said in a soothing tone. "They all get scared, but you don't need to be."

Florence did not know why, but she was suddenly upset that Kony was holding her baby. He'd just lost most of his family. But Florence had no pity for him.

Don't hurt my baby, she thought, trying to control her breath. *Please don't hurt him.*

The Great Teacher began to hum to Kenneth, whose cries slowed. Kony began to sing softly then. "Don't cry, little boy. Teacher is not a hyena come to snatch you away."

Then he began to rock Kenneth and to spin in slow circles, humming again, before suddenly lifting the baby high overhead. "He's a good little boy," he sang. "A good little boy."

Florence saw emotions rippling across the Great Teacher's face: joy and grief and anger, one after the other as he held the boy high and swiveled in his tracks.

At last, Kony lowered Kenneth slowly, held the baby's cheek to his own, and sang, "Teacher had good little boys once just like you. Just like you."

Rubbing Kenneth's back, he continued to pivot until he saw Florence and stopped. For a moment she recognized nothing familiar, nothing human in his eyes. It was like looking into dark wells that had no bottom.

The Great Teacher smiled oddly at her then. "I remember my boys at this age. There's something about it. So innocent, but so ready to get into trouble."

Florence nodded. "Yes, Teacher."

"What is his name?"

"Kenneth, Teacher."

"Ahh. And who is his father?"

She swallowed and then said, "Commander Opoka. Your signaler. I am Betty, his wife."

Kony's eyes went dark and fathomless again.

"Whose love did you crave as a child, Betty?"

"Teacher?"

"Whose love did you crave? Your father's? Or your mother's? The love you did not get enough of. Quick answer. No right or wrong."

"My father, I guess," she said, feeling awkward. "My mother and I were very close."

"Hmmm," he said, nodding and lifting Kenneth up and down once more. "I don't remember my sons being this heavy. How old is he?"

"Almost three, Teacher."

"Three and still such a chub cheek," he said to Kenneth in a squeaky voice. "Would Kenneth like to come home with Teacher? Would he?"

A pit opened in Florence's stomach. It grew huge when he smiled weirdly at her.

"What do you think, Commander Tony's wife, Betty, who longed for her father's love?"

She didn't know what to say at first, but then said, "I think a child belongs with his mother and father, Teacher."

"But he's such a big boy. So heavy. Teacher could take him off your hands. Give you a rest from having to raise him alone. Give him a father's love so he does not crave it later in life."

Florence was having trouble breathing. "He's not heavy to me, Teacher. I would carry him forever and a day if I had to. And so would Commander Opoka."

Kenneth began to squirm in Kony's arms and reached out for her. The Great Teacher's smile ebbed away. There was a moment when she did not know what he was going to do. Then he held Kenneth out to her. "A baby boy does need his mommy. And daddy. Opoka is here, by the way."

Florence was happy for that as she came over cautiously, dropped the hoe, and took Kenneth in her arms. Suddenly, she was shaking so hard inside, she thought she was going to get dizzy and faint.

"Can I use your hoe?" Kony asked.

It took a moment to penetrate her thinking. "Hoe, Teacher?"

"You were weeding."

She nodded in a panic. "I will finish now."

He said, "I will finish for you. Go home, find your husband. Enjoy your little boy. They grow so fast at this age. And tell your husband, bum shoulder or not, we leave in the morning."

With that, the Great Teacher squatted, picked up the hoe, then walked toward the cabbage patch and began to dig at the weeds, deftly at first with quick flicks of his wrists, and then more savagely as Florence left the field under the watchful eyes of the bodyguards. The last she saw of Kony, he was bringing the hoe high overhead like an axe and smashing it down on the cabbage heads, one after the other.

———

"I think he's losing his mind, Anthony," Florence said that evening after they reunited and the boys were sleeping.

"I think he lost it a long time ago," Anthony replied, rubbing his shoulder, which had been bothering him since the fire.

Feeling her frustration build, Florence said, "He was taunting me, Anthony. He was threatening to take Kenneth from us and adopt him."

"Or he is still mourning all the little boys he lost," Anthony said.

"A strange, sick way to do it."

"I can't argue."

"He kept asking me whose love I craved as a little girl."

"He asked me the same thing the first time I met him. He was trying to get inside your head, figure out what makes you *you*."

"I don't want him in my head," Florence insisted. "It's no good, Anthony. We live under him, under his spirits, with no control over our own lives. How will Kenneth go to school? How will we have any life if we stay here?"

Ever since rejoining Kony inside Control Altar, Anthony had been troubled by many of the same questions. He did not want Florence, Kenneth, or Boniface living under the Great Teacher's rule for any longer than they had to.

"He says we are moving tomorrow," Anthony said. "I don't know how yet, but I will send for you, get you out of here."

"But what about you?" Florence demanded.

Flashing on the Great Teacher's promise to hunt him down no matter where he went, Anthony said, "Once you and the boys are out, I'll follow."

———

In early April 2003, Kony ordered the roving bands of General Matata's battalion to rendezvous with General Tabuley's forces in the mountains west of Agoro, Uganda. For months, he'd had them splintered into smaller fighting units. But now the LRA's supreme commander wanted at least two full battalions on hand to strike again.

General Tabuley had lost yet another signaler, so Anthony was serving two masters and had little time to move around. But on the third day after he arrived in the Agoro mountains, he went for a walk through the various encampments, with Corporal Leonard trailing.

He ran into Patrick near General Matata's camp.

"I thought you were dead!" Patrick said when he saw Anthony.

"I thought the same about you!" Anthony said, and laughed, happy they were still friends and alive. He lowered his voice. "Where's Albert?"

Patrick looked over, saw Leonard standing about twenty meters away, and understood. He turned his head so Anthony's handler could not see his mouth and muttered, "Transmitting. Before I forget, what's the name of your village back home?"

"Rwotobilo."

"Thought so," Patrick said, gesturing over at a girl about fourteen who was stooped over a cooking pot near General Matata's shelter. "Iris. She's from there, I think."

Anthony frowned. He did not remember an Iris in Rwotobilo. He walked over to her, grateful that Patrick intercepted Leonard and started asking him questions.

"You are Iris?" Anthony said quietly to the girl.

She looked up at him, saw his rank, and got nervous. "Yes, Commander."

"How long have you been in the LRA?"

"Three months."

"Where were you captured?"

"They took me from a refugee camp outside Gulu."

"Not Rwotobilo?"

"My family lived near the primary school in Rwotobilo before we went to the camp."

Feeling excited, Anthony said, "I went to that school. Did you know the Opoka family?"

Iris nodded. "George Opoka used to own a store near the school."

Anthony beamed at her. "He is my father! You have seen him?"

"I saw him the day before I was captured. Are you Anthony, or Albert?"

Feeling good and warm inside, he said, "Anthony. He is good, my father?"

She smiled. "He told my father he wants to go back to his fields, like all of us."

That made Anthony feel even better. "I don't suppose you knew my mother. Acoko Florence? She was gone from Rwotobilo when I was taken."

Iris's face fell a little. "She came back to your dad one Christmas night."

Anthony's heart soared, and tears welled in his eyes. "She did?"

Iris nodded. Her eyes had gone a little dull. "But about four years ago, an LRA soldier with a big scar on the right side of his face attacked your compound."

Anthony registered the big scar and thought, *Bacia!*

"Your father escaped," Iris went on. "Your grandfather died. Acoko managed to hit the scarred guy with her hoe, but he beat her head bad with his gun. Omera George took care of her in the camp, but she finally died from the injuries about two years ago."

In four sentences, the vision of his mother and father together again, the vision that he'd nurtured long before his kidnapping, was there and then gone. His mother was gone. She was in the stars. *And Bacia was responsible.*

"I'm sorry, Anthony," Iris said.

"I am, too," he said, swallowing at a ball of grief and anger growing in his throat. "But thank you for telling me."

He turned and walked away, wanting to go off by himself to mourn.

But as he was going to ask General Tabuley to use an alternate signaler for a few hours, he heard a jet coming, and then another. He and every other LRA soldier on the hill took cover.

In total, seven attack jets fired fourteen missiles at the fortifications Kony was having built before the jets arrived, UPDF snipers started killing LRA boys from long range, and the mortar shelling started from teams that had entered the area undetected.

"Opoka!" General Tabuley shouted.

Anthony knew he had no time to grieve or to be angry now. He ran toward his commander, already falling into his role as head of all battlefield communications. It was a job he was inherently good at, and he was quickly caught up in the ebb and flow of combat.

But then the fighting turned savage, with hand-to-hand combat on the hillsides and bombs being dropped from above before the attack helicopters came with the autocannons again, killing scores of LRA boys young and old while Kony broadcast orders from an encampment on high, sheltered as usual with his wives.

On the second morning, as the LRA was rapidly losing ground, the Great Teacher announced he was heading north, deeper into the mountains, where he would better hear the spirits, leaving Tabuley and Matata to counterattack and fade. Then he ordered Anthony to stay with Tabuley.

Leaving was the move that broke whatever hold Kony still had over Anthony's will and mind. *He's a coward*, he thought. *He's no war dog. He's an out-and-out coward who couldn't fight his way out of a pigsty.*

———

Anthony slipped away from Corporal Leonard and saw Patrick and Albert during a lull in the fighting the following evening. "I need to talk to you both," he said. "In private."

His old friend looked around, shrugged, and pointed over to a stand of trees on the hillside. When they were out of hearing, Anthony looked at Albert. "My mother is dead."

His half brother's eyes went wide. "Acoko Florence? No."

"Two years ago," he said. "Bacia clubbed her with his gun when he and another guy tried to kidnap Dad."

"I'm sorry," Albert said. "Dad?"

"He escaped Bacia."

"That's saying something," Patrick said. "Bacia goes psycho when people run. But I'm sorry about your mom, Opoka. That's rough."

Anthony swallowed hard. "You've already saved me so many times, I probably don't have the right to ask you this again, Patrick. And even by asking I'm endangering your life, Albert."

"Out with it," Albert said. "I have to get back."

"I want you to help Betty and my sons escape."

Patrick acted insulted. "I told you before. No. They'd be killed. We'd be killed."

"Please, they're going to die if they *don't* escape," Anthony insisted. "Museveni won't give up. This is a lost cause, but Kony won't release Betty because of me."

Patrick said, "He thinks you'll run if she's gone."

Anthony nodded.

Patrick said, "I just can't do it."

"Neither can I," Albert said.

Anthony remembered the dying shopkeeper for a moment before he said, "I used to think of the Great Teacher as this huge, wild dog with Kony's snarling head. But now, he's just a man who's gotten everything he's ever wanted through fear. The truth is, he's a coward, first to run from a fight. The second people stop being terrified of him is when he's done. But sorry I asked, brothers. Like I said, I had no right."

He turned and walked away.

"Hey, Anthony," Albert called after him. "I get it. I'll try to figure out a way."

Patrick said, "Yeah, I don't know when. I don't know how. But we will pull every trick we can to get Betty and your boys out."

Chapter Thirty-Seven

Fourteen long months later, in stifling heat and humidity, Florence bent over yet again and hoed rows of a new yam field deep in the bush behind the newest LRA center for the wounded.

She was almost twenty-one by that point, a captive for more than six years, and had fallen into despair, believing that the power of love had failed her, believing that she and her boys might never escape the clutches of Joseph Kony and the Lord's Resistance Army.

She'd only seen Anthony three times in the past year and a half. Their last meeting was nearly seven months ago. And every time they'd managed to be together, that goon Corporal Leonard had been lurking about, watching Anthony, trying to listen in on their conversations.

He kept assuring her that his brother and Patrick were working on her escape.

"I saw Patrick again several weeks ago," Anthony had said back then. "He and Albert think they've got it figured out. Now they just have to have a reason to be where you are."

Busting a clod of dirt, Florence laughed bitterly to herself. *A reason to be where I am.* She didn't even know where she was, not really. For more than a year, she and the boys and her band of women, children, and guards had been chased out of one attempt at a permanent encampment after another.

As a result, her sons had had no routine, no certainty in their lives other than her love. For months, she'd had no idea where their next meal or bed would be. And the UPDF continued to hunt them because Kony continued to kill innocent people. Back in February, one of his battalions attacked a refugee camp north of Lira, near her hometown, killing two hundred innocent people.

After a year of near-constant attack and fleeing, they had finally shaken the Ugandan army patrols that hounded them and come here, a place as far off a road as they could find. Huts were built for the women, and then the little hospital for the long-term wounded was constructed. There were two hundred people living in the encampment. If you could call it living.

She and the boys were subsisting on adyebo half the time. Day after day, month after month, the hunger, the burden, and the relentless tedium of her situation had simply become overwhelming. Every day Florence felt like she suffered from sunup to sundown. No matter how often she tried to do some of the things the dying shopkeeper had taught Anthony to combat her misery, she got no relief. Or maybe she wasn't doing it right? Florence didn't know, and it made her want to sit down and cry, and—

"Betty?"

She heard the man's voice call softly from the forest to her right and became frightened. "Who's there?"

"Quiet. It's Anthony's friend."

She almost squealed, "Patrick?"

"Shhhh," the big man said, taking a step from the shadows so he could see her. "Do you still want to go?"

She dropped her hoe. "Right now?"

"Tomorrow," he said. "I have to be here this evening with my new commander and his men. Stick to your routine today and first thing in the morning. Be near the southwest sentry at ten hundred but do not draw attention to yourself. You're out walking with your kids. You've got your gun and your hoe. They expect these things. But no pack. No bag. Nothing that says you're going somewhere. Got it?"

"Yes," Florence said. "What about Albert?"

"He had to stay with General Matata, but he wishes you good luck. I'll whistle when it's time to go. And you have to do what I tell you at all times. Okay?"

She nodded.

"We're going to have to do some running."

Florence smiled. "Good. I am ready."

He turned away and vanished without another word, leaving Flo breathless.

———

She was going home! At last! And the boys as well!

How is Patrick going to do it? How far are we going to have to run? Will he help carry Kenneth if he can't keep up? Her oldest had just turned four after all. Those unanswered questions and a dozen others occupied her mind the rest of the day and well into the night as she cooked double portions of their remaining food, fuel for herself and the boys. Kenneth and Boniface, a toddler now, passed out soon afterward. But she felt so full after eating she had trouble sleeping. She kept tossing and turning, despite knowing she had to rest if they were going to run a long way.

But why in the morning? Why not try at night? The moon's almost half-full. If we had to, we could see well enough.

Florence finally eased her anxieties by clinging to a memory that had helped her during the past year of separation. She thought of Anthony's smile that first time they met near the well at Nesitu, and how indignant she'd been when he'd walked away from her. She remembered walking away from him when he came courting.

It always made her laugh.

———

Hearing a giggle, Florence woke with a start to see it was broad daylight and her hut was empty. Fearing she'd missed Patrick, she groped around, found the Casio wristwatch Anthony had bought for her on their honeymoon. Half past seven.

Thank you, thank you, she thought, feeling her heart slow. Patrick's words echoed in her head. *Stick to your routine. Nothing that says you're going somewhere.*

Florence dressed quickly in her only dress and sandals and went outside, finding Kenneth tickling Boniface, who was squirming as he laughed.

"Hungry?"

"Yes," Boniface said.

"A lot," Kenneth said.

She went to the stream, got water in her plastic jug and in her canteen. She built a small fire and reheated some bread she'd made the day before. She smeared it with honey one of the soldiers had taken from a hive and given to her the week before. She made sure she and the boys drank plenty of water and that they'd all peed.

It was a quarter to ten when they finished. After getting her AK-47 from the hut, she wrapped several scarves around her waist and hung her canteen across her chest. It was hot enough. No one would question her carrying it. She picked up her hoe.

"Let's go for a little walk," she said, trying again to slow her heart, which had started to hammer in her chest.

Boniface yawned. "Tired, Mama."

Florence shouldered her gun, bent down, and picked him up. Boniface wrapped his legs around her waist and laid his head against her shoulder, sucking his thumb as she walked casually toward the southwest corner of the encampment, seeing other women tending fires and their children. She nodded to them, smiled, and kept moving.

The field where she'd been weeding the day before was close to the southwest corner of the encampment. She crossed the field and walked down a path through the trees that led to an overlook where the sentry usually stood. Looking ahead, Florence saw Patrick was already there, towering over and talking to the young soldier on duty. She felt like she did not want the sentry to see them, so she stepped off the path and walked into the bush several meters and stood there, holding Boniface in one arm and Kenneth's hand.

She whispered, "We're going to stay here until Daddy's friend says we can come out. It's important we stay quiet."

A few minutes later, she heard footsteps and pulled Kenneth close to her. The sentry walked by with his gun on his shoulder, yawning and looking happy to be relieved of duty. He disappeared back toward the yam field. Florence and the boys stayed where they were until they heard Patrick whistle once, sharply.

"Here we go," she said, and urged Kenneth out of the brush onto the trail.

Ahead of them, a girl a few years younger than Florence came out of the forest on the other side of the trail, followed by two boys, one who looked in his early teens and another closer to the girl's age. Beyond them, Patrick was making windmill motions with his arms.

"We're going to run a little now, okay, Kenneth?"

"I run like Daddy."

"That's right," Florence said, quickening their pace, letting go of Kenneth's hand, and running after the girl and the two boys.

They reached Patrick.

Florence gestured to the others. "Who are they?"

"Albert's friends. They want freedom, just like you," he whispered. "No talking now."

He picked up several palm fronds and gestured with his chin to a game trail that dropped off the side of the overlook into dense jungle. The others didn't move, so Florence did, carrying Boniface and hurrying onto the switchback trail that led downhill. She paused at the first turn to make sure Kenneth was behind her, and to see Patrick sweeping the trail clean of their tracks.

That spurred Florence to move even faster on the steep sidehill until she reached the bottom, which was dimmer and steamy. She paused for the others to catch up.

"What are you stopping for, Betty?" Patrick said, pushing by them. "The next sentry comes on duty in fifteen minutes."

Once he got to the front, Patrick moved at a relentless pace, hacking aside vines with a machete and urging them to keep going as hard and as fast as they could. Boniface complained he wanted to get down, but Florence held him tight and stayed close enough to see Patrick's back. And Kenneth was doing great, running barefoot on the now-muddy trail.

The girl and the older boy were staying with them as well, but the younger kid was having trouble keeping up as they splashed down through a stream and up the other side. For the next kilometer, the way was flat and boggy, and the younger boy fell twice on the uneven footing. They crossed two more streams before the boy said, "I gotta rest!"

Patrick stopped, looked back, angry, before they heard a horn blow three times in quick succession from back there, up on the overlook where the sentry had been posted.

"They know!" Patrick growled. "The manhunters are coming! Keep up or die!"

Florence had taken a quick pause to tie little Boniface to her back with one of the scarves. When Patrick turned and ran, she pushed Kenneth after him.

"Stay with Patrick," she said. "I'm right behind you."

Kenneth saw how scared she was, turned, and, arms pumping, ran after his father's friend. They ran for a solid hour before Florence's oldest could not go on. Patrick got him piggyback, and they kept the torrid pace for another hour before they slowed to a fast walk.

"Where are we going, Patrick?" she heard Kenneth ask.

"A road, eventually," he said. "LRA hunters hate roads."

"How far?" asked the girl, Cynthia. She was right behind Florence and breathing hard.

"Eighteen, twenty kilometers?" Patrick said.

"I'll never make it, Marcus," the younger boy said.

The older boy turned to look at him. "You have to, Daniel."

Patrick kept the pace steady for the next hour. At intersections, he had them walk side trails, then jump into the jungle and loop back onto the main trail.

"Why?" Cynthia asked.

"To throw them off," Patrick grunted. "Slow them."

Daniel, the younger boy, said, "But we don't know they're still chasing us."

"You don't, but I do."

———

It took them three more hours to cover ten kilometers. When the cover grew less dense, more savanna, Patrick intentionally left the trail and used a compass to guide them south-southwest through elephant grass and acacia thickets and the occasional swampy area, where they encountered muck and the bugs were thick and swarming.

As the sun got low in the west, they came to an open area about a half kilometer long with much shorter vegetation, no more than thigh high after hours of bushwhacking and taking game trails through grass that was over their heads. On the other end of the natural field, some four hundred meters off, a line of trees loomed.

Daniel had once again fallen behind. So had Cynthia and Marcus, who were strung out behind Florence, who still had Boniface on her back. Kenneth was walking, managing to take three steps for every one of Patrick's.

Everyone else was tired, but Florence was as alert as she'd ever been. *We're going home. We're almost eight hours into our escape. We've done it. We're going home!* She called up an old memory—her mother's face by her bed that Christmas Eve when Josca had come to rescue her from the measles ward—and felt flooded with joy. It would not be long now before she was in her mother's arms again.

"How far is that road now?" Cynthia called.

"Six, seven kilometers?" Patrick said. "If we stay on this bearing, we can't miss it."

A burst of shots rang out behind them. Florence startled, then started running, looking over her shoulder and seeing little Daniel back there, staggering, blood pouring from his mouth.

"They're on us!" Patrick yelled, then grabbed Kenneth and took off in a dead sprint toward that line of trees.

Flooded with adrenaline, Florence ran even harder. Several guns fired, all going off at once. She heard a scream, looked back, and saw Cynthia clutching at her leg before falling. There was no sign of Marcus, the older boy.

Sprinting now, Florence stayed with Patrick, ignoring the stitch in her side, ignoring the bullets until the group came over a rise about two hundred meters from the trees. The light was low. But she saw movement at the edge of the shadows. Patrick did, too, skidded to stop, put Kenneth down, and took a quick look through his binoculars.

"UPDF!" he said.

The shooting intensified behind them even as the Ugandan army patrol opened up from the trees in front of them. Florence saw flames bursting out of the muzzles of a dozen submachine guns, and tracers coming their way and more shots behind her. They were caught in a cross fire.

"Mama!" Kenneth screamed before Patrick tackled him.

It's over, she thought as she dove for the ground. *After everything, love loses.* Something smashed her head.

Florence saw stars before it all went to darkness.

Chapter Thirty-Eight

June 13, 2004
Kidepo Valley National Park, Uganda

Anthony finished his late-afternoon radio call, then set about putting out his solar panels for the batteries. He didn't mind. He was deep in a vast park of rugged, broken country, out on a cliff that looked down on a flat where fifty elephants were on the march, trumpeting as they went to water.

And he'd just heard from Brigade Commander Dominic Ongwen himself that some of General Matata's men had gone to a rendezvous at the encampment where Florence and the boys had been eking out a living. That meant that Patrick or Albert or both had been there as well. For all he knew, his family was already gone, already free. Not even Corporal Leonard's presence was a bother. Not today.

They have to be out by now. Their plan was perfect. Call off a tired sentry, slip out a back door, and don't head for the nearest road, but the road they won't think of, and then stay on that road until they reach safety.

He knew it was the right thing to get her out. Too many people he knew in the LRA had been killed. His longtime commander, General Charles Tabuley, had died in combat the November before. Now he walked back toward his bivouac, smelling something savory on the wind. He found his friend Iris preparing a stew for Brigade Commander Ongwen, who had stolen her from General Matata after discovering her cooking skills.

"You've got a spring in your step," Iris said when Anthony walked by grinning.

"Why not?" he said. "It's a beautiful day, not a cloud in the sky. Bunch of elephants back there playing music."

"And here I just want to go home," Iris said quietly.

"We all do," he said, equally quiet. "We just have to be patient."

"I've been here more than a year."

"Almost ten for me."

"Ten?" she said. "How do you do that?"

Before he could reply, he saw Commander Ongwen and General Bunyi, a squat, neckless man, walking toward them, somber, looking everywhere but at him.

"Opoka," Ongwen said.

"Signal Commander," Bunyi said. "We'd like to talk to you for a moment in private."

Anthony saluted, said, "Yes, sir. Where, sir?"

They started off with Corporal Leonard trailing until the senior officers told him to remain behind. Anthony's minder looked ready to argue, but then sat where he was with a sullen expression. They led Anthony to a log by a stream they used for water.

He felt calm, unthreatened. He'd been expecting a visit from someone eventually to tell him that Betty had run with his sons. He was prepared to act shocked, depressed. He was prepared to tell the truth as the officers knew it, that he had not seen his wife and boys in almost seven months, and they had not spoken on the radio, either. And no, of course he would not consider running.

"Anthony," General Bunyi began. "Commander Ongwen just spoke with General Matata over his radio."

Which meant they had talked to Albert as well. Anthony cocked his head to one side, trying to seem puzzled but calm. "Yes?"

Ongwen cleared his throat. "Your wife tried to escape four days ago with three recent LRA recruits. Patrick Lumumba chased them with manhunters."

He glanced at Bunyi, who said, "Lumumba staggered back into Matata's camp a few hours ago, badly wounded, shot through the right side of his neck. Just missed his carotid artery. He said he almost caught up to Betty and the others, and the manhunters were right behind him when they all ran into a UPDF patrol and there was a battle."

Ongwen cleared his throat, and then said, "They were caught in a cross fire. Lumumba was shot and knocked out."

Bunyi said, "He didn't come around until the following afternoon. He was in a ditch, left for dead. The patrol was gone, the manhunters were dead, and I'm terribly sad to say, so were Betty and your two sons."

Anthony didn't know what to say at first. Was this Patrick adding to the story? *But he was shot in the neck, just missed the carotid. There's no faking that.* He leaned forward, feeling right on the edge of breakdown, trying to be the leopard in its cave, trying not to crumble while the dog beast snarled and tried to ram his shoulders through the entrance.

"That's not true. That can't be right," he said.

Bunyi put his hand on Anthony's back. "It's true, Commander Tony. Lumumba said there was a toddler strapped to her back and a boy about four beside her. There were birds on them."

———

Anthony slowly wrapped his hands and forearms around his head, feeling worse than he had being dragged off from Rwotobilo a decade before, like he had been cut loose from the only things anchoring him in this life.

Don't cry, he kept telling himself. *Don't let them see you cry.*

Finally, he looked up at them through filmy eyes. "Did he bury them?"

Ongwen nodded.

"Does he remember where?"

"I don't know."

Memories of Florence danced in his head. The way she clapped. The way her body shook when she laughed. Her eyes so bright when she talked about the boys, or about home, her mother and father, and school. Her dream of being a nurse. Such a good, good human.

Gone.

He could not bring himself to think about Kenneth and Boniface, shot down before they could even become themselves.

"Are you going to run, Opoka?" Ongwen asked.

Anthony stared dully at the commander. "Does it matter, sir?"

Ongwen and Bunyi glanced at each other.

Bunyi said, "We don't want to hunt you, Opoka. You're one of us."

"Again, does it matter, General?"

"It does to me. Is there anything we can do? Anything?"

Anthony thought about asking to be released. But why? Would going home be worth anything without Florence or Kenneth or Boniface? No, he decided. There was nothing for him there now. His mother was dead. His grandfather was dead. George was living in a camp. And there was nothing here for him now except signaling and his own—

"Opoka?" Ongwen said.

He smelled something savory in the wind again and had an impulsive thought. "If you wish me to remain, release your cook, the girl, Iris."

"The cook?" Bunyi said. "What is she to you, Anthony?"

"My little sister by my father's second wife," he lied. "Release her, and I will fight with you and the Great Teacher until the end."

"I don't know," Ongwen said. "That Iris is a great cook."

The general seemed torn as well.

"Please, General," Anthony said. "Let at least one good thing come of this."

General Bunyi thought for a moment, and then said, "Done. We will call the chief in Taan Valley to come get her. Do you want to tell your sister?"

Anthony could not stop his lower jaw from trembling as he nodded and got up. "Thank you, General. Brigade Commander."

He felt unbalanced as he walked away from them back toward the encampment, smelling Iris's cooking, his body and mind as tortured as they'd been after being hit by the rocket grenade.

Birds, Anthony thought, and had to fight not to puke.

Iris was stirring when Anthony returned. "Gather your things. You're going home."

She dropped the wooden spoon into the pot. "What?"

"General Bunyi is releasing you because I told him you were my little sister."

Iris gazed at him in wonder. "Why would they do that? Why would you do that?"

"Betty and Kenneth and Boniface were killed by the UPDF when they were trying to escape. I told the general I would not try to run if they let you go."

She ran up to him, hesitated, and then hugged him. "I'm so sorry, Commander. But thank you. You are a good man, and when I see your father, I will tell him that."

He patted her on the back, staring off into the middle distance. "Better to tell them I'm dead. Better to tell them there was no hope for me after my family died." Then he pulled back from her. "Have a good life, Iris."

Anthony walked alone to the cliff where his batteries had been charging in the sun. The elephants had watered and moved on. He wondered if the fall from there was enough to end the suffering that stretched out endlessly before him.

Can't do it, he thought bitterly. *Those bastards won't release Iris if I'm already dead.*

Then he thought of Florence and the boys as he'd walked away from them the last time, how they'd all waved goodbye, even Boniface. Anthony felt his heart shatter, and he lay on his side on the clifftop, letting his loss go in long, gut-wrenching croaks and sobs.

———

Anthony had never known grief like this, so internal and wrenching it felt like he and Florence had been like two young trees growing together, side by side, their roots entwined. And now Flo and her roots had been torn out of the ground beneath his feet. And Kenneth and Boniface. And the birds. He couldn't shake that image from his mind.

I did that. I asked Patrick to take them. I thought it was safe, but I sent my own family to their deaths. And the birds.

For weeks, the signal commander mourned. Grief was like a fog that crept after him wherever he went. The only relief he got was thinking of Iris and how the morning after he gained her release, he had stood out on the cliff and watched her walk down the valley where the elephants had trumpeted, going to meet the local village chief, bound for Rwotobilo and the three big, crisscrossing trees he would never see again.

Anthony went through his duties even as he was being tortured inside. After the LRA was flushed out of the wilds of the national park by Ugandan army helicopters, he almost welcomed the attacks and the fact that they were back on the run, pursued, rarely staying in one place more than a night or two. Firefights with UPDF patrols were common and lethal in the months after his family was killed. Boy soldiers died all around him, and there were many times he thought sure his time had come at last. But somehow none of the bullets, mortars, bombs, and missiles connected to end his misery.

In mid-July, Kony once again summoned Anthony to his side. To the young man's disgust, the Great Teacher said nothing about the death of his wife and sons.

"We're going back to Bin Rwot to get the food that's cached there," Kony said. "Then to the Katire hills, where we will rendezvous with General Matata and two battalions. You know the area?"

Feeling numb inside, Anthony said, "North side of the Imatongs, bottom of the U, above the town of Katire. We went through there leaving Gong One training camp."

The Great Teacher nodded. "I had large caches of weapons, ammo, and uniforms brought into those hills during the past year. We can last a long time there. And it's a great place for an ambush."

Surrounded by one hundred of his bodyguards, and General Vincent's elite soldiers, Kony, his wives and children, Anthony, and four hundred others marched north yet again. Ten days later they reached Rubangatek, which was virtually deserted. But the food was there. They found another cache full in Bin Rwot, which held a few more LRA holdouts, most of them with serious wounds. He saw Lily limping toward him.

She looked at him wearily but attempted a smile. "Hello, Signaler."

"Hello, Lily. It's good to see you."

Lily snorted derisively. "And yet Teacher barely sees me."

"I'm sorry. How's your leg?"

"Worse than your shoulder," she said, and appeared to be fighting not to cry.

"You will stay here?"

"I can't keep up, and I've been replaced, so there's no choice, is there?"

He hesitated, not knowing what to say, then thought of his father asking what a good human would say.

"I wish you the best, Lily," he said finally. "I really do."

She limped past him, saying, "And here I go expecting the worst."

He watched her a moment, remembering her as the kindest of the Great Teacher's wives, and felt sorry for her lot in life before turning his grieving thoughts to Florence and the boys.

They left Bin Rwot and headed into the Imatongs. In some ways, the ordeal was worse than Anthony remembered from his first two trips through those rugged mountains. In most ways, he did not care. He welcomed the punishment.

Early August in the highlands is usually dry. But the rains came early. Soaking wet at times, they crossed three passes at altitudes close to three thousand meters.

Finally, weeks after they had set out from Uganda, Anthony stood with Kony and his senior commanders high on a mountainside looking north on the clearest day in a week. Far below them, they could see the lazy U shape of the broad, long, green valley formed by the two arms of the Imatong range, both of them coming together to cradle the town of Katire.

The Great Teacher ordered General Vincent and Brigade Commander Ongwen to send their men down to retrieve the caches stored in caves above the town, and to bring them up to a long bench that stretched into timber at close to twenty-five hundred meters in altitude. Other LRA boys were ordered to clear the undergrowth in the forest so huts could be built.

At eleven that same morning, Anthony tuned in the shortwave and the FM radios they'd received from the Sudanese military. From the shortwave, he heard his brother Albert say that General Matata's forces were less than ten kilometers from Katire. Kony told them to start climbing to his position and then listened to an FM radio report out of Juba that described "a great victory in Uganda's Operation Iron Fist."

The announcer said, "Ugandan army gunships and ground troops attacked the Lord's Resistance Army rebel group this morning at their barrack strongholds at Rubangatek and Bin Rwot, southeast of Juba. Against fierce LRA resistance, the aerial and ground assault ultimately prevailed against the rebel group led by messianic warlord Joseph Kony. Scores of LRA were killed, the barracks destroyed, and several of Kony's slave wives were rescued from captivity along with their children. The Ugandan and Sudanese governments hope this begins the process of stamping out the LRA and Kony for good."

The Great Teacher threw back his head and laughed caustically. "Messianic warlord? Fierce LRA resistance? Slave wives? We left the wounded who could not make the march. And my wives are with me. These are all lies. They attacked empty barracks. What is this nonsense, Opoka? I am not there. I am here, on the other side of the Imatongs with a growing army."

"You are, Teacher," Anthony said.

"Turn that off," Kony said, gesturing at the FM radio. "I need to think."

He'd no sooner said that than the shortwave began to crackle. Ongwen was sending up a message in code from the caves above the town of Katire.

Anthony translated the code and read it. "Teacher, the caches have been raided."

"What?!" Kony thundered.

"There's more," Anthony said, cowering as he read on. "We can see through binoculars that the townspeople looted them. They are wearing our uniforms. There are sacks of our grain outside many of the homes. Weapons and ammunition, too. Orders?"

For several minutes, Kony stood there fuming down at the town far below, his hands clenching into fists and relaxing, clenching into fists and relaxing.

At last, he looked at Anthony and said, "First, to Matata: Stop climbing. Proceed to Katire. Second, to Commander Ongwen: This cannot be tolerated. The government of Sudan has underestimated me, and the people of Katire have underestimated the LRA. Kill anyone who has stolen from us and retrieve what is ours. Round them up and do it in a memorable way."

Anthony swallowed hard as he began to code the message. "You are sure, Teacher?"

Kony backhanded him hard across the face, drew his pistol, and put it to Anthony's head. "Don't you ever question my judgment, Opoka. Do you understand?"

The blow stunned Anthony, but he was focused on the muzzle of the Great Teacher's pistol, how cold it felt. He wanted to tell him to just do it. Put a bullet in his brain and end the suffering for good.

Instead, hatred boiling through him, he said, "I am sorry, Teacher. It won't happen again."

The gun stayed where it was.

"Joseph," his wife Evelyn said, "don't. Opoka's a good man and he's lost his family."

For what seemed an eternity, Kony kept the gun there, but then drew it away.

"Translate and send, Signaler," he said coldly. "It's all you are good for. Translate and send. And you are no longer my radioman, no longer our nation's future minister of communications. I intend to reassign you for good."

With that, Kony stalked away with his young wife, who looked dreadfully thin. Anthony fought not to tremble. He knew he'd just had a close shave with death. The Great Teacher executed people for less.

It took him twice the usual time to encode Kony's orders and send them. Ongwen almost immediately replied. "Received, Teacher. Memorable it will be."

Anthony stood there not knowing what to do. He told Corporal Leonard, who was eating, that he needed to get a better line of sight for a transmission for the Great Teacher. Then he took his lightweight radio, his rifle, and his binoculars, and hiked out to an outcropping that gave him a better view of the town below and the hundred LRA soldiers scrambling down the mountainside.

Sweeping into Katire from several angles, Ongwen's gunmen began retrieving uniforms, food, guns, and ammo from the townspeople. If someone was found with any goods that had been cached in the caves, they were separated and moved to the east end of the town. Anyone who tried to resist was shot.

Suddenly, there appeared to be many more soldiers in the town than Ongwen had left with. Anthony realized Matata's soldiers had to be there now, which likely meant that Patrick and Albert might be down there as well. He tried to spot his brother and old friend through the binoculars, but Katire was too far to put a face or a build on any figure or movement.

The number of people at the east end of town had grown to almost one hundred when he heard Ongwen on the radio, ordering his men to crowd them into a tight group. Then he heard him call for "four SPG-9s" to be brought forward.

Anthony got a sickening feeling in his stomach. The SPG-9 was a Soviet-made, 73 mm recoilless rifle, often used as a lightweight antitank weapon. It shot a hollow-charge round that blew and shattered on impact.

"Why?" he muttered to himself, and then could not watch when LRA boys carried the portable antitank guns to the edge of the town about one hundred meters from the now-tight knot of people.

The recoilless rifle shots, even at that distance, were booming, startling sounds of mechanized war. When he forced himself to look through the binoculars again, Anthony could see scores of bodies torn apart. Other men and women wandered around wounded, maimed, screaming silently, or trying to run for the bush. Before they could make it to cover, other LRA boys cut them down with machine guns.

Then he heard Ongwen on the radio boasting: "That's what you get when you steal from the Great Teacher and his holy! A memorable punishment!"

Sitting there on the outcropping, Anthony hung his head and cried. He knew that after being spared by Kony, he could not be seen showing emotion like this. But he could not stop crying. When he tried to calm himself by thinking of his father and the late Mr. Mabior and the things they'd taught him, he cried even harder.

How could any of it explain being part of this insanity, this mass murder to send a message? Kony didn't have to give that order. He could have told Ongwen to go get their supplies back and left it at that. No, the Great Teacher had to kill, and he had to kill in a way no one expected. Did anyone or anything matter to him except his own gain?

"No one matters to him," Anthony blubbered softly. "Florence was right. We are his slaves. I am his slave."

He could not take it any longer when he heard radio chatter from Ongwen to his men, ordering them to take the rest of the people who'd stolen from Kony into a side canyon away from town and dispose of them. Anthony told himself that his father's dream had not come true, that he had not grown up to become a good human.

In fact, he was not human anymore. Not even a leopard in his mind.

Anthony Opoka, Commander Tony of the LRA, was an empty, wind-up war machine.

It felt like there was nothing in his heart, no humanity, no soul to him anymore as he shut down the radio and climbed down off the rocky outcropping and trudged back toward that bench where Kony wanted Control Altar's camp built.

"What happened out there?" Leonard asked. "You were acting strange."

"I saw strange things," Anthony said, and gathered his radio batteries to charge them.

———

Two hours later, while charging his radio batteries, Anthony saw Albert at a distance climbing the hillside. Through the binoculars, he looked shell-shocked. Patrick was fifty meters behind Albert, a grim expression on his face.

Anthony could see the livid wound on the side of his friend's neck and thought, *Birds.*

He knew he should invent a reason to go to General Matata's encampment, to find Patrick and hear the story of the failed escape of his family.

But for once, Anthony lacked the courage.

Chapter Thirty-Nine

Because a replacement signaler had not yet been chosen, Anthony was ordered to stay within fifteen meters of Kony, who said little to him other than to direct orders to one commander or another over the battlefield radios.

Long into the following day, Anthony watched as the Great Teacher relentlessly drove the thousand-plus child soldiers he had at his disposal. He had two hundred of them creating fortifications on the hillsides above Katire. He had three hundred ferrying land mines and digging trenches where the explosives were laid across trails that laced the hillsides. He sent another three hundred to positions north of the town, and east and west of the road to Torit.

They were not done placing the land mines until late in the day. After dark, the Great Teacher had the mining crew retreat to higher, cliffy country and wait. But he kept the boys building the fortifications hard at work all night.

Slowly, through the numbness, Anthony realized what Kony was up to. He had cynically ordered the mass murder to bring a retaliation. It was as he had said before they started marching more than a month before—Katire was a great place for an ambush.

He was with the Great Teacher at dawn the next day, when the LRA leader looked down through his binoculars, watching as the first Sudanese officials came along the lonely, bumpy road from Torit. Forward LRA scouts reported seeing many of the town's survivors talking to the officials and gesturing toward the still-unburied bodies festering outside the east end of town and up at the LRA boys still digging on various hillsides. The Sudanese hurried off.

Kony kept the boys hard at work until dark, when he ordered the fortifications fitted with scarecrows and booby-trapped. Then the boys made their way gingerly up the mountain, taking with them the little flags that marked the positions of the mines.

———

Shortly after dawn the following morning, August 14, a line of open-topped lorries filled with UPDF and Sudanese soldiers appeared on Torit Road. The scouts reported they were accompanied by a large communications truck with long whip antennae.

"Airpower is definitely coming," Kony said, watching through binoculars.

"Depending on where they stop, we'll have a say in that," General Vincent said.

The convoy came to a halt half a kilometer shy of town. Soldiers poured from the lorries. Mortar teams assembled and began shelling the hills above town and all around the decoy fortifications.

"They're shooting too low," the Great Teacher said, smiling.

"Burning their munitions," General Vincent agreed.

Kony looked at Anthony. "Order all commanders to hold their fire until they see the UPDF starting to climb below us."

Anthony relayed that message and the next one from Kony, which came amid renewed mortar rounds whistling and exploding harmlessly on the flanks of the lower hillsides: "Get someone in position to take out that communications truck on my call."

Ongwen came back almost immediately to say he had two recoilless rifle teams working their way into range.

Two UPDF gunships appeared in the skies from the north, flanking Torit Road as they chugged south, up and over the town of Katire, where they opened fire with heavy machine guns, raking the low hills and the areas around the fortifications.

They made two passes before Ongwen called to say his boys were in position.

"Hold fire," Kony said, watching as Ugandan and Sudanese forces began advancing on the town, with the helicopters circling overhead.

They faced zero resistance, of course, and soon were through the town and massing for a frontal assault uphill. The Great Teacher let them come until they were halfway up to the dummy soldiers in the dummy fortifications before ordering those on the flanks to stay in cover and spread out. LRA boys filtered down through the trees east and west of Torit Road and took positions north of the lorries, sealing off any escape.

The foot soldiers continued to climb the hillside. The first few reached the empty fortifications and saw the scarecrows before the helicopters swung off to refuel and reload at lorries parked farther up the valley. A minute later, the first booby trap went off. Ten seconds after that, the first land mine detonated.

"Now, Ongwen," Kony said.

Anthony sent the message. From a low knoll northeast of the town, the recoilless rifles fired in tandem, the hollow-charge rounds hitting not bodies this time but the communications truck fore and aft, blowing gaping holes in the sides of it before the sound of the double hit rolled up the mountainside.

"Snipers," the Great Teacher said. "And General Matata, move forward."

Anthony relayed the orders through Albert. The LRA boys hiding on the cliffs above the fortifications began raining fire down on the still-advancing Ugandan and Sudanese forces. Heard from above, the peppering of the light arms contrasted with the low thunder of the land mines that went off sporadically as the enemy tried to work higher. Matata moved his forces down the mountain to support the snipers.

Kony stared strangely at Anthony, and then said, "Sing for them, Signaler." "Teacher?"

"On your goddamned radio," he said. "Sing '*Polo, polo, yesu Lara*' to give them strength."

Seeing the man was in one of his insane phases, Anthony keyed the microphone and began to sing.

Polo, polo, yesu Lara.
Heaven, heaven, Jesus save me.
Heaven should come to rescue us in our lives,
And we shall never leave the way to heaven.
Polo, polo, yesu Lara.
Heaven, heaven, Jesus save me.

Faced with a frontal assault from above and from their flanks by a larger-than-expected LRA force, the UPDF and Sudanese soldiers fought ferociously. Kony's boys kept the helicopter gunships at bay by firing shoulder-launched missiles at them.

For nearly five hours, the battle went on. When Anthony wasn't relaying orders, he was singing under the steel gaze of the Great Teacher. Finally, around 10:00 a.m., the Ugandans began to retreat downhill and through Katire.

As they exited the town, hustling back toward the lorries, Kony ordered the LRA soldiers on both sides of Torit Road to open fire. Scores of Ugandan army men died in the first minutes of fighting, which became boxed into the streets of the town. A gunship roared in, firing on LRA positions and then trying to rescue survivors.

The helicopter was fifty meters from landing, when one of Brigade Commander Ongwen's men came up out of deep grass, aimed a rocket grenade, and fired it. The missile caught the underbelly of the helicopter and exploded. The chopper lurched hard at the impact, stuttered, and then spiraled down into a crop field, where it disintegrated in a fireball.

LRA soldiers up and down the mountain began to cheer, ululate, and sing. Anthony could hear their voices below and above him, like some twisted and triumphant boys' choir. Soon afterward, the surviving Ugandan and Sudanese forces gave up.

Ongwen radioed that he was prepared to take them all to that canyon where he'd taken the other townspeople.

"No," Kony replied. "Take their weapons, put them back in their trucks, and let them go. I want word of this brutal defeat to reach Juba and Khartoum and then Kampala and Museveni as fast as possible so they will think twice before trying to assault the LRA ever again."

———

The Great Teacher was in high spirits the rest of the day and into the night, back to teasing his wives and greeting Ongwen as a hero. It took everything in Anthony's power not to let his loathing show as Kony made a general broadcast to other LRA commands in southern Sudan and northern Uganda, boasting of the victory and how thorough it had been.

Anthony slept fitfully and was already up when the LRA's supreme commander emerged from his shelter with binoculars around his neck. He told Anthony to bring the Cascina.

Anthony followed Kony to that outcropping he himself had sat on during the civilian massacre days before. *Did he see me come out here? Did Leonard see me crying and report me?*

As Anthony dug in his pack for his antenna wire, the Great Teacher stood at the edge overlooking Katire and the valley.

"My kingdom, for now," Kony said. "I truly am a man blessed by God and guided by spirits, Opoka. Yesterday was proof that my cause—our cause—is just. I didn't just win yesterday. I showed mercy yesterday, releasing those men. But I also humiliated Museveni, made him grovel, made him start to imagine—against his will, I might say—that despite his every effort, I am building a bigger army than ever, right here in my mountain fortress, with thousands of new recruits and the fields below to feed and train them. All of them will be marching on Kampala someday soon. And then, the worst imagining of all for Museveni, the thought of me, Joseph Kony, riding into the capital in victory, with my minister of communications by my . . ."

They both had become aware of a distant roar that was growing louder until they picked up the glint high in the air and well up the valley. Along with Kony, Anthony raised his binoculars. He saw two sleek fighter jets coming right at them at near supersonic speeds.

"Those are MiG-21s!" the Great Teacher yelled. "Ugandan colors on the tail!"

Anthony dropped his binoculars to find the LRA leader hustling past him, yelling, "Bring the radio, call for standby, we're under—"

The jets were already on them. From a kilometer away, they each fired a missile.

Anthony saw the contrail of one before it struck amid General Matata's encampment far across the mountainside. Before he could think of Albert or Patrick, the second hit close to Control Altar with a force and sound unlike any he had ever faced before. The near blast punched him in the chest, boxed his ears, and passed through him like a giant wave that seemed to shake his brain.

Kony was knocked right off his feet.

Instinct kept Anthony moving, shouldering the radio pack, grabbing the Great Teacher under the armpit and hauling him to his feet even as the jets came around again. Seeing them swing into position, he shoved the LRA leader down and fell beside him, hearing the now-unmistakable rush of two more missiles fired and seeking targets.

The first struck the mountainside near Control Altar. So did the second. The ground beneath them humped and trembled at each explosion. Anthony was hit two more times by that brain-and-body-shaking wave that left him stunned, unable to think straight or move.

Now it was the Great Teacher pulling him to his feet and saying something. Dizzy, dazed, Anthony did not hear Kony at first. Then the LRA leader began to scream loud enough that he understood him through the ringing in his ears.

"They're going to come back!" he said. "Radio for retreat! We have to get out of here!"

He was relieved when, after he announced the retreat, Albert said, "Roger that, Nine Whiskey."

———

The Great Teacher's instincts were sound. Two more times that morning, the UPDF fighter jets returned to fire missiles. A total of twelve blasted the mountainside as Kony and what was left of the LRA took to deep, forested draws where they could not be seen from the air, heading back up into the Imatong range with plans to traverse it straight south, rendezvous with the rest of his soldiers, and finally cross into Uganda to make Museveni pay for what he'd done.

There had been no time to count casualties, but Anthony saw at least a hundred bodies on the hillsides, most of them aged twenty and under, and other LRA boys so badly wounded they had to be left behind. He'd been unable to think during the early part of the withdrawal. He stumbled along behind Kony, just stepping where the Great Teacher stepped, and hoping that somehow one of Museveni's missiles would take them both out.

But the aerial attacks stopped. In the meantime, they kept climbing until they reached a meadow high in the mountains where a great many LRA soldiers were gathering along with the women and children. He looked at them, trying to imagine Florence alive and coming out from behind them, Kenneth at her side, Boniface in her arms.

But then a cloud of small black birds erupted from the forest to his left about sixty meters, and he was so upset he wanted to go down on his knees, puke, and die. It felt as if life was not just making him suffer. It was torturing him.

General Matata came out of the trees where the birds had flushed followed by Albert, bent over under the weight of his radio pack. Corporal Leonard came up, stood a few meters away, his face bleeding and filthy from combat, staring at the ground.

"Have you seen Evelyn?" Kony asked, on his feet, but seeming dazed, disconnected somehow.

"No, Teacher," Anthony said as Patrick exited the woods, filthy, blood on his uniform.

"She was behind me about an hour ago. I saw her."

The signaler nodded as the Great Teacher wandered off to ask others about his wife.

Patrick noticed him and walked away from Albert and Matata. As he came closer, Anthony kept staring at the nasty red scar on the side of his neck.

"I thought you were dead," Anthony said.

"I thought you were dead, too," Patrick said, looking as exhausted as Anthony felt.

"I know you want to tell me what happened, but I can't hear it. Not now. Maybe not ever."

"I understand," Patrick said softly, sadly, before taking a step closer and muttering, "except this is a story you might want to hear. Let's go in the trees, take a leak."

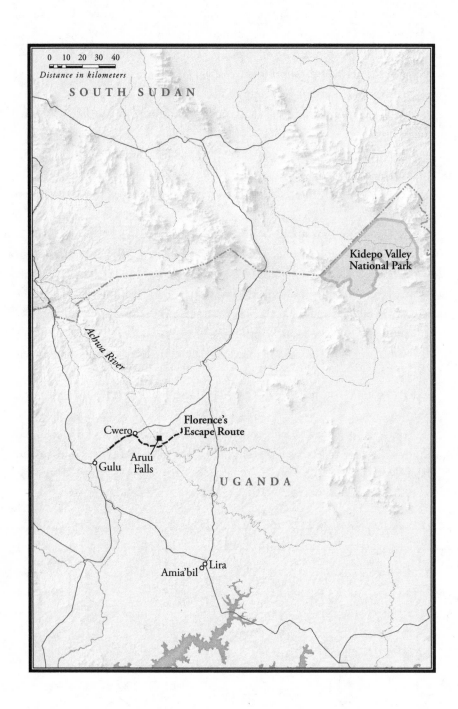

0 10 20 30 40
Distance in kilometers

SOUTH SUDAN

Kidepo Valley
National Park

Achwa River

Cwero

Florence's
Escape Route

Aruu
Falls

Gulu

UGANDA

Amia'bil Lira

Chapter Forty

The Ugandan army patrol opened up from the trees in front of them. Florence saw flames bursting out of the muzzles of a dozen submachine guns, and tracers coming their way and more shots behind her. They were caught in a cross fire.

"Mama!" Kenneth screamed before Patrick tackled him.

It's over, she thought as she dove for the ground. *After everything, love loses.*

Something smashed her head.

Florence saw stars before it all went to darkness.

Time slowed. She felt herself slipping into . . .

"Mama!" Kenneth cried, shaking her. "Mama, wake up!"

Florence stirred while the battle still raged, looked up, saw the vague outline of her oldest son kneeling over her, and then heard Boniface crying on her back. She reached up to her head, felt a gash and blood all down her face.

"Where's Patrick?"

"I don't know," Kenneth said. "He crawled away."

"Crawled away?"

"Betty!" Patrick hissed. "Hands and knees, all of you, and come toward me."

Florence sat up, felt the sharp, bloody corner of a rock next to her, took another one of her scarves, and tied it around her forehead before pushing Kenneth forward and following him until he stopped after about twenty meters.

"There's a shallow stream here," Patrick said. "C'mon, Kenneth. I'll get you down."

Florence saw him lift her oldest son in the light afforded by the half-moon. Then he helped her and Boniface down into water halfway up her shins.

Patrick said, "Kenneth, hold on to the back of my shirt. Florence, you hold the back of his shirt. And keep your heads down!"

They crouched and moved forward with the stream's current while the UPDF patrol and the LRA manhunters continued to wage war on each other. After negotiating several tight spots, including one that brought them unnervingly close to the flank of the Ugandan army unit, they were finally around the patrol and could leave the streambed.

Patrick checked her forehead, said she could use stitches, but rewrapped the scarf tight for her. "Are you good?"

"How far?"

"Another five klicks."

"Let's go," she said, ignoring the pounding headache she had.

———

Two hours later, they reached a dirt road close to a pond. "Stay hidden there," Patrick said, pointing to a clump of trees on the opposite side of the road. "Rest."

"Where are you going?"

"To scout the road ahead before we commit."

He loped off. Florence went to the trees. She got Boniface off her back and nursed him while Kenneth cuddled up next to her and slept. She thought she was too wound up from being in battle to sleep, but she was out cold when Patrick shook her awake three hours later.

"I've got a bike. We can move faster. Leave the gun. You're done with that now."

Florence looked at the AK-47, remembering that many LRA soldiers had been executed for losing their weapons. But Patrick was right. She was done with that now.

She took out the banana clip, cleared the action, and tossed the gun and the magazine in the pond. Then she retied Boniface to her back, feeling him fall asleep almost immediately, and went to Patrick, Kenneth, and the bike.

It was a rickety one-speed single-seater with no fenders. Patrick had Florence sit sideways on the frame in front of him with Kenneth balanced on the handlebars.

"I don't know about this," Florence said.

"No choice now," Patrick said, and after several false starts, he had them making wobbly progress down the road.

The night was cloudless with that half-moon high overhead, so they did not need Patrick's flashlight to ride the ten kilometers to the village of Cwero and a better road, which they reached at two o'clock in the morning. They turned left. Florence saw a sign that said "Gulu, 30K." Even though she was dead tired, even though her head ached from the cut and her butt had gone numb from sitting on the bar between the seat and the handles, her heart began to race, not with excitement but with raw fear.

She'd heard stories from women who'd escaped, only to be recaptured. Many were refused welcome by their families and lived on the streets with a mark of shame on them. Others described fellow escapees being shot on sight when they came out of the bush.

They rode for two hours before Patrick stopped.

"This is as far as I go," he said. "You keep walking down this road for another kilometer or two. You'll come to a police barracks."

"Police?" she said, feeling sick to her stomach.

"It's all right. We heard on Mega FM that they declared an amnesty for LRA people who make it out. Tell the police you want to go to a place called World Vision in Gulu. They help child soldiers."

"What about you?" she said, lifting Kenneth down off the handlebars.

"I'm going back," he said. "I have to sell them a story that you died in the firefight. That should give Anthony a chance to escape himself."

"You'll come with him?"

Patrick shook his head. "My parents are dead. The LRA is all I know."

"Thank you, Patrick."

"No thanks are necessary. I've owed your husband for a long, long time now."

———

Anthony's heart felt like it had grown four sizes in the last five minutes. He wanted to scream for joy but didn't dare. Grinning, tears coming down his cheeks, he said, "And then what?"

"I told Florence not to admit to anyone but the police that she was LRA, and I left."

"I don't know whether to slug you or hug you. I really thought they were dead."

"You had to, or it wouldn't have worked. I had to lie to Albert, too."

"He doesn't know?"

"I had to sell it, Opoka."

"But the birds on their bodies? Man, I had nightmares."

"Sorry."

"What about your neck?"

"Bad luck coming north. Encountered another UPDF patrol and got shot for real."

Anthony shook his head. "And you walked back. Glad you made it."

"So am I. And I'm glad for Betty."

Anthony wiped the tears from his eyes, wondering where Florence had gone from a desolate road near a police barracks.

What does it matter? They're alive!

———

"Mama, I'm so tired," Kenneth whined as Patrick rode the bike away. "I can't walk anymore."

Florence considered ducking into some trees and sleeping until it was light out. But daylight would bring traffic to the road, more chances for people to question her. She knew she was filthy, covered in blood, and decided she was better off going to the police barracks as fast as she could.

"Just a little farther," she said, and took his hand, and they set off alone.

As dawn came on and she neared the barracks, she slowed and stopped. For years she'd been told that anyone associated with the Ugandan military or police would shoot an LRA soldier on sight. For a long time, she stood in the shadows down the road, looking at the building, trying to fight off the shaking in her body as it reacted to the confusion in her mind.

For reasons she did not understand, she was taken by the vivid memory of Kony dressed as a woman after the fire that took his wives, how he'd toyed with her about taking Kenneth, and how he'd hacked the cabbage heads as she'd hurried away, carrying her baby to safety.

As the memory faded, she heard the Great Teacher's voice whisper, *You'll never be safe. You can't go back. They know you're all murderers, and—*

"Mama? You said we're going home," Kenneth said. "Where is it?"

Florence felt her old anger at Kony build, felt it steel her before she said, "Through the front doors of that building, little man."

The four-year-old began tugging on her arm. "Then let's go. I'm hungry."

"I, too, Mama," Boniface said on her back.

She closed her eyes for a second, summoned her courage, and, holding Kenneth's hand once more, she went up the walkway toward a porch. A door opened. A man in a police uniform came out, holding a cup of coffee and smoking a cigarette. He saw her, and his free hand went to his sidearm in a holster.

"Please," she said in a slight stammer. "My name is Florence Okori. I was kidnapped by the LRA in February 1998 outside Lira. These are my sons, Kenneth and Boniface. We wish to surrender and be taken to World Eyesight in Gulu."

That made him relax a little. "World Vision in Gulu. Wait here. I will get a female officer to take you there."

"Oh," she said, her heart still pounding in her chest. "Can I get food and water for my boys at World Vision in Gulu?"

"I think that can happen right here."

———

Florence, Kenneth, and Boniface ate oatmeal with brown sugar and toast with jam, the first real sweets the boys had ever eaten, and the first she had had since her honeymoon with Anthony. A medic in the police station cleaned her forehead wound and sewed it up before they climbed into the back of a Land Rover and were driven into Gulu.

The boys were dumbfounded. They'd never seen a city before, the bustle, the cars, the horns, the music, the whirling scents of spices and food cooking.

For Florence, it came as a slap to her nervous system. For more than six years, she'd been living in remote areas, always under guard, always under the threat of harsh punishment. Seeing what life looked like outside the LRA—women shopping in the markets, men working on motorcycles, students heading to school—made her all the more aware that over a quarter of her life had been spent in captivity.

Florence felt shaky getting out of the truck and being led to the building that housed World Vision. The policewoman introduced her to a man and woman working at the front desk. They asked her where she'd lived in the LRA, and she told them that she'd lived longest in Rubangatek and Bin Rwot in southern Sudan.

The woman said, "Wait here."

She soon returned with three women who had stayed in the LRA barracks at Rubangatek after Kony left. To her astonishment, one of them was her old friend Palmer, who shrieked when she saw Florence and hugged her. The other women knew her as well and vouched for her. And they were all so clean and healthy looking!

With Palmer and the other women there, Florence was excited, but deep inside, she remained afraid for herself and for her children. She really didn't know if she could trust the people in charge. But once she'd been vouched for, the staff welcomed her with open arms. They gave her and the boys a little room with a bed, sheets, blankets, and new clothes.

She took the first hot shower of her life, put on a new dress, and had her hair cut. She had trouble sleeping on a mattress the first night and finally fell asleep on the floor.

On her second day at World Vision, Florence was tested for disease. She agreed enthusiastically to have the boys vaccinated against measles, polio, and typhus. And she attended counseling sessions where she and other women, including Palmer, shared their experiences in the LRA. Palmer, it turned out, had run after a UPDF helicopter killed her husband. She'd never had children with him and made it to Gulu the month before.

Over the course of the next week, Florence told more and more of her story in the group sessions. She and Palmer laughed when she described them both refusing to sleep with Okaya, and then sobered when describing the beatings. Gradually, she relaxed. She could see what the counselors were talking about, that most of her thoughts about returning to her old life were based on fear and the reminders of all the traumatic things she'd experienced.

Those lessons hit home again and again when helicopters passed over the World Vision compound and the LRA children, including her own kids, started screaming and running to hide.

———

Late in the second week, she received devastating news. Counselors had tried to contact her parents through officials in Lira. The officials had found J. Okori and C. Okori on a list of those who had died during a flash flood the year before.

Florence cried off and on for two days. After everything, she'd come home to learn her mother and father were gone. How could they be dead? How was that fair? How was any of her experience in the LRA fair? Were any of her family left? Or was she a total orphan now, a single mother of two with nowhere to go and a husband still in captivity?

The bitterness that had seized Florence's heart after her abduction and before her escape returned in full force. She found herself spending long parts of her days hating Joseph Kony again, blaming him for everything stolen from her, six years of her life, her dream of being a nurse, her innocence, her youth. In many ways, she felt like she had not been freed at all, that she was still a victim of the Great Teacher's warped mind.

For a week, Florence wallowed in loathing, suffered in Rush, in inner Violence, in Lack, and in Fear. Sensing her misery, Kenneth crawled up in her lap on the seventh day and said, "Don't be sad, Mama. I and Boniface are here."

Something about the way he said it, so sweet and innocent and caring, made her feel grateful for both boys, and that eased her misery a bit. Then she thought of Anthony and how he'd rescued her from this terrible bitterness before, and she felt grateful for having met him, for having grown in love with him, and for having her two wonderful boys with him. Her suffering eased even more.

Then she had an out-of-the-blue odd thought that she thoroughly rejected at first. But the more she considered it, the more she knew it was true. And when she felt good about that, her misery almost entirely vanished.

Florence wondered and fretted about this for hours over the course of her last week at World Vision, but did not share it with her counselors, or even Palmer. But then, the day before she was set to transfer to a refugee camp for mothers and children, she remembered Miss Catherine and her mother saying that if you can become still enough to listen to your heart in times of trouble, you will hear the voice of a greater power telling you how to proceed.

She went into a quiet corner of the compound, put her hands over her heart, closed her eyes, and prayed for inner stillness and a way to be free of Kony and everything that had happened to her in captivity.

She stayed there for the longest time, hearing nothing but the distant laughter of children playing, until an idea seized her so thoroughly that she swore she'd been spoken to by a force beyond herself. Florence popped open her eyes, unsure if she could do *that* to Joseph Kony, as evil a man who had ever walked the earth as far as she was concerned, kidnapper of boys and girls by the tens of thousands and murderer of the countless who did not survive his regime.

I can't do it. I can't do that.

But then Flo was again seized out of nowhere by the memory of the Great Teacher dressed as a woman that day in the field after his wives and his children were burned alive, and how he'd held Kenneth and toyed with her emotions, and how he'd taken the hoe from her almost as an afterthought, and how he'd beaten the cabbage heads with it as she hurried to get her baby far away from his wrath.

But suddenly, she saw that scene quite differently, from Kony's perspective, from the dark depths of the abyss he lived in after his wives and children were burned to death. The agony of it rocked her to her core, left her shaking and frightened.

Refusing to dwell there, she crawled her way out of the Great Teacher's miseries and thought of her boys again, and then of Anthony, and how happy she was to have met and chosen him as her husband. He was a good man, a good husband, a good father.

And I love him. And the power of love is stronger than anything.

With those two thoughts dominating her, Florence closed her eyes and summoned Kony from that day in the field, when he'd asked her whose love she'd craved as a child.

Frozen for a moment in the terror of reliving that experience, she nevertheless summoned courage and looked directly into the Great Teacher's eyes, became lost in his fathomless grief for a second time. As she did, she spoke to Kony, uttered words she did not think possible, and as she did, the image of him beating cabbage heads and the inner terror it provoked in her began to shrink and to dissolve.

When they were gone, she opened her eyes and felt lighter than she had in years.

"I felt freed," she told Palmer and the other women at her final counseling session. "I feel free. I don't ignore what he did to Anthony and the way he made me and our boys live, but there's no longer hatred for him in my heart. Joseph Kony no longer controls me in any way."

Palmer and the other women were in tears as they clapped for her.

———

From World Vision, Florence, Kenneth, and Boniface were taken to the Lira Rakeli displaced persons camp for mothers with children, which was about ten kilometers from the city of Lira and nineteen from the village of Amia'bil. There were dozens of former LRA women there to make her comfortable enough to ignore the hostile stares of other women who'd been evacuated from their homes and sent to the camp because of the Lord's Resistance Army.

Florence and the boys were given a hut of their own, and more clothes and food. She settled in, unwilling or unable to think about the future beyond each day. She focused on the boys and how they were filling out with all the good food they were getting and how easily they made friends with the other children. That in and of itself was amazing to her, considering the circumstances of their lives before and during the escape.

One morning as she was bent over, sweeping up the ashes from the breakfast fire, she heard a man say, "Florence Okori? Is that you?"

Florence stood up, looked over, and saw her father standing there.

She collapsed on the ground, sobbing first in confusion and then in joy as Constantine bent over her and patted her on the back. "Florence. It's okay now."

She looked up at him, blubbering, "People in Lira said you were on a list of people who died in a flood last year."

"What?" He laughed and shook his head. "Why would they look for us in Lira? You know we live in Amia'bil, and we are both very much alive and so happy you are, too."

"Mama is good?"

"And can't wait to see you."

It turned out that Constantine and Josca had heard her name mentioned the evening before on a Lira radio station that kept tabs on returning LRA members. Her father had set out to see her at dawn.

"Papa," she said when Kenneth and Boniface came over. "These are my sons."

Her father's face pulsed with confusion and then hardened. "You are a mother?"

"I am, Papa, and I love them. Boys, this is your grandfather."

Boniface hid his face in the loose fabric of her dress. But Kenneth walked forward and put out his hand. "Nice to meet you, sir. I am Kenneth."

Constantine pursed his lips, but then shook his little hand. The hardness remained, however, as he said, "Nice to meet you, too, Kenneth. Would you like to meet your mama's mama?"

Florence put her face in her hands and was overcome for several minutes in the sure understanding that all the things that she'd written in her mental book of dreams, all the hopes of going home, of finding her way back to life, were finally coming to pass.

———

They got permission for Florence and the boys to leave the camp with Constantine for two days. They took a jitney to Lira, and another to the outskirts of Amia'bil, where Josca was waiting by the side of the road for them.

She and Florence fell crying into each other's arms.

"I never stopped praying for this moment," Josca said. "Not once. Not once."

Florence was overcome and couldn't voice a thing until her father said, "These are Florence's sons, Kenneth and Boniface."

As Josca pulled back from her long-lost daughter, Florence saw there was deep disapproval sewn through her mother's face even though she said, "You're back. That's what is important."

She squeezed Florence's hands, then threw her arms wide, went forward, and scooped up both boys, saying, "You can call me Josca, or Granny."

Boniface thought that was funny. "Granny?"

"That's right," Josca said. "And you, little man? What will you call me?"

Kenneth smiled. "Granny Josca?"

"Okay, Granny Josca it is," Florence's mother said, turning and heading into Amia'bil, carrying them both. "We'll go to see Granny Josca's house, and I will make your mother's favorite chicken and yams. And you'll see where she used to draw water from the stream and where she went to school."

"Mama," Florence called after her as she followed, still sniffling beside her father. "They've eaten so much, they're heavy. You don't have to carry them both."

Josca turned and smiled back at her. "Florence, these are your children, my grandchildren. I would carry them forever."

Chapter Forty-One

January 22, 2005
South of Zapi, Uganda

Still deep in the bush, Anthony felt enchained by that point. He had known the story of his family's escape for more than five months, and he had been unable to make a run for it.

Corporal Leonard had seemed to sense a change in him almost immediately and had become even more insistent about keeping close tabs on Anthony during the long march across the top of the Imatong range and back into Uganda.

And the entire way, Kony had fretted about Evelyn and used her situation as a threat.

Kony kept saying, "But I have my best men out tracking her. It's only a matter of time. Isn't that right, Commander Tony?"

Anthony knew the man was trying to get inside his head again and decided not to let him.

"No one gets away from them, Teacher," he said. "Especially Sergeant Bacia and Corporal Leonard."

"That's right. No one escapes," Kony said.

Anthony, however, wondered if he'd blown it. If Evelyn and her kids had not been caught yet, why hadn't he run earlier?

After they had crossed into Uganda, Kony suddenly wanted to slip in and hide in the deep bush of his childhood, near Odek, where he could sneak up on Awere Hill and recontact the spirits.

"They will speak to me there," Kony said. "They always have on Awere."

The LRA leader had seemed almost giddy as they got close. But ten kilometers from Odek, scouts radioed that Ugandan army soldiers were watching the village. And they had sharpshooters up on the hill where the myth of the Great Teacher had begun with a chance thunderstorm.

Anthony read the decoded report out loud to him. "Villagers in Odek say they are waiting for Kony on the hill because they believe he will try to go there to regain his spirit power."

The LRA's supreme commander said nothing, but his chin trembled at the anger he was trying to contain. They were so close Kony could see his beloved rock-topped hill out there in the mist, which he gazed at for a long time, blinking every once in a while.

The UPDF are ahead of him, Anthony thought. *They're anticipating all his moves.*

———

Corporal Leonard's attention had gotten more acute a month earlier, in December 2004. Once they abandoned the idea of returning to Odek, and with the UPDF targeting the Great Teacher above all, Kony assigned Anthony to General Bunyi and went into hiding with his wives and the bodyguards of Control Altar high in the mountains of north-central Uganda, south of the Imatong range.

Since the beginning of Operation Iron Fist nearly three years before, Kony had ordered his top commanders to carry cheap FM radio receivers so they could listen to Ugandan radio stations and hear what their military was saying about the fight and where it was headed. General Bunyi, Dominic Ongwen, and by extension Anthony and Corporal Leonard had been listening almost every evening to Mega FM, a station out of Gulu, since their return to Uganda.

On Tuesday and Thursday evenings, the station featured two people who wished to speak to the child soldiers still being held by the LRA. It was normally someone's mother saying that they were still loved and still wanted.

It's all lies, Ongwen usually said, and turned it off before the "boo-hoo" started. The Butcher of Katire could not stand women crying and whimpering.

But on the Thursday before Christmas, Ongwen and Bunyi were eating as the broadcast began and made no move to turn the radio off. Anthony was sitting a few feet away, staring into a small campfire. Corporal Leonard hovered nearby.

"Hello to all the LRA soldiers in our listening area," the announcer began. "As we do every Tuesday and Thursday night here on Mega FM, we let friends and loved ones say hello. Tonight, we'll start with a friend from World Vision services here in Gulu."

There was silence for several moments before a woman said, "Now?"

"Now," the announcer said.

"Anthony?" the woman said, causing Anthony, the two officers, and his minder to stare at the radio. "This is your mother, Florence. Please come home, Anthony. Thank you."

After an awkward pause, the announcer came back on, said, "Well, there, nice and concise. Thank you, Florence."

Ongwen turned off the radio. He and Bunyi were watching Anthony, who stayed still.

"Is your mother named Florence, Anthony?" General Bunyi asked.

He nodded, acting sad and bewildered. "My mother's name was Acoko Florence. But this is some cruel joke or meant for another Anthony, because I know for a fact that my mother died of head injuries in an IDP camp near Gulu almost four years ago."

Ongwen stared at him longest before saying, "That true, Commander Tony?"

Anthony gazed unwavering into Ongwen's eyes. "Iris? My sister? The cook you released back in June? She held my mother as she died. She helped bury her before she was captured."

Ongwen went back to his food. And then so did Bunyi.

For Anthony to carry on the rest of the evening as if nothing had happened took every bit of acting skill perfected over more than a decade of keeping his true thoughts and emotions to himself. The senior officers bought his response whole. But Corporal Leonard acted like a suspicious dog at his every move until the officers took to their mats to sleep.

Anthony wanted to go off somewhere, jump up and down, screaming for joy. *That wasn't Acoko! That was my Florence! My Betty! I'd know her voice anywhere!*

Instead, once again, Anthony buried his true self deep, ignored his minder, and lay down on his mat. He pulled his blanket up over his shoulder and head, so he could grin madly at the warm golden sensation building in his heart.

Florence. The boys. They made it!

———

In the days following the radio broadcast, they had moved again and again. Anthony studied their position every night on General Bunyi's maps as he was broadcasting, looking for an opportunity to run.

But Corporal Leonard's suspicions had only heightened. Whenever Anthony moved more than thirty meters from his radio, his handler was there questioning him.

Just a few minutes before, he'd gone to use the latrine without notifying the corporal.

"What are you doing, Commander Tony, going off on your own?" Leonard demanded on his return. "You know I'm ordered to watch you."

"I know, but I really don't like you, Corporal," Anthony said. "You stink all the time."

"If you weren't a commander, I'd beat your ass."

"And if you had a brain, you'd be lonesome," Anthony said.

Leonard looked like he really wanted to beat Anthony's ass.

But then the Great Teacher walked into their camp dressed as a woman with Yango, General Vincent, and two of Kony's newest "wives," neither of them older than fifteen. To Anthony, who had not seen the LRA's supreme commander in months, Kony had aged well beyond his forty-four years. Beneath his shawl, his dreadlocks and beard were graying, his cheeks were gaunt, and his eyes were sunken and rheumy. He had developed a tic in his left cheek, and Anthony wondered if he was on some kind of drug.

Kony said, "You will take a fifth of all the food you have and bring it to Yango. Control Altar is going on a long trek. The spirits of Jumma Driscer and silly Cilindi have directed me to find a new sanctuary to revive the Ten Commandments and the mission of the holy. You will know exactly where when I call for you to join me."

The Great Teacher appeared ready to leave, when he caught sight of Anthony sitting there beside Corporal Leonard.

"Commander Tony," he said, smiling as if greeting an old friend, and then affecting sadness. "I am sorry for the loss of Betty and your sons. I know what you have been through."

Anthony nodded stiffly. Kony had known the story of their supposed fate for a few months, and this was his first mention of it.

"Thank you, Teacher. I appreciate it."

Kony gazed at him with those bloodshot eyes for a long moment. "You were always my best signaler. The best signaler. I promote you, Captain Opoka. And I want you to know you are back in the running for minister of communications in my government."

Anthony felt nothing warm, nothing rare from the praise. "You are very kind, Teacher. I am honored."

For some reason, the Great Teacher gazed a few moments at Anthony, seeming to sense that inside, his former signaler felt indifferent to the compliment, the promotion, the promise of future power. Then Kony turned and left the camp, his wives and his security chief in tow.

Anthony did not know why, but he felt in his gut that it would be the last time he'd see the man who had taken a decade of his life and turned him into an empty, soulless war machine. He was glad. In his mind and heart, he never wanted to lay eyes on the Great Teacher again.

———

March 6, 2005
Lototuru, Uganda

For almost six weeks, Anthony looked for an opportunity to escape. He studied the moon, waiting for a dark night. But then General Bunyi led him and four hundred other fighters northeast through the wilderness toward the Sudan border, trying to draw the Ugandan army's attention away from Joseph Kony and the favored few of Control Altar, who were all headed northwest.

Twice during the new moon in February, Anthony thought he was going to get his chance and make a break for it. But both times, Corporal Leonard had once again seemed to sense his restlessness and refused to leave his side for any reason.

"You can try, Captain Tony," Leonard said one day, out of the blue. "But I'm still one of the best manhunters in the LRA."

"I have no idea what you're talking about," Anthony said.

He knew, however, that Leonard relished the idea of tracking him down and killing him before he could reach civilization.

I have to get him out of the picture, Anthony thought.

He considered waiting until the UPDF attacked again, and then fragging Leonard in the heat of battle and running while everyone else was distracted. But he could very well collide with another Ugandan army patrol the way Florence and Patrick had during her escape.

Besides, when it came down to it, he decided he could not kill a fellow soldier in cold blood in order to escape. If he was going to go, it would not be as the war machine, or as the leopard. He would run as a human, a good one, a person he could live with and love.

Finally, after weeks of considering ways to neutralize his minder, a plan hatched in his head, a scheme even a good human could live with. On the regular broadcast one evening, he called to General Matata's signaler.

"Fourteen Charley, this is Nine Whiskey, come back."

"Nine Whiskey, this is Fourteen Charley. Over."

"Remember that place from years and years ago, with three big trees on a hill, the three biggest trees around, growing so close their trunks crisscrossed?"

There was a silence long enough for Anthony to trigger his mic. "Fourteen Charley?"

Albert's voice sounded thick and hoarse when he replied, "I remember, Nine Whiskey. You couldn't miss seeing them from a long way off."

"Maybe I'll see you there, Fourteen Charley."

After another pause, Albert said, "Unlikely, Nine Whiskey. Six Bravo has ordered us in another direction."

Anthony closed his eyes. "Roger that, Fourteen Charley. Good luck."

"I wish you more than luck, Nine Whiskey. I wish you a long life. So does the big man."

"I wish you a long life, too, Fourteen Charley. To both of you."

Albert said, "Over and out."

The transmission ended, cutting Anthony off from the only two people who still tied him to the LRA.

"What was all that about?" Corporal Leonard said. "Some hill with three big trees?"

"Northeast of here," Anthony said. "You know the one. We camped near them last year. Great place to get a strong radio signal."

Leonard said nothing, but Anthony felt his minder's constant attention on him as he ate and then settled down to sleep.

———

Before dawn the following day, Anthony got up with the tin cup he drank with and slipped off toward a trench latrine. He gritted his teeth and then plunged the tin cup into the waste and then poured most of it out.

He returned to his mat and lay there, quickly taken by the fear of Corporal Leonard discovering his plan before he could execute it. There were suddenly so many ways it could go wrong; he froze and almost opted not to go through with it.

But then he remembered Mr. Mabior, the dying shopkeeper in Torit, telling him about the fourth and most potent form of suffering.

"Fear stops most people from living the life they were meant to live," Mabior said. "They cling to what is, rather than embrace what could be. Do you know why?"

Younger Anthony had shaken his head. "Not really."

"Loss of identity."

"I don't understand."

"Fear is almost always based on trying to protect your identity, the person you believe you really are inside. You fear that change will change that inner person. In the extreme, the change you fear most is death. But it could be as trivial as changing jobs. But fear is fear, and like the other forms of suffering, it disconnects you from the powers of your ancestors and the universe."

Anthony had frowned, confused.

The dying shopkeeper had shifted uncomfortably before he said, "Have you ever made a good decision while you were afraid?"

"Many times, in battle."

"I would suggest those were reactions. I'm talking about having the time to make a good decision. If you were afraid, did you make a good one?"

After thinking about that a moment, Anthony shook his head.

"How could you? You were disconnected. If you are connected, you will make a good decision. Get it?"

Anthony had nodded and listened as Mr. Mabior told him, "Extinguish the suffering of Fear by closing your eyes, breathing deep, and saying seven times, 'I am you. You are me. We are one.' And when you are done, you'll take seven more deep breaths, and say, 'I am one with all that ever was or will be. And I will be cared for.'"

———

Lying there on his mat as the sun began to rise, Anthony did the breathing exercise and repeated the phrases the shopkeeper had told him. Then, remembering Catholic mass from his childhood, he prayed to Jesus to help him, too. After he was done, he no longer felt helpless and doubtful. Indeed, as he sat up and looked around, he knew in his heart that this was his day.

Corporal Leonard was already up and crouched by a fire ring. Anthony glanced over and saw his minder's canteen and tin cup sitting there.

Getting to his feet, Anthony grabbed his radio pack, got the antenna wire, and made a show of hanging it. Partway through the process, Leonard stood, farted, and then wandered off toward the pit latrine.

Anthony waited until he was out of sight, then moved to get his tin cup. After checking to make sure the corporal was not returning, he got the man tracker's canteen and poured water from it into his fouled tin cup. He swirled it and then poured the fouled liquid into Leonard's cup, swirled it again, and then poured a little of it back into the canteen and closed it. Then he tossed the remains and put the canteen and tin cup back exactly where he'd found them. Anthony breathed deep again and returned to his early-morning signaler routine.

General Bunyi arrived a few minutes later with a stack of topographical maps in a tube. Corporal Leonard returned as the general was sending messages over the radio to General Vincent, who was with Kony and Control Altar.

"We have left Uganda for Congo," Vincent said in a coded message. "The Great Teacher is establishing a new holy order here. We are going to build a new training ground deep inside Garamba National Park."

Anthony coded and decoded Vincent's TONFAS while keeping track of Leonard's actions. The corporal had gotten the campfire going and just stood there a moment, warming his hands before reaching for his canteen and tin cup.

Once he was pouring, Anthony gave his full focus to General Bunyi's reply, asking when Kony wished the rest of the LRA to follow to Congo. Vincent responded that Matata and his surviving troops were already on the march there.

The order for Bunyi's forces to come would be given once the training camp was in place.

Leonard set the canteen and cup down and returned to his fire.

Before signing off, Bunyi told Vincent they were getting low on food. The general left, and Commander Tony stayed stone-faced as he dismantled and repacked his radio and then put a pot of water from his own canteen on the fire. He used it to clean and sterilize his tin cup. Then he waited.

All day long, as he went about his business, he kept track as the corporal drank from his cup and canteen. He thought it might get to Leonard that day, but it wasn't until the middle of the following morning that he saw the corporal rubbing his stomach.

Around noon, Anthony got out a pouch of rice and beans left over from the night before. He offered some to Leonard. The corporal's nostrils flared, and he shook his head.

Anthony was eating when the corporal got a stricken look about him. He hurried off several meters and vomited violently.

"Oh God," he moaned when the spasm subsided.

Then he got that stricken look again and took off for the latrine.

Five times in the next hour, his minder puked and shit until he was as weak as a newborn lamb, sweating, lying on his mat in the fetal position and grunting at cramps. Every once in a while, he'd try to drink from his canteen, only to provoke another wave of sickness.

Anthony almost felt sorry for him.

———

His minder was out cold around four that afternoon when Anthony picked up his rifle and pack and went to General Bunyi's bivouac. He told the general that Leonard had fallen ill from food poisoning.

"I also spoke with a few locals in the bush this morning," Anthony went on. "There are two villages close to here with large fruit and vegetable gardens, including corn ready to pick. I could take a group to raid, General."

Bunyi nodded. "An old friend of yours suggested the same thing just a little while ago. Ahh, here he is now."

Anthony glanced over at the soldier ambling their way and felt his stomach plunge. He had kept track of the man's ruthless exploits but had not seen him in almost ten years.

His mother's killer was older now, late thirties, first flecks of gray in his afro. And there was a newer scar below his left eye to complement the brutal one across his right cheek that had faded little with time.

"Sergeant Bacia," General Bunyi said, "Captain Opoka will take twenty soldiers to get food. Go with him. Keep an eye on things."

It took everything in Anthony to remain calm. Bacia obviously remembered Anthony and got a foul look about him for a moment. Anthony understood. More than a decade before, the manhunter had caught a boy trying to run, and now he was to be commanded by that same boy. But then the sergeant seemed caught in a memory that made him smile a moment.

"I'll do that, General," Bacia said. "Nothing like a good raid."

On the one hand, Anthony could not believe his bad luck. He'd managed to neutralize Corporal Leonard, one of the LRA's best trackers, only to be saddled with the very best manhunter in Kony's army, a legend who enjoyed running down and killing escapees.

Why do these things always happen to me? Anthony wondered miserably. *I was getting a clean break, and now my situation is worse. Much worse. You're an idiot, Opoka!*

On the other hand, here was Bacia, the psycho who killed his mother. Anthony felt the thrill of possible revenge pulse through him. That would be better, wouldn't it? Kill the manhunter and then escape?

He remembered the dying shopkeeper then and realized that if he continued with this line of inner Violence, of seeking justice above all, he'd continue to suffer and he'd make bad choices.

After taking a deep breath, he accepted his circumstances and said, "Should I leave the radio with you, General? I will be able to carry more in an empty pack."

"Smart, Captain," Bunyi said, and turned back to his maps.

After taking a long look at one of the maps that showed their position, Anthony assembled his company of twenty and left the encampment with Sergeant Bacia walking in his footsteps. The villages were roughly nine kilometers south and four kilometers apart. When they were two kilometers beyond the camp, he stopped and divided the group into two ten-person units.

"Bad move, Captain Opoka," Sergeant Bacia said. "Better to swarm. In and out."

"My call," Anthony said calmly. "If you'd like to lead the other group, I'm fine with it."

He could tell Bacia wanted to do just that. But the manhunter said, "The general asked me to keep an eye on you because Leonard is sick."

"Then we go together," Anthony said, deciding at that moment that he could not stay a good human and escape. He was going to have to isolate and kill the man in order to run. The fact that Bacia had caused his mother's death only made it better.

Inside, Commander Tony went cold. As if sensing an unseen threat, behind him the manhunter shifted his rifle off his shoulder and cradled it in his arms as they marched on.

About ninety minutes before sunset, Anthony and his men were a kilometer away from their target village and crops when he stopped them.

"We should have left two hours ago," Bacia complained. "We'll finish picking in the dark with flashlights."

"Not if we work hard."

He drew a picture in the dirt, showing how the village sat on a plateau, and the position of the gardens. He divided the troops again, this time into five groups of two, and showed them all where he wanted them on the crude map. He gave them twenty-five minutes to get into position.

"And us?" Bacia asked skeptically.

Anthony showed him a location slightly southwest of the village. "We'll be going straight into the crop fields, so we know what's there first."

The sergeant's eyebrows went up, and he nodded. "Makes sense."

Then Anthony had an idea. Maybe he didn't have to kill the man. Maybe there was a better option.

He purposefully made a grimace and belched before he and Bacia started across the west side of the plateau. Anthony kept stopping every few minutes to breathe slowly.

"What's going on, Captain?" Bacia demanded.

"Stomach's getting a little queasy."

"You eat what Leonard ate?"

Anthony nodded uncertainly. "But wouldn't I have gotten sick already?"

"Maybe your gut's stronger."

"Not feeling strong now," Anthony said, belched again, and pressed on.

They got into position with five minutes to spare. Grimacing, Anthony drank from his canteen, waited a minute, then groaned as he turned toward the manhunter. "Gonna be sick."

"Well, don't puke on me," Bacia said, disgusted, and backed up.

Anthony spun around, made a show of rushing over and into some bushes where he could still see pieces of his new minder through the branches. Which meant Bacia was seeing pieces of him. He hunched over with his back to the tracker, stuck his fingers down his throat, gagged, and then vomited up the water and food he'd had earlier.

He made himself heave a few more times for show, then opened his canteen, threw water on his brow so it looked like he was sweating badly. He staggered out of the bushes, looking at Bacia with a dazed expression. Then he doubled over and moaned.

Two shots went off in the village.

"We gotta go, Captain," his minder said.

"Can't," Anthony groaned, unbuckling his pants. "I gotta shit."

"Right here?"

"Go lead them," he gasped. "I'll be right there."

Bacia looked skeptically at him until Anthony hobbled over behind a thick bush and pulled his pants down around his ankles.

Another shot went off.

"They don't know what they're doing!" Anthony said, squatting down and then making wet farting noises.

"Damn it," the sergeant barked. "I swear to God if you run, Opoka, I will track you down and kill you, and I will like it. I don't care whose signaler you used to be."

"I couldn't run if my life depended on it," Anthony said, and made gagging noises.

The fourth shot and shouts from the village did it.

Bacia grabbed his rifle and pack and hustled that way and out of sight. Anthony kept groaning for a full minute before pulling up his pants and grabbing his rifle. Leaving the pack behind, he trotted toward the southwest corner of the plateau.

From the top of the escarpment, he looked out over broken country mottled with rocky hills, dense thickets, and grassy expanses, some already in shadow. The sun had begun its long sink toward the horizon. From a look at General Bunyi's topo maps that afternoon, he believed he was 150 kilometers northeast of Rwotobilo. He glanced at the position of the sun, calculated southwest.

And then, some ten years and six months after being kidnapped by the LRA, trying to escape, being recaptured, surviving the bayonet, and deciding that he would die in the bush, never to see his family again, Anthony Opoka threw all those haunting memories into the winds of his past.

He fixed an image of Florence and the boys in his mind, committed his heart to their love, and began to run.

Chapter Forty-Two

Anthony scrambled down the steep side of the plateau, sliding on rocks, jumping over bushes, until he reached level ground and opened up his stride. He believed he'd have at least a twenty-minute head start before Sergeant Bacia discovered him missing.

But the tracker was a suspicious man and true to his nature. Anthony was no more than five hundred meters out from the bottom of the plateau when he heard a bullet zip by him before hearing the muzzle report.

He's on to me! Anthony thought, and fought the urge to sprint. He didn't want to burn all his energy when there was a dog like Bacia behind him. Instead, the district champ began zigzagging and lengthened his stride into a lope that would let him put more ground between him and the tracker.

Three quick shots went off, followed by a bellow from back up on the plateau.

He's calling the others!

At eight hundred meters, and still loping, he looked back and saw Bacia and six LRA fighters sliding down the side of the escarpment. Anthony did not panic. He stayed at his pace, strongly aware of the sun and the light, still an hour from full darkness.

Stay ahead of them until the stars are out, he thought. *That's all you need to do.*

———

At the kilometer mark, he started up a hill that he knew was going to expose him. He charged and was halfway up when he heard more shots. Several pinged off rocks near him.

That was enough to drive Anthony up and over the summit. He began to sprint and leap on the descent, racing the end of day, trying desperately to create a bigger gap between himself and his pursuers. There were more trees and lengthening shadows on the flat on the far side of the hill. He stayed in the darker landscapes as he slowed back into that steady lope.

He started up the next rise, looked back, and saw all seven men. But one was way out in front, pulling away from two others, with four lagging. The lead man was now six hundred meters behind him.

That's Bacia. It's gotta be.

Anthony got angry then, dug deep, and took the entire hillside in one sustained, frantic pull. When he reached the top, the manhunter shot at him wild from the middle of the flat and missed by half a meter. Sprinting the descent again, the signaler hit the third bottom as the sun began to finally vanish on the western horizon.

Gimme darkness, man.

Loping for the third time, he tried to run in the dimmer shadows beneath the trees, but they soon gave way to an opening about five hundred meters across and covered in thigh-high elephant grass. He hated the idea of going in there. He'd be exposed. And he'd be breaking grass stalks, leaving signs Bacia would be able to follow. But Anthony had no choice.

He leaped into the grass and turned on the speed, knowing that until night robbed the manhunter of a shot, he was going to be a wide-open target. He kept his knees pumping high across the grassy expanse, quads and calves cramping, lungs burning, trying not to panic at the threat that at any moment, he could be gunned down from behind.

———

The shot finally came twenty minutes later when he was a hundred meters from scattered trees on the far side of the meadow. The bullet passed so close he heard it snap past his ears long before the report of Bacia's gun echoed behind him.

He hit the forest, debated ambushing the manhunter, but thought that was what the sergeant might expect and want. A man like Bacia would come into these trees on full hunting alert.

Better to outlast him.

Anthony sucked it up once more and ran on, aware of the light fading, but not fast enough. And then the trees thickened, and it was almost too dark.

He slowed, nervous, letting his eyes adjust, but kept pushing forward until he broke free of the dense bush into another long, grassy opening, this one becoming murkier by the moment. Anthony ran straight into it. Even if Bacia used his flashlight to track him, he knew he was gaining the advantage now second by second.

Two hundred meters out, he slowed near one of several trees. Night had fully fallen.

As his father had taught him the evening of his first lesson in being a good human, Anthony scanned the sky until he saw three silver stars appear on the glowing horizon and knew that was west, then turned and found his single bright star in the east. Facing southwest, he forged on, telling himself that the stars guiding him held the souls of his ancestors and the spirits of his children to come.

Anthony ran all night at a steady pace, feet spread wide for balance, using his naturally strong peripheral vision and every bit of the weak moonlight to avoid hitting trees and limbs. He spooked animals, prayed he didn't step on snakes, and fell multiple times, tearing his clothes and bruising his body, while brush and thorn raked his face and hands. But he never stopped, and he never released his two-handed grip on his gun.

Before dawn, he exited the wilderness, crossed a road near Lokung, and plunged back into dense bush. He kept moving southwest by the stars until the sun had risen. He found a running stream, filled his canteen, and drank all of it twice before burying himself in a thicket, sitting up against a tree trunk, facing his back track, the AK-47 in his lap.

He slept an hour, then ran two more before again sleeping over his back trail. He kept up that cycle of running and resting all day and through the next night, crossing the Palabek–Labongo road at three in the morning.

Exhausted and hungry at dawn, Anthony searched for food and found a wild mango tree in a dense thicket. Even though its fruit was hardly ripe, he gorged, then sat with his back against a nearby rock facing his back trail once more and fell deep into sleep.

He tried to get up and run two hours later but couldn't. He slept for another three hours before continuing. But his stamina was dwindling. For every two hours he pushed on, he needed an hour of rest.

Late the third night of his escape, more than forty hours after Bacia last shot at him, Anthony slowed down, telling himself it was finally safe enough to sleep longer. He forded a small stream and climbed the far bank before collapsing against the base of a tree sixty meters beyond the waterway, rifle in his lap, facing his back trail yet again.

———

A soft cry, a mew, roused him from a dead sleep in the twilight before dawn.

Groggy, lethargic, Anthony tried to open his eyes but couldn't. His head began to nod. He felt himself swirling back down into darkness until a branch snapped.

He came wide awake, moved the safety lever on the AK-47 down, and began to slowly move the rifle to his left shoulder, wanting the forestock resting on his knees before he moved the gun in the direction of that snap. As he did, he scanned the bush left to right. Mosquitoes whined around his head. Biting flies tried to crawl up his nose.

He eased the rifle to his left shoulder and over his knee, but before he could swing the barrel and find his sights, the head and shoulders of Sergeant Bacia were right there in the creek bottom at one o'clock. His gun was already up, aiming at Anthony.

"Got you," the manhunter said, grinning, climbing slowly up the bank about fifty meters away. "I told you I would, Opoka. I told you that you'd never get away from me. Your mother sure didn't. Bitch gave me this other scar before I clubbed her so hard I heard her skull crack."

Anthony felt Violence erupt in him, wanted justice, wanted to swing his gun and take his chances at killing the man before he was shot down.

But that cry came again, that mew that had roused him, followed by a louder one, scared and lonely. Brush rustled along the creek bank to Anthony's eleven o'clock.

Bacia had heard the soft crying, too, and flicked his eyes off the gun sights and his prey. His own eyes darting from the manhunter to the mewing, Anthony started to move his gun again before he spotted the source of the noise.

Two spotted kittens crawled over the bank and up onto the trunk of a downed tree, where they began to wail piteously again.

Bacia took his eyes off them. "Drop the gun, Opoka, or die right now."

Anthony let the gun fall at his side.

"Yeah," the manhunter said, moving toward Anthony now, ignoring the kittens as they cried. "This is good. This is real nice and—"

Anthony heard a crack in the brush to his right. Bacia heard it, too, and tried to get turned around. But the blur of fury coming at him was simply too fast.

———

With a primal roar, the female leopard exploded from the brush, fangs bared, took two bounds, and then leaped. She sank her front claws into the sergeant's chest, snapping at his throat as he fell from the impact, and spinning her rear claws against his shirt, tearing through it and into his belly.

The manhunter screamed and tried to fight off the cat.

Anthony grabbed his gun, tried to aim. But Bacia's lower abdomen was already flayed open, hemorrhaging, and she had her mouth locked into the side of his neck before he could shoot. The manhunter screamed for mercy and found none.

The leopardess held him pinned until his legs stopped twitching. Then she released his neck and stood up over the body for several long moments, panting, her muzzle, throat, and rear legs brightly blooded.

The kittens called again.

She left Bacia without another look, crossed quickly to her kittens, and nuzzled them. She picked up the smaller and noisier of the two by the nape of the neck and moved toward a bamboo thicket at ten o'clock and out eighty meters. The larger kitten complained but followed its mother.

At the edge of the bamboo, she dropped the kitten to sniff the air and wait for her other cub to catch up. She pivoted her head in Anthony's direction for several moments, still panting a little. He could barely breathe and prayed she could not see him trembling.

And then, like ghosts of the forest, they were gone. Awestruck, Anthony sat there for a long time, shaking now, and listening to the odd pop and snap as the leopards moved toward their beds.

Realizing there could still be trackers behind Bacia, he stood up, giving a glance at the ghastly end of his mother's killer before sneaking out of the other side of the thicket and starting southwest again at a trot.

———

Anthony jogged, ran, and marched on and off for most of the third afternoon and on through the fourth night, finding himself climbing a steep hill as the first fingers of sunlight slowly erased the stars from the sky. He neared the crest, figuring he'd find a safe place to rest for the day, somewhere up high where he could see far and spot any tracker on his trail long before he became a close threat.

When he reached the top of the hill, however, it looked oddly familiar to him—the rocky top, the hills in the west across a broad valley checkered with crop fields lying fallow. He kept walking across the long ridge and gazing all around until it dropped off toward a river in the near distance. He stopped, studying his immediate surroundings, including a ledge to his right.

Anthony stared at the ledge, his mind searching until it found the right memory.

He saw the silhouette of the thumb-sucker and heard him say, *I'm James.*

His head whipped around. He saw his younger self going behind the ledge, right to the edge of a steep slope, to take a pee.

I will find this hill again.

The day was already turning ferociously hot and muggy. The glare from the sun made it hard to see. Anthony put his hand to his brow, unsure as he peered off into the far southwest, trying to match an image he'd burned in his mind more than a decade before. It was not there, nor in the south-southwest as he expected.

But when he looked more to the west-southwest, he spotted his match. There, on a distant hill, three crisscrossing trees towered above all others.

Home, Anthony thought, and started to cry. *It's right there.*

Part of him could not believe it, and he closed his eyes to make sure. But when he opened them and put his hand to his brow, he saw the huge, crisscrossing trees again and got so excited that all thoughts of sleep were banished. He was going all the way home.

Right now.

———

The closer Anthony got to Rwotobilo, the more farms and homes he encountered, forcing him to stay in the thicker cover. Even though he'd had to wade the same river they'd come across on a rope line more than a decade before, he knew he was filthy and bloodied from the run. He didn't want villagers to see him and report him to the UPDF or shoot at him if they had weapons.

But oddly, he saw no villagers, no farmers, and soon realized that the entire valley where he'd grown up appeared empty. Then he remembered that Museveni had ordered everyone into camps while his army hunted the LRA.

Anthony did not go straight at the three big trees that marked his home in the last four kilometers, and instead headed at an off angle to the east before he climbed a ridge and soon saw his school and the field where he'd won his first footrace. He remembered himself older, walking the road in front of the school with his brothers Albert and Charles, who were bouncing up and down after he'd been named head boy.

A lifetime ago. A whole other person.

He stayed in the grass and bushes, moving toward home, peeking into the yard around every neighbor's hut in between and seeing no one. Most of the fields lay untilled. Here and there, chickens, cows, and goats wandered unchecked. The place felt deserted.

But when he was almost to the turnoff to the Opoka family compound, he saw an older man limping down the road, carrying a hoe over his shoulder.

Anthony stashed his gun in the high grass and stepped out in front of the man with his hands up. The man looked frightened. "You going to kill me, son?"

Anthony shook his head. "I just want to go home."

"Where's home?"

He pointed several hundred meters away to the crisscrossing trees. "Over there. Do you know George Opoka? Omera George?"

"I do. But he's not here. He's in a camp somewhere. West of Gulu, I think."

"He's my father."

"Mmm," the man said, turning angry. "We're all in camps because of you types."

"I was kidnapped, sir," Anthony said. "I was in prison. For more than ten years. They did this to me." Then he opened his blouse and showed him his shoulder.

The man recoiled and then looked at him in sharp reappraisal. "If you are who you say you are, did you have an uncle who lived near here?"

"Paul. My father's brother. He lived over there by the three big trees."

He nodded. "I think he may be here. He got permission to work his fields as long as he's back in the camp at night. Same as me."

Anthony heard a helicopter coming and fought the urge to run. "Could you do me a favor? Go and tell my uncle Paul that Anthony is here."

The man hesitated, but after he saw the desperation in Anthony's face as the helicopter approached, he said, "I'll go see if he's still around."

He limped off toward the Opoka compound. Anthony got his gun, hustled deep into the high grass and then into the shadows of bushes that he hid beneath to avoid being seen from the air. They'd shoot him on sight.

He relaxed when the gunship was gone. His eyes got heavy. He slept.

———

"Anthony?" he heard a voice call, waking him. "Are you here?"

Leaving the gun, he crawled out from under the bush and stood up, seeing his uncle Paul standing there on the road, a little grayer as he grinned and clapped. "My God, it is you!"

Anthony pushed through the grass, feeling the tears coming yet again as he rushed into his uncle's arms.

"It's so good to see you," Anthony choked.

Paul had tears in his eyes, too. "We thought you were dead for the longest time. Until a girl from down the road here told us you set her free."

"Iris," he said. "I did."

They pulled back from each other.

"You grew," Paul said. "You're a man."

"Ten and a half years."

His uncle wiped his eyes. "Let me go tell the UPDF to come here to receive you."

Anthony had not really thought beyond going home and trying to find Florence. And the Ugandan army had been his enemy for more than a decade. He pondered for a few minutes and saw it was the only move he had.

"Tell them there is an important LRA fighter who wishes to give himself up," he said. "I'll be waiting right here for them."

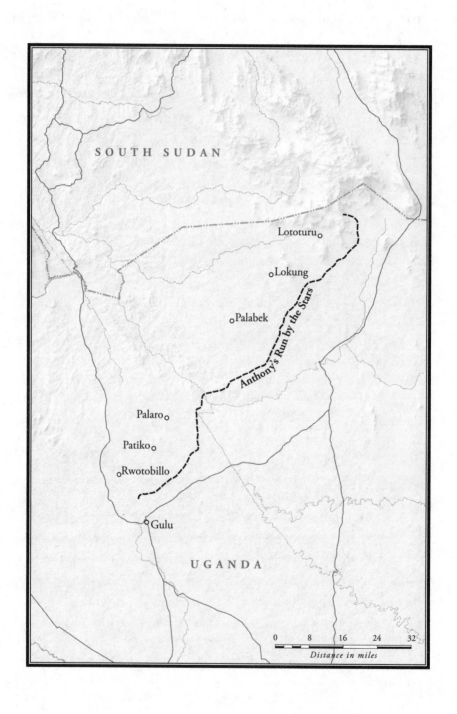

Chapter Forty-Three

Before leaving Anthony, his uncle gave him some raw cassava roots he'd just dug up and apologized he didn't have more to offer.

"I've had less," Anthony said, gratefully taking the roots and returning to the bushes.

He stayed there for two more days and nights, eating the raw roots, drinking from the ditch, and sleeping. Late the second afternoon, when he was sure he was alone, he slipped into his family's compound and stood before his mother's old hut, hating the fact that Sergeant Bacia had been the one to end her life. Refusing to think of the manhunter again, he remembered that first evening George taught him about the stars and being a good human, and Acoko later that same night saying that his father was a good man, but wrong about certain things.

Life isn't all about happiness, Anthony. It's about survival. Sometimes life is so hard you just have to survive it.

"I did, Mom," he said, hugged her in his mind, and went back to his hiding spot.

An hour after the signaler awoke on the third morning, March 14, 2005, he was beginning to think he was going to have to go to Gulu to give himself up when he heard the unmistakable sound of many boots marching in cadence.

He got his gun, eased out on the road, and stood there, watching a detachment of thirty-five Ugandan army soldiers coming at him, rifles held at port arms. Try as he might, he could not control the fear erupting through him. He was sure they'd come to shoot him down, or at least to beat him senseless before they dragged him off to prison and showed him that photograph taken the night that they all had to step on the thumb-sucker.

One of the soldiers said something when they were fifty meters from Anthony. They fanned out, went to their knees, aiming their rifles at him.

Terrified now, he thought, *All this way, and I'm going to die right back where I started.*

Then a UPDF lieutenant stepped forward and said in a soft voice in English, "Put the gun down, Anthony."

For several moments, Anthony hesitated. The gun was his power. From the moment he was given the rifle after marching unarmed into battle at the Dinka barracks, he had been shown time and again what happened to soldiers of the Lord's Resistance Army who lost their weapons. He'd seen boys executed. He'd seen others driven to madness.

The lieutenant took another step, said softly, "Put it down, son. Enough is enough."

Anthony bent over, put the gun in the dirt, and stepped back from it. He felt so anxious doing it that he started to cry all over again.

The lieutenant, who turned out to be a low-level intelligence officer, walked to him unarmed, palms open. "Don't cry. You're safe now. You are going to rejoin your life."

———

They marched Anthony back to Gulu in handcuffs. He was taken to a building on the grounds of a UPDF barracks. The lieutenant tried to interrogate him in English, but after more than a decade in the bush, the signaler wasn't understanding much. When he spoke to the officer in Acholi, the man told him that unfortunately his native tongue was Swahili.

They had to use multiple translators, and though he took copious notes, the lieutenant seemed unimpressed with his story. When the Ugandan officer told him he was going to be taken to a jail cell, Anthony felt anxious as he asked, "How long? I mean, how many years do you think, for what I have done?"

The lieutenant shrugged. "Depends on what Kampala says, but being an LRA commander, if you were, you'll probably serve twenty."

He stared at the interpreter and then the officer. "Twenty years?"

"I'm sorry. Like I said, it depends on Kampala."

Anthony was shocked to his core as they handcuffed him and led him away.

Twenty years.

I was only gone for ten.

But I was a commander. I did serve Kony.

Anthony was put in a cell by himself. When the steel gate had been locked shut behind him, he sat on the edge of the metal bunk, put his head in his hands, and felt himself sliding into the darkest hours of his life.

Prison for twenty years. Twice the amount of time he'd spent fighting in the LRA.

But locked away like this in a cement box. No bush or savanna to march through. No rain to smell on the wind. No stars to see at night.

Not the leopard in his cave. The leopard in his cage.

Thinking back on all the hardship he'd endured, all the bad things that had happened to him in the last decade, Anthony tried to imagine who he would be, leaving prison after suffering twenty more years without freedom—old, broken, probably more than half-mad.

He thought of Florence.

Is she in prison, too? Are the boys? For how long? Twenty years?

Then he considered the likelihood that, as a woman, she would be treated better. If she wasn't in prison, where was she? With her parents?

Then he became convinced that even if Florence was with her parents, she would never wait for him. *Not for twenty years. No one waits for twenty years.*

Those thoughts haunted him even after guards took him to shower and shave. The thoughts tortured him even after he'd been given the best meal he'd had since his abduction. He tried to lie on the cot and sleep.

But an endless, figure-eight loop of his personal miseries played behind his eyes, showing him being dragged away from Rwotobilo, the flash of the camera after he stepped on the dead thumb-sucker, the bayonet, marching and singing toward the bullets unarmed, the agony of the rocket-grenade fin, the mental cruelties of Joseph Kony, and Dominic Ongwen's atrocities at Katire. The last time he saw Florence and the boys. The loop always began and ended with the deepening certainty that he must have done something truly evil in his childhood to have deserved this fate.

Anthony finally fell asleep on the cement floor, after telling himself that suicide would be a better choice than spending two more decades of feeling like this, helpless and alone.

———

For two days, the leopard paced in his cage, pondering whether to live and hope for freedom someday or to kill himself and attain it now.

That was what he wanted, wasn't it?

Freedom?

Anthony decided freedom was what he wanted more than he'd wanted anything in his entire life. The simple freedom to live his life the way he wanted, to make all decisions for himself. As a young teenager, he'd just begun to taste freedom from his parents when he was taken. For ten and a half years, he'd had no freedom, not really. There had almost always been someone watching him, telling him what to do. It had been even worse with Kony, he realized. Being inside Control Altar for so long had imprisoned his mind in ways that he was only beginning to sense and understand.

And now, twenty years before I know real freedom. If I live that long.

His mood and thoughts sank lower by the hour. Somewhere in his mind, he knew he should think about the things the dying shopkeeper had told him. But he ignored those impulses, tossed them aside as total nonsense.

How do you not suffer when your life has been taken away from you all over again?

One of the jailers came to him after breakfast on the third morning.

"You have a visitor."

In handcuffs again, Anthony was led back into an interrogation room and saw George standing there and was overwhelmed.

His father rushed to hold him as they both shook with emotion.

"I tried every day to be a good human, Dad," Anthony choked. "But it was hard to be that person in the LRA."

"I don't care," George said, tears streaming down his face. "My boy is home. That's all that matters now."

Anthony did not have the heart then to tell his father he was going to spend the next two decades in prison. He gave George the broad strokes of his life in the LRA. His dad told him about the second attack on their compound and how he escaped and how Acoko had fought the LRA soldier with the cheek scar, wounding him with the hoe before being clubbed, and how she'd lingered in and out of health for almost two years before passing.

"She would have been proud of you," he said.

"I don't know about that, Dad."

"No, she would have. I am. I can tell, despite everything, that you are still her Anthony, my Anthony."

"I'm a different Anthony, Dad."

George couldn't speak for several moments, then looked at him with hope in his eyes. "And your brother Albert?"

"He was alive two weeks ago. I talked to him on the radio."

"Then he could escape, too," George said, nodding. "And we all can be together again."

"That won't happen for a while. I have to pay for the things I did in the LRA."

"For how long?"

Anthony swallowed against the ball of emotion swelling in his throat. "They're saying twenty years, Dad."

"What?" George said, shocked. "No. That's so wrong. It's—"

Before his father could finish, a Ugandan army officer Anthony had never seen before entered the room. "I'm afraid you're going to have to leave for now, Mr. Opoka. Your son has an important visitor who has flown in from Kampala."

———

UPDF General Hugo Adamo was bigger than Patrick, a great slab of a man with a boxy head and a chest like a buffalo's. He was dressed in camo, had a gravelly voice and a no-bullshit manner as he sat down at the table opposite Anthony, folding his massive hands and staring the signaler in the eyes before speaking in Acholi.

"Are you Commander Tony?"

"Yes, sir," Anthony said.

"What's your call handle?"

"Nine Whiskey."

"Prove it," the Ugandan army general said, and slid a piece of paper across the table. "That's a transcript of an LRA intercept made ten days ago. Tell me what it says."

Anthony studied the paper. It was a TONFAS coded message.

He looked up at General Adamo. "Can you unlock my handcuffs and get me a pencil and another piece of paper?"

The general called for the handcuffs to be removed and a pencil and paper.

While they waited, Adamo said, "I heard you were wounded pretty bad a few times."

Anthony nodded, unbuttoned the shirt he'd been given, and showed him his shoulder.

Adamo recoiled and shook his head. "Damn, son, how do you live through something like that? You must be one tough sonofabitch."

Anthony smiled at the praise, felt the rare warmth, and then flashed on Kony and felt suspicious of it.

"I am lucky more than tough," he said. "A little left, and I would have been dead."

The officer who'd brought him to the room returned with several pieces of paper and two pencils. Five minutes later, Anthony looked up and said, "It's a message from General Vincent, telling General Matata to start moving his men toward the border with northeast Congo. There are also specific coordinates for a rendezvous that was supposed to take place four days ago."

Adamo took the translated message, read it, and sat back, a smile slowly curling his lips.

"Well then, this wasn't a wild-goose chase after all."

"General?"

"I was skeptical when we got a report in Kampala that Joseph Kony's personal radioman had escaped, but I had to take the chance, fly up, and see for myself."

General Adamo questioned him for almost four hours. Anthony answered as truthfully as he could. He even volunteered the story of the thumb-sucker.

The general shook his head. "We have heard this kind of story time and again, pretending to take photos of you, telling you we received them when we did not. We believe they did it to most of the LRA abductees, baptizing you in blood, brainwashing you into believing that after that point, no one cared about you in your old life anymore. I'm sorry you had to go through it."

Anthony hung his head and nodded. "Still doesn't make it okay."

"No, it doesn't," Adamo said. "But you had no say in the matter, did you?"

He felt angry, and said, "None. You weren't supposed to think for yourself. Ever."

"But you did?"

"Yes, and I kept it all to myself. And three other people I trusted. My brother Albert and Patrick Lumumba. And my wife."

"You're lucky you had them. They in or out?"

"Florence and my sons escaped. Patrick and Albert? I don't know where they are."

"A lot of LRA guys like you who've escaped, they leave their bush wives and kids be. Start their lives over fresh. Once they've paid their debt to the government, that is."

Anthony did not know what to make of the first part of that, but Adamo's last few words caused him to take a deep breath.

"Is it true I am going to serve twenty years in prison for what I have done?"

"Twenty years in prison? Well, that's up to you."

"I don't understand."

"You can spend twenty years in a Ugandan prison or serve twenty years as a soldier in the UPDF. Your choice."

Anthony stared at the general. "Twenty years in the UPDF?"

"Got to be some way for you to pay for your sins."

"What would I—"

The same Ugandan officer who'd ended his talk with George knocked and entered. "Sorry to interrupt, General. But you're needed on the phone. It's urgent."

General Adamo glanced at his watch and then at Anthony. "Think about it, make your decision, and I'll be back to talk to you tomorrow."

As the general was getting up, Anthony said, "I'm sorry, sir, what exactly would I do for twenty years in the army with a shoulder like this?"

Adamo tilted his head. "Does it matter? You'll do what you're told, one way or another."

———

A guard returned him to his cell, and he sat there on the bunk, his brain lurching in a dozen directions and directed by a dozen voices before he heard one louder than the rest say in an oily, mocking tone, *"Does it matter? You heard him. You'll do what you're told, one way or another."* One way or another, you are going to prison, Commander Tony.

That was true. Okay, real prison sounded a lot worse. But twenty years in the UPDF was a severe sentence any way you looked at it, maybe even a death sentence. It certainly was not freedom. Not in the way Anthony wanted freedom.

He would be controlled. He would have to follow orders blindly, do whatever he was told to do, even if he disagreed with the orders. Once more, he would have to keep his thoughts to himself. Once again, he would have to be the leopard in his cave.

Better than a cage, he thought.

Or was it? And what about Florence and the boys? What about the general saying that many other escaped LRA soldiers let their "bush wives" be? That they started their lives fresh? As if the marriage never existed? As if the children never existed?

That oily voice said, *Well, why not? If you're going to be in prison in the army for twenty years, do you really want to also be in the prison of a marriage at the same time? You should forget them altogether. Start a new life.*

Anthony desperately wished his father were there so he could talk to him. Then he remembered George telling him before his abduction that the worst thing in life you could be was a soldier. And here he'd spent ten years in combat. And here he might spend twenty more in uniform.

The oily voice said, *Forget them all. Act like you're accepting the twenty-year army sentence, play the leopard in his cave, and when you get the chance, make another run for it. But this time, leave Uganda and run to Kenya. Go there, get across the border. Start over in total freedom, Commander Tony.*

It sounded so easy, so enticing. The idea of having total freedom made him feel good inside, really good, as if the things he'd done in the LRA would not matter, as if his wounds and handicap would not hinder him, as if liberty alone would make him whole and strong in a way he'd never been allowed.

I'm doing it, Anthony decided. *I'm leaving it all behind. I'll run the first chance I get.*

He got off the bunk and began doing deep squats and lunges. He would need to stay in shape if he was going all the way to Kenya. And did he even need to run all the way? He could take a jitney or a bus and get off near the border. The run would be shorter. Freedom would be easier than he thought.

But within minutes, doubts began to creep in.

Then he allowed himself thoughts of Florence, of the way she made him smile every time he saw her. And the boys, how they made him proud, how he had wanted freedom for them, a life out from under the thumb of Kony.

Forget them. Lie to the general tomorrow morning. Take the army deal and run the first chance you get. It's the only way to freedom that does not take two decades of your life.

Anthony thought about abandoning Florence and the boys, never seeing them again, and he felt sick inside. Then he thought about spending twenty more years in uniform, controlled and manipulated beneath one general's thumb or another, and he felt equally nauseous.

There's no good answer.

He wished he had asked the dying shopkeeper about this oily voice of suffering, the one that pointed out so many paths that there seemed no clear way forward, no right action to be taken other than blindly running for freedom.

He wished again that his father were there to counsel him. But he had no one.

He had to make this decision alone, and the weight of that felt crushing. His heart ached at every route that lay before him, and he felt himself trapped and spiraling down into despair.

Maybe you were right the other day. Maybe suicide is the best way out. Instant freedom.

For several moments, he really thought about killing himself and ultimately decided that would be the coward's path. But when he thought about the other paths he might take, he felt the despair again and the helplessness.

He remembered that first evening out with George when his father told him he was special, raised the rare warmth in him, and pointed out the stars that had led his escape from the Great Teacher. He bowed his head and wished to God that all the glimmering stars in the sky, the souls of his ancestors and the spirits of the unborn, could come together to show him the right direction to take.

Then he recalled walking in the darkness back to their compound after that first lesson, how he'd marveled at his dad's ability to see the path forward when it was nearly pitch black.

George's words came back to him more powerful than any voice of suffering, and more brilliant than any light in any sky.

It all comes down to this, Anthony. Whenever you are confused about anything in life, not sure what to do, ask yourself this question.

Sitting there in his cage, contemplating every tortuous step that lay before him, Anthony said, "What would a good human do?"

Chapter Forty-Four

March 19, 2005
Lira, Uganda

Florence climbed off the jitney from Amia'bil and walked through the city, carrying a new notebook and feeling anxious and unsure of herself. The government had recently given her a slot in a vocational program that would soon lead to work, but she was focused on unfinished business when she entered a building near the high school and went through the door of the District Education Office.

A clerk looked up and smiled at her.

"Is it here?" Florence asked.

"Came yesterday," the clerk said. She went for a manila file on her desk, found an envelope, and brought it over to the counter.

Florence picked up the envelope. "You don't know what it says?"

"Not my business, is it?"

"I guess not," she said, turning to leave. "Thank you."

"You're not going to open it and tell me after all the strings I had to pull for you?"

"Oh," Florence said. "Yes, I guess."

The clerk crossed her arms. "Unless you don't want me to know?"

Florence tore open the envelope. Her hands shook so hard removing the folded sheet of paper that she put it on the counter. "I can't. You read it."

The woman picked up the paper and unfolded it. As her eyes scanned down the page, the clerk's grin grew. "Florence Okori, national secondary education exams, top ten percent!"

"No!" Florence said, grabbing it from her. Then she saw it for herself and shook the letter and smiled through her tears. "I did it. I did. I could have . . . I could have . . ."

"You could have what?"

"Been a nurse," Florence said, sniffling. "That was my dream growing up."

"You can still become a nurse with those kinds of grades."

"I have two sons now," she said, shrugging and wiping at her tears and then smiling. "But this is good enough. Knowing I passed my exams like this is good enough."

———

Florence walked back through the city to the jitney stand near the big open-air market, the envelope with her exam results tucked between the cover and the first page of the notebook she'd bought the week before, her latest book of dreams, which she cradled over her heart as she had as a girl, as if the writing in it had the power to change her future.

She found a bus that would drop her outside Amia'bil, paid, got on, and found a seat near a window, wondering how much school would cost. It wasn't like she could leave the boys with her mother and go off to try to become a nurse, could she? Who was going to pay for it all?

These questions and thoughts consumed her as the bus made frequent stops, letting more people off than on the farther they got from Lira. Florence was sitting alone and feeling just a little sad when she decided, *No, I am done with my nursing dream. Kenneth and Boniface are my life now. I care for them like Miss Catherine cared for me. And they are more than—*

Florence heard a woman somewhere behind her say, "Look at her, sitting there all proud of herself, one of Kony's whores come home."

A second woman said, "I don't know why her mother let her back in."

Florence felt like she did during the beating she'd taken from Okaya's men after she and Palmer had refused to sleep with him, punched, humiliated, and helpless, a useless, throwaway thing. Her hands shook as she lowered her notebook from her chest.

The first woman said, "If it was my whoring daughter coming back with bastard brats, she wouldn't be living under my roof."

"Or eating my food. Ever."

Florence flipped open the cover. She turned over the envelope holding her exam results and read what she'd written there on the first page the night after buying the notebook.

The second woman said, "I would not let my husband near her."

"Who knows what he'd catch," the first woman said, and cackled.

Florence cleared her throat and, in a loud, firm voice, began to read. "I am Florence Okori Opoka, and these are my dreams. No one can take them from me. Only I can let them go or hold them tight. Only I can write them down. Only I can say them out loud or hold them secret in my heart. Only I and God can make them come true."

The bus had fallen silent. It pulled over outside Amia'bil. Florence shut her notebook, got up, glared at the two women, whom she recognized from her mother's church, and then got off without a word. She did not look back as she walked down the hill to her family's compound, still shaking inside at what had happened.

In some ways, it did not surprise her. She'd heard of other women who'd been spit on and shunned after their return from captivity. Even her parents at times made cruel remarks about her life in the LRA, as if she'd had any say in being kidnapped. And they flat-out refused to let her or the boys talk about Anthony or their time in captivity. As far as Josca and Constantine were concerned, Anthony did not exist. And neither had Major Okaya. In their minds, her past had been swept clean, and her sons born of immaculate conception. The few times Florence had said otherwise, it had led to angry shouting and threats of being thrown out on the streets to starve. She'd learned not to mention Anthony when she was anywhere around them. She knew her parents still loved her, but like the women on the bus, they made her feel less of herself.

Florence heard the boys laughing and giggling before she saw them playing with her cousin Jasper, who had escaped during a firefight six months before and gone through the same kind of rehabilitation as Florence.

"Mama!" two-and-a-half-year-old Boniface cried when he saw her, and hugged her legs.

"Well?" Jasper said, still walking with a slight limp from his old leg wound.

"Top ten percent," she said, grinning.

"You did it, Flo!"

"Yes, I did," she said, chin up, her smile widening. "And I'm not going to be sad and think about what could have been."

"Good for you. Must make you proud, though."

Florence raised her chin even higher. "It does. I remember how hard those tests were."

"I do, too. It was all you could think about."

"And all you could think about was your music on the radio."

"Still do," he said. "One of the best things in life."

"What's number one this week?"

"On BBC? 'All About You' by McFly. But I've been listening to Saida Karoli from Tanzania. Her song 'Maria Salome' is like being hypnotized."

At dinner, Florence told her parents about the scores and showed them the proof. Josca congratulated her. So did her father. But it felt stale, forced, as if they were suffering the weight of what she had lost, or sensed the hateful things said to her on the bus ride home. A cloud seemed to hang over the meal. Even the boys were strangely quiet.

———

As they finished, Jasper said, "It's almost time for the show."

Florence shrugged. "I don't know if I'm up for it."

"Well, we have cleanup duty, and *I'm* listening," her cousin said.

Constantine and Josca walked off because the pleas always popped their delusions, reminded them of what Florence had gone through in the LRA. Jasper fetched his new radio and tuned it to the Lira station that served as a repeater for the Mega FM broadcast of the show Florence had appeared on shortly after escaping. She had not missed an episode since and was ordinarily interested in who else had made it out of the Great Teacher's control.

But after her bus ride, she wanted to erase Kony from her mind. At least for tonight.

Instead, she was washing dishes in a big tub when the announcer came on, saying, "All you LRA soldiers out there in listener land who are still foolishly fighting for Joseph Kony, listen up. We have someone here who wants to talk to you, someone you know very well."

There was a pause before she heard a voice say, "This is Nine Whiskey, repeat, Nine Whiskey, Commander Tony calling all stations!"

Florence stood there dumbfounded for a moment before going wild, throwing her soapy hands over her head and shrieking, "He's alive! He's come in from the bush!"

She ran over closer to the radio, feeling like her heart was going to explode, when Anthony said, "I am calling to tell you that you will not be mistreated. Lay down your guns and run away from the LRA. Again, you will not be mistreated if you abandon the Great Teacher, who is deserting you, deserting Uganda, escaping into the Congo. Let him go. Let that evil man go his way. Your family waits for you. It is time to come home and be a good human again. And Betty the Nurse, if you can hear me, this is Signal Commander Tony, Nine Whiskey, Nine Whiskey, over and out."

Chapter Forty-Five

Florence was so happy she had a hard time standing still.

Anthony is alive! He is out! And he called to me!

"You should write to him," Jasper said after hugging her. "Send him a picture of you and the boys through the Red Cross. They'll do that, you know."

"You're right!" she said. "That's good. I will."

"And in the meantime, I wouldn't say anything about it to your parents. Your father, especially."

Constantine came by later and asked what all the yelling had been about. Florence just said an old friend had managed to escape the LRA. He walked off without interest.

The next day, she took the boys in their cleanest clothes to a studio in Lira and had a portrait shot. She paid for a print and put it in an envelope with a letter telling Anthony that she and the boys were doing well and could not wait to see him.

Florence heard nothing for almost three weeks, and she began to wonder if Anthony was having second thoughts about finding her. Then a social worker from World Vision came to the compound to check on Florence, Kenneth, and Boniface and to deliver a letter from Anthony.

"He made me help him write it," the woman said, smiling. "He was so excited to hear from you he could barely calm down."

"Who?" Constantine said, coming up with her mother. "Who wrote you a letter?"

Florence hesitated, and then said, "Anthony. He was my husband in the bush."

Josca got angry. "I'm sorry, Florence, but he was not your husband. You were too young. You were forced. This is wrong."

Constantine said, "He took you as his slave. I refuse to let you see him. He corrupted you!"

"He did not," she shot back angrily. "And I was no slave, and I was not forced to marry Anthony. I was given the choice, and I chose him. Do you know why? Because he told me he loved me. Do you know what else? I don't have to open this letter to know that he still loves me. And I love him."

Constantine was still fuming, shutting down, so Florence turned to her mother. "You've always said there is nothing more powerful than love, Mama."

Josca's jaw was set. "I know, but your father and I are—"

The social worker said, "Mr. and Mrs. Okori, I have come to know Anthony Opoka. He *is* a good person. He's helping—"

"I don't care, and Florence is forbidden from contacting him," Constantine snarled, and started to stalk away.

The social worker called after him, "Mr. Okori, you should understand that there are many LRA soldiers who had wives and children in the bush, and when they came out, they decided to abandon them and start their lives over. Anthony Opoka is not doing that. He really does love your daughter and your grandsons."

Her parents said nothing more about it for almost a day, but then Josca came to her and said, "You may see this man, Florence. You may invite him here. But we absolutely do not recognize your marriage."

———

A month later, Anthony rode east in a jitney toward Lira, feeling as free and as happy as he ever had.

That night in the cage, when he had asked himself what a good human would do in his predicament, the answer had come to him not as some oily voice in his brain but as a sudden understanding in his heart. He decided to forgo the ideal of total freedom, to embrace love, and to use it not only to survive but to thrive through the coming decades in the Ugandan army.

The next morning, when he was brought from his cell to see General Adamo in the interrogation room, he told the general he'd take whatever position was available in the UPDF for the next twenty years.

Adamo had smiled. "Good choice."

"Thank you, sir."

The general's smile faded. "But where to assign you? Maintenance? Latrine cleaning?"

Something died deep inside Anthony, but he nodded. "I think I can do that one-handed."

The general was quiet a moment, as if pondering his next move, before looking Anthony right in the eye. "You hate Joseph Kony?"

"For more than ten years."

"You think he should be caught? Brought to justice?"

"Yes, sir. I do. I would testify against him."

"I think you'd be a star witness. But in the meantime, I think you can serve in ways other than cleaning latrines."

He sighed with relief. "Anything, sir."

The general opened a file on the table, tapped a meaty finger on the message Anthony decoded the day before. "The TONFAS. I want you reading, decoding, and analyzing every intercept we get. Would you like to join the team we've got hunting the Great Teacher?"

Anthony was shocked by this sudden turn of events and fortune, but bobbed his head, smiling. "Very much, sir."

They let him go an hour later with enough cash to buy dinner in a restaurant for George, his uncle Paul, and his younger brother Charles, who had managed to escape two abduction attempts by the LRA over the years and grown up to become a teacher.

That was a meal of rare warmth, Anthony thought as the jitney got closer to Amia'bil. He smiled. Not only was he going to see Florence and his sons soon, but he had learned just that morning that his appeal on the Gulu station had prompted hundreds of escaping LRA boys and girls to stream out of the bush in the weeks afterward, so many that World Vision and the other aid groups helping to rehabilitate the child soldiers were all struggling to keep up.

But he put those happy thoughts aside for the moment because the driver called out that Amia'bil was the next stop. Anthony sat in a rear seat and craned his neck to see over the other passengers until he spotted Florence standing there by the road.

He scrambled from his seat with the presents he had bought for her, barely able to contain his emotions, which threatened to buckle him when he got out and saw she was already crying, grinning, and coming to him with open arms.

Anthony grabbed Florence, hugged her, and kissed her, overwhelmed by his good fortune, flooded with bliss at their reunion.

"It is a miracle, isn't it?" Anthony whispered in her ear.

"I feel it in every bit of me."

He pulled back, tears rolling down his cheeks as he nodded, and said, "We made it because of this feeling."

"I know," she said, her lip trembling. "And that's a miracle any way you look at it."

"Where are the boys?"

"Waiting with my parents, who I am warning you are very against the idea of us. They don't recognize our marriage, but they are roasting a chicken for you."

"Another miracle, any way you look at it."

Florence laughed, wiping at her tears. "I missed you."

He sobered. "I thought you and the boys were dead for the longest time."

"What? No!"

He nodded. "Patrick had to do it. I can see that now. But my heart wasn't just broken when I heard you and the boys had died. It was gone. There was a hole in my chest."

"But he told you eventually?"

"And then you were all I could think about."

"Let's go see Kenneth and Boniface. You won't believe how much they've grown."

———

Anthony was shocked to see Boniface up and going wobbly after a puppy, and then almost overwhelmed when Kenneth saw him, ran to him, and hugged him. He met Constantine and Josca, who barely spoke and eyed him suspiciously, and then various sisters and cousins, including Jasper, whom he was happy to see alive.

Though Florence's parents remained cold and remote, he won over the rest of her family with his easy smile, his soft way of talking, and his obvious tenderness toward Florence.

"She talked about you all the time," Anthony told Josca as the chicken roasted over an open fire. "And how you carried her when she was sick as a girl."

Josca nodded politely.

"And she knew all the plants to help heal the wounded because of you," he told Constantine after they'd all eaten and everyone except Josca had had a few beers.

Her father nodded but would not look at him. "She used to follow me when I'd go gathering. We always thought she'd become a nurse."

"In a way, she did," Anthony said. "Another reason why I love your daughter and wish to marry her, according to your wishes and traditions."

Constantine said nothing for a long time, then got up and went off with his wife. When they returned, Florence's father said, "My daughter says you are a good man, but we do not know that. If you want to marry her, we expect this dowry to be paid."

Then he pulled out a handwritten list and gave it to Anthony.

He read it, felt heavy in his gut, and said, "Excuse me for saying so, sir, but it's a lot for what the army is paying me."

"Florence is a lot of woman. If you love her, prove it to us."

"And then you will marry her the proper way," Josca said. "In a church."

"Papa, this is unfair," Florence said angrily after reading the list.

Constantine said, "It was unfair we lost you for so many years. We won't lose you again."

"Mama?"

But Josca would not meet her eyes as she said, "I love you, Flo, but it's how we feel."

Seeing the frustration build in Florence, Anthony said, "Okay, Mr. and Mrs. Okori, I don't know how, I don't know when, but I promise I will figure out a way to give you all this in return for your daughter's hand. And then we will get married in a church."

———

For three years, Anthony translated the TONFAS and helped General Adamo and others to root out the last LRA strongholds in Uganda, setting aside a portion of his small monthly salary to go toward the dowry's conditions. And after work every day for three years, he went into the bush with another man to cut down trees and burn them to make charcoal he sold to buy the livestock and other things Florence's father had demanded. Anthony's visits to his family once a month in Amia'bil were the highs of his life and leaving them his lows.

He and Florence began appearing regularly on Mega FM radio, calling more and more child soldiers home from the bush. She started volunteering to help in rehabilitation, teaching the returnees about the power that finally set her soul free after so many years of hatred in captivity.

Anthony had struggled with the idea at first. How could you do that to a man like Kony? After everything he'd seen the Great Teacher do?

But over a few months, she convinced him. "You taught me about the four voices of suffering, and they have helped me. But doing this to Kony helped me even more."

Anthony tried at last and was shocked by how unlocked he felt. "I get it now," he told Florence. "I can do this and still testify against him. Against all of them."

Florence put her hand over her heart, and said, "You can. And you will."

In 2006, the International Criminal Court in the Hague filed charges against the Great Teacher, General Vincent, Brigade Commander Dominic Ongwen, and Deputy Army Commander Okot Odhiambo. All four men were charged with crimes against humanity and war crimes, including the forced enlistment of children, murder, rape, and sexual slavery.

General Vincent, shaken by the indictments, tried to negotiate a truce. Kony attended two of the meetings under a guarantee of his safety. His escaped wife, Evelyn Amony, helped negotiate for Uganda. Ultimately the Great Teacher withdrew from the talks and retreated deep into Congo's Garamba National Park. For going behind his back to try to forge another peace treaty, Kony executed General Vincent in 2007.

That same year, Anthony learned that Albert had died in combat on the Uganda-Congo border. His younger brother never made it out of the LRA.

Anthony and his father and surviving brothers and sisters were devastated.

The hunt for the Great Teacher had resumed and was still ongoing in October 2008, when Anthony finally met Constantine's dowry demands. But Joseph

Kony was absolutely not on his mind when he rented a truck and a jitney on a bright, sunny day and set out. Together with many members of his extended family and fellow escaped LRA soldiers now fighting for the Ugandan army, Anthony drove from Rwotobilo, through Gulu and Lira, and stopped just outside Amia'bil to unload.

He was dressed in his finest uniform when they drove five cows and six goats, carried four chickens in cages, slung several new farming tools over their shoulders, and marched singing into the cheering village, where Anthony handed it all over to Constantine and Josca along with five hundred US dollars.

"You are a good man, Anthony," Constantine said.

"And a good human, I hope," Anthony said, grinning.

Then he put Florence on his good arm and led them all to the packed local Catholic church, where Josca acted as maid of honor and George as the best man, and in front of their children and families, they exchanged vows and finished by asking each other a simple question.

"See my happiness?" Anthony said.

"I do," Florence said. "See my happiness?"

"I do."

And when they kissed, the church lustily roared its approval.

When the time came for a sermon, the priest said, "Normally, I never miss an opportunity to say something, but I'm going to stand aside. Mr. and Mrs. Opoka have something to say."

They held hands when they turned to face their family and friends.

"First of all," Anthony said. "I want to thank my father, George, for taking the time when I was a little boy to teach me how to read the stars, how to tell right from wrong, and how to become a good human. And to my late mother, Acoko, who taught me to survive."

In the front row, George put his hand over his heart and nodded.

Anthony looked at Florence's family. "And I want to thank you, Constantine and Josca, for teaching Florence many of the same things."

Her mother and father, who had come to like Anthony over the past three years, now bobbed their heads and smiled at him.

Florence cleared her throat, gazed at her mother, father, and then George. "But it wasn't just that you taught us how to be good people. Those are just rules, like Kony had rules. Things to be broken if they're taught with cruelty. But when you taught us as young children, you did it out of deep, deep love. And we felt it, deeply, both of us. And so we remembered what you taught us."

Anthony said, "Kony tried to make us inhuman. He taught us everything that was the opposite of what this church teaches, what a good human believes, and how we were both raised and loved. But they beat his rules into you until you felt like everything before the LRA was a happy dream that you needed to forget in order to survive. There were times when I couldn't remember the happy dream at all. But then I met Florence at a water hole, and for once, I did not know what to say."

"And then he walked away from me!" Florence said, eyes wide, hands on her hips. "Can you believe that?"

The whole church started laughing.

"So I went to see her and talk to the commander who was looking out for her, and she walked away from me!" Anthony said, acting as confused as he'd been that day, and provoking another storm of laughter and claps.

"I had to," Florence said, looking around. "Am I right, ladies?"

The women started cheering and clapping.

Anthony gazed at her. "But I came back a third time, and she said yes."

"I can't say we fell in love at first sight."

"Well, *you* can't."

"I know, but I saw it differently," Florence said playfully before sobering. "But I did grow in love with Anthony. Very fast. I found I could share secrets with him that you had to keep bottled up in the LRA."

Anthony nodded. "And as our love grew, the memories of how we were deeply loved as children returned, and we found ourselves telling each other the way we were raised, what we were taught at home, in school, in church, and by all the kind people in our lives. It all came flooding back: what it was to be a good human, to believe in the goodness of another person, to treat others as you expect to be treated."

"Those memories of love saved us," Florence said, choking back emotion. "They formed the basis of our spiritual resistance to what Kony stood for. They helped us keep straight what was right and what wasn't, what really mattered when it mattered, and guided us when we needed to be guided. And because we started believing in love and those things again, we started believing in the dream of a better future for our boys, one where they would not grow up the slave or the soldier of a madman."

Anthony said, "I'm not going to go into it here, but it also helped that we had learned from a dying man that there is a big difference between pain and suffering. Pain is physical, like getting shot. Suffering is mental, the result of paralyzing voices in your head that can be quieted if you can learn to recognize them and then call them out by name."

"A difficult thing to understand and do at first, but it works," Florence said, and held his hand again. "There's something else we've found that works even more."

She described being at World Vision, free from captivity, but imprisoned by hatred and bitterness for Joseph Kony.

"But then, one day, I admitted that I loved Anthony so much I was grateful to Kony for bringing us together. And strangely, the miserable thoughts drifted away. Not gone, but softened.

"A week later, I was still thinking about how I'd felt better after thanking Kony for giving me Anthony, when another strange thought entered my head. And my first reaction was, 'No. No, I cannot do that. Not to him. Not to Kony.'"

She put her other hand over her heart as she gazed all around. "But then I felt I just had to do this. I closed my eyes. I put my hand here. I saw Kony in my mind. I said to him, 'I am deeply sorry for whatever happened to make you the way you are. When I think of you now, I feel pity, not anger. And for everything you did to us, I forgive you, with love, from the bottom of my heart.'"

Flo's face was aglow. "I am here to tell you that the image of Kony faded away to nothing. Nothing. It was a miracle. It is a miracle. By forgiving him with love, I was let out of the invisible prison of hatred and bitterness the Great Teacher built for me. By forgiving Kony with love, I was finally free."

People started clapping and patting their wet eyes with tissues.

Anthony said, "Florence told me all this soon after we reunited, and I rejected it immediately. Forgive that mad dog Kony? That hyena? With love? How is that even possible?" He paused, looked around. "But Florence can be pushy."

"What?"

He laughed. The audience laughed.

Anthony said, "Flo kept at me, and finally I was able to thank and forgive Kony because he'd given me the loves of my life. It was true—after I did, I felt like I was free of him. I still want to testify against him, but I am free of that man."

Florence looked down at her mother and father. "I guess we're saying that if love is the most powerful force in the universe, then gratitude and forgiveness are a close second and third."

Josca's eyes brimmed with tears as she nodded. Constantine gripped his wife's hand and bobbed his head as well.

Anthony said, "And when you live by these three forces, no matter what has happened to you, life does become a miracle. A daily miracle."

"As far as we are concerned, our life, our story, it's one long incredible miracle," Florence said, beaming before looking at Anthony. "We done?"

"Just one more thing," Anthony said, before looking at the audience with a dead-serious expression. "Never, ever get between a mama and her kittens."

"You're asking for it if you do!" Florence said, and started laughing.

Anthony raised her hand overhead and said, "And now we have to celebrate!"

The audience clapped and stood. They sang a favorite hymn as Anthony and Flo walked down the aisle with Kenneth and Boniface.

Outside, Florence said it was her happiest day ever, that Anthony truly was the man of her dreams. Anthony told people he felt like Florence had given him the heart of a leopard, able to take on anything in life if he just believed and acted from that heart.

Anthony was about to head for the Okori compound when he heard a hoarse male voice say, "Hey, Opoka. Sorry I missed the ceremony."

He looked over his shoulder and was puzzled to see a big man, clean-shaven, hair tight to his head, wearing a crisp UPDF uniform. His eyes had this intense curiosity as they danced over Anthony and Florence.

Before Anthony could say anything, the soldier said, "I heard about your epic escape. Then again, you were always good at running. And rescuing people from river floods."

"Patrick!" Anthony shouted, and ran to his old friend. "You're out!"

"Two months," Patrick said, slapping him on the back. "I thought someone would have told you, but when I found out you didn't know and that you and

Betty, uh, Florence were getting married, I decided to surprise you. I just got here a little too late. As usual."

Anthony grinned, threw back his head, and howled. "It's never too late! Florence, look who is here. Patrick!"

Florence began to cry again as she came toward him. "Our guide out of darkness."

"More like your bicycle thief," Patrick said, and hugged and congratulated her.

And then, as Anthony had promised Florence on their first honeymoon in Sudan so many years before, they and their families and friends returned to the Okori compound in Amia'bil, where, for three days straight, they feasted and drank and sang and danced in wild celebration of the new chance at life gifted to Commander Tony and Betty the Nurse by the greatest power of all.

AUTHOR'S NOTE

Over the course of Joseph Kony's thirty-year reign of terror in northern Uganda, southern Sudan, and Congo, the Lord's Resistance Army is believed to have kidnapped as many as thirty-seven thousand boys and girls and an equal number of adults and attempted to turn the males into fearsome, soulless soldiers and the females into slaves, sexual and otherwise.

The LRA's atrocities and the Ugandan government's scorched-earth policies led to more than a million people being displaced from their homes and crowded into refugee camps. There are no firm numbers available on how many innocent people were killed or maimed as Kony built his child armies, but some experts believe more than ten thousand died at his hand.

In 2008, the US State Department designated Kony a "global terrorist." Later that same year, President George Bush authorized the use of US military advisers in the LRA conflict. With Anthony Opoka translating TONFAS messages and offering insight into the Great Teacher's troubled mind, the Ugandan, Congolese, and Sudanese governments united to launch Operation Lightning Thunder. Hoping to end the LRA for good, they aerially attacked and destroyed many LRA camps in the Garamba National Park in northeast Congo.

But, yet again, Kony got away and ordered retaliation attacks. In the following eighteen months, Dominic Ongwen and the remains of his brutal Sania Brigade killed more than a thousand Congolese citizens, kidnapped hundreds of new child soldiers, and displaced hundreds of thousands of innocent civilians who fled the rumor and fact of the LRA.

In the ensuing years, Anthony and Florence had two daughters, Juliet and Sandra. Florence became consumed with raising her growing family. Her dream of becoming a nurse became a fond but faded memory replaced by dreams for her children. When she could, she continued to appear with Anthony on the radio, calling child soldiers in from the bush. She also volunteered as a counselor to help LRA women reintegrate into society and to find their way back into their families' good graces through the powers of love, gratitude, and forgiveness. And she taught her sons and daughters about those same powers and, like her mother before her, how an education could unlock the doors to their future. She also stayed close to her friend Palmer.

In 2011, after the US Congress passed legislation meant to disarm the LRA and capture Kony so he could be put on trial for crimes against humanity, President Obama sent more than one hundred military and intelligence advisers to Uganda in what was known as Operation Observant Compass. They created forward-operating bases near the border with Congo and hunted Kony and the remainder of his army in some of the most inaccessible terrain on earth.

Once again, Kony's former signaler was a big part of the effort.

But because he was quiet, reserved, not given to talking about himself, Anthony's story might never have been heard by the outside world. Then Michael Patrick Mulroy entered his life, or, rather, Anthony entered Mulroy's.

Mick Mulroy had been a US Marine and then a CIA special activities paramilitary operations officer and one of the earliest Americans into Afghanistan after 9/11 and into Iraq before the second Gulf War. Mulroy became the CIA's chief of station in Uganda in 2013. Soon after his arrival in Kampala, Mulroy arranged to visit two remote joint US and Uganda special operations bases along the border with Congo.

Anthony was assigned to go along as a cultural adviser to the Americans.

The first thing Mulroy noticed when they were introduced was that Anthony held his right wrist with his left hand when he shook hands. When they arrived in the bush, Mulroy immediately saw the respect that everyone hunting Kony showed to Anthony. Then Anthony, a veteran of near nonstop combat for a decade, heard about Mulroy's own service history and was highly impressed.

On the tarmac of the airstrip, after they returned to Kampala, Mulroy thanked Anthony and stuck out his hand. Again, Anthony used his left hand to guide his right.

"What happened?" Mulroy asked.

"Injury, big injury," Anthony replied.

"Did this happen when you were in the army, fighting the LRA?"

"No, Mick," he said, smiling. "I was fighting *for* the LRA. I was Kony's radioman."

————

Over the course of the next year, in bits and pieces, Mulroy got Anthony's story out of him. The CIA man was repeatedly shocked and moved by the tale, and through its telling, they became the best of friends, *omeras* in Acholi, brothers in any language. Mulroy also came away from the experience a staunch opponent of using children in war and a firm believer that the story of Florence and Anthony Opoka could end the practice.

Mulroy started using his iPhone to film mostly Anthony talking about the story, since Florence's English-speaking abilities had not yet caught up to her husband's. He showed some of the footage to an old friend, Eric "Olly" Oehlerich, then a squadron commander in US Navy SEAL Team Six with responsibility for Africa and the Middle East. Oehlerich was equally moved by the story of love conquering one of the most brutal situations he'd ever heard of and volunteered to help Mulroy do more interviews and to put together a rough documentary based on the story.

Enter Mark Rausenberger, another CIA special activities paramilitary operations officer, whose exploits were among those depicted in the film *12 Strong*, about the first team of Americans going into Afghanistan on horseback to fight Al Qaeda and the Taliban after 9/11.

Like Oehlerich, after seeing the rough footage, Rausenberger became fascinated by the story and repulsed by the practice of kidnapping children and forcing them into war. He offered to buy software to give their effort a more professional edit, then taught himself to use the software and did much of the job himself.

In early 2015, LRA Brigade Commander Dominic Ongwen, the Butcher of Katire, was captured and brought to the Hague to be tried on sixty-one counts of war crimes and crimes against humanity. Many Ugandans and Sudanese appeared against Ongwen, but none more forceful or damning than Anthony Opoka. The signaler was flown to Brussels and the International Criminal Court twice in the following years and spent days testifying under oath against Ongwen.

By then, the three Americans had spent over a thousand man-hours condensing the story into an intense fifteen-minute documentary and were planning on using it to start raising money to end child soldiering when tragedy struck. Rausenberger was killed during a CIA paramilitary operation in the Philippines.

Mulroy was crushed and then touched when Florence had twin boys shortly after Rausenberger's death and the Opokas named them Mick and Mark. Mulroy became the twins' godfather.

The documentary and the move to end child soldiering took a back burner for a brief time as Mulroy made a video about Rausenberger that was shown at his memorial and sent to many of his friends in May 2016. The video mentioned his involvement in the documentary, and people began asking to see it.

Mulroy and Oehlerich were asked to speak about counterinsurgencies at Yale University later that same year. They talked about child soldiering and showed the documentary, which included Anthony revealing his shoulder. When the film ended, there was stunned silence in the auditorium. They got similar reactions when they showed the video at other seminars.

But then Mulroy was offered a senior job in the US Department of Defense, and Oehlerich was entering his final years as SEAL Team Six squadron commander. Again, their effort to use the story to end child soldiering had to be set aside. Someone told them a book should be written about Anthony and Florence, and they agreed, but neither man had the time or inclination to pursue the idea.

The hunt for Kony had begun to wind down. Anthony was transferred to an antipoaching team that worked in Uganda's national parks. And the story languished until April 2019, when Alan Hayes, a dear friend of my family, died suddenly after surgery in Salt Lake City.

Both my sons had lived with Alan for years while trying to make the US Ski Team, and rushed to Salt Lake, where they were met by other men who had once lived in Hayes's little house near the University of Utah, including SEAL Team Commander Oehlerich.

As my sons and Oehlerich worked to get their late house-dad's estate in order, there were nights spent drinking and telling Alan stories and others. One that Oehlerich told grabbed my oldest son, Connor, who is also a novelist.

"Dad," Connor said in a phone call the next day, "I think I just heard your next book. It takes place in Africa, and I believe it meets your criteria for stories about humanity."

Those two facts had my attention immediately. After graduating from college, I was a Peace Corps volunteer in Niger, West Africa, an experience that influenced me profoundly. I taught English to the children of nomads in an oasis on the southern edge of the Sahara. I learned how to adapt to cultures far different from my own. I saw firsthand what it was like when students did not know where their next meal was coming from. And every day they gave me lessons in resilience and good humor that still remain with me.

In short, I had been looking for a story set in Africa for a long time, and Connor knew it. He also knew that after writing *Beneath a Scarlet Sky* and *The Last Green Valley*, I was more interested than ever in telling stories that were inherently moving, inspiring, healing, and perhaps transformative for me and for my readers.

"Give me the gist of it," I said.

"No," he said. "I think you need to hear this one from Olly and Mick."

———

That summer, Oehlerich was turning over command of his squadron in SEAL Team Six, retiring from the military after twenty-plus years of service, and moving his family home to Whitefish, Montana. Mulroy left the Pentagon and also moved to Whitefish, so it was not until September 2019 that the three of us were able to get together at my home in Bozeman.

They gave me the barest outline of the story and how they heard it, and not only was I amazed, but I also was moved to chills.

"How do people live through something like that?" I asked.

"Well, silver stars in the sky," Oehlerich said, gesturing up with one finger.

Mulroy smiled, said, "Silver stars, magic mushrooms, and the power of love, Olly."

The retired SEAL commander laughed. "And don't forget mama leopard giving birth in combat and fighting her way out with an AK-47."

"Who could forget that?" the ex-CIA man said.

Okay, by then, not only was I moved, but I was also hooked, and became even more so when I learned that Anthony was one of the main witnesses in the crimes-against-humanity trial of Dominic Ongwen at the Hague and Oehlerich and Mulroy showed me their mini documentary. I was dumbfounded, in tears, and feeling like there was even more to the tale, deeper dimensions I could sense. I knew right then I wanted to write it, and even more so when they explained their purpose in seeing the story told.

Mulroy said, "We showed the documentary to a few people, and somehow Hollywood found out about it. But they wanted to make us the central figures, and we were absolutely not the central figures, and we refused. This is a story about Anthony and Florence and their remarkable humanity. We want to see their story used to show people what the human heart is capable of and to put an end to this kind of warfare. We want it all to be for the greater good."

"Hundred percent," Olly said.

"Even better," I said. "I'm in."

We agreed right off that, at a minimum, 22.5 percent of the book's proceeds would go to the Opoka family and to end child soldiering, with those percentages quickly rising and eventually doubling if the story proved successful. I also agreed to help pay for the Opoka children's education.

And right from the outset, we decided that while most of the books written about Joseph Kony and the LRA had ended up being about the author trying unsuccessfully to find and explain the Great Teacher, this book would be different. It would be written for and about the children.

Before they left that first meeting, I asked, "What about Kony? Where is he?"

"He could still be hiding out in that national park in Congo," Mulroy said. "But the best intelligence I've seen suggests that he went mad from syphilis and died in 2018."

———

Mulroy, Oehlerich, and I were supposed to go to Uganda to research the story more fully in June 2020, but COVID-19 shut down all travel to Africa.

In February 2021, as I was reading everything I could find about Joseph Kony and the Lord's Resistance Army, the International Criminal Court sided with the testimony of Kony's signaler and convicted Dominic Ongwen on all sixty-one counts, including war crimes, crimes against humanity, and the crime of forced marriage. Anthony felt vindicated and victorious, that justice had been done, but he also felt cheated because he never got the chance to testify in court against the Great Teacher.

We finally got a window of opportunity in June 2021, flew to Kampala, and drove north to Gulu and on into the bush near the border with what is now South Sudan.

Over the course of fifteen days, I extensively interviewed Florence and Anthony, who was still serving in the Ugandan army with the rank of major. The Opokas were warm, intelligent, gracious, thoughtful, and painfully honest.

They were also extremely funny and loved to laugh, joke, and entertain. They had warm, loving relationships with their children, siblings, friends, and parents, whom we were blessed to spend time with out in Rwotobilo, in the shade of the three big trees, and in the Okori compound in Amia'bil. Being in many of the pivotal places in the story with Anthony and Florence, including on Awere Hill, where Kony first called storms, we were all moved to tears more times than I could count.

Anthony had excellent recall for all manner of detail about his journey, the Lord's Resistance Army, and all the military paraphernalia that surrounded it. He was dead serious when he talked about Kony. He lit up every time he spoke about Flo.

I was honored that after several days, Florence trusted me enough to open up and work with a wonderful female translator to explain in detail the worst parts of her own harrowing journey, her belief in the power of love, and that birth in a firefight in the river bottom; how she'd run with Patrick and the boys; and how she'd freed herself from hatred and from Kony through love, gratitude, and forgiveness.

She is without question one of the most remarkable humans I have ever met.

I was also able to talk at length with George Opoka, who spoke about trying to raise good humans, the wonder of stars, and the importance of a loving, involved father in a young boy's life; and with Josca and Constantine Okori, who told me about Florence's measles and how the time in the hospital changed her, and how they'd never given up hope of seeing her again.

More than fifty other people, including Anthony's brother Charles and his uncle Paul, came forward to tell their part in the tale. We spoke with other family members as well and survivors, victims, NGO aid workers, therapists, historians, government officials, friends, enemies, and innocent bystanders. As I had suspected, the story of Anthony and Florence and their time in the LRA grew deeper dimensions and wider vistas every day.

Indeed, near the end of our time in Uganda, Anthony received tragic news. Patrick Lumumba, his old friend, running rival, and repeated savior in the LRA, had died in combat, fighting insurgents in Mozambique. Anthony was heartbroken.

By the time we left Uganda, I was convinced that Mulroy was right, that the story of Anthony and Florence could help end the barbaric practice of child soldiering. But I also felt deeply inspired by their journey, healed in a way, and transformed in others, and I wanted to bring that experience to life for the reader.

While I was able to spend time with many of the major characters involved, others had already died, so I was forced to use secondhand knowledge and my imagination to tell their parts in the tale. And because there were so many critical people in the story who literally had the same names, I condensed those characters into composites for the sake of narrative clarity.

I also recreated conversations and identified emotions and motives based on thirty-year-old memories. And I invented several characters and events to depict and illuminate certain, known LRA practices, among them forcing kids to walk on other kids who could not keep up on the rails and taking fake photos as proof of guilt.

What you have read, then, is not straight narrative nonfiction, nor creative nonfiction, but historical fiction based on my understanding of the events, culture, and people who survived the Lord's Resistance Army.

Any factual mistakes or mischaracterizations are mine alone.

———

While the LRA has been stopped, there are believed to be as many as three hundred thousand child soldiers currently being forced to fight around the world. The United Nations believes child soldiering has become a global security issue because radicalized, militant, dehumanized children grow up to be radicalized, militant, dehumanized adults. As such the office of Special Representative of the Secretary-General for Children and Armed Conflict was formed to monitor and help end the practice.

Also seeking to end the practice permanently and to rehabilitate any child coerced into combat, Mulroy and Oehlerich founded a nonprofit as this novel was being written.

They named the organization simply End Child Soldiering. Working with UNICEF and the office of the Special Representative of the Secretary-General, the nonprofit evaluates on an annual basis where the greatest need is in the world, and then delivers money directly to NGOs on the ground, working with children trying to escape combat and find stability on the other side of war.

You have already contributed to the cause by buying this book, and we thank you. If you were moved by the story of Anthony and Florence Opoka and wish to give more to end the use of kids in combat, we invite you to make donations at https://endchildsoldiering.com. or to the Grassroots Reconciliation Group, which works with former child soldiers, at https://grassrootsgroup.org.

AFTERWORD

ANTHONY OPOKA

I was born in the village of Rwotobilo in northern Uganda. Like all young boys, I always looked up to my father, George. He cared for all his brothers, his sister, and his cousins who lived in the village, and he was known for being wise and kind.

He taught me to be a good human, to always be fair to others, and to move at night by the stars. I loved my childhood.

In 1994, when I was fourteen, the LRA abducted me and my brother. I talked them into letting another brother go. I went through a crucible every morning for weeks, forced to keep up on the rails, and to run through the mountains. Those who couldn't make the run were killed, and their bodies were stacked next to the river. In the evenings, we would sit nearby, absorbing the stench of their bodies.

It was a nightmare, and it still is.

I repeatedly told myself, "I will not quit; I will not be in that pile in the morning." Somehow, I survived. I became a fighter and a good one, even though I was just a child fighting men. I was taught to fight without concern for my own life and to believe in the power of our leader, Joseph Kony.

During one battle, I was struck in the chest and arm by the rear fin of an RPG. It tore through my skin, my muscle, and my bone. Blood was everywhere. I fell to the ground, struggling to remain conscious. I knew the soldiers we were fighting would kill me on sight.

I was placed in a morgue and left for dead. Thankfully, a medic saw my eyes move the cloth on my face and took me to be treated. It was a long recovery.

With a wounded arm, I worried about how I could still be of value to the LRA and whether they would keep me alive. While recovering, I would sit out all night staring at the sky and wondering whether I would survive. I taught myself to navigate at night, becoming invaluable to the LRA. The Ugandan military had begun a new campaign, sending helicopter gunships to kill anything in their path. We could only move at night, and I had the skills that my unit needed.

The leadership came to rely on me. As well as mapping the stars in the sky, I also served as a radio operator to several senior officers, including Kony. The LRA spoke in coded messages they called TONFAS. These codes were heavily guarded. I was beside the senior commanders as they went into battles against the Ugandan military and against the South Sudanese military.

One day, I was cleaning my radios by a small stream. A young lady came walking to gather water. Her name was Florence.

FLORENCE OPOKA

I was born in a remote village in northern Uganda named Amia'bil. My childhood was difficult. My legs were paralyzed due to measles, so my mother had to carry me everywhere she went, and through that, she taught me the power of love. Thankfully, this paralysis would eventually pass.

We were poor but happy. I studied hard at night, using the light of our fire, to advance past primary school. Nobody in my family had made it this far in school before. Eventually, the test day came to go on with school, and I was pleased with how I did. I couldn't wait for the results.

But before I got them, LRA soldiers burst into my hut in the middle of the night. My brother tried to fight them off, but he couldn't. I was pulled into the open yard. They pulled off my clothes and threw me in a group with the other villagers who had been abducted.

They took us into the bush away from our village. I was taught how to be a soldier and a medic. Eventually, we went into battle, where I saw terrible injuries. I stayed alive but was basically floating through life, feeling nothing about all the death around me.

I was forced to marry a much older man—a senior LRA commander. I hated him. I refused to lie with him, taking beatings instead before I gave in. One day, he went to fight and didn't return.

Then I met Anthony. I was fetching water from a local well and saw a young man taking care of his radio. We started chatting—the rest you know already.

I did not look at my life and our story as something with value that others would want to know. But helping with this book gave what Anthony and I went through so much more meaning, and I began to see that people would want to know what happened to us and how we survived. Today, I hope our story can spread the power of love, heal people, and help keep children out of wars forever.

ANTHONY OPOKA

Mick Mulroy was the CIA leader in Uganda during the American mission against the LRA, called Operation Observant Compass. Mick and I were both cultural advisers on the mission. I had joined the Ugandan military by that point.

I first met Mick in a remote base. He came up and shook my hand. He noticed I held my right wrist with my left hand when shaking and asked if I had an injury. I told him about my time in combat with the LRA.

Although Mick and I were from different places and people, we were alike in many ways and became lifelong friends. Mick had served in combat, and we shared a bond as soldiers. We started working closely to help bring LRA soldiers out of the bush by convincing them they would be welcomed back. For example, we worked with a famous singer, Jose Chameleone, to create a song called "Come Home."

Mick and I also repeatedly deployed with special operations to try and find the leader of the LRA, Joseph Kony, and to bring more soldiers out of the bush. I knew Kony very well from my time with the LRA. Mick and I worked very closely with the US military officers and officials working with the Ugandan military.

From 2011 to 2017, the United States conducted Operation Observant Compass in the African countries of Uganda, the Central African Republic, South Sudan, and the Democratic Republic of the Congo. The mission was to defeat the Lord's Resistance Army. Although unsuccessful in the capture of Kony, by the end of the mission, the LRA ranks were reduced to two hundred or fewer holdouts, and most of its senior leaders were killed or in custody.

Florence and I became good friends with Mick; his wife, Mary Beth; their daughter, Mary Grace; and their son, Walton. We stayed with them at their home in Kampala from time to time. Mick and I started working on a study about the history of the LRA, the guerrilla tactics they used, and all of the Ugandan military tactics against them before the United States entered the struggle. They would travel with me to my village and Florence's and spoke to many former fighters.

We began to tell the story of the LRA through our eyes, and Mick told me that he believed our story should be recorded. Mick began to film it with his iPhone on multiple trips to my village. We even reenacted many of the events with my village family. I did not know where it would go or what we would turn it into.

In 2015, it was time for Mick and his family to return to America. I was sad to see them go. Mick was my *omera*, my brother. He said to me that my story would be told, and it was. Mick showed the video to a friend of his named Mark Rausenberger. Mark was committed to making something out of it. Mick, Mark, journalist Zack Baddorf, and Olly worked hard to make the video we took into a documentary.

They called me often and asked me questions to ensure accuracy. One sad day, Mick called and told me that Mark had died in the Philippines. I knew he had a wife, Julie, and two daughters, Molly and McKenna, and I was very sad for them. When Florence and I had twins, we named them Mark and Michael. They are both Mick's godsons now.

We kept working on the documentary with Mick and Olly. They showed it at several events in the United States. One day, I was told that Olly had shown it to a famous writer, Mark Sullivan, from Montana and that he wanted to write a book based on the story. Mick, Olly, and Mark then came to Uganda and stayed with me to review the story in detail. Florence and I took them to places where we had lived and fought for the LRA.

It is a story that we hope will be known, not for us, but for every child soldier. Florence and I will always work with Mick, Olly, and Mark to help end the use of child soldiers. I helped them with this effort to ensure that those who are forced to fight can finally find peace and come home.

Through our story, Florence and I have found meaning in the time we spent in the LRA, and we hope to leave the world a better place than we endured.

And those who are wise shall shine like the brightness of the sky above; and those who turn many to righteousness, like the stars forever and ever.

—Daniel 12:3

ACKNOWLEDGMENTS

Thanks first and foremost to Anthony Opoka and Florence Okori Opoka for opening up and telling their story to me. It was life-changing and life-affirming to hear firsthand how love can conquer the worst hardships and obstacles.

I am grateful to my son, Connor, for bringing my attention to their tale, and to Mick Mulroy and Eric "Olly" Oehlerich for filling in enough details about what Anthony and Florence endured—and how their story could help end child soldiering—that I felt compelled to go to Uganda to hear it in full.

My research in Uganda was invaluably aided by Magdalen Amony of the Grassroots Reconciliation Group in Gulu, who is an expert in the rehabilitation of child soldiers. She provided critical context as the Opokas told their story and served as my full-time English–Acholi translator when interviewing Florence. Ms. Amony also arranged for me, Mick, and Olly to watch fifty former captives of Joseph Kony perform a moving play in which they acted out their kidnappings, the terror of their time in the Lord's Resistance Army, and their escape and reunion with their families. Thank you for all the help and patient guidance.

Sitting in the shade of the three big trees that lord over the village of Rwotobilo, George Opoka described teaching his son, Anthony, about life, how to navigate by the stars, and how, when faced with a quandary, to ask the question, "What would a good human do?" I was also helped by Charles Opoka, who told me how he was saved by Anthony the night of his brother's kidnapping, and by Frank Opoka, who summoned up the emotions of finding his nephew alive after ten years in captivity. You all made the book better.

So did Florence's late father, Constantine Okori, who prior to his death talked about his daughter's time in the hospital with the measles, her fascination with natural healing herbs, and her dreams of being a nurse. Florence's mother, Josca Achola Okori, cooked us an incredible meal of yams and chicken stew in Amia'bil, and reiterated her belief that nothing in the universe is stronger than the power of love. She got tears in her eyes when she described cradling Florence on the way home from the hospital on Christmas Eve—and how she told her daughter that she would have carried her forever if she'd had to.

Former Ugandan military intelligence officer Tony Awany gave me insight into the long hunt for Joseph Kony and other LRA commanders, the importance of Anthony in that effort, and the power of Anthony's testimony at the Hague in the war crimes trial. I appreciate it.

My depiction of life in the LRA would not have been the same without the works of Evelyn Amony, Jimmie Briggs, Tim Allen, Koen Vlassenroot, Peter Eichstaedt, David Axe, and Tim Hamilton; the recollections of many of the friends, family, and strangers we talked to in Uganda, including John Opoka, Anne Opoka, and Gwen Okori; and the assistance of three female cousins of Joseph Kony, who met with me in his home village of Awere and answered all my questions, but asked not to be named. Thank you all.

I spent a lot of time talking about the story with my Oneness teachers, Sri Krishnaji and Sri Preethaji. They in turn gave me a deep understanding of the spiritual journeys taken by Anthony and Florence that I hope resonates throughout the book. I am in their debt for this aspect of the narrative and a thousand other gifts. Bless you both.

My agents, Meg Ruley and Rebecca Scherer at the Jane Rotrosen Agency, understood the power of the Opokas' story before I even wrote it, and supported me and the project through the entire publishing process. I am lucky to have them in my corner.

Despite a pandemic that delayed the research, writing, and delivery of this book by more than a year, my incredible editor at Lake Union, Danielle Marshall, never wavered in championing the novel from proposal through final edits. Thank you and everyone else at Amazon Publishing who stepped forward to support *All the Glimmering Stars*.

Special shoutouts go out to developmental editor David Downing, whose keen eye has once again elevated one of my manuscripts; to Chantelle Aimée Osman, who oversaw the creation of the maps; and to Jen Bentham, Angela Elson, and J. E. Lightning, who caught all my screwups.

And finally, to Courtney Greenhalgh, Shara Alexander, and Bill McGowan: I deeply appreciate your efforts to bring worldwide attention to Anthony and Florence's story and to the cause of bringing an end to the use of children in combat.

ABOUT THE AUTHOR

Photo © 2023 Amelia Anne Photography

Mark Sullivan is the acclaimed author of more than twenty novels, including the #1 Amazon Charts, *Wall Street Journal*, and *USA Today* bestseller *Beneath a Scarlet Sky* as well as the #1 *New York Times* bestselling Private series, which he writes with James Patterson. Mark has received numerous accolades for his work, including the WHSmith Fresh Talent Award, and he has written both a *New York Times* Notable Book and a *Los Angeles Times* Best Book of the Year. He grew up in Medfield, Massachusetts, and graduated from Hamilton College with a BA in English before working as a volunteer in the Peace Corps in Niger, West Africa. Upon his return to the United States, Mark earned a graduate degree from the Medill School of Journalism at Northwestern University and began a career in investigative reporting before turning to fiction. An avid skier and adventurer, he lives with his wife in Bozeman, Montana, where he remains grateful for the miracle of every moment. For more information, visit www.marksullivanbooks.com.

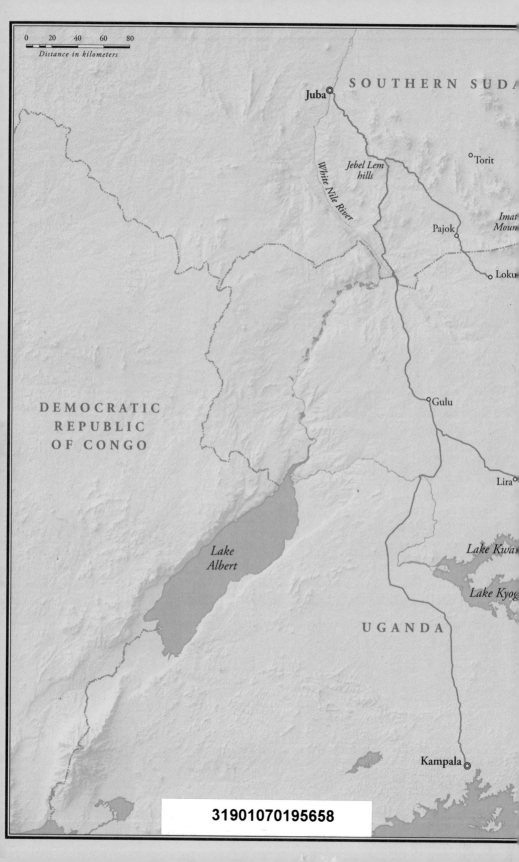

SOUTHERN SUDAN

Juba

Torit

Jebel Lem hills

White Nile River

Pajok

Imat Moun

Loku

DEMOCRATIC
REPUBLIC
OF CONGO

Gulu

Lira

Lake
Albert

Lake Kwa

Lake Kyog

UGANDA

Kampala

0   20   40   60   80
Distance in kilometers